D0465052

THE EMPIRE OF ISHER

Also by A. E. van Vogt

The War Against the Rull

Slan

THE EMPIRE OF ISHER

A. E. VAN VOGT

A TOM DOHERTY ASSOCIATES BOOK
NEW YORK

THE EMPIRE OF ISHER

An Orb Edition
Published by Tom Doherty Associates, LLC
175 Fifth Avenue
New York, NY 10010

ISBN 0-7394-1124-1

Printed in the United States of America

CONTENTS

THE WEAPON SHOPS OF ISHER

PROLOGUE

I

MAGICIAN BELIEVED TO HAVE HYPNOTIZED CROWD

JUNE 11, 1951—Police and newspapermen believe that Middle City will shortly be advertised as the next stopping place of a master magician and they are prepared to extend him a hearty welcome if he will condescend to explain exactly how he fooled hundreds of people into believing they saw a strange building, apparently a kind of gunshop.

The building seemed to appear on the space formerly, and still, occupied by Aunt Sally's Lunch and Patterson Tailors. Only employees were inside the two aforementioned shops, and none noticed any untoward event. A large, brightly shining sign featured the front of the gunshop, which had been so miraculously conjured out of nothingness; and the sign constituted the first evidence that the entire scene was nothing but a masterly illusion. For from whichever angle one gazed at it, one seemed to be staring straight at the words, which read:

FINE WEAPONS
THE RIGHT TO BUY WEAPONS
IS THE RIGHT TO BE FREE

The window display was made up of an assortment of rather curiously shaped guns, rifles as well as small arms; and a glowing sign in the window stated:

THE FINEST ENERGY WEAPONS
IN THE KNOWN UNIVERSE

Inspector Clayton of the Investigation Branch attempted to enter the shop, but the door seemed to be locked. A few moments later, C. J. (Chris) McAllister, reporter of the *Gazette-Bulletin*, tried the door, found that it opened, and entered.

Inspector Clayton attempted to follow him, but discovered that the door was again locked. It is believed that McAllister went through to the back, as several spectators reported seeing him. Immediately after his reappearance, the strange building vanished as abruptly as it had appeared.

Police state they are baffled as to how the master magician created so detailed an illusion for so long a period before so large a crowd. They are prepared to recommend his show, when it comes, without reservations.

(Author's Note: The foregoing account did not mention that the police, dissatisfied with the affair, attempted to contact McAllister for a further interview, but were unable to locate him. Weeks have passed; and he has still not been found.

What *did* happen to McAllister from the instant that he found the door of the gunshop unlocked?)

There was a curious quality about the gunshop door. It was not so much that it opened at his first touch as that, when he pulled, it came away like a weightless thing. McAllister had the impression that the knob had freed itself into his palm.

He stood very still, startled. The thought that came finally had to do with Inspector Clayton who, a minute earlier, had found the door locked. The thought was like a signal. From behind him boomed the voice of the Inspector:

"Ah, McAllister, I'll handle this now."

It was dark inside the shop beyond the door, too dark to see anything, and somehow, his eyes wouldn't accustom themselves to the intense gloom. Pure reporter's instinct made him step forward toward the blackness that pressed from beyond the rectangle of door. Out of the corner of one eye, he saw Inspector Clayton's hand reaching for the door handle that his own fingers had let go a moment before. And he knew instantly that if the inspector could prevent it, no reporter would get inside that building. His head was still turned, his gaze more on the police officer than on the darkness in front; and it was as he began another step forward that the remarkable thing happened.

The door handle would not allow Inspector Clayton to touch it. It twisted in some queer way, in some *energy* way, for it was still there, a strange, blurred shape. The door itself, without visible movement it was so swift, was suddenly touching McAllister's heel. Light, almost weightless, was that touch; and then, before he could think or react to what had happened, the momentum of his forward movement had carried him inside. As he breasted the darkness, there was a sudden, agonized tensing along his nerves. Then the door shut tight, the brief, unexpected agony faded. Ahead was a brightly-lit shop; behind—were unbelievable things!

For McAllister, the moment that followed was one of blank impression. He stood, body twisted awkwardly, only vaguely conscious of the shop's interior, but tremendously aware in the brief moment before he was interrupted of what lay beyond the transparent panels of the door through which he had just come.

There was no unyielding blackness anywhere, no Inspector Clayton, no muttering crowd of gaping spectators, no dingy row of shops across the way. It was not even the same street. There was *no* street. Instead, a peaceful park was visible. Beyond it, brilliant under a noon sun, was the skyline of a vast city. From behind him, a husky, musical, woman's voice said:

"You will be wanting a gun?"

McAllister turned. The movement was automatic reaction to a sound. And because the affair was still like a dream, the city scene faded almost instantly; his mind focused on the young woman who was advancing slowly from the rear section of the store. Briefly, his thought wouldn't come clear. A conviction that he ought to say something was tangled with first impressions of the girl's appearance. She had a slender well-shaped body; her face was creased with a pleasant smile. She had brown eyes, and wavy brown hair. Her simple frock and sandals seemed so normal at first glance that he gave them no further thought. He was able to say:

"What I can't understand is why the police officer, who tried to follow me, couldn't get in. And where is he now?"

To his surprise, the girl's smile became faintly apologetic: "We know that people consider it silly of us to keep harping on that ancient feud." Her voice grew firmer. "We even know how clever the propaganda is that stresses the silliness of our stand. Meanwhile, we never allow any of *her* men in here. We continue to take our principles very seriously."

She paused as if she expected comprehension from him. But McAllister saw from the slow puzzlement creeping into her eyes that his face must look as blank as the thoughts behind it. *Her men!* The girl had spoken the words as if she were referring to some personage, and in direct reply to his use of the word, police officer. That meant *her* men, whoever she was, were policemen; and they weren't allowed in this gunshop. So the door was hostile, and wouldn't admit them. An emptiness struck into McAllister's mind, matching the hollowness that was beginning to afflict the pit of his stomach, a sense of unplumbed depths, the first staggering conviction that all was not as it should be. The girl was speaking in a sharper tone:

"You mean you know nothing of all this, that for generations the gunmaker's guild has existed in this age of devastating energies as the common man's only protection against enslavement? The right to buy guns—" She stopped, her narrowed eyes searching him; then: "Come to think of it, there's something very peculiar about you. Your outlandish clothes—you're not from the northern farm plains are you?"

He shook his head dumbly, more annoyed with his reactions every passing second. But he couldn't help it. A tightness was growing in him now, becoming more unbearable instant by instant, as if somewhere a vital mainspring was being wound to the breaking point.

The young woman went on more swiftly: "And come to think of it, it is astounding that a policeman should have tried the door, and there was no alarm."

Her hand moved. Metal flashed in it, metal as bright as steel in blinding sunlight. There was not the slightest hint of an apology in her voice as she said: "You will stay where you are, sir, until I have called my father. In our business, with our responsibilities, we never take chances. Something is very wrong here."

Curiously, it was at that point that McAllister's mind began to function clearly. The thought that came paralleled hers. How had this gunshop appeared on a 1951 street? How had he come here into this fantastic world? Something was very wrong indeed.

It was the gun that held his attention. It was a tiny thing, shaped like a pistol, but with three cubes projecting in a half circle from the top of the slightly bulbous firing chamber. He began to feel shaken, looking at it, for that wicked little instrument, glittering there in her browned fingers, was as real as herself.

"Good Heaven," he whispered. "What the devil kind of a gun is it? Lower that thing and let's try to find out what all this is about."

She seemed not to be listening. He noticed that her gaze was flicking to a point on the wall somewhat to his left. He followed her look in time to see seven miniature white lights flash on. Curious lights! He was fascinated by the play of light and shade, the waxing and waning from one tiny globe to the next, a rippling movement of infinitesimal increments and decrements, an incredibly delicate effect of instantaneous reaction to some supersensitive barometer. The lights steadied; his gaze reverted to the girl. To his surprise, she was putting away her gun. She must have noticed his expression.

"It's all right," she said coolly. "The automatics are on you now. If we're wrong about you, we'll be glad to apologize. Meanwhile, if you're still interested in buying a gun, I'll be happy to demonstrate."

So the automatics were on him, McAllister thought. He felt no relief at the information. Whatever the automatics were, they wouldn't be working in his favor. The young woman putting away her gun in spite of her suspicions spoke volumes for the efficiency of the new watchdogs. He'd have to get out of this place, of course. Meanwhile, the girl was assuming that a man who came into a gunshop would, under ordinary circumstances, want to buy a gun. It struck him, suddenly, that of all the things he could think of, what he most wanted to see was one of those strange guns. There were incredible implications in the very shape of the instruments. Aloud he said:

"Yes, by all means show me." A thought occurred to him. He added, "I have no doubt your father is somewhere in the background making some sort of study of me."

The young woman made no move to bring out any weapons. Instead, she stared at him in puzzlement.

"You may not realize it," she said slowly, "but you have already upset our entire establishment. The lights of the automatics should have gone on the moment Father pressed the buttons, as he did when I called him. They didn't! That's unnatural, and yet—" her frown deepened—"if you were one of *them*, how did you get through that door? Is it possible that *her scientists* have discovered human beings who do not affect the sensitive energies? And that you are but one of many such, sent as an experiment to determine whether or not entrance could be gained? Yet that isn't logical either. If they had even a hope of success, they wouldn't risk the chance of throwing away an overwhelming surprise. In that case, you would be the entering wedge of an attack on a vast scale. She is ruthless, she's brilliant; and she craves complete power over poor fools like you who have no more sense than to worship her and the splendor of the Imperial Court."

The young woman paused, with the faintest of smiles. "There I go again, making a political speech. But you can see that there are at least a few reasons why we should be careful about you."

There was a chair in one corner. McAllister started for it. His mind was calmer. "Look," he began, "I don't know what you're talking about. I don't even know how I came to be in this shop. I agree with you that the whole thing requires explanation, but I mean that differently than you do."

His voice trailed. He had been half lowered over the chair, but instead of sinking into it, he came erect, slowly, like an old, old man. His eyes fixed on lettering that shone above a glass case of guns behind her. He said hoarsely:

"Is that—a calendar?"

She followed his gaze, puzzled: "Yes, it's June third. What's wrong?"

"I don't mean that. I mean—" He caught himself with an effort. "I mean those figures above that; I mean—what year is this?"

The girl looked surprised. She started to say something, then stopped and backed away. Finally: "Don't look like that! There's nothing wrong. This is eighty-four of the four thousand seven hundreth year of the Imperial House of the Isher. It's quite all right."

II

Very deliberately McAllister sat down, and the conscious wonder came: Exactly how *should* he feel? Not even surprise came to his aid. The events were beginning to fall into a kind of distorted pattern. The building front superimposed on those two 1951 shops; the way the door had acted. The great exterior sign with its odd linking of freedom with the right to buy weapons. The actual display of weapons in the window, the finest energy weapons in the known universe! . . . He grew aware that the girl was talking earnestly with a tall, gray-haired man who was standing on the threshold of the door through which she had originally come. There was a tenseness in the way they were talking. Their low-spoken words made a blur of sound in his ears, strange and unsettling. McAllister could not quite analyze the meaning of it until the girl turned, and said:

"What is your name?"

McAllister gave it.

The girl hesitated, then: "Mr. McAllister, my father wants to know what year you're from!"

The gray-haired man stepped forward. "I'm afraid," he said gravely, "that there is no time to explain. What has happened is what we gunmakers have feared for generations: that once again would come one who lusted for unlimited power; and who, to attain tyranny, must necessarily seek first to destroy us. Your presence here is a manifestation of the energy force that she has turned against us—something so new that we did not even suspect it was being used against us. But I have no time to waste. Get all the information you can, Lystra, and warn him of his own personal danger." The man turned. The door closed noiselessly behind his tall figure.

McAllister asked: "What did he mean—personal danger?"

He saw the girl's brown eyes were uneasy as they rested on him. "It's hard to explain," she began in an uncomfortable voice. "First of all, come to the window and I'll try to make everything clear. It's all very confusing to you, I suppose."

McAllister drew a deep breath. "Now we're getting somewhere."

His alarm was gone. The gray-haired man seemed to know

what it was all about. That meant there should be no difficulty getting home again. As for all this danger to the gunmaker's guild, that was their worry, not his. He stepped forward, closer to the girl. To his amazement, she cringed away as if he had threatened her. As he stared blankly, she laughed humorlessly; and finally she said:

"Don't think I'm being silly; don't be offended—but for your life's sake, don't touch any human body you might come in contact with."

McAllister was conscious of a chill. Then, suddenly, he felt a surge of impatience at the fear that showed in the girl's face. "Now look," he began, "I want to get things clear. We can talk here without danger, providing I don't touch, or come near you. Is that right?"

She nodded. "The floor, the walls, every piece of furniture—in fact the entire Shop is made of non-conducting material."

McAllister had a sense of being balanced on a tight rope over a bottomless abyss. He forced calm onto his mind. "Let's start," he said, "at the beginning. How did you and your father know that I was not of—" he paused before the odd phrase, then went on—"of this time?"

"Father photographed you," the girl said. "He photographed the contents of your pockets. That was how he first found out what was the matter. You see, the sensitive energies themselves become carriers of the energy with which you're charged. That's what was wrong. That's why the automatics wouldn't focus on you, and—"

"Energy—charged?" said McAllister.

The girl was staring at him. "Don't you understand?" she gasped. "You've come across seven thousand years of time. And of all the energies in the universe, time is the most potent. You're charged with trillions of trillions of time-energy units. If you should step outside this Shop, you'd blow up Imperial City and half a hundred miles of land beyond.

"You—" she finished on an unsteady, upward surge of her voice—"you could conceivably destroy the Earth!"

III

He hadn't noticed the mirror before. Funny, too, because it was large enough, at least eight feet high, and directly in front of him on the wall where, a minute before (he could have sworn) had been solid metal.

"Look at yourself," the girl was saying soothingly. "There's nothing so steadying as one's own image. Actually, your body is taking the mental shock very well."

He stared at his image. There was a paleness in the lean face that stared back at him. But his body was not actually shaking as the whirling in his mind had suggested. He grew aware again of the girl. She was standing with a finger on one of a series of wall switches. Abruptly, he felt better. "Thank you," he said quietly. "I certainly needed that."

She smiled encouragingly; and he was able now to be amazed at her conflicting personality. There had been on the one hand her inability a few minutes earlier to get to the point of the danger, an incapacity for explaining things with words. Yet obviously her action with the mirror showed a keen understanding of human psychology. He said: "The problem now is, from your point of view, to circumvent this Isher woman and get me back to 1951 before I blow up the Earth of . . . of whatever year this is."

The girl nodded. "Father says that you can be sent back, but as for the rest, watch!"

He had no time for relief at the knowledge that he could be returned to his own time. She pressed another button. Instantly, the mirror was gone into metallic wall. Another button clicked. The wall vanished. Before him stretched a park similar to the one he had already seen through the front door, obviously an extension of the same gardenlike vista. Trees were there, and flowers, and green, green grass in the sun.

One vast building, as high as it was long, towered massively dark against the sky and dominated the entire horizon. It was a good quarter mile away; and incredibly, it was at least that long and that high. Neither near that monstrous building, nor in the park, was a living person visible. Everywhere was evidence of man's dynamic labor, but no men, no movement. Even the trees stood motionless in that breathless sunlit day.

"Watch!" said the girl again, more softly.

There was no click this time. She made an adjustment on one of the buttons, and the view was no longer so clear. It wasn't that the sun had dimmed its bright intensity. It wasn't even that glass was visible where a moment before there had been nothing. There was still no apparent substance between them and that gemlike park. But the park was no longer deserted.

Scores of men and machines swarmed out there. McAllister stared in amazement; and then as the sense of illusion faded, and the dark menace of those men penetrated, his emotion changed to dismay.

"Why," he said at last, "those men are soldiers, and the machines are—"

"Energy guns!" she said. "That's always been their problem. How to get their weapons close enough to our shops to destroy us. It isn't that the guns are not powerful over a very great distance. Even the rifles we sell can kill unprotected life over a distance of miles, but our gunshops are so heavily fortified that, to destroy us, they must use their biggest cannon at point-blank range. In the past, they could never do that because we own the surrounding park, and our alarm system was perfect—until now. The new energy they're using affects none of our protective instruments; and, what is infinitely worse, affords them a perfect shield against our own guns. Invisibility, of course, has long been known, but if you hadn't come, we would have been destroyed without ever knowing what happened."

"But," McAllister exclaimed sharply, "what are you going to do? They're still out there, working—"

Her brown eyes burned with a fierce, yellow flame. "My father has warned the guild. And individual members have now discovered that similar invisible guns are being set up by invisible men outside their Shops. The council will meet shortly to discuss defences."

Silently, McAllister watched the soldiers connecting what must have been invisible cables that led to the vast building in the background; foot thick cables that told of the titanic power that was to be unleashed on the tiny weapon shop. There was nothing to be said. The reality out there overshadowed sentences and phrases. Of all the people here, he was the most useless, his opinion the least worthwhile. He must have said so, but he did not realize that until the familiar voice of the girl's father came from one side of him.

"You're quite mistaken, Mr. McAllister. Of all the people here you are the *most* valuable. Through you, we discovered that the Isher were actually attacking us. Furthermore, our enemies do not know of your existence, therefore have not yet realized the full effect produced by the new blanketing energy they have used. You, accordingly, constitute the unknown factor. We must make immediate use of you."

The man looked older, McAllister thought. There were lines of strain in his lean, sallow face as he turned to his daughter, and his voice, when he spoke, was edged with sharpness: "Lystra, Number Seven!"

As the girl's fingers touched the seventh button, her father explained swiftly to McAllister, "The guild supreme council is holding an immediate emergency session. We must choose the most likely method of attacking the problem, and concentrate individually and collectively on that method. Regional conversations are already in progress, but only one important idea has been put forward as yet and—ah, gentlemen!"

He spoke past McAllister, who turned with a start. Men were coming out of the solid wall, lightly, easily, as if it were a door and they were stepping across a threshold. One, two, three—thirty.

They were grim-faced men, all except one who glanced at McAllister, started to walk past, and then stopped with a half-amused smile.

"Don't look so blank. How else do you think we could have survived these many years if we hadn't been able to transmit material objects through space? The Isher police have always been only too eager to blockade our sources of supply. Incidentally, my name is Cadron—Peter Cadron!"

McAllister nodded in a perfunctory manner. He was no longer genuinely impressed by the new machines. Here were the end-products of the machine age; science and invention so advanced that men made scarcely a move that did not affect, or was not affected by, a machine. A heavy-faced man near him said: "We have gathered here because it is obvious that the source of the new energy is the great building just outside this Shop—"

He motioned toward the wall which had been a mirror and then the window through which McAllister had gazed at the monstrous structure in question. The speaker went on: "We've known, ever since the building was completed five years ago, that it was a power building aimed against us; and now from it new energy has flown out to engulf the world, immensely potent energy so strong that it broke the very tensions of time, fortunately only at this nearest gunshop. Apparently, it weakens when transmitted over distance."

"Look, Dresley," came a curt interruption from a small, thin man, "what good is all this preamble? You have been examining the various plans put forward by regional groups. Is there, or isn't there, a decent one among them?"

Dresley hesitated. To McAllister's surprise, the man's eyes fixed doubtfully on him, his heavy face worked for a moment, then hardened. "Yes, there is a method, but it depends on compelling our friend from the past to take a great risk. You all know what I'm referring to. It will gain us the time we need."

"Eh!" said McAllister, and stood stunned as all eyes turned to stare at him.

IV

It struck McAllister that what he needed again was the mirror to prove to himself that his body was putting up a good front. His gaze flicked over the faces of the men. The gunmakers made a confusing pattern in the way they sat, or stood, or leaned against glass cases of shining guns; and there seemed to be fewer than he had previously counted. One, two—twenty-eight, including the girl. He could have sworn there had been thirty-two. His eyes moved on, just in time to see the door of the back room closing. Four of the men had gone to whatever lay beyond that door.

He shook his head, puzzled. And then, consciously drawing his attention back, stared thoughtfully at the faces before him. He said: "I can't understand how any one of you could even think of compulsion. According to you, I'm loaded with energy. I may be wrong, but if any of you should try to thrust me back down the chute of time, or even touch me, that energy in me would do devastating things—"

"You're damned right!" chimed in a young man. He barked irritably at Dresley: "How the devil did you ever come to make such a psychological blunder? You know that McAllister will have to do as we want to save himself; and he'll have to do it fast!"

Dresley grunted. "Hell," he said, "the truth is that we have no time to waste in explanation and I just figured that he might scare easily. I see, however, that we're dealing with an intelligent man."

McAllister's eyes narrowed over the group. This was phony. He said sharply, "And don't give me any soft soap about being intelligent. You fellows are sweating blood. You'd shoot your own grandmothers and trick me into the bargain, because the world you think right is at stake. What's this plan of yours that you were going to compel me to participate in?"

It was the young man who replied. "You are to be given insulated clothes and sent back to your own time—"

He paused. McAllister said: "That sounds okay so far. What's the catch?"

"There is no catch!"

McAllister stared. "Now, look here," he began, "don't give me any of that. If it's as simple as that, how the devil am I going to be helping you against the Isher energy?"

The young man scowled blackly at Dresley. "You see," he said, "you've made him suspicious with that talk of yours about compulsion." He faced McAllister. "What we have in mind is an application of a sort of an energy lever and fulcrum principle. You are to be the weight at the long end of a kind of energy 'crowbar,' which lifts the greater weight at the short end. You will go back five thousand years in time; the machine in the great building, to which your body is tuned and which has caused all this trouble, will move ahead in time several months."

"In that way," interrupted another man before McAllister could speak, "we should have time to find another counteragent. There must be a solution, else our enemies would not have acted so secretly. Well, what do you think?"

McAllister walked slowly over to the chair that he had occupied previously. His mind was turning at furious speed, but he knew with a grim foreboding that he hadn't the technical knowledge necessary to safeguard himself. He said slowly:

"As I see it, this is supposed to work something like a pump handle. The lever principle, the old idea that if you had a lever long enough, and a suitable fulcrum, you could move the Earth out of its orbit."

"Exactly!" It was the heavy-faced Dresley who spoke. "Only this works in time. You go five thousand years, the building goes—"

His voice faded, his eagerness drained from him as he caught the expression in McAllister's face.

"Look!" said McAllister. "There's nothing more pitiful than a bunch of honest men engaged in an act of dishonesty. You're strong men, the intellectual type, who've spent your lives enforcing an idealistic conception. You've always told yourselves that if the occasion should ever require it, you would not hesitate to make drastic sacrifices. But you're not fooling anybody. *What's the catch?*"

V

It was startling to have the suit thrust at him. He had noticed the men emerge from the back room; and it came as a shock to realize that they had gone for the insulated clothes before they could have known that he would use them. McAllister stared grimly at Peter Cadron, who held the dull, grayish, limp thing toward him, and said in a tight voice:

"Get into this, and get going! It's a matter of minutes, man! When those guns out there start spraying energy, you won't be alive to argue about our honesty."

Still he hesitated. The room seemed insufferably hot. Perspiration streaked down his cheeks and he felt sick with uncertainty. Somewhere in the background a man was saying:

"Our first purpose must be to gain time, then we must establish new shops in communities where they cannot be easily attacked. Simultaneously, we must contact every Imperial potential who can help us directly or indirectly, and finally we must—"

The voice went on, but McAllister heard no more. His frantic gaze fell on the girl, standing silent and subdued near the front door. He strode toward her; and either his glare or presence was frightening, for she cringed and turned white.

"Look!" he said. "I'm in this as deep as hell. What's the risk in this thing? I've got to feel that I have some chance. Tell me, what's the catch?"

The girl was gray now, almost as gray and dead looking as the suit Peter Cadron was holding. "It's the friction," she mumbled finally, "you may not get all the way back to 1951. You see, you'll be a sort of 'weight' and—"

McAllister whirled away from her. He climbed into the soft almost flimsy suit, crowding the overall-like shape over his neatly pressed clothes. "It comes tight over the head, doesn't it?" he asked.

"Yes!" It was Lystra's father who answered. "As soon as you pull that zipper shut, the suit will become completely invisible. To outsiders, it will seem just as if you have your ordinary clothes on.

The suit is fully equipped. You could live on the moon inside it."

"What I don't get," complained McAllister, "is why I have to wear it. I got here all right without it." He frowned. His words had been automatic, but abruptly a thought came. "Just a minute," he said, "what becomes of the energy with which I'm charged when I'm bottled up in this insulation?"

He saw by the stiffening expressions of those around him that he had touched on a vast subject.

"So that's it!" he snapped. "The insulation is to prevent me losing any of that energy. That's how it can make a 'weight.' I have no doubt there is a connection from this suit to that other machine. Well, it's not too late."

With a desperate twist, he tried to jerk aside, to evade the clutching hands of the four men who leaped at him. But they had him instantly, and their grips on him were strong beyond his power to break. The fingers of Peter Cadron jerked the zipper tight, and Peter Cadron said:

"Sorry, but when we went into that back room, we also dressed in insulated clothing. That's why you couldn't hurt us. And remember this: There's no certainty that you are being sacrificed. The fact that there is no crater in *our* Earth proves that you did not explode in the past, and that you solved the problem in some other way. *Now, somebody open the door, quick!*"

Irresistibly, he was carried forward. And then—

"Wait!"

It was the girl. Her eyes glittered like dark jewels and in her fingers was the tiny, mirror-bright gun she had pointed in the beginning at McAllister. The little group hustling McAllister stopped as if they had been struck. He was scarcely aware. For him there was only the girl, and the way the muscles of her lips were working and the way her voice suddenly cried: "This is utter outrage. Are we such cowards—is it possible that the spirit of liberty can survive only through a shoddy act of murder and gross defiance of the rights of the individual? I say no! Mr. McAllister must have the protection of the hypnotism treatment; surely so brief a delay will not be fatal."

"Lystra!" It was her father; and McAllister realized by his swift movement how quickly the older man grasped every aspect of the situation. He stepped forward and took the gun from his daughter's fingers—the only man in the room, McAllister thought, who could dare approach her in that moment with the certainty she would not fire. For hysteria was in every line of her face; and the tears that followed showed how dangerous her stand might have been against the others.

Strangely, not for a moment had hope come. The entire action seemed divorced from his life and his thought; there was only the observation of it. He stood there for a seeming eternity, and, when emotion finally came, it was surprise that he was not being hustled to his doom. With the surprise came awareness that Peter Cadron had let go of his arm, and stepped clear of him.

The man's eyes were calm, his head held proudly erect. He said, "Your daughter is right, sir. At this point we rise above our fears, and we say to this unhappy young man: 'Have courage! You will not be forgotten. We can guarantee nothing, cannot even state exactly what will happen to you. But we say, if it lies in our power to help you, that help you shall have.' And now—we must protect you from the devastating psychological pressures that would otherwise destroy you, simply but effectively."

Too late, McAllister noticed that the others had turned their faces away from that extraordinary wall—the wall that had already displayed so vast a versatility. He did not even see who pressed the activating button for what followed.

There was a flash of dazzling light. For an instant he felt as if his mind had been laid bare; and against that nakedness the voice of Peter Cadron pressed like some engraving stamp: "To retain your self-control and your sanity—this is your hope; this you will do in spite of everything! And, for your own sake, speak of your experience only to scientists or to those in authority whom you feel will understand and help. Good luck!"

So strong remained the effect of that brief flaring light that he felt only vaguely the touch of their hands on him, propelling him.

He felt himself falling.

ONE

The village at night made a curiously timeless picture. Fara walked contentedly beside his wife along the street. The air was like wine; and he was thinking dimly of the artist who had come up from Imperial City, and made what the telestats called—he remembered the phrase vividly—"a symbolic painting reminiscent of a scene in the electrical age of seven thousand years ago."

Fara believed that utterly. The street before him with its weedless, automatically tended gardens, its shops set well back among the flowers, its perpetually hard, grassy sidewalks, and its street lamps that glowed from every pore of their structure—this was a restful paradise where time had stood still.

And it was like being a part of life that the great artist's picture of this quiet, peaceful scene before him was now in the collection of the empress herself. She had praised it, and naturally the thrice-blest artist had immediately and humbly begged her to accept it. What a joy it must be to be able to offer personal homage to the glorious, the divine, the serenely gracious and lovely Innelda Isher, one hundred eightieth of her line.

As they walked, Fara half turned to his wife. In the dim light of the nearest street lamp, her kindly, still youthful face was almost lost in shadow. He murmured softly, instinctively muting his voice to harmonize with the pastel shades of night: "She said—our empress said—that our little village of Glay seemed to her to have in it all the wholesomeness, the gentleness, that constitutes the finest qualities of her people. Wasn't that a wonderful thought, Creel? She must be a marvelously understanding woman."

They had come to a side street, and what he saw about a hundred and fifty feet along it stopped his words. "Look!" Fara said hoarsely.

He pointed with rigid arm and finger at a sign that glowed in the night, a sign that read:

FINE WEAPONS
THE RIGHT TO BUY WEAPONS
IS THE RIGHT TO BE FREE

Fara had a strange, empty feeling as he stared at the blazing sign. He saw that other villagers were gathering. He said finally, huskily, "I've heard of these shops. They're places of infamy against which the government of the empress will act one of these days. They're built in hidden factories and then transported whole to towns like ours and set up in gross defiance of property rights. That one wasn't there an hour ago." His face hardened. His voice had a harsh edge in it as he said, "Creel, go home."

He was surprised when Creel did not move off at once. All their married life, she had had a pleasing habit of obedience that had made life a wonderful thing. He saw that she was looking at him wide-eyed, and that it was a timid alarm that held her there. She said, "Fara, what do you intend to do? You're not thinking of—"

"Go home!" Her fear brought out all the determination in his nature. "We're not going to let such a monstrous thing desecrate our village. Think of it—" his voice shivered before the appalling thought—"this fine, old-fashioned community, which we had resolved always to keep exactly as the empress has it in her picture gallery, debauched now, ruined by this . . . this thing—but we won't have it; that's all there is to it."

Creel's voice came softly out of the half-darkness of the street corner, the timidity gone from it: "Don't do anything rash, Fara. Remember it is not the first new building to come into Glay—since the picture was painted."

Fara was silent. This was a quality of his wife of which he did not approve, this reminding him unnecessarily of unpleasant facts. He knew exactly what she meant. The gigantic, multitentacled corporation, Automatic Atomic Motor Repair Shops, Inc., had come in under the laws of the State with their flashy building, against the wishes of the village council, and had already taken half of Fara's repair business.

"That's different!" Fara growled finally. "In the first place people will discover in good time that these new automatic repairers do a poor job. In the second place it's fair competition. But this Weapon Shop is a defiance of all the decencies that make life under the House of Isher such a joy. Look at the hypocritical sign: 'The right to buy weapons—' Aaaaahh!" He broke off with, "Go home, Creel. We'll see to it that they sell no weapons in this town."

He watched the slender woman-shape move off into the shadows. She was halfway across the street when Fara called after her: "And if you see that son of ours hanging around some street corner, take him home. He's got to learn to stop staying out so late at night."

The shadowed figure of his wife did not turn; and after watching her for a moment moving against the dim background of softly glowing street lights, Fara twisted on his heel and walked swiftly toward the shop. The crowd was growing larger every minute, and the night air pulsed with excited voices. Beyond doubt, here was the biggest thing that had ever happened to the village of Glay.

The sign of the Weapon Shop was, he saw, a normal-illusion affair. No matter what his angle of view, he was always looking straight at it. When he paused in front of the great display window, the words had pressed back against the storefront, and were staring unwinkingly down at him. Fara sniffed once more at the meaning of the slogan, then turned to the sign in the window. It read:

THE FINEST ENERGY WEAPONS
IN THE KNOWN UNIVERSE

A spark of interest struck fire inside Fara. He gazed at the brilliant display of guns, fascinated in spite of himself. The weapons were of every size, ranging from tiny little finger pistols to express rifles. They were made of every one of the light, hard, ornamental substances: glittering glassein, the colorful but opaque Ordine plastic, viridescent magnesitic beryllium. And others. It was the deadly extent of the destructive display that brought a chill to Fara. So many weapons for the little village of Glay, where not more than two people to his knowledge had guns, and those only for hunting.

Why, the thing was absurd, fantastically mischievous, and threatening.

Somewhere behind Fara a man said: "It's right on Lan Harris's lot. Good joke on that old scoundrel. Will he raise a row!"

There was a titter from several men, that made an odd patch of sound on the warm, fresh air. And Fara saw that the man had spoken the truth. The Weapon Shop had a forty-foot frontage. And it occupied the center of the green, gardenlike lot of tightfisted old Harris. Fara frowned. Clever, these Weapon Shop people, selecting the property of the most disliked man in town, giving everybody an agreeable titillation. But the cunning of it made it vital that the trick should not succeed. He was still scowling anxiously when he saw the plump figure of Mel Dale, the mayor. Fara edged toward him hurriedly, touched his hat respectfully, and said, "Where's Jor?"

"Here." The village constable elbowed his way through a little crowd of men. "Any plans?" he said.

"There's only one plan," said Fara boldly. "Go in and arrest them."

The two men looked at each other, then at the ground. It was the big constable who answered shortly, "Door's locked. And nobody answers our pounding. I was just going to suggest we let the matter ride until morning."

"Nonsense!" Astonishment made Fara impatient. "Get an axe and we'll break down the door. Delay will only encourage such riffraff to resist. We don't want their kind in our village for a single night. Isn't that so?"

There was a hasty nod of agreement from everybody in his immediate vicinity. Too hasty. Fara looked around puzzled at eyes that lowered before his level gaze. He thought: "They are all scared. And unwilling." Before he could speak, Constable Jor said:

"I guess you haven't heard about those doors or these Shops. From all accounts, you can't break into them."

It struck Fara with a sudden pang that it was he who would have to act here. He said, "I'll get my atomic cutting machine from my shop. That'll fix them. Have I your permission to do that, Mr. Mayor?"

In the glow of the Weapon Shop window, the plump man was sweating visibly. He pulled out a handkerchief, and wiped his forehead. He said: "Maybe I'd better call the commander of the Imperial garrison at Ferd, and ask them."

"No!" Fara recognized evasion when he saw it. Suddenly, the conviction came that all the strength in this village was in him. "We must act ourselves. Other communities have let these people get in because they took no decisive action. We've got to resist to the limit. Beginning this minute. Well?"

The mayor's "All right!" was scarcely more than a sigh of sound. But it was all Fara needed. He called out his intention to the crowd, and then, as he pushed his way out of the mob, he saw his son standing with some other young men staring at the window display.

Fara called: "Cayle, come and help me with the machine."

Cayle neither stirred nor turned. Fara paused, half inclined to make an issue of it, then hurried on, seething. That wretched boy! One of these days he'd have to take firm action there. Or he'd have a no-good on his hands.

The energy was soundless and smooth. There was no sputter, no fireworks. It glowed with a soft, pure white light, almost caressing the metal panels of the door. But after a minute it had still not affected the material. Fara refused to believe the failure, and played the boundlessly potent energy on that resisting wall. When he finally shut off his machine, he was perspiring freely. "I don't understand it," he gasped. "Why—no metal is supposed to stand up against a steady flood of atomic force. Even the hard metal plates used inside the blast chamber of a motor take the explosions in what is called infinite series, so that each one has unlimited rest. That's the theory, but actually steady running crystallizes the whole plate after a few months."

"It's as Jor told you," said the mayor. "These Weapon Shops are—big. They spread right through the empire, *and they don't recognize the empress.*"

Fara shifted his feet on the hard grass, disturbed. He didn't like this kind of talk. It sounded sacrilegious. And besides it was nonsense. It must be. Before he could speak, a man in the crowd said, "I've heard it said that that door will open only to those who cannot harm the people inside."

The words shocked Fara out of his daze. His failure had had a bad psychological effect. He said sharply, "That's ridiculous! If there were doors like that, we'd all have them. We—"

What stopped his words was the sudden realization that *he* had not seen anybody try to open the door; and with all this reluctance around him it was quite possible that no one had tried. He stepped forward, grasped at the doorknob, and pulled. The door opened with an unnatural weightlessness that gave him the fleeting impression that the knob had come loose into his hand. With a gasp, Fara jerked the door wide open.

"Jor," he yelled, "get in!"

The constable made a distorted movement—distorted by what must have been a will to caution, followed by the instant realization that he could not hold back before so many. He leaped awkwardly toward the open door. And it closed in his face.

Fara stared stupidly at his hand, which was still clenched. And then, slowly, a thrill coursed along his nerves. The knob had withdrawn. It had twisted, become viscous, and slipped amorphously from his straining fingers. Even the memory of the sensation gave him a feeling of unnormal things. He grew aware that the crowd was watching with silent intentness. Fara reached angrily for the knob, but this time the handle neither turned nor yielded in any way. The obstacle brought his determination back in force. He motioned to the constable.

"Go back, Jor, while I pull."

The man retreated, but it did no good. And tugging did not help. The door would not open. Somewhere in the crowd, a man said darkly, "It decided to let you in, then it changed its mind."

"What foolishness are you talking!" Fara spoke violently. "*It* changed its mind. Are you crazy? A door has no sense."

Fear put a quaver into his voice. Shame at his alarm made him bold beyond his normal caution. Fara faced the Shop grimly. The building loomed there under the night sky, in itself bright as day, alien and menacing, and no longer easily conquerable. He wondered what the soldiers of the empress would do if they were invited to act. And, suddenly, he foresaw flashingly that even they would be able to do nothing. Fara was conscious of horror that such an idea could enter his mind. He shut his brain tight.

"The door opened for me once," he said wildly. "It will open again."

It did. Gently, without resistance, *with* that same sensation of weightlessness, the strange, sensitive door followed the tug of his fingers. Beyond the threshold was dimness, a wide, darkened alcove. Behind him, Mayor Dale said:

"Fara, don't be a fool. What will you do inside?"

Fara was amazed to realize that he had stepped across the threshold. He turned, startled, and stared at the blur of faces. "Why—" he began blankly; then he brightened—"Why, I'll buy a gun, of course."

The brilliance of his reply, the cunning implicit in it, dazzled him for half a minute longer. The mood yielded slowly as he found himself in the dimly lighted interior of the Weapon Shop.

TWO

It was preternaturally quiet inside. No sound penetrated from the night out of which he had come. Fara walked forward gingerly on a carpeted floor that deadened his footsteps. His eyes accustomed themselves to the soft lighting, which came like a reflection from the walls and ceiling. He had expected ultranormalness. The ordinariness of the atomic lighting acted like a tonic to his tensed nerves. He glanced around with gathering confidence. The place looked normal enough. It was a shop, scantily furnished. There were showcases on the walls and on the floor, lovely things, but nothing unusual, and not many of them—a dozen. There was in addition a double door leading to a back room.

Fara tried to keep one eye on that door as he examined several showcases, each with three or four weapons either mounted or arranged in boxes or holsters. With narrowed eyes, he estimated his chances of grabbing one of the weapons from a case, and then, the moment someone came, force him outside where Jor would perform the arrest. Behind him, a man said quietly, "You wish to buy a gun?"

Fara turned with a jump. Brief rage flooded him at the way his plan had been wrecked by the arrival of the clerk. The anger died as he saw that the clerk was a fine looking, silver-haired man, older than himself. That was disconcerting. Fara had an immense and almost automatic respect for age. He said at last, lamely, "Yes, yes, a gun."

"For what purpose?" said the man in his quiet voice. Fara could only look at him. He wanted to get mad. He wanted to tell these people what he thought of them.

But the age of this representative locked his tongue. He managed speech with an effort of will. "For hunting." The plausible words stiffened his mind. "Yes, definitely for hunting. There is a lake to the north of here," he went on more fulsomely, "and—"

He stopped, scowling at the extent of his dishonesty. He was not prepared to go so deeply into prevarication. He said curtly, "For hunting."

Fara was himself again. He hated the man for having put him so completely at a disadvantage. With smoldering eyes he watched the old fellow click open a showcase and take out a green-shining rifle. As the man faced him, weapon in hand, Fara was thinking: "Pretty clever, having an old man as a front." It was the same kind of cunning that had made them choose the property of Miser Harris. He reached for the gun; but the man held it out of his reach.

"Before I can even let you test this," he said, "I am compelled by the bylaws of the Weapon Shops to inform you under what circumstances you may purchase a gun."

So they had private regulations. What a system of psychological tricks to impress the gullible.

"We Weapon Makers," the clerk was saying mildly, "have evolved guns that can, in their particular range destroy any machine or object made of what is called matter. Thus whoever possesses one of our weapons is more than a match for any soldier of the empress. I say more because each gun is the center of a field of force which acts as a perfect screen against immaterial destructive forces. That screen offers no resistance to clubs or spears or bullets, or other material substances, but it would require a small atomic cannon to penetrate the superb barrier it creates around its owner.

"You will readily comprehend," the man went on, "that such a potent weapon could not be allowed to fall, unmodified, into irresponsible hands. Accordingly, no gun purchased from us may be used for aggression or murder. In the case of the hunting rifle, only such specified game birds and animals as we may from time to time list in our display windows may be shot. Finally, no weapon can be resold without our approval. Is that clear?"

Fara nodded. For the moment, speech was impossible to him. He wondered if he ought to laugh out loud, or curse the man for daring to insult his intelligence. So the gun mustn't be used for murder or robbery. So only certain birds and animals could be shot. And as for reselling it, suppose—suppose he bought this thing, took a trip of a thousand miles, and offered it to some wealthy stranger for two credits—who would ever know? Or suppose he held up a stranger. Or shot him. How would the Weapon Shop ever find out? He grew aware that the gun was being held out to him stock first. He took it, and had to fight the impulse to turn the muzzle directly on the old man.

"How does it work?" he asked.

"You simply aim it, and pull the trigger. Perhaps you would like to try it on a target we have."

Fara swung the gun up. "Yes," he said triumphantly, "and you're it. Now, just get over there to the front door, and then outside." He raised his voice, "And if anybody's thinking of coming through the back door, I've got that covered, too." He motioned jerkily at the clerk. "Quick now, move! I'll shoot! I swear I will."

The man was cool, unflustered. "I have no doubt you would. When we decided to attune the door so that you could enter despite your hostility, we assumed the capacity for homicide. However, this is our party. You had better adjust yourself accordingly, and look behind you."

There was silence. Finger on trigger, Fara stood moveless. Dim thoughts came of all the *half-things* he had heard in his days about the Weapon Shops; that they had secret supporters in every district, that they had a private and ruthless hidden government, and that once you got into their clutches, the only way out was death. But what finally came clear was a mind picture of himself, Fara Clark, family man, faithful subject of the empress, standing here in this dimly lighted store, deliberately fighting so vast and menacing an organization. He forced courage into his sagging muscles. He said, "You can't fool me by pretending there's someone behind me. Now, get to that door."

The firm eyes of the old man were looking past him. The man said quietly, "Well, Rad, have you all the data?"

"Enough for a primary," said a young man's voice behind Fara. "Type A-7 conservative. Good average intelligence, but a Monaric development peculiar to small towns. One-sided outlook fostered by the Imperial schools present in exaggerated form. Extremely honest. Reason would be useless. Emotional approach would require extended treatment. I see no reason why we should bother. Let him live his life as it suits him."

"If you think," Fara said shakily, "that that trick voice is going to make me turn, you're crazy. That's the left wall of the building. I know there's no one there."

"I'm all in favor, Rad," said the old man, "of letting him live his life. But he was the prime mover of the crowd outside. I think he should be discouraged."

"We'll advertise his presence," said Rad. "He'll spend the rest of his life denying the charge."

Fara's confidence in the gun had faded so far that, as he listened in puzzled uneasiness to the incomprehensible conversation, he forgot it completely.

The old man said persistently: "I think a little emotion might have a long-run effect. Show him the palace."

Palace! The word tore Fara out of his paralysis. "See here," he began, "I can see now that you lied to me. This gun isn't loaded at all. It's—"

His voice failed him. His body went rigid. There was no gun in his hand.

"Why, you—" he began wildly. And stopped again. His mind heaved with imbalance. He fought off the spinning sensation, thought finally, tremblingly: Somebody must have sneaked the gun from him. That meant there was someone behind him. The voice was no mechanical thing. He started to turn. And couldn't. He struggled, pushing with his muscles. And couldn't turn, couldn't move, couldn't budge. The room was growing curiously dark. He had difficulty seeing the old man. He would have shrieked then if he could. Because the Weapon Shop was gone.

He was standing in the sky above an immense city. Standing in the sky, and nothing around him but air, and blue summer heaven, and the city a mile, two miles below. His breath seemed solidly embedded in his lungs. Sanity came back as the remote awareness impinged on his mind that he was actually standing on a hard floor, and that the city must be a picture somehow focused directly into his eyes.

For the first time, with a start, Fara recognized the metropolis below. It was the city of dreams, Imperial City, capital of the glorious Empress Isher. From his great height he could see the grounds of the silver palace, the Imperial residence itself. The last tendrils of his fear were fading now before a gathering fascination and wonder. The fear vanished as he recognized with a thrill that the palace was drawing nearer at tremendous speed. "Show him the palace!"

they had said. The glittering roof flashed straight at his face. The solid metal of it passed through him.

His first sense of imminent and mind shaking desecration came as the picture paused in a huge room, where a score of men sat around a table at the head of which sat a young woman. The inexorable, sacrilegious, limitlessly powered cameras that were doing the photographing swung across the table and caught the woman full face.

It was a handsome face, but there was passion twisting it now, as she leaned forward and said in a voice at once familiar—how often Fara had heard its calm, measured tones on the telestats—and distorted. Distorted by anger and an insolent certainty of command. That caricature of a beloved voice slashed across the silence as clearly as if he were there in the great room:

"I want that traitor killed, do you understand? I don't care how you do it, but I want to hear by tomorrow night that he is dead."

The picture snapped off and instantly Fara was back in the Weapon Shop. He stood for a moment, swaying, fighting to accustom his eyes to the dimness. His first emotion was contempt at the simpleness of the trickery. A motion picture. What kind of a fool did they think he was, to swallow something as transparently unreal as that? Abruptly, the appalling depravity of the scheme, the indescribable wickedness of what was being attempted here brought red rage.

"Why, you scum!" he flared. "So you've got somebody to act the part of the empress, trying to pretend that—Why, you—"

"That will do," said the voice of Rad. Fara shook as a big young man walked into his line of vision. The alarmed thought came that people who would besmirch so vilely the character of Her Imperial Majesty would not hesitate to do physical damage to Fara Clark. The young man went on in a steely tone, "We do not pretend that what you saw was taking place this instant in the palace. That would be too much of a coincidence. But it was taken two days ago. The woman is the empress. The man whose death she ordered is a former adviser whom she considered a weakling. He was found dead in his apartment last night. His name, if you care to look it up in the news files, was Banton Vickers. However, let that pass. We're finished with you."

"But I'm not finished," Fara said in a thick voice. "I've never heard or seen so much infamy in all my life. If you think this town is through with you, you're crazy. We'll have a guard on this place day and night, and nobody will get in or out."

"That will do." It was the silver-haired man. "The examination has been most interesting. As an honest man, you may call on us if you are ever in trouble. That is all. Leave through the side door."

It was all. Impalpable forces grabbed him, and he was shoved at a door that appeared miraculously in the wall, where seconds before had been the palace. He found himself standing in a flower garden, and there was a crowd to his left. He recognized his fellow townsmen, and that he was outside.

The nightmare was over. As he entered his house half an hour later, Creel said, "Where's the gun?"

"The gun?" Fara stared at his wife.

"It said over the 'stat a few minutes ago that you were the first customer of the new Weapon Shop."

Fara stood, remembering what the young man had said: "We'll advertise his presence." He thought in agony: His reputation! Not that his was a great name, but he had long believed with a quiet pride that Fara Clark's motor repair shop was widely known in the community and countryside. First, his private humiliation inside the Shop. And now this lying to people who didn't know why he had gone into the store.

He hurried to the telestat, and called Mayor Dale. His hopes crashed as the plump man said:

"I'm sorry, Fara. I don't see how you can have free time on the telestat. You'll have to pay for it. They did."

"They did!" Fara wondered if he sounded as empty as he felt.

"And they've paid Lan Harris for his lot. The old man asked top price, and got it. He phoned me to transfer the title."

"Oh!" Fara's world was shattering. "You mean nobody's going to do anything? What about the Imperial garrison at Ferd?"

Dimly, he was aware of the mayor mumbling something about the empress's soldiers refusing to interfere in civilian matters. "Civilian matters!" Fara exploded. "You mean these people are just going to be allowed to come here whether we want them or not, illegally forcing the sale of lots by first taking possession of them?" A thought struck him. "Look," he said breathlessly, "you haven't changed your mind about having Jor keep guard in front of the Shop?"

The plump face in the telestat plate grew impatient. "Now, see here, Fara, let the constituted authorities handle this matter."

"But you're going to keep Jor there," Fara said doggedly.

The mayor looked annoyed. "I promised, didn't I? So he'll be there. And now, do you want to buy time on the telestat? It's fifteen credits for one minute. Mind you, as a friend, I think you're wasting your money. No one has ever caught up with a false statement."

Fara said grimly, "Put two on, one in the morning, one in the evening."

"All right. We'll deny it completely. Good night."

The telestat went blank; and Fara sat there. A new thought hardened his face. "That boy of ours—there's going to be a showdown. He either works in my shop or he gets no more allowance."

Creel said, "You've handled him wrong. He's twenty-three, and you treat him like a child. Remember, at twenty-three you were a married man."

"That was different," said Fara. "I had a sense of responsibility. Do you know what he did tonight?"

He didn't quite catch her answer. For a moment he thought she said: "No. In what way did you humiliate him first?"

Fara felt too impatient to verify the improbable words. He rushed on, "He refused in front of the whole village to give me help. He's a bad one, all bad."

"Yes," said Creel in a bitter tone, "he's all bad. I'm sure you don't realize how bad. He's as cold as steel, but without steel's strength or integrity. He took a long time, but he hates even me now because I stood up for you for so long when I knew you were wrong."

"What's that?" said Fara, startled; then gruffly: "Come, come, my dear, we're both upset. Let's go to bed."

He slept poorly.

THREE

There were days when the conviction that this was a personal fight between himself and the Weapon Shop lay heavily on Fara. Though it was out of his way, he made a point of walking past the Weapon Shop on his way to and from work, always pausing to speak to Constable Jor. On the fourth day, the policeman wasn't there.

Fara waited patiently at first, then angrily. He walked finally to his shop and called Jor's house. Jor wasn't home. He was, according to his wife, guarding the Weapon Store. Fara hesitated. His own shop was piled with work, and he had a guilty sense of having neglected his customers for the first time in his life. It would be simple to call up the mayor and report Jor's dereliction. And yet he didn't want to get the man into trouble.

Out in the street, he saw that a large crowd was gathering in front of the Weapon Shop. Fara hurried. A man he knew greeted him excitedly: "Jor's been murdered, Fara!"

"Murdered!" Fara stood very still, and at first he was not clearly conscious of the thought that was in his mind: Satisfaction! Now, even the soldiers would have to act. He realized the ghastly tenor of his thoughts, but pushed the sense of shame out of his mind. He said slowly, "Where's the body?"

"Inside."

"You mean those . . . scum—" In spite of himself, he hesitated over the epithet. It was difficult to think of the silver-haired Weapon Shop man in such terms. His mind hardened. "You mean, those scum killed him, then pulled his body inside?"

"Nobody saw the killing," said another man, "but he's gone and hasn't been seen for three hours. The mayor got the Weapon

Shop on telestat, but they claim they don't know anything about him. They've done away with him, that's what, and now they're pretending innocence. Well, they won't get out of it as easily as that. Mayor's gone to phone the soldiers at Ferd to bring up some big guns."

Something of the excitement that was in the crowd surged through Fara, the feeling that big things were brewing. It was the most delicious sensation that had ever tingled along his nerves, and it was all mixed with a strange pride that he had been so right about this, that he at least had never doubted that here was evil. He did not recognize the emotion as the full-flowering joy that comes to a member of a mob. But his voice shook as he said, "Guns? Yes, that will be the answer, and the soldiers will have to come, of course."

Fara nodded to himself in the immensity of his certainty that the Imperial soldiers would now have no excuse for not acting. He started to say something about what the empress would do if she found out that a man had lost his life because the soldiers had shirked their duty, but the words were drowned in a shout:

"Here comes the mayor! Hey, Mr. Mayor, when are the atomic cannons due?"

There was more of the same general meaning as the mayor's car landed lightly. Some of the questions must have reached His Honor, for he stood up in the open two-seater, and held up his hand for silence. To Fara's astonishment, the plump-faced man gazed at him with accusing eyes. He looked around him, but he was almost alone; everybody else had crowded forward. Fara shook his head, puzzled by that glare, and then flinched as Mayor Dale pointed a finger at him and said in a voice that trembled, "There's the man who's responsible for the trouble that has come upon us. Stand forward, Fara Clark, and show yourself. You've cost this town seven hundred credits that we could ill afford to spend."

Fara couldn't have moved or spoken to save his life. The mayor went on, with self-pity in his tone, "We've all known that it wasn't wise to interfere with these Weapon Shops. So long as the Imperial government leaves them alone, what right have we to set up guards, or act against them? That's what I've thought from the beginning, but this man . . . this . . . this Fara Clark kept after all of us, forcing us to move against our wills, and so now we've got a seven-hundred credit bill to meet and—"

He broke off with, "I might as well make it brief. When I called the garrison, the commander laughed and said that Jor would turn up. And I had barely disconnected when there was a money call from Jor. He's on Mars." He waited for the shouts of amazement to die down. "It'll take four weeks for him to come back by ship, and we've got to pay for it, and Fara Clark is responsible."

The shock was over. Fara stood cold, his mind hard. He said finally, scathingly, "So you're giving up, and trying to blame me all in one breath. I say you are all fools."

As he turned away, he heard Mayor Dale saying that the situation was not completely lost as he had learned that the Weapon Shop had been set up in Glay because the village was equidistant from four cities, and that it was the city business the Shop was after. This would mean tourists, and accessory trade for the village stores.

Fara heard no more. Head high, he walked back to his shop. There were one or two catcalls from the mob, but he ignored them. The worst of it, as the days passed, was the realization that the people of the Weapon Shop had no personal interest in him. They were remote, superior, undefeatable. When he thought of it, he felt a vague fear at the way they had transferred Jor to Mars in a period of less than three hours, when all the world knew that the trip by fastest spaceship could never be made in less than twenty-four days.

Fara did not go to the express station to see Jor arrive home. He had heard that the council had decided to charge Jor with half of the expense of the trip, on the threat of losing his job if he objected. On the second night after Jor's return, Fara slipped down to the constable's house, and handed the officer one hundred and seventy-five credits. He returned home with a clearer conscience.

It was on the third day after that the door of his shop banged open and a man came in. Fara frowned as he saw who it was: Castler, a village hanger-on. The man was grinning. "Thought you might be interested, Fara. Somebody came out of the Weapon Shop today."

Fara strained deliberately at the connecting bolt of a hard plate of the atomic motor he was fixing. He waited with a gathering annoyance that the man did not volunteer further information. Asking questions would be a form of recognition of the worthless fellow. A developing curiosity made him say finally, grudgingly, "I suppose the constable promptly picked him up?"

He supposed nothing of the kind; but it was an opening.

"It wasn't a man. It was a girl."

Fara knitted his brows. He didn't like the idea of making trouble for women. But the cunning devils! Using a girl, just as they had used an old man as a clerk. It was a trick that deserved to fail; the girl was probably a hussy who needed rough treatment. Fara said harshly, "Well, what's happened?"

"She's still out, bold as you please. Pretty thing, too."

The bolt off, Fara took the hard plate over to the polisher, and began patiently the long, careful task of smoothing away the crystals that heat had seared on the once shining metal. The soft throb of the polisher made the background to his next words, "Has anything been done?"

"Nope. The constable's been told, but he says he doesn't fancy being away from his family for another month or so, and paying the cost into the bargain."

Fara contemplated that for a minute, as the polisher throbbed on. His voice shook with suppressed fury when he said finally, "So they're letting them get away with it. It's all been as clever as hell. Can't they see that they mustn't give an inch before these . . . these trangressors? It's like giving countenance to sin."

From the corner of his eye, he noticed that there was a grin on the face of the other. It struck Fara suddenly that the man was enjoying his anger. And there was something else in that grin—a secret knowledge. Fara pulled the engine plate away from the polisher. He faced the ne'er-do-well. "Naturally, that sin part wouldn't worry you much."

"Oh," said the man nonchalantly, "the hard knocks of life make people tolerant. For instance, after you know the girl better, you yourself will probably come to realize that there's good in all of us."

It was not so much the words, as the I've-got-secret-information tone that made Fara snap, "What do you mean—after I get to know the girl better! I won't even speak to the brazen creature."

"One can't always choose," the other said with enormous casualness. "Suppose he brings her home."

"Suppose who brings who home?" Fara spoke irritably. "Castler, you—" He stopped. A dead weight of dismay plumped into his stomach; his whole being sagged. "You mean—" he said.

"I mean," replied Castler with a triumphant leer, "that the boys aren't letting a beauty like her be lonesome. And, naturally, your son was the first to speak to her." He finished: "They're walkin' together now on Second Avenue, comin' this way."

"Get out of here!" Fara roared. "And stay away from me with your gloating. Get out!"

The man hadn't expected such an ignominious ending. He flushed scarlet, then went out, slamming the door. Fara stood for a moment, stiffly. Then, with jerky movements, he shut off his power and went out into the street. The time to put a stop to that kind of thing was—now!

He had no clear plan, simply a determination to end an impossible situation. It was all mixed up with his anger against Cayle. How could he have had such a worthless son, he who paid his debts and worked hard, and tried to be decent and live up to the highest standards of the empress?

He wondered if there mightn't be bad blood on Creel's side, not from her mother, of course—Fara added the qualification hastily. There was a fine, hard-working woman, who would leave Creel a tidy sum one of these days. But Creel's father had disappeared when she was a child.

And now, Cayle with this Weapon Shop girl, who had let herself be picked up—he saw them as he turned the corner onto Second Avenue. They were heading away from Fara. As he came up, the girl was saying:

"You have the wrong idea about us. A person like you can't get a job in our organization. You belong in the Imperial service, where they can use young men of good appearance and ambition."

Fara was too intent for her words to mean anything. He said harshly, "Cayle!"

The couple turned, Cayle with the measured unhurriedness of a young man who had gone a long way on the road to acquiring steel-like nerves; the girl was quicker, but dignified.

Fara had a feeling that his anger was self-destroying, but the violence of his emotions ended that thought even as it came. He said thickly, "Cayle, get home at once."

He was aware of the girl looking at him curiously from strange, gray-green eyes. No shame, he thought, and his rage mounted, driving away the alarm that came at the sight of the flush that was creeping into Cayle's cheeks.

The flush faded into a pale, tight-lipped anger as Cayle half-turned to the girl and said, "This is the childish old fool I've got to contend with. Fortunately, we seldom see each other. We don't even eat our meals at the same table. What do you think of him?"

The girl smiled impersonally. "Oh, we know Fara Clark. He's the mainstay of the empress in Glay."

"Yes," the boy sneered. "You ought to hear him. He thinks we're living in heaven, and the empress is the divine power. The worst part of it is that there's no chance of his ever getting that stuffy look wiped off his face."

They walked off; and Fara stood there. The extent of what had happened drained anger from him as if it had never been. There was the realization that he had made a mistake. But he couldn't quite grasp it. For long now, since Cayle had refused to work in his shop, he had felt this building up to a climax. Suddenly, his own uncontrollable ferocity stood revealed as a partial product of that deeper problem. Only, now that the smash was here, he didn't want to face it.

All through the day in his shop, he kept pushing it out of his mind, kept thinking: Would this go on now, as before, Cayle and he living in the same house, not even looking at each other when they met, going to bed at different times, getting up, Fara at six-thirty, Cayle at noon? Would *that* go on through all the days and years to come?

Creel was waiting for him when he arrived home. She said: "Fara, he wants you to loan him five hundred credits, so that he can go to Imperial City."

Fara nodded wordlessly. He brought the money back to the house the next morning, and gave it to Creel, who took it into Cayle's bedroom.

She came out a minute later. "He says to tell you goodbye."

When Fara came home that evening, Cayle was gone. He wondered whether he ought to feel relieved. But the only sensation that finally came was a conviction of disaster.

FOUR

He had been caught in a trap. Now he was escaping.

Cayle did not think of his departure from the village of Glay as the result of a decision. He had wanted to leave for so long that the purpose seemed part of his body hunger, like the need to eat or drink. But the impulse had grown dim and undefined. Baffled by his father, he had turned an unfriendly eye on everything that was of the village. And his obstinate defiance was matched at every turn by the obdurate qualities of his prison—until now.

Just why the cage had opened was obscure. There was the Weapon Shop girl, of course. Slender, her gray-green eyes intelligent, her face well formed and carrying about her an indefinable aura of a person who had made many successful decisions, she had said—he remembered the words as if she were still speaking them—"Why, yes, I'm from Imperial City. I'm going back there Thursday afternoon."

This Thursday afternoon *she* was going to the great city, while he remained in Glay. He couldn't stand it. He felt ill, savage as an animal in his desire to go also. It was that, more than his quarrel with his father, which made him put pressure on his mother for money. Now, he sat on the local carplane to Ferd, dismayed to find that the girl was not aboard.

At the Ferd Air Center, waiting for the Imperial City plane, he stood at various vantage points and looked for Lucy Rall. But the crowds jamming toward the constant stream of interstate planes defeated even his alert eyes. All too soon his own vast machine glided in for a landing. That is, it seemed too soon until he saw the plane coming toward him. A hundred feet high at the nose, absolutely transparent, it shimmered like a jewel as it drew up in the roadstead.

To Cayle there came a tremendous excitement. Thought of the girl faded. He clambered aboard feverishly. He did not think of Lucy again until the plane was hurtling along over the evergreen land far below. He leaned back in his comfortable chair then, and wondered: What kind of a person was she, this girl of the Weapon Shops? Where did she live? What was her life as a member of an almost rebel organization? . . . There was a man in a chair about ten feet along the aisle. Cayle suppressed an impulse to ask him all the questions that bubbled inside him. Other people might not realize as clearly as he himself did that, though he had lived all his life in Glay, he wasn't really village. He'd better not risk a rebuff.

A man laughed. A woman said, "But, darling, are you sure we can afford a tour of the planets?" They passed along the aisle, Cayle assessing the casualness with which they were taking the trip.

He felt enormously self-conscious at first, but he also gradually grew casual. He read the news on his chair 'stat. With idle glances he watched the scenery speeding by below, adjusting his chair scope for enlarged vision. He felt quite at home by the time the three men seated themselves opposite him and began to play cards.

It was a small game for tiny stakes. And, throughout, two of the men were never addressed by name. The third one was called "Seal." Unusual name, it seemed to Cayle. And the man was as special as his name. He looked about thirty. He had eyes as yellow as a cat's. His hair was wavy, boyish in its unruliness. His face was sallow, though not unhealthy-looking. Jeweled ornaments glittered from each lapel of his coat. Multiple rings flashed colored fire from his fingers. When he spoke it was with slow assurance. And it was he who finally turned to Cayle and said:

"Noticed you watching us. Care to join us?"

Cayle had been intent, automatically accepting Seal as a professional gambler, but not quite decided about the others. The question was, which one was the sucker?

"Make the game more interesting," Seal suggested.

Cayle was suddenly pale. He realized now that these three were a team. And he was their selected victim. Instinctively, he glanced around to see how many people were observing his shame. To his relief, nobody at all was looking. The man who had been sitting ten feet away was not in sight. A stout, well-dressed woman paused at the entrance of the section but turned away. Slowly the color trickled back into his face. So they thought they had found someone who would be an easy mark, did they. He stood up, smiling.

"Don't mind if I do," he said.

He sat down in the vacant chair across from the yellow-eyed man. The deal fell to Cayle. In quick succession and honestly, he dealt himself a king down and two kings up. He played the hand to the limit and, even with the low stakes, eventually raked in about four credits in coins.

He won three out of the next eight games, which was below average for him. He was a callidetic, with temporary emphasis on automatic skill at cards, though he had never heard the word. Once, five years before when he was seventeen, while playing with four other boys for credit-twentieths, he won nineteen out of twenty games of showdown. Thereafter, his gambling luck, which might have rescued him from the village, was so great that no one in Glay would play with him.

In spite of his winning streak now, he felt no sense of superiority. Seal dominated the game. There was a commanding air about him, an impression of abnormal strength, not physical. Cayle began to be fascinated.

"I hope you won't be offended," he said finally, "but you're a type of person who interests me."

The yellow eyes studied him thoughtfully, but Seal said nothing.

"Been around a lot, I suppose?" said Cayle.

He was dissatisfied with the question. It was not what he wanted. It sounded less than mature. Seal, mere gambler though he was, towered above such a naive approach. But he replied this time. "A bit," he said noncommittally.

His companions seemed to find that amusing. They both guffawed. Cayle flushed, but there was a will in him to know things. "To the planets?" he asked.

No answer. Seal carefully studied the cards that were down, then raised a credit-fortieth. Cayle struggled against the feeling that he was making a fool of himself. Then, "We all hear things," he said apologetically, "and it's sometimes hard to know what's true and what isn't. Are any of the planets worth going to?"

The yellow eyes studied him now with amusement. "Listen, fella," said Seal impressively, "don't go near them. Earth is the heaven of this system and if anybody tells you that wonderful Venus is beckoning, tell 'em to go to hell—that's Venus. Hell, I mean. Endless sandstorms. And one day, when I was in Venusburg, the temperature rose to eighty-four centigrade." He finished, "They don't tell you things like that in the ads, do they?"

Cayle agreed hastily that they didn't. He was taken aback by the volubility of the reply. It sounded boastful like—he couldn't decide. But the man was abruptly less interesting. He had one more question.

"Are you married?" he asked.

Seal laughed. "Married! Listen, my friend, I get married every place I go. Not legally, mind you." He laughed again, significantly. "I see I'm giving you ideas."

Cayle said, "You don't have to get ideas like that from other people."

He spoke automatically. He hadn't expected such a revelation of character. No doubt Seal was a man of courage. But the glamour was gone from him. Cayle recognized that it was his village morality, his mother's ethics, that were assessing the other. But he couldn't help it. For years he had had this conflict between his mother's credos and his instinctive awareness that the world outside could not be compressed into the mores that encompassed village life.

Seal was speaking again, heartily. "This boy is really going to be somebody in ever-glorious Isher, eh, boys? And I'm not overstating, either." He broke off. "Where do you get all those good cards?"

Cayle had won again. He raked in the pot, and hesitated. He had won forty-five credits, and knew he had better quit before he caused irritation. "I'm afraid I'll have to stop," he said. "I've some things to do. It's been a pleas—"

He faltered, breathless. A tiny, glittering gun peered at him over the edge of the table. The yellow-eyed man said in a monotone, "So you think it's time to quit, eh?" His head did not turn, but his voice reached out directly at his companions. "He thinks it's time to quit, boys. Shall we let him?" It must have been a rhetorical question, for the henchmen merely grimaced.

"Personally," the leader went on, "I'm all in favor of quitting. Now, let me see," he purred. "According to the transparency his wallet is in his upper right hand breast pocket and there are some fifty-credit notes in an envelope pinned into his shirt pocket. And then, of course, there's the money he won from us in his trouser pocket."

He leaned forward and his strange eyes were wide open and ironic. "So you thought we were gamblers who were going to take you, somehow. No, my friend, we don't work that way. Our system is much simpler. If you refused to hand over, or tried to attract somebody's attention, I'd fire this energy gun straight into your heart. It works on such a narrow beam that no one would even notice the tiny hole in your clothing. You'd continue to sit right there, looking a little sleepy perhaps, but who would wonder about that on this big ship, with all its busy, self-centered people?" His voice hardened. "Hand it over! Quick! I'm not fooling. I'll give you ten seconds."

It took longer than that to turn over the money but apparently the continuity of acquiescence was all that was required. He was allowed to put his empty pocketbook back into his pocket and several coins were ignored. "You'll need a bite before we land," Seal said generously.

The gun disappeared under the table and Seal leaned back in his chair with an easy relaxation. "Just in case," he said, "you decide to complain to the captain, let me tell you that we would kill you instantly without worrying about the consequences. Our story is simple. You've been foolish and lost all your money at cards." He laughed and climbed to his feet, once more imperturbable and mysterious. "Be seeing ya, fellow. Better luck next time."

The other men were climbing to their feet. The three sauntered off and, as Cayle watched, they disappeared into the forward cocktail bar. Cayle remained in his chair, hunched and devastated.

His gaze sought the distant clock—July 15, 4784 Isher—two hours and fifteen minutes out of Ferd and an hour, still to Imperial City.

With closed eyes Cayle pictured himself arriving in the old city as darkness fell. His first night there, that was to have been so thrilling, would now be spent on the streets.

FIVE

He couldn't sit still. And three times, as he paced through the ship, he paused before full length energy mirrors. His bloodshot eyes glared back at him from the lifelike image of himself. And over and above the desperate wonder of what to do now, he thought: How had they picked him for victim? What was there about him that had made the gang of three head unerringly toward him?

As he turned from the third mirror he saw the Weapon Shop girl. Her gaze flicked over him without recognition. She wore a soft blue tailored dress, and a strand of creamy pearls around her tanned neck. She looked so smart and at ease that he didn't have the heart to follow her. Hopelessly, Cayle moved out of her line of vision and sank into a seat.

A movement caught his distracted gaze. A man was slumping into a chair at the table across the aisle. He wore the uniform of a colonel in Her Imperial Majesty's Army. He was so drunk he could hardly sit, and how he had walked to the seat was a mystery rooted deep in the laws of balance. His head came around, and his eyes peered blearily at Cayle.

"Spying on me, eh?" His voice went down in pitch, and up in volume. *"Waiter!"*

A steward hurried forward. "Yes, sir?"

"The finest wine for my shadow n'me." As the waiter rushed off, the officer beckoned Cayle. "Might as well sit over here. Might as well travel together, eh?" His tone grew confidential. "I'm a wino, y'know. Been trying to keep it from the empress for a long time. She doesn't like it." He shook his head sadly. "Doesn't like it at all. *Well, what're you waiting for? C'mon over here.*"

Cayle came hastily, cursing the drunken fool. But hope came too. He had almost forgotten, but the Weapon Shop girl had suggested he join the Imperial forces. If he could obtain information from this alcoholic and join up fast, then the loss of the money wouldn't matter. "I've got to decide," he told himself. He distinctly thought of himself as making a decision.

He sipped his wine presently, more tense than he cared to be, eyeing the older man with quick, surreptitious glances. The man's background emerged slowly out of a multitude of incoherent confidences. His name was Laurel Medlon. Colonel Laurel Medlon, he would have Cayle understand, confidant of the empress, intimate of the palace, head of a tax collecting district.

"Damned, hic, good one, too," he said with a satisfaction that gave more weight to his words than the words themselves.

He looked sardonically at Cayle. "Like to get in on it, eh?" He hiccoughed. "Okay, come to my office—tomorrow."

His voice trailed. He sat mumbling to himself. And, when Cayle asked a question, he muttered that he had come to Imperial City ". . . when I was your age. Boy, was I green!" He quivered in a spasm of vinous indignation. "Y'know, those damned clothing monopolies have different kinds of cloth they send out to the country. You can spot anybody from a village. I was sure spotted fast . . ."

His voice trailed off into a series of curses. His reminiscent rage communicated itself to Cayle.

So that was it—his clothes!

The unfairness of it wracked his body. His father had consistently refused to let him buy his suits even in nearby Ferd. Always Fara had protested, "How can I expect the local merchants to bring their repair work to me if my family doesn't deal with them?" And having asked the unanswerable question, the older man would not listen to further appeals.

"And here I am," Cayle thought, "stripped because that old fool—" The futile anger faded. Because large towns like Ferd probably had their own special brand of cloth, as easily identifiable as anything in Glay. The unfairness of it, he saw with reaching clarity, went far beyond the stubborn stupidity of one man.

But it was good to know, even at this eleventh hour.

The colonel was stirring. And, once more, Cayle pressed his question. "But how did you get into the army? How did you become an officer in the first place?"

The drunken man said something about the empress having a damned nerve complaining about tax money. And then there was something about the attack on the Weapon Shops being a damned nuisance, but that wasn't clear. Another remark about some two-timing dames who had better watch out made Cayle visualize an officer who maintained several mistresses. And then, finally came the answer to his question.

"I paid five thousand credits for my commission—damn crime . . ." He gabbled again for a minute, then, "Empress insists on giving them out for nothing right now. Won't do it. A man's got to have his graft." Indignantly, "I sure paid plenty."

"You mean," Cayle urged, "commissions are available now without money? Is that what you mean?" In his anxiety, he grabbed the man's sleeve.

The officer's eyes, which had been half closed, jerked open. They glared at Cayle suspiciously. "Who are you?" he snapped. "Get away from me." His voice was harsh, briefly almost sober. "By God," he said, "you can't travel these days without picking up some leech. I've a good mind to have you arrested."

Cayle stood up, flushing. He staggered as he walked away. He felt shaken and on the verge of panic. He was being hit too hard and too often.

The blur faded slowly from his mind. He saw that he had paused to peer into the forward cocktail bar. Seal and his companions were still there. The sight of them stiffened him and he knew why he had come back to look at them. There was a will to action growing in him, a determination not to let them get away with what they had done. But first he'd need some information.

He spun on his heel and headed straight for the Weapon Shop girl, who sat in one corner reading a book, a slim, handsome young woman of twenty years or so. Her eyes studied his face as he described how his money had been stolen. Cayle finished, "Here's what I want to know. Would you advise me to go to the captain?"

She shook her head. "No," she said, "I wouldn't do that. The captain and the crew receive a forty percent cut on most of these ships. They'd help dispose of your body."

Cayle leaned back in his seat. He felt drained of vitality. The trip, his first beyond Ferd, was taking toll of his strength. "How is it," he asked finally, straightening, "that they didn't pick you? Oh,

I know you probably aren't wearing village-type clothes, but how do they select?"

The girl shook her head. "These men," she said, "go around surreptitiously using transparencies. The first thing they discover is, if you're wearing a Weapon Shop gun. Then they leave you strictly alone."

Cayle's face hardened. "Could I borrow yours?" he asked tautly. "I'll show those skunks."

The girl shrugged. "Weapon Shop guns are tuned to individuals," she said. "Mine wouldn't work for you. And, besides, you can use it only for defense. It's too late for you to defend yourself."

Cayle stared gloomily down through the myradel floor. The beauty below mocked him. The splendor of the towns that appeared every few minutes merely deepened his depression. Slowly the desperation came back. It seemed to him suddenly that Lucy Rall was his last hope and that he had to persuade her to help him. He said, "Isn't there anything that the Weapon Shops do besides sell guns?"

The girl hesitated. "We have an information center," she said finally.

"What do you mean—information? What kind of information?"

"Oh, everything. Where people were born. How much money they have. What crimes they've committed or are committing. Of course, we don't interfere."

Cayle frowned at her, simultaneously dissatisfied and fascinated. He had not intended to be distracted but for years there had been questions in his mind about the Weapon Shops.

And here was somebody who knew.

"But what do they do?" He said insistently. "If they've got such wonderful guns why don't they just take over the government?"

Lucy Rall smiled and shook her head. "You don't understand," she said. "The Weapon Shops were founded more than two thousand years ago by a man who decided that the incessant struggle for power of different groups was insane and the civil and other wars must stop forever. It was a time when the world had just emerged from a war in which more than a billion people had died and he found thousands of people who agreed to follow him. His idea was nothing less than that whatever government was in power should not be overthrown. But that an organization should be set up which would have one principal purpose—to ensure that no government ever again obtained complete power over its people. A man who felt himself wronged should be able to go somewhere to buy a defensive gun. You cannot imagine what a great forward step that was. Under the old tyrannical governments it was frequently a capital offense to be found in possession of a blaster or a gun."

Her voice was taking on emotional intensity now. It was clear that she believed what she was saying. She went on earnestly. "What gave the founder the idea was the invention of an electronic and atomic system of control which made it possible to build indestructible Weapon Shops and to manufacture weapons that could only be used for defense. That last ended all possibility of Weapon Shop guns being used by gangsters and other criminals and morally justified the entire enterprise. For defensive purposes a Weapon Shop gun is superior to an ordinary or government weapon. It works on mind control and leaps to the hand when wanted. It provides a defensive screen against other blasters, though not against bullets but since it is so much faster, that isn't important."

She looked at Cayle and the intentness faded from her face. "Is that what you wanted to know?" she asked.

"Suppose you're shot from ambush?" Cayle asked.

She shrugged. "No defense." She shook her head, smiling faintly. "You really don't understand. We don't worry about individuals. What counts is that many millions of people have the knowledge that they can go to a Weapon Shop if they want to protect themselves and their families. And, even more important, the forces that would normally try to enslave them are restrained by the conviction that it is dangerous to press people too far. And so a great balance has been struck between those who govern and those who are governed."

Cayle stared at her in bitter disappointment. "You mean that a person has to save himself? Even when you get a gun you have to nerve yourself to resist? Nobody is there to help you?"

It struck him with a pang that she must have told him this in order to show him why she couldn't help him.

Lucy spoke again. "I can see that what I've told you is a great disappointment to you. But that's the way it is. And I think you'll realize that's the way it has to be. When a people lose the courage to resist encroachment on their rights, then they can't be saved by an outside force. Our belief is that people always have the kind of government they want and that individuals must bear the risks of freedom, even to the extent of giving their lives."

There must have been an expression on his face, a reflection of the strain that was in him. For she broke off. "Look," she urged, "let me alone for a while to think over what you've told me. I won't promise anything. But I'll give you my decision before we reach our destination. All right?"

He thought it was a nice way of getting rid of him. He stood up, smiling wryly, and took an empty seat in an adjoining salon. Later, when he glanced in the doorway, the corner where she had been sitting was unoccupied.

It was that that decided him. She was evading the problem. He had been tensing again and now he climbed to his feet and headed for the forward bar.

He came upon Seal from behind and struck him a cruel blow on the side of the face. The smaller man was plummeted out of his stool and knocked to the floor. His two companions jumped to their feet. Cayle kicked the nearer man in the groin, mercilessly. The fellow moaned, and staggered, clutching his stomach.

Ignoring him, Cayle dived at the third man who was trying to get his gun from a shoulder holster. He struck the gambler with the full weight of his body and from that moment the advantage was his. It was he who secured the gun, struck savagely with it at the man's groping hand and drew blood and a cry of pain, followed by a mad scramble to break free.

Cayle whirled, in time to see Seal climb to his feet. The man rubbed his jaw and they stood staring at each other.

"Give me back my money," said Cayle. "You picked the wrong man."

Seal raised his voice. "Folks, I'm being robbed. This is the most barefaced—"

He stopped. He must have realized that this was not a matter of being clever or reasonable. He must have realized it for he suddenly held up his hands and said quickly, "Don't shoot, you fool! After all, we didn't shoot you."

Cayle, finger on trigger, restrained himself. "My money?" he snapped.

There was an interruption. A loud voice said, "What's going on here? Put up your hands, you with the gun."

Cayle turned and backed toward the near wall. Three ship's

officers with portable blasters stood just inside the door, covering him. Not once during the argument that followed did Cayle lower his own gun.

He told his story succinctly and refused to surrender. "I have reason to believe," he said, "that the officers of a ship on which such incidents can occur are not above suspicion. Now, quick, Seal, my money."

There was no answer. He sent a swift look to where Seal had been—and felt a sense of emptiness.

The gambler was gone. There was no sign of the two henchmen.

"Look," said the officer who seemed to be in command, "put up your gun and we'll forget the whole matter."

Cayle said, "I'll go out of that door." He motioned to his right. "When I'm through there I'll put up my gun."

That was agreeable and Cayle wasted no time. He searched the ship, then, from stem to stern, but found no sign of Seal or his companions. In a fury, he sought out the captain. "You scum, you," he said coldly, "you let them get away in an airboat."

The officer stared at him coolly. "Young man," he said finally, satirically, "you are discovering that the ads are right. Travel is very educational. As a result of being aboard our ship, you have become more alert. You have discovered within yourself qualities of courage hitherto unsuspected. Within the space of a few hours, in short, you've grown up a little. The value of that in terms of survival cannot be estimated. In terms of money, you've paid a small amount. If you should desire, at some future date to pay an additional gratuity, I shall be happy to give you my address."

Cayle said, "I'll report you to your firm."

The officer shrugged. "Complaint forms are available in the lounge. You'll have to attend a hearing at our Ferd office at your own expense."

"I see," said Cayle grimly. "It works out very nicely for you, doesn't it?"

"I didn't make the rules," was the reply. "I just live under them."

Quivering, Cayle walked back to the salon where he had last seen the Weapon Shop girl. But she was still not in sight. He began to tense himself for the landing, now less than half an hour away.

Below he could see that the shadows of approaching darkness were lengthening over the world of Isher. The whole eastern sky looked dark and misty as if out there, beyond the far horizon, night had already come.

A few minutes after Cayle had walked away from her, the girl closed her book and strolled in a leisurely fashion into a private telestat booth. She locked the door, then pulled the switch that disconnected the instrument from the main board in the captain's cabin.

She took one of the rings from her finger, manipulated it into a careful integration with the government 'stat. A woman's face took shape on the screen, said matter-of-factly, "Information Center."

"Connect me with Robert Hedrock."

"One moment, please."

The man's face that came almost immediately onto the screen was rugged rather than handsome but it looked sensitive as well as strong and there was a pride and vitality in every muscular quirk, in every movement, that was startling to see. The personality of the man poured forth from the image of him in a ceaseless, magnetic stream. His voice, when he spoke, was quiet though resonant:

"Coordination department."

"This is Lucy Rall, guardian of Imperial Potential, Cayle Clark." She went on to describe briefly what had happened to Cayle. "We measured him as a callidetic giant and are watching him in the hope that his rise will be so rapid that we can use him in our fight to prevent the empress from destroying the Weapon Shops with her new time weapon. This is in accord with the directive that no possibility be neglected provided there is someone available to do something about it. I think he should be given some money."

"I see." The virile face was thoughtful. "What is his village index?"

"Middling. He may have a hard time in the city for a while. But he'll get over his small town attitudes quickly. The trouble he is involved in now will toughen him. But he needs help."

There was decision on Hedrock's face. "In such cases as this the smaller the amount of money the greater the subsequent gratitude—" he smiled—"we hope. Give him fifteen credits and let him regard it as a personal loan from you. Provide no other protection of any kind. He's on his own completely. Anything else?"

"Nothing."

"Goodbye then."

It required less than a minute for Lucy Rall to restore the 'stat to its full government status.

SIX

Cayle watched the face of the landlady as she looked him over. *This* decision was out of his hands.

He actually thought of it as that—a decision. The question was, would she spot him as village? He couldn't be sure. Her expression, when she nodded, was enigmatic. The room she rented him was small but it cost only a credit-fourth a day.

Cayle lay down on the bed and relaxed by the rhythm system. He felt amazingly well. The theft of his money still stung but it was no longer a disaster. The fifteen credits the Weapon Shop girl had given him would tide him over for a few weeks. He was safe. He was in Imperial City. And the very fact that the girl had loaned him money and given him her name and address must prove something. Cayle sighed with pleasure, finally, and went out to get some supper.

He had noticed an automat at the corner. It was deserted except for a middle-aged man. Cayle bought a steak from the instantaneous cooking machine, and then deliberately sat down near the other diner.

"I'm new here," he said conversationally. "Can you give me a picture of the city? I'd appreciate it."

It was a new tack, for him, admitting naivete. But he felt very sure of himself, and very convinced that he needed data more than he needed to protect his own self-conscious pride. He was not too surprised when the stranger cleared his throat importantly and then said:

"New to the big city, eh? Been anywhere yet?"

"No. Just arrived."

The man nodded, half to himself, a faint gleam of interest in his gray eyes. Cayle thought cynically: "He's wondering how he can take advantage of me."

The other spoke again, his tone half-ingratiating now. "My name is Gregor. I live just around the corner in a skytel. What do you want to know?"

"Oh," Cayle spoke quickly, "where's the best residential district? Where's the business section? Who's being talked about?"

Gregor laughed. "That last—the empress, of course. Have you ever seen her?"

"Only on the 'stats."

"Well, you know then that she's just a kid trying hard to be tough."

Cayle knew nothing of the kind. Despite his cynicism, he had never thought of any member of the ruling family of Isher except in terms of their titles. Automatically, he rejected this man's attempt to make a human being out of Imperial Innelda.

He said, "What about the empress?"

"They've got her trapped in the palace—a bunch of old men who don't want to give up power."

Cayle frowned, dissatisfied with the picture. He recalled the last time he had seen the empress on the 'stats. It was a willful face as he remembered it; and her voice had had in it great pride as well as determination. If any group was trying to use her as a tool, then they had better watch out. The young empress had a mind of her own.

Gregor said, "You'll want to try the games. That's on the Avenue of Luck. And then there's the theatres, and the restaurants, and—"

Cayle was losing interest. He should have known better than to expect that a casual acquaintance in a cheap residential district would be able to tell him what he wanted to know. This man had a small mind. What he had to say would not be important.

The man was continuing: "I'll be very happy to take you around. I'm a little short myself right now but—"

Cayle smiled wryly. So that was the extent of this man's machinations. It was part of the corrupt pattern of Isher life, but in this case such a mean and miserable part that it didn't matter. He shook his head and said gently:

"I'll be happy to go out some other time. Tonight, I'm kind of tired—you know, long trip—just got in."

He applied himself to his food, not at all unhappy. The conversation had done him no harm; in fact, he felt slightly better. Without ever having been in Imperial City, he had a better idea than Gregor as to what was, and what was not, sensible.

The meal cost more than he had expected. But even that he decided not to regret. After his experiences on the plane he needed sustenance. He went out onto the street contentedly. The neighborhood swarmed with children, and though it was already dark the play went on relentlessly.

Cayle paused for a moment to watch them. Their ages seemed to vary from about six to twelve years. Their play was of the group-rhythm type taught in all the schools, only this was heavily overlaid with a sex-motif that he had never seen before. He was startled, then rueful.

"Good heavens!" he thought. "I had the reputation for being a devil of a fellow. To these kids I'd be just plain naive."

He went up to his room, conscious that the young man over whom the elders of Glay had many times shaken their heads was really a simple, honest soul. He might come to a bad end but it would be because he was too innocent, not the other way around.

It disturbed him. In Glay there had been a certain pleasure in defying the conventions. In Glay he had thought of himself as being "city." Lying on the bed he knew that was true up to a point only. He lacked experience and knowledge, automatic response and awareness of dangers. His immediate plans must include remedies for these weaknesses. The vagueness of the purpose disturbed him. He had an uneasy feeling that he was making stop-gap decisions, that somehow he was not comprehending the main decision he must make one of these days.

He drifted into sleep, worrying about it. Twice, when he stirred on the edge of wakening, the thought was still there, unpleasant, urgent, a jarring background to his first night in the city of dreams. He awoke tired and unhappy. Only gradually did the uneasiness wear off.

He avoided the expensive automat, eating breakfast for a credit-eighth in a restaurant that offered personal service and featured "home" cooking. He regretted his miserliness. The weight of the indigestible meal on his stomach did not lighten until he was in the Penny Palace, an ornate gambling establishment on the world famous Avenue of Luck.

According to a guidebook which dealt exclusively with the avenue and its games, the Penny Palace owners "have put up glitter signs which modestly claim that it is possible for anyone to come in with a penny and walk out with a million, meaning, of course, a million credits." Whether or not this good fortune has ever been achieved the signs do not indicate.

The write-up concluded generously, "The Penny Palace has the distinction of having more fifty-fifty games for the number of machines it has in operation than any other establishment on the Avenue of Luck."

It was that plus the low stakes that interested Cayle. His immediate plans did not include walking out "with a million." He wanted five hundred credits to begin with. After that—well, then he could afford to enlarge his horizon.

He laid his first bet on a machine that pumped the words *odd* and *even* into a swirling pool of light. When ten of each had been pumped into the pool the liquid-looking stuff suffered a chemical change, after which it would support only one of the words on its surface. All the others sank through a screen and vanished.

The winning words floated easily face up and somehow set in motion the paying mechanism or the collecting mechanism. The bettors either saw their bets vanish with a click or else their winnings would slide automatically to the square before which they stood. Cayle heard the click of defeat.

He doubled his bet and this time won. He withdrew his original stake, and played with the coin he had won. The intricate lights fused, the pump squished, then up floated the word *even.* The pleasant sound of money sliding softly toward him assailed Cayle's ears. It was a sound that he was to hear often during the next hour and a half for, despite the fact that he played cautiously and only with pennies, he won just over five credits.

Tired at last he retreated to a connecting restaurant. When he came back into the "treasure room," as it was called, he noticed a game that was played in an even more intimate fashion by the player himself.

The money went into a slot, releasing a lever, and when this was pulled a light sequence was set up. The movement was very rapid but it resolved swiftly into red or black. The game was thus but another variation of the odd and even sequence, since the player had the same fifty-fifty chance of winning.

Cayle slipped a half credit coin into the proper slot, pulled the activating lever—and lost. His second guess was equally wrong, and his third, also. The fourth time his color shimmered into place and he had his first win. He won the next ten straight, lost four, then won seven out of another ten series. In two hours, by playing carefully, limiting his luck rather than forcing it, he won seventy-eight credits.

He withdrew to one of the bars for a drink, and pondered his next move. So many things to do—buy a new suit, protect his winnings, prepare for another night and pay back the money Lucy Rall had loaned him.

His mind poised, titillated. He felt comfortable and very sure of himself. A moment later he was putting through a 'stat call to the Weapon Shop girl.

Making more money could wait.

She came in almost immediately. "I'm out on the street now," she answered his request.

Cayle could see what she meant. Her face almost filled the screen. Extens-stats magnified from a tiny image. People used them on the street, keeping them connected with their home 'stats. One of the fellows in Glay had one.

Before Cayle could speak, the girl said, "I'm on my way to my apartment. Wouldn't you like to meet me there?"

Would he!

Her apartment turned out to be a four room affair, unique only in the abundance of automatic devices. After a quick look around, it was clear to Cayle that Lucy Rall never did a stroke of housework. What puzzled him, however, was that the place seemed unprotected. The girl came out of her bedroom dressed for the street and shrugged at his comment.

"We Weapon Shop people," she said, "live just like anyone else, usually in the nicer residential districts. Only our Shops and—" she hesitated—"a few factories and, of course, the Information Center are protected from interference."

She broke off. "You said something about buying a suit. If you wish I'll help you select it. I've only two hours, though."

Cayle held the door open for her, exhilarated. The invitation to her apartment must have a personal meaning. Whatever her duties for the Weapon Shops, they couldn't possibly include inviting obscure Cayle Clark to her apartment, even if only for a few moments. He decided to assume that she was interested in him as an individual.

They took a carplane, Lucy pushing the button that brought the machine down to pick them up.

"Where are we going?" Cayle asked.

The girl smiled, and shook her head. "You'll see," she said. When they were in the plane, she pointed up. "Look," she said.

An artificial cloud was breaking out in the sky above. It changed colors several times, then vividly through it shone the letters: HABERDASHERY PARADISE.

Cayle said, "Why, I saw their ad last night."

He had forgotten but now he remembered. The streamers of lights had soared aloft the night before as he walked from the automat to his rooming house. Advertising Paradise. Informing males of every age that here was the place to buy, here the retail establishment that could furnish anything in men's clothing any hour of the day or night, anywhere on earth, Mars, or Venus and, for a trifling extra cost, anywhere in the inhabited Solar System.

The ad had been one of hundreds—and so, in spite of his need for clothes, the name didn't remain in his memory.

"It's a store worth seeing," Lucy said.

It seemed to Cayle that she was enjoying his enjoyment. It made him feel a little naive—but not too much. What was important was that she was going with him. He ventured, "It's so kind of you to help me."

Haberdashery Paradise turned out to be more impressive than its ads. The building was three blocks long and eighty stories high. So Lucy told him; and added, "We'll go to the main sections quickly, then buy your suit."

The entrance to Paradise was a hundred yards wide, and thirty stories high. An energy screen kept the weather out but its doorless vastness was otherwise without barriers. It was easy to press through the harmless screen into the domed anteroom. The Paradise not only supplied beach clothing—it supplied a beach with a quarter of a mile of surging water tumbling from a misty horizon onto acres of sand, complete with seashells, complete with the rich, tangy smell of the sea itself. Paradise not only supplied ski outfits, it supplied startlingly lifelike mountains with a twisting half-mile of snow-covered slope.

"Paradise is a COMPLETE STORE," said one flashing sign to which Lucy called his attention. "If there is anything you do not see that fits in with our slogan, 'Everything for the Man,' ask for it. We have it at a price."

"That includes women," Lucy said matter-of-factly. "They charge the same for women as they do for their suits, anywhere from five credits to fifty thousand. You'd be surprised how many women of good family register when they need money. It's all very discreet, of course."

Cayle saw that she was looking at him thoughtfully. And that he was expected to make a comment. It was so direct that he was startled. He said hastily, "I shall never pay money for a woman."

It seemed to satisfy her, for they went from there to the suits. There were thirty floors of suits but each floor had its own price range. Lucy took him to the twenty-thirty credit floor and pointed out to him the difference in weave between "city" cloth and the cloth of his own suit. For thirty-two credits he bought a suit, shirt, tie, socks and shoes.

"I don't think," said Lucy practically, "you should go any higher than that yet."

She refused his offer of the credits he owed her. "You can pay me that later on. I'd rather you put it in the bank now, as a reserve fund."

It meant he would see her again. It seemed to mean she wanted to see him again.

"Better hurry and change," said Lucy. "I'll wait."

It was that that decided him to try to kiss her before they separated. But when he came out, her first words dashed this determination. "I didn't realize how late it was," she said. "It's three o'clock."

She paused to look at him, smiled. "You're a big, strong, handsome man," she said. "Did you know? But now, let's hurry."

They separated at the Gargantuan entrance, Lucy hurrying to a carplane stop, leaving him empty behind her. The feeling departed slowly. He began to walk at a quickening pace.

By the time he came to where the Fifth Interplanetary Bank sat heavily on the base from which its ethereal spires soared to a height of sixty-four stories, ambition was surging in him again. It was a big bank in which to deposit the tiny sum of fifteen credits but the money was accepted without comment, though he was required to register his fingerprints.

Cayle left the bank, more relaxed than he had been at any time since the robbery. He had a savings account. He was suitably dressed. There remained one more thing before he proceeded to the third phase of his gambling career.

From one of the public carplanes he had located the all-directional sign of a Weapon Shop, nestling in its private park near the bank. He walked briskly up the beflowered pathway, and he was almost at the door when he noticed the small sign, which he had never seen before in a Weapon Shop. The sign read:

ALL METROPOLITAN WEAPON SHOPS
TEMPORARILY CLOSED
NEW AND OLD RURAL SHOPS OPEN AS USUAL

Cayle retreated reluctantly. It was one possibility he had not expected, the fabulous Weapon Shops being closed. He turned as a thought came. But there was no indication as to when the Shops would reopen, no date, nothing at all but the one simple announcement. He stood frowning, experiencing a sense of loss, shocked by the silence. Not, he realized, that that last should be bothering him. In Glay it was always silent around the Weapon Shop.

The feeling of personal loss, the what-ought-he-to-do-now bewilderment grew. On impulse, he tried the door. It was solid and immovable. His second retreat began, and this time he carried through to the street.

He stood on a safety isle undecided as to what button to push. He thought back over the two and a half hours with Lucy and it seemed a curious event in space-time. He felt appalled, remembering how drab his conversation had been. And yet, except for a certain directness, a greater decisiveness, her own conversation left no dazzling memories.

"This is it," he thought. "When a girl puts up with a dull fellow for an afternoon, she's felt something."

The pressures inside him grew stronger, the will to action telescoping his plans, impelling him to swift activity. He had thought—Weapon Shop, more gambling, then Army District Headquarters commanded by Colonel Medlon—over a period of a week. The Weapon Shop had to be first because Weapon Shops did not open for Imperial agents, whether soldiers or merely government employees.

But he couldn't wait for that now. He pressed the button that would bring down the first carplane going toward District Number Nineteen.

A minute later he was on his way.

SEVEN

District Nineteen headquarters was an old style building of the waterfall design. The pattern was overdone, the design renewing itself at frequent intervals. Stream after marble stream poured forth from hidden crevices and gradually merged one with another.

It was not a big building, but it was big enough to give Cayle pause. Its fifteen stories and its general offices, filled with clucking file machines and clerks, were impressive. He hadn't pictured such a field of a authority behind the drunken man on the plane.

The building directory listed civil functions and military functions. Cayle presumed that he would find Colonel Medlon somewhere behind the heading: STAFF OFFICES, PENTHOUSE.

A note in brackets under the listing said: *Secure pass to penthouse elevator at reception desk on 15th floor.*

The reception department took his name, but there was a subdued consultation before a man attached it to a relayer and submitted it for the examination of an inner office authority. A middle-aged man in captain's uniform emerged from a door. He scowled at Cayle. "The colonel," he said, "doesn't like young men." He added impatiently, "Who are you?"

It didn't sound promising. But Cayle felt his own stubbornness thickening in his throat. His long experience at defying his father made it possible for him to say in a level voice, "I met Colonel Medlon on a plane to Imperial City yesterday and he insisted I come to see him. If you will please inform him that I am here—"

The captain looked at him for a full half minute. Then, without a word, he went back into the inner sanctum. He emerged, shaking his head but more friendly. "The colonel says that he does not remember you but that he will give you a minute." He lowered his voice to a whisper. "Was he—uh—under the influence?"

Cayle nodded. He did not trust himself to speak. The captain said in a low, urgent voice, "Go inside and push him for all he's worth. A very important personage has called him twice today and he wasn't in. And now you've got him nervous. He's frightened of what he says when he's under. Doesn't dare touch a drop when he's in town, you know."

Cayle followed the backstabbing captain, with one more picture of the Isher world taking form in his mind. Here was a junior officer who appeared to be maneuvering for his superior's job.

He forgot that as he stepped out of the penthouse elevator. He wondered tensely if he were capable of handling this situation. The gloomy feeling came that he wasn't. He took one look at the man who sat behind a great desk in the corner of a large room and the fear that he would be thrown bodily out of the Nineteenth District Headquarters evaporated.

It was the same man as on the ship, but somehow shrunken. His face, which had seemed bloated when he was drunk, looked smaller. His eyes were thoughtful, and he drummed nervously on his desk.

"You may leave us alone, Captain." His voice was quiet and authoritative.

The captain departed with a set look on his face. Cayle sat down.

"I seem to recall your face now," said Medlon. "Sorry, I guess I had been drinking a little." He laughed hollowly.

Cayle was thinking that what the other had said about the empress must be highly dangerous for a man of his position. Aloud, he said, "I did not receive the impression of anything unusual, sir." He hesitated. "Though, when I think of it, you were perhaps too free with your confidences." Once more he paused. "I thought it was your position that made it possible for you to speak so strongly and so freely."

There was silence. Cayle had time for cautious self-congratulation but he did not delude himself. This man had not risen to his present position by being afraid or simpleminded.

"Uh—" said Colonel Medlon finally, "what did we—uh—agree on?"

"Among other things, sir," said Cayle, "you told me that the government was in need of officers and you offered me a commission."

"I do not," said Colonel Medlon, "recall the offer." He seemed to be bracing himself. "However, if I did so far forget myself as to make such an offer I have very regretfully to inform you that I have no authority to make you an officer. There is a regular procedure with regard to commissions, completely out of my hands. And since the positions are held in great esteem, the government has long regarded them as a source of financial return. For instance, a lieutenancy would cost you five thousand credits even with my influence behind you. A captaincy would disturb you to the extent of fifteen thousand credits, which is quite a sum for a young fellow to raise and—"

Cayle had been listening with a developing wryness. Looking back over his words it seemed to him that he had done his best with the material. He just wasn't in a position to make use of Medlon's indiscretions. He said with a twisted smile, "How much is a colonelcy?"

The officer guffawed. "Young fella," he said jovially, "it is not paid for in money. The price comes out of your soul, one black spot at a time."

He broke off, earnestly, "Now, look," he said. "I'm sorry if I was a little free with Her Majesty's commissions yesterday, but you understand how these things are. And just to show you I'm not a welsher, even when I'm not responsible, tell you what I'll do. You bring five thousand credits here at your convenience in, say—well, two weeks, and I'll practically guarantee you a commission. How's that?"

For a man who owned less than forty credits, it was a fairly futile attempt at a solution. If the empress had actually ordered that commissions not be sold in future, the command was being ignored by corrupt henchmen. Cayle had his second insight into the Imperial Innelda's situation.

She and her advisers were not all-powerful. He had always thought that only the Weapon Shops restrained her government. But the net was caught in was more intangible than that. The vast mass of individuals who served her will had their own schemes, their own desires, which they pursued with more ardor than they served the woman to whom they had sworn allegiance.

The colonel was rustling papers on his desk. The interview was over. Cayle was about to say some final word, when the telestat on the wall behind Medlon lighted up. The face of a young woman came onto the screen.

"Colonel," she said curtly, "where the hell have you been?"

The officer stiffened. Then turned slowly. But Cayle did not need the uneasy reaction of the other man to realize who the woman was.

He was looking at the empress of Isher.

EIGHT

Cayle, who had been sitting down, climbed to his feet. It was an automatic movement. Motivating it was an awareness that he was an intruder. He was halfway to the door when he saw that the woman's eyes were watching him.

"Colonel," he mumbled, "thank you for the privilege—"

His voice was a sick sound in his ears and he stopped in shame. And then he felt a surge of doubt, a disbelief that such an event could be happening to him. He looked at the woman with eyes that momentarily questioned her identity. At that moment Medlon spoke.

"That will be all, Mr. Clark," he said, too loudly.

It was the loudness that brought Cayle out of his blur of emotional reaction. He was still ashamed of himself but it was a shame of something that had happened, not of what was happening. He had a sudden picture of himself, tall and well-dressed, and not too bad looking, standing here before a drink-wrecked caricature of a man, and before *the* woman of Isher. His gaze touched her face in the 'stat without flinching. He bowed slightly, an instinctive gesture that made him feel even better.

He had no doubt now of her identity. At twenty-five the empress Innelda was not the world's most beautiful woman. But there was no mistaking her long, distinctive face and green eyes. It was the face of the Isher family of emperors and empresses. Her voice, when she spoke again, was her 'stat voice, familiar to anyone who had ever listened to her anniversary greetings—so different, though, to have her speaking directly at him.

"What is your name, young man?"

It was Medlon who answered, quickly, his voice tense but calm. "An acquaintance of mine, Your Majesty." He turned to Cayle. "Goodbye, Mr. Clark. I enjoyed our conversation."

"I said, *what is your name?*" The woman ignored the interruption.

It was spoken so straight at him that Cayle shrank. But he gave his name.

"And why are you in Medlon's office?"

Cayle caught Medlon's eye. A tense eye, it was, striving to attract his attention. A remote part of his brain had admired Medlon's skillful earlier words. His admiration faded. The man was in a panic. Deep inside Cayle a hope started. He said, "I was inquiring about the possibility of obtaining a commission in Your Majesty's armed forces."

"I thought so," said the empress in a level voice. She paused. She looked thoughtfully from Cayle to Medlon, then back to Cayle. Her skin was a smooth, light tan in color. Her head was proudly held. She looked young and alive and gloriously confident. And something of her experience in handling men showed then. Instead of asking Cayle the next question, she gave Medlon a way out.

"And may I ask, Colonel, what your answer was?"

The officer was rigid, perspiring. But in spite of that his voice was calm and there was even an edge of joviality in it as he said, "I informed him, Your Majesty, that his commission would require about two weeks to put through." He laughed deprecatingly. "As you know, there is a certain amount of red tape."

Cayle felt himself riding a tide that was lifting him higher and higher. Because the benefits of this were for him. He felt an unnatural admiration for the empress—she was so different from what he had expected. It amazed him that she would restrain herself so as not to embarrass one of her officers virtually caught in a misdemeanor.

The restraint did not keep the sarcasm out of her voice, however, as she said, "Yes, Colonel, I know but too well. This whole rigmarole is only too familiar to me." Passion replaced the sarcasm. "Somehow or other, the young men who normally buy their way into the army have heard that something is up and so they remain away in droves. I am beginning to suspect there is a pro-Weapon Shop conspiracy to put off the few likely prospects who do turn up."

Her eyes flashed with green fires. It was apparent that she was angry and that the restraints were off. She turned to Cayle.

"Cayle Clark," she said in a ringing voice, "how much were you asked to pay for your commission?"

Cayle hesitated. Medlon's eye was a terrible thing to see, it was so dark. His half-turned head seemed unnatural in the way it was twisted. The message in that abnormal eye needed no words. The colonel was regretting everything he had said to the prospective lieutenant of Her Majesty's Imperial Army.

The appeal was so great that Cayle felt repelled. He had never before experienced the sensation of having a man completely at his mercy. It made him cringe. Abruptly, he didn't want to look. He said, "Your Majesty, I met Colonel Medlon on the Inter-State yesterday and he offered me a commission without any strings attached."

He felt better for the words. He saw that the officer was relaxing and that the woman was smiling with pleasure.

"Well, Colonel," she said, "I'm glad to hear that. And, since it answers in a satisfactory fashion what I was going to talk to you about, you have my felicitations. That is all."

The screen clicked into blankness. Colonel Medlon sank slowly back into his chair. Cayle walked forward, smiling. The colonel said in a level voice, "It has been a pleasure to meet you, young man. But now, I am very busy. I certainly hope I shall be hearing from you in the next two weeks with the five thousand. Goodbye."

Cayle did not move immediately, but the bitterness of the defeat was already upon him. Out of the darkness of his thoughts came the consciousness that to him had come an improbable opportunity. And he had nullified it by being weak. He had believed that an amoral wretch would be grateful for being saved from exposure. He saw that the colonel, looking quite jaunty, was eyeing him with amusement.

"The empress doesn't understand the problem involved in ending a system of paid commissions." Medlon shrugged. "I have nothing to do with it myself. I can no more alter it that I can cut my throat. One man would destroy himself bucking it." He hesitated. A sneer came into his face. "My friend," he said, "I hope this has been a lesson to you in the economics of personal advancement." He finished curtly. "Well, good day."

Cayle decided against attacking the man physically. This was a military building, and he had no intention of being arrested for assault where he could not properly defend himself. In his mind he marked the colonel down for further attention at a later date.

Darkness was settling over the city of the Ishers when he finally emerged from District Nineteen Headquarters. He looked up at the cold fixed stars through a mist of ads, and felt much more at home than he had the night before. He was beginning to see his way through the maze of existence on this world. And it seemed to him that he had come through very well, considering his ignorance. All around him, the sidewalks began to give off the sunlight they had absorbed during the day. The night waxed brighter as the heavens above grew darker. He became more confident as he walked. He had been right to attack Seal regardless of risks, and he had been right to hold back on Medlon. Seal was an individual out in the open as he was, and basically no one cared what happened to him. But the colonel could call on the power of Isher law.

He had not intended to return to the Avenue of Luck until morning. But now having, it seemed to him, resolved his inner doubts, he changed his mind. If he could win five thousand credits and buy a commission, the treasures of Isher would start pouring in his direction. And Lucy Rall—he mustn't forget Lucy.

Even one day was too long to wait.

NINE

Cayle had to push his way through throngs of human beings in order to enter the Penny Palace. The size of the crowds encouraged him. In this mass of money-hungry humanity he would be like a piece of driftwood in a vast ocean.

He did not hesitate. He had looked over the games earlier and he headed straight toward the one he wanted for his final bid for fortune. It would be important, he thought, to gain a playing position and stick to it.

The new game paid odds as high as a hundred to one and as low as five to one. It worked in a comparatively simple fashion, though Cayle, who knew something of the energies, having worked in his father's shop since before he was fifteen, realized there was electronic intricacy behind the deceptive appearance of artlessness. A ball of force was the core. It was about an inch in diameter and it rolled erratically inside a larger plastic ball. Faster, faster, faster it darted over the inner surface, until its speed transcended the resistance of matter. Then, like the pure force it was, it burst the limitations of its prison. Through the plastic it plunged, as if there were nothing there, as if it were a beam of light that had been imprisoned by an unnatural physical law in an almost invisible cage.

And yet, the moment it was free, it grew afraid. It changed color, subtly, swiftly, and it slowed. Its speed of escape must have been miles a second but so great was its fear that it stopped completely after traveling less than three feet.

It began to fall. And until that moment of fall, until it almost touched the table, it gave an illusion of being everywhere. It was an illusion entirely inside the minds of the players, a product of enormous velocity and mental hallucination. Each player had the conviction that the ball was flying straight toward him, that when it fell it would fall into the channel he had activated with a number. It was inevitable that the majority of the gamblers were due for disappointment when the ball, its mission accomplished, dropped into a channel and activated the odds mechanism.

The very first game in which Cayle participated paid him thirty-seven credits for his one. He raked in his winnings with an attempt at casualness but the shock of victory overflowed along his nerves in spasms of excitement. He placed a credit each in four channels, lost, then bet the same numbers again and won ninety credits. During the next hour he won on an average once in five times. He recognized that this luck was phenomenal even for him—and long before the hour was up he was risking ten credits in each channel that he played.

At no time did he have an opportunity to count his money. At intervals, he would thrust a handful of credits into the automatic changer and receive large bills, which he would press into an inner pocket. Not once did he draw on his reserves. After awhile, he thought in a curious panic, "I must have three or four thousand credits. It's time to quit. It's not necessary to win the whole five thousand in one night. I can come back tomorrow and the day after and day after that."

It was the speed of the game that confused him. Each time the impulse came, that it was time to think of stopping his play, the ball would start to whirl and he would hastily drop money into several channels. If he lost, irritation would come, and a greedy determination not to leave behind even a penny of his winnings.

If he won, it seemed ridiculous to stop in the middle of the most amazing streak of luck that he could ever hope to have. Wait, he told himself, till he lost ten in a row . . . ten in a row . . . ten . . . Somewhere along there he had a glimpse of a wad of forty or fifty one-thousand credit notes which he had put in his side pocket. There was more money in other pockets—and again and again, without being more than blurrily aware of the fact, he would strew large bills at random in various channels. How much he couldn't remember. Nor did it matter. The machine always counted accurately and paid him the right odds.

He was swaying now like a drunken man. His body seemed to be floating above the floor. He played on in an emotional mist almost oblivious of others. He did become conscious that more and more players were riding his luck, calling up his numbers in their own channels. But that was unimportant and personally meaningless. He did not come out of his daze until the ball plunked down like a dead thing in its cage. He stood stolid, waiting for the game to begin again, unaware that he had anything to do with its stopping until a plump, dark man came forward.

The stranger said with an oily smile, "Congratulations, young man, we welcome your patronage. We are happy for you—but for these other ladies and gentlemen we have bad news. The rules of this house, which are conspicuously posted in our fine establishment, do not permit luck riders, as we call them. This fortunate young man's trend of luck has been definitely established. Henceforth, all other bets must be placed before the 'winner' makes his choice. The machine has been set to react accordingly. So do not cause yourself disappointment by making a last-second wager. It will not work. And now, good luck to all of you and especially to you, young man."

He waddled off, still smiling. A moment later, the ball was whirling again.

It was during the third game that Cayle thought out of nothingness: "Why, I'm the center of attention." It startled him. He had come out of that oblivion on which he had counted to maintain his security. "I'd better slip out of here as quietly as possible," he thought.

He turned from the table—and a pretty girl threw her arms around him, pressed tightly against him and kissed him.

"Oh, please, let me have some of your luck. Please, please."

He disentangled himself blankly, the original impulse forgotten. "I was going to do something," he remembered and laid several bets while he frowned over the elusive memory. He was aware that newcomers were jostling up to the table, sometimes forcibly crowding out the less resourceful and determined of those who had been there first. Once, when he noticed a particularly violent ejection of a vociferously protesting player, the warning thought ticked again in his head that he and this table were now plainly marked by a thousand avid eyes.

He couldn't recall just what it was he wanted to do about that. There seemed to be a lot of women around, plucking at him with their fingers, kissing him if he turned his head, and he had a sense of an over-abundance of their perfume.

He couldn't move his hands without a woman's bare skin being available for his touch—naked arms, naked backs, and dresses cut so low in front that he was constantly having his head drawn down into soft, daintily perfumed bosoms. When he bent an inch for a natural reason the ever-present hands pulled him the rest of the way.

And still the night and his luck did not end. He had a sense of too much pleasure, too much applause at every spin, at every win. And whether he won or not women flung themselves into embraces with him and either kissed him commiseratingly or in a frenzy of delight. Wild music played in the background. He was twenty-three years old and the attack on every sense of his body overwhelmed his caution. When he had won uncountable thousands of credits the doors of the Penny Palace closed and the roly-poly man came over and spoke curtly.

"All right," he said, "that's enough. The place is cleared of strangers and we can stop this nonsense."

Cayle stared at him, and the clock of danger was ticking so loudly that his whole brain hummed with the sound. "I think," he mumbled, "I'll go home."

Somebody slapped his face—hard. "Again," said the plump man. "He's still riding an emotional jag." The second blow was harder. Cayle came out of his haze with a sharp comprehension that he was in deadly peril.

"What's going on here?" he stammered. His eyes appealed to the people who had been cheering him only minutes before. The people whose presence had lulled him . . . It was impossible that anything would be done against him while they were around.

He whirled on the plump man. And then stood rigid as rough hands grabbed him and rougher hands probed in the pockets of his clothes relieving him of his winnings. As from a great distance he heard the plump man speak again.

"Don't be naive. There is nothing unusual about what has happened. All the regular players have been squeezed out. Not only out of the game, but out of the building. The thousand people in here now are hired for such occasions and cost us ten credits each. That's only ten thousand altogether, and you won from fifty to a hundred times as much as that." He shrugged. "People don't realize the economics of such things. Next time, don't be so greedy." He smiled an oily smile. "That is, if there is a next time."

Cayle found his voice. "What are you going to do?"

"You'll see." His voice went up. "All right, men, take him to the truckplane and we'll open up again."

Cayle felt himself irresistibly hustled across the room and into a dark corridor. He was thinking in despair that, once again, he had put himself into a position where other men decided his fate.

INTERLUDE

McAllister, reporter from 1951, realized that he was lying on a sidewalk. He climbed to his feet. A group of curious faces gawked at him; and there was no park, no magical city of the future. Instead, a bleak row of one-story shops made a dull pattern on either side of the street.

A man's voice floated toward him out of a blur of other sounds: "I'm sure it's the reporter who went into that weapon shop."

So he was back in his own time. Perhaps even the same day. As he moved slowly away, the same penetrating voice said, "He looks kind of sick. I wonder what—"

He heard no more. But he thought, "Sick!" These people would never understand how sick. But somewhere on Earth must be a scientist who could help him. The record was that he hadn't exploded.

He was walking rapidly now, and clear of the crowd. Once, he looked back, and saw that the people were dispersing in the aimless fashion of folk who had lost their center of interest. McAllister turned a corner, and forgot them.

"I've got to decide."

The words were loud, close. It took a moment to realize that he had spoken them.

Decide? He hadn't thought of his position as requiring a decision. Here he was. Find a scientist . . . If that was a decision, he had already made it. The question was, who? Memory came of his old physics professor at City College. Automatically, he turned into a phone booth and fumbled for a nickel. With a sickening sense of disaster, he remembered that he was dressed in an all-enclosing, transparent suit, and that his money was inside. He drew back, then stopped, shaken. *What was happening?*

It was night, in a brilliant, glowing city. He was standing on the boulevard of an avenue that stretched jewel-like into remote distance. It was a street that flamed with a soft light gleaming up from its surface—a road of light, like a river flowing under a sun that shone nowhere else, straight and smooth.

He walked along for uncomprehending minutes, fighting a wild hope, but at last the thought forced through to his consciousness: Was this again the age of Isher and the gunmakers? It could be. It looked right, and it meant they had brought him back. After all, they were not evil, and they would save him if they could. For all he knew, weeks had passed in their time.

He began to hurry. Find a Weapon Shop. A man walked by him, and McAllister turned and called after him. The man paused curiously, and looked back, then continued on his way. McAllister had a brief picture of dark, intense eyes, and a visualization of a person on his way to a marvellous home of the future. It was that that made him suppress his impulse to run after the man.

Afterwards, he realized he should have. It was the last person he saw on all those quiet, deserted streets. It must have been the in-between hour before the false dawn, and no one was abroad. Oddly, it was not the absence of human life that disturbed. It was the fact that not once did he see a Weapon Shop.

In spite of that, his hope mounted. Soon it would be morning. Men would come out of these strange, glowing homes. Great scientists of an age of wizard scientists would examine him, not in a frenzy of haste, with the fear of destruction hanging over their heads. But quietly, in the sanity of super-laboratories.

The thought ended. He felt the *change.*

He was in the center of a blinding snowstorm. He staggered from the first mighty, unexpected blow of that untamed wind. Then, bracing himself, he fought for mental and physical calm.

The shining, wondrous night city was gone. Gone also the glowing road. Both vanished, transformed into this deadly, wilderness world. He peered through the driving snow. It was daylight, and he could make out the dim shadows of trees that reared up through the white mist of blizzard less than fifty feet away. Instinctively, he pressed toward their shelter and stood finally, out of that blowing, pressing wind. He thought: "One minute in the distant future; the next—where?"

There was certainly no city. Only trees, and uninhabited forest and a bitter, primeval winter. How long he stood there, while those winds blew and that storm raged, he had no idea. He had time for a thousand thoughts, time to realize that the suit protected him from the cold as if there was no cold; and then—

The blizzard was gone. And the trees. He stood on a sandy beach. Before him stretched a blue, sunlit sea that rippled over broken, white buildings. All around, scattered far into that shallow, lovely sea, far up into the weed-grown hills, were the remnants of a once tremendous city. Over all clung an aura of incredible age, and the silence of the long-dead was broken only by the gentle, timeless lapping of the waves.

Again came that instantaneous transition. More prepared this time, he nevertheless sank twice under the surface of the vast, swift river that carried him on and on. It was hard swimming, but the insulated suit was buoyant with the air it manufactured each passing second. And, after a moment, he began to struggle purposely toward the tree-lined shore a hundred feet to his right. A thought came, and he stopped swimming. "What's the use!" The truth was as simple as it was terrible. He was being shunted from the past to the future. He was the "weight" on the long end of an energy seesaw; and in some way he was slipping further ahead and further back each time. Only that could explain the catastrophic changes he had already witnessed. In an hour would come another change.

It came. He was lying face downward on green grass. When he looked up, he saw a half dozen low-built buildings on the horizon of grass. They looked alien, unhuman. But his curiosity was not about them. A thought had come: How long, actually, did he remain in one particular time?

He kept an eye on his watch; and the time was two hours and forty minutes. That was his last curiosity. Period after period, as the seesaw jerked on, he remained in his one position, water or land, it made no difference to him. He did not fight it. He neither walked nor ran nor swam nor even sat up . . . Past—future—past—future—

His mind was turned inward. He had a vague feeling that there was something he ought to do, inside his skin, not outside. Something about a decision he had believed he must make. Funny, he couldn't recall what it was.

Beyond doubt, the gunmakers had won their respite. For at the far end of this dizzy teeter-totter was the machine that had been used by the Isher soldiers as an activating force. It too teetered past, then future, in this mad seesaw.

But that decision. He'd really have to try to think about it . . .

TEN

At ten minutes of midnight, July 16, 4784 Isher, the door of the coordination department of the Weapon Makers, in the Hotel Royal Ganeel, opened. Robert Hedrock came out and strode along a wide bright corridor that stretched off into the distance ahead of him. He moved with an almost catlike alertness but actually his attention was not on his surroundings.

Little more than a year ago he had applied for Weapon Shop membership, his given reason being that he expected a crisis between government and Weapon Shop forces and that he desired to be on the Weapon Shop side. His papers were in order, the *Pp* machine gave him so high a rating in every mental, physical and moral category that his file was immediately brought to the attention of the Weapon Shop executive council. From the beginning he was on special duty and his assignment to the coordination department during an emergency was merely a normal step in his meteoric rise to Weapon Shop power.

Hedrock was aware that a few members of the council and a number of the top executives considered his ascent too rapid and not in the best interests of the Weapon Shops. That he was even regarded by some as a mysterious figure, though no sinister connotations were intended by the critics. No one actually questioned the verdict of the *Pp* machine in his favor, which puzzled him at times. At some later date, he decided, he would investigate the machine much more carefully and discover just why normally skeptical men accepted its judgements without question.

It had proved inordinately simple for him to fool it, lie to it, tell it his carefully doctored story.

True, he had special control of his mind and abnormal technical knowledge of machine reaction to biological processes. There was also the overruling fact of his friendliness to the Weapon Shops—which undoubtedly helped. The *Pp* machine, he had been told, had the Weapon Shop door's unique sensitivity for recognizing hidden hostility. And its basic structure included the ability, also built into every gun, to recognize and react within limitations. Like the weapons that would not kill except in self-defense, or under other restrictions, its intricately acute electronic senses perceived minute differences in the reactions of every part of the examined body. It was an invention that had been developed since the last time he had been a member of the Weapon Shops a hundred-odd years before. It was new to him. And their dependence on it made it necessary for Robert Hedrock, Earth's one immortal man, friend of the Weapon Shops, to make sure it was as effective a safeguard as they thought.

But that was for later. It was the least of the problems confronting him. He was a man who had to make up his mind, how soon was not yet clear—but all too soon it seemed to him. The first great attack of the youthful empress had already closed the Weapon Shops in every large city on Earth. But even that was secondary compared to the problem of the endless seesaw. He could not escape the conviction that only he, of all the human beings on Earth, was still qualified to make the decision about *that.* And he still had not an idea of what to do.

His thought reached that point, as he came to the door marked *Private—Executives Only*, his destination. He knocked; waited the necessary seconds, then entered without further preliminary.

It was a curious arranged room in which he found himself. Not a large room, by Isher standards, but large enough. It was so close to being a two hundred-foot cube that Hedrock's eyes could not detect the difference. Its most curious feature was that the door, through which he entered, was about a hundred feet above the floor with the ceiling an equal distance higher. There was a platform just inside the door. From it projected an energy plane. Hedrock stepped into one of the pairs of insulators on the platform. The moment he felt them grip his shoes he walked out onto the vaguely glowing latticework of force.

In the center of the room (center on height-depth as well as length-width level) seven Weapon Shop councilors were standing around a machine that floated in a transparent plastic case. They greeted Hedrock briefly, then returned their attention to the machine. Hedrock watched them silently, conscious of their intense, unnormal depression. Beside him Peter Cadron whispered, "It's almost time for another swing."

Hedrock nodded. And slowly, as he gazed at the wizard mechanism floating in its vacuumized case, their absorption communicated itself to him. It was a map of time. A map of inter-crossed lines so finely drawn that they seemed to waver like heat waves on a torrid day.

Theoretically the lines extended from a central point into the infinite past and the infinite future (with the limitation that the mathematics employed, infinity was almost zero). But after several trillion years the limitation operated to create a blurred effect, which was enhanced by the unwillingness of the eyes to accept the image. On that immense ocean of time, the shadowy shapes, one large and very near the center, one a mere speck on the curving vastness of the map, lay moveless. Hedrock knew that the speck was a magnified version of the reality, which was too small to make out with the naked eye. The image had been so organized that its every movement was followed by a series of magnifiers. These instruments were attuned to separate sensitive energies and adjusted automatically to the presence of additional onlookers.

As Hedrock watched with pitying eyes both shadows moved. It was a movement that had no parallel in macrocosmic space—a movement so alien that the vision could not make an acceptable image. It was not a particularly swift process but, in spite of that, both shadows—withdrew. Where? Even the Weapon Shop scientists had never quite decided that. They withdrew and then slowly reappeared, but now their positions were reversed, with variations.

They were farther out. The large shadow, which had been wavering one month and three days from the center in the *past*, was suddenly a month and three days and a few hours in the *future*. The tiny speck, which had been ninety-seven billion years in the future, reversed to about one hundred and six billion years in the past.

The time distance was so colossal that Hedrock shrank in spite of himself and half turned to Cadron. "Have they figured out his energy potential?"

Cadron nodded wearily. "Enough to destroy the planet." He groaned. "Where in the name of space are we going to release it?"

Hedrock tried to picture that. He had not been among those who talked to McAllister, the reporter from the twentieth century. His understanding of what had happened had been pieced together from fragmentary accounts. And one of his purposes in coming to this room now was to learn the details.

He drew Cadron aside and frankly asked for information. Cadron gazed at him with a wry smile. "All right," he said, "I'll tell you. The truth is, all of us are ashamed of the way we acted."

Hedrock said. "Then you feel that McAllister should not have been sacrificed?"

Cadron shook his head. "No, that isn't exactly what I mean." His frown deepened. "I guess the best method is to tell you the whole story—briefly, of course."

He began. "The girl attendant of the Greenway Shop heard someone come and went out to attend to him. The customer was a queer looking chap in outlandish clothes. It turned out that he was a newspaper reporter from the twentieth century A.D. He was so obviously disconcerted, so fascinated by the showcases with their energy guns. And he gave an account of a Weapon Shop having appeared in a street in the little city in which he lived. I can imagine the sensation it caused but the truth is that everybody thought it was an illusion of some kind.

"It seemed solid, of course. But when the police tried to open the door, naturally it wouldn't open. McAllister, with a reporter's curiosity, finally tried the door himself. For him, of course—he not being a police or government official—it opened immediately. He went inside.

"He admitted to the attendant experiencing a sense of tension as he crossed the threshold and, though he didn't know it, it was at that moment that he picked up the first measure of time-energy, the equivalent of approximately seven thousand years—his weight being the other factor. When the attendant told her father—who was in charge of the Shop—what had occurred, he realized immediately that something was wrong. In a few minutes he had verified that the shop was being subjected to titanic energy pressure. He discovered that the source of the energy was the huge government building on an adjoining street. He immediately called the Weapon Makers into council.

"By the time we arrived on the scene a swift decision was necessary. McAllister had enough time-energy locked up in his body to destroy the entire city—that is if he ever stepped outside our insulated shop without himself being insulated. Meanwhile, the pressure from the government building against our Shop continued unabated. At any moment it might succeed in precipitating the Shop itself into the time stream, and there was reason to believe that other attacks would be made at any moment on our Shops everywhere. No one could guess what the result would be. To cut a long story short we saw a way to gain time by focusing the energy of the building upon McAllister and tossing him back into his own time. We could do this by putting him into an insulated space suit which would prevent him from exploding until we could develop a mechanism for that purpose.

"We knew that he would seesaw back and forth in time, shifting the government building and its energies out of this space-time area."

Cadron shook his head gloomily. "I still don't see what else we could have done. We were compelled to act swiftly in a field where no great knowledge is available, and the fact that we merely got out of the frying pan and into the fire was just our hard luck. But personally I feel very badly about the whole thing."

"Do you think McAllister is still alive?" Hedrock asked.

"Oh yes. The suit into which we put him was one of our supers, complete with an eight ring food-making device, and there's a cup in it that's always full of water. The other facilities are equally automatic."

He smiled a twisted smile. "We had an idea, completely false as it turned out, that we could save him at some later date."

"I see," said Hedrock. He felt depressed. It was unfortunate but all the decisions had been made before he had even heard of the danger.

The newsman was now the juggernaut of juggernauts. In all the universe there had never been anything like the power that was accumulating, swing by swing, in his body. Released, the explosion would rock the fabric of space. All time would sigh to its echoes and the energy tensions that created the illusion of matter might collapse before the strain.

"What's the latest about the building?" Hedrock asked.

Cadron was more cheerful. "It's still within its critical limits. We've got to make our decision before it reaches the danger stage."

Hedrock was silent. The matter of what the decision should be was a sore point with him, who was obviously not going to be asked. He said finally, "What about the men who are working on the problem of slowing the swings and bringing the seesaw back this way?"

Another man answered that. "The research is abandoned. Science four thousand seven hundred and eighty-four has no answer. We're lucky enough to have made one of our shops the fulcrum. We can set off the explosion anywhere in the past or future. But which? And when? Particularly when?"

The shadows on that cartograph made no movement, gave no sign. *Their* time of action was not yet.

ELEVEN

The strain attendant on watching another swing faded. The men were turning away from the map, and there was a murmur of conversation. Somebody said something about using the opportunity to acquire all the possible data on time travel. Councilor Kendlon remarked that the body's accumulation of energy was fairly convincing proof that time travel would never be popular.

It was Dresley, the precise, the orderly, who finally remarked, "Gentlemen, we are here as delegates of the council to listen to Mr. Hedrock's report of the counterattack against the empress. In his report some weeks ago he was able to give us administrative details. And you will recall that we found his organization set-up to be efficient in the extreme. Mr. Hedrock, will you now bring us up to date?"

Hedrock glanced from person to person thoughtfully. He saw that they were watching him, and that raised his necessity level. His problem, it seemed to him, was to make up his own mind about the seesaw, then carry out his decision without regard for the attitude of his nominal superiors. It would be difficult.

He began succinctly, "Since the first directive was given me, we have set up one thousand two hundred and forty-two new Shops, primarily in small villages, and three thousand eight hundred and nine contacts have been established, however tenuous in some cases, with Imperial government personnel, both military and civil."

He explained briefly his system of classifying the various individuals into groups on the basis of vocation, degree of importance and, what was more important, pitch of enthusiasm for the venture into which the empress had precipitated her adherents.

"From three scientists," Hedrock went on, "who regard the Weapon Shops as an integral part of Isher civilization, we gained in the first ten days the secret of the science behind the time-energy machine in so far as that science is known to the government. We discovered that, of the four generals in charge of the enterprise, two were opposed to it from the beginning, a third was won over when the building disappeared—but the fourth, General Doocar, the man in charge, unfortunately will not abandon the attack until she does. He is an empress man in the sense of personal loyalty transcending his own feelings and opinions."

He paused, expecting them to comment. But no one said anything. Which was actually the most favorable response of all. Hedrock continued, "Some thousands of officers have deserted the Imperial forces, but only one member of the Imperial Council, Prince del Curtin, openly opposed the attack after the execution of Banton Vickers who, as you know, criticized the whole plan. And the prince's method of disapproval has been to withdraw from the palace while the attack is in progress.

"Which brings us," said Hedrock, "to the empress herself." He summarized her character for them. The glorious Innelda, an orphan since her eleventh birthday, had been crowned when she was eighteen and was now twenty-five. "An age," said Hedrock grimly, "which is an in-between stage in the development of the animal man to human man levels."

He saw that they were puzzled by his reiteration of facts they all knew. But he had no intention of condensing his account. He had his own formula for defeating the empress and he wanted to state it at least once in as skillful a fashion as possible. "At twenty-five," he said, "our Innelda is emotional, unstable, brilliant, implacable, impatient of restrictions on her desires and just a bit unwilling to grow up. As the thousands of reports came in, it seemed to me finally that our best method of dealing with such a person was to leave channels along which she could withdraw gracefully when the crises came."

He looked around, questioningly. He was keenly aware that, with these men he dared not try to put his ideas over in a disguised form. He said frankly, "I hope that council members will not take it amiss if I recommend for their consideration the following basic tactic. I am counting on some opportunity occurring of which we can take advantage and so bring her whole war machine to a stop.

My assumption is that once it has stopped the empress will busy herself with other matters and conveniently forget all about the war she started."

Hedrock paused in order to give weight to his next words. "My staff and I will watch anxiously for the opportunity and will call your attention to anything that seems to have possibilities. And now, are there any questions?"

The first few were minor. Then a man said, "Have you any notion as to what form this so-called opportunity will take?"

Hedrock said carefully, "It would be difficult to go into all the avenues that we are exploring. This young woman is open on many fronts to persuasion and to pressure. She is having a hard time with recruits for the army. She is still subject to the connivances and intrigues of a group of older people who are reluctant to accept her as an adult. They withhold information from her. Despite her efforts to keep in touch with what is going on, she is caught in an old, old net: Her communication with the real world is snarled up." Hedrock finished, "In one way or another we are trying to take advantage of these various weaknesses."

The man who had already spoken said, "This is only a formula."

"It is a formula," said Hedrock, "based on my study of the character of the empress."

"Don't you think you had better leave such studies to the *Pp* machine experts and to the No-men?"

"I examined all the Weapon Shop data on the lady before offering my suggestion."

"Still," said the man, "it is up to the elected council to make decisions in such matters."

Hedrock did not back down. "I have made a suggestion," he said, "not a decision."

The man said nothing more. But Hedrock had his picture of a council of very human members, jealous of their prerogatives. These people would not easily accept his decision, when he finally made it, on the problem of the seesaw drama that was being played to its still undetermined conclusion in ever remoter bends of time.

He saw that his audience was becoming restless. Eyes turned involuntarily toward the time map and several men glanced anxiously at their watches. Hastily Hedrock withdrew from the room with its almost invisible energy floors. Watching that pendulum could become a drug. The brain itself would be weakened by the strain of attending a mechanism which recorded the spasms of real bodies in their movements through time itself.

It was bad enough to know that the building and the man were swinging steadily back and forth.

He arrived back in his office just in time to catch a 'stat call-up from Lucy.

". . . in spite of my efforts," she said, "I was forced out of the Penny Palace. And when the doors shut I knew what was going to happen. I'm afraid he was taken to one of the Houses of Illusion, and you know what that means."

Hedrock nodded thoughtfully. He noted sharply that the girl seemed disturbed by her experience. "Among other things," he said slowly, "the illusion energies have some qualifying effect on callidity. The nature of the modification cannot be determined without subsequent measurement but it can be stated with reasonable certainty that his luck will never again take the direction of success at gambling."

He had delayed his reaction while he examined her face. Now he said with decision, "It is unfortunate that Clark has fallen prey to all these pitfalls of the city so easily. But since he was never more than a long-run possibility we can let him go without regret, particularly—and this cannot be stressed too often—as even the slightest interference in the natural progression of his life would cause later suspicion that would nullify any good he might do us.

"You may accordingly consider yourself detached from him. Further instructions will be given you in due course." He paused. "What's the matter, Lucy? Got an emotional fixation on him?"

Her expression left no doubt of it. Hedrock pressed on quietly, "When did you discover it?"

Whatever resistance had been in her, whatever fear of discovery, was gone. "It was when those other women were kissing him. You mustn't think," she added hastily, "that disturbed me. He'll go through quite a lot of it before he settles down."

"Not necessarily," said Hedrock earnestly. "You'll have to resign yourself to the House of Illusion but it has been my observation that a fair percentage of men emerge from such an experience hard as steel in some respects but rather weary of worldliness."

He realized from her face that he had said enough. The groundwork for her future action was established. Results would follow in the natural course of events. He smiled a friendly smile. "That's all for now, Lucy. Don't let it get you down."

Her image and his faded from the screen in a flash.

Robert Hedrock glanced out of the door of his office several times during the next hour. At first the corridors seemed very busy. Gradually the activity died down and at last the corridor was clear.

He acted now with decision but without haste. From a wall safe he took the micro-film plans of the time control machine—the one in the room where he had talked to the Weapon Shop councilors a little more than two hours before. He had requested Information Center to send them to him and they had done so without comment. There was nothing unusual in their compliance. As head of the coordination department he had access to all the scientific knowledge of the Weapon Shops. He even had an explanation as to why he wanted the plans in the event that he were asked. He wanted to study them, so his story would go, in the hope that some solution would suggest itself. But his reasons were private and his purpose personal.

With the films in his pocket he headed along the corridor toward the nearest stairway. He went down five flights and came to a section of the Hotel Royal Ganeel that was not occupied by the Weapon Shops. He unlocked an apartment door, went inside, and locked the door behind him.

It was an imposing suite, as befitted an executive of the Weapon Shops—five rooms and a tremendous library. He went straight to the library, closed and locked the door, then carefully examined the place for spying devices. There were none, which was what he expected. As far as he knew he was not under suspicion. But he never took unnecessary chances.

Swiftly he held one of the rings on his finger against an ordinary looking electric socket. A loop of metal slid out. He inserted his finger into the loop and pulled. What happened in that moment was an ordinary enough Weapon Shop phenomenon. He was transmitted by a Weapon Shop matter transmitter a distance of about eleven hundred miles into one of his numerous laboratories. What was out of the ordinary about the action was that the presence of the transmitter was not known to the Weapon Shop Council. The laboratory had for centuries been one of his many closely-guarded secret retreats.

He decided that he could safely remain an hour. But that all he could hope to do in one night was to make another print of the microfilm. Building a duplicate machine would require many visits such as this. As it turned out he had time to make an extra print of the plans. Very carefully he put the additional copy into a vault filing case, there to join the tens of thousands of other diagrams and plans to which, over a period of several thousand years, he had given an AA priority.

At the end of the hour, Earth's one immortal man, founder of the Weapon Shops, possessor of secrets unknown to any other living human being, returned to the library of his apartment in the Hotel Royal Ganeel.

Presently he was back in his office, five flights farther up.

TWELVE

Lucy Rall emerged from the government 'stat booth, and she was hurrying through an alcove when she caught a glimpse of herself in an energy mirror. She stopped. The outside lights beckoned. The sidewalks were aglow with a brightness that defied the night. But she stood there in front of the reverse image of herself and stared at her pale face and tensed eyes.

She had always thought of herself as good looking, but the face that confronted her was too drawn to be pretty. She thought, *Is that what Mr. Hedrock saw?*

Out on the street, finally, she walked uncertainly along. She had made her call from a booth in one of the gambling palaces and the flashing brilliance of the famous Avenue of Luck was unabated. Magic street still, alive with swarms of human moths fluttering from one light source to another. The lights themselves blazed day and night, but the crowds would gradually fade away as the darkness of the upper skies waned. It was time for her also to go home. But she lingered in an unnatural indecision, knowing she could do nothing, wondering what she could do. The inner conflict drained her strength and twice within an hour she paused for energy drinks.

There was something else, also, a sense of personal disaster. She had always taken it for granted that she would eventually marry a Weapon Shop man. All through school and college, when her own application for membership was already approved, she had considered all others—the ordinary people—as outsiders. She thought with a piercing comprehension, "It was that moment on the ship when he was in trouble. I was sorry for him."

He was in deeper trouble now. If she could possibly locate the

House he had been taken to, she would—what? Her mind paused. She felt astounded at the forcefulness of the idea that came. Why, it was ridiculous. If she went to one of those places she would have to go through with an illusion, mentally *and* physically.

It seemed to her, shakily, that the Weapon Shops would separate her from their organization for even considering such a thing. But when her mind automatically flashed back over the fine print of the documents she had signed, she couldn't recall any prohibition. In fact, some of the sentences, as she remembered them, were positively sensational when examined in her present situation:

". . . Weapon Shop people may marry according to their desire . . . participate in, or partake of, any vice or pleasure of Isher for personal reasons . . . There are no restrictions on the use made of a member's spare time by the member . . .

"It is, of course, taken for granted that no member will wish to do anything that might harm his or her standing with the *Pp* machine . . . as everyone has been clearly told . . . periodic examinations by the *Pp* will determine the status of a member's continuance with the shops . . .

"In the event that a member is discovered to have fallen below the requirements in any vital degree, the Weapon Shops will relieve the individual of all Weapon Shop memories and information the possession of which by unauthorized persons might be dangerous to the Shops . . .

"The following vices and pleasures, when pursued with too much ardor, have proven in the past to be initial steps in the severance of relations . . ."

Among those she remembered as being mildly dangerous for women was "Houses of Illusion." She couldn't recall clearly but it seemed to her there had been a footnote in connection with that listing. Something about the danger not being in the pleasure itself but in the knowledge that the men in such places were nearly always unwilling slaves. Repeated experiences caused penetration of the ego with the result that what began as a search for a comparatively normal sensual adventure ended with the ever bolder participation of the ego.

She came out of her intent memory reverie to realize that she was walking rapidly toward the special flash signal of a 'stat station. Within a minute she had her connection with the Weapon Shop Information Center. A few seconds later she tucked a 'stat duplicate of the 2,108 addresses of Houses of Illusion in her purse, and headed for the Penny Palace.

Her decision was made and from that moment she had not a thought of drawing back.

Inside the Penny Palace she saw things that Cayle could not possibly have observed without having the knowledge that she had. The play, she saw, was almost back to normal. A few of the hired people were still ostentatiously playing at games that would otherwise have been bare of players. The moment enough legitimate pleasure seekers were risking money on a machine the hirelings withdrew casually. Lucy headed toward the rear of the great room, pausing frequently and pretending to watch the play at various games. She carried a Weapon Shop nullifier in her purse. So she opened and shut doors leading to the manager's office without setting off the Imperial-type alarms.

Inside she depended entirely on her ring alarm to warn her of the approach of anyone. Coolly but swiftly she searched the office. First she pressed the machine-file activator, pecking out the key word *illusion*. The file screen remained blank. She clicked off the word *house*. No response.

Surely he had the address of the House or Houses with which he dealt. In a fury she snatched up the 'stat book and operated its activators. But there, too, *house* and *illusion* produced no response. Was it possible this man Martin—she had found his name on various documents—had connections with only a few Houses and had their numbers in his head? Grimly, she realized it was very possible indeed.

She had no intention of leaving before she had exhausted all the possibilities of her position. She made a quick examination of the contents of the desk. Finding nothing she settled into the comfortable chair and waited. Not for long. Her finger tingled as the ring alarm went off. She turned it, first toward one of the two doors, then the other. The active response came from the same door through which she had entered nearly fifteen minutes earlier. Whoever it was would now be in the corridor, his hand reaching for the office door.

The door opened, and the roly-poly man came in. He was humming softly to himself. The big desk and the chair in which she was sitting were so placed that he was inside before he saw that he had a visitor. He blinked at her with sea-blue eyes, a fatty little man who had somehow, long ago, conquered all fear. The piglike eyes switched to the gun in her fingers, then back to her face, greedily.

"Pretty girl," he said at last.

It was obviously not a complete reaction. Lucy waited. And finally it came, a purring question with an overtone of snarl. "What do you want?"

"My husband."

From all angles that seemed to Lucy the best identification to make of herself. It was natural that there might be a Mrs. Cayle Clark in the background.

"Husband?" echoed the man blankly. He looked genuinely puzzled.

Lucy said in a monotone, "He was winning. I waited in the background, keeping an eye on him. Then I was forced out by a pushing crowd. When I tried to get back in the doors were locked. And when they opened he wasn't there. I put two and two together and here I am."

It was a long speech, but it covered the subject. It gave the picture of a worried, determined wife. And that was very important. It would be unfortunate if he suspected that the Weapon Shops were interested in Cayle Clark. She saw that understanding had come to the piglike man.

"Oh, you mean him." He laughed curtly, his eyes watchful. "Sorry, young lady, I merely called a truckplane service that had contacts. What they do with the people they pick up I don't know."

Lucy said precisely, "What you mean is you don't know the address to which they took him but you know the kind of place. Is that correct?"

He stared at her thoughtfully, as if trying to make up his mind about something. Finally, he shrugged. "House of Illusion," he said.

The fact that she had guessed that did not make the confirmation less valuable. Just as his apparent frankness did not mean that he was telling the truth. Lucy said, "I notice there's a Lambeth in the corner over there. Bring it here."

He brought it instantly. "You'll notice," he said, "I'm not resisting."

Lucy made no reply. She picked up the Lambeth cone and pointed it at the fat man. "What is your name?"

"Harj Martin."

The Lambeth needles remained stationary. Martin it was.

Before she could speak, the man said, "I'm prepared to give you all the information you want." He shrugged. "Doesn't mean a thing to me. We're protected. If you can locate the House your husband was taken to, go ahead. But you should know the Houses have their own methods of getting rid of men when the police are called in."

There was a nervousness in his manner that interested Lucy. She looked at him with bright eyes. "You must be making plans," she said. "You would like to reverse our positions." She shook her head deprecatingly. "Don't try it. I would shoot."

"It's a Weapon Shop gun," Martin said, pointedly.

"Exactly," said Lucy. "It won't shoot unless you attack me."

That wasn't strictly true. Weapon Shop members had special guns, that would shoot under fewer restrictions than the guns sold to consumers.

Martin sighed. "Very well," he said. "The name of the firm is Lowery Truckplanes."

The Lambeth needles indicated the name was correct. Lucy backed toward the door. "You're getting off easy," she said. "I hope you realize that."

The fat man nodded, licking his lips. She had a final mental picture of his blue eyes watching her warily, as if he still hoped to catch her off guard.

No further words were spoken. She opened the door, slipped through, and half a minute later was safely out on the street.

Anton Lowery was a blond giant who lifted himself sleepily from his pillow and stared stupidly at Lucy. He made no attempt to get up. He said finally, "I don't know where they would have taken him. It's just transportation business with us, you understand. The driver calls up Houses at random, until he finds one that can use a man. We don't keep records."

He sounded vaguely indignant. Like an honest trucker whose business ethics were being questioned for the first time. Lucy wasted no time arguing the matter.

"Where can I locate the driver?" she asked.

It seemed the driver had gone off duty at 2 A.M. and was not due back for another sixty-six hours. "It's these unions," said Mr. Lowery. "Short hours, big pay and plenty of time off." Giving her the information seemed to bring him a satisfaction, a sense of victory over her that detracted considerably from the indignation in his tone.

"Where does he live?" Lucy asked.

He hadn't the faintest idea. "Might get that from the union," he suggested. "They don't give us addresses."

It turned out that he couldn't remember the name of the union. The Lambeth, which she had brought with her from the Penny Palace, verified his statements one by one. Lucy sagged. In three days Cayle would be initiated into the sordid life of the Houses of Illusion. The dark thought aroused her to abrupt anger.

"Damn you!" she said savagely. "When the driver reports back to work, you get the address of the House from him. I'll call you ten minutes after he's due back and you'd better have the information."

Her tone and manner must have been convincing. For Anton Lowery assured her hastily that he had no objection to her gaining the information and would personally see to it that she got it. He was still protesting as she left his bedroom.

Outside Lucy had another energy drink at a corner automat—and realized it wasn't enough. Her watch showed a few minutes to 5 A.M. And her tense body told her it was time to go home to bed.

She reached her apartment without incident. Wearily, she undressed, and heavily climbed between the sheets. Her last conscious thought was: *Three days . . . Would the time pass more slowly for the man who was enduring continuous pleasure? Or for herself who knew that pleasure prolonged was the greatest pain of all?*

She slept on that thought like an overtired child.

THIRTEEN

As soon as she had the address of the House she called up Hedrock. He listened thoughtfully to her account, then nodded.

"Good work," he said. "We'll back you up. I'll send a warship over, very high up. And if we don't hear from you in a reasonable time we'll raid." He hesitated. "I hope you realize that the only way we can justify such action is if you leave no doubt in Clark's mind that your reasons are purely personal. Are you prepared to go that far?"

He didn't need to ask the question. The haggard face that stared at him from the 'stat screen left no doubt of the extent of her fixation. This girl was emotionally wrought up. He felt a qualm of pity, and yet, he realized, he was not responsible for her feelings. He had merely recognized them, and used his knowledge of psychology to intensify her pursuit. A callidetic of the measurement of Cayle Clark would yet make himself felt in Isher. The chance that the impact would affect the war itself was not impossible. Once started on the right path, the pace of activity, the pattern of callidity, would be a direct moving cube, piling up so fast that no human brain would grasp the extent of what was happening until afterwards.

If only there were some way of discovering what form it would take—Hedrock shook himself inwardly. He was not given to wishful thinking. They would simply have to watch Clark's movements and hope that they would recognize the moment when it arrived. He saw that the girl was waiting for him to speak again. His thoughts grew instantly sharp. He said, "What time is your appointment? Tonight or tomorrow?"

"Tonight at ten-thirty." She managed a grim smile. "The receptionist insisted I be on time. Apparently, they can hardly handle the business they get."

"Supposing he isn't among those available at that time—what will you say?"

"I gather that there is a complete illusion break at that time. The men and women are then allowed to select partners. However, if he shouldn't be available, I shall not be either. I shall be very finicky."

"Do you think Clark will recognize you?" He saw that she didn't understand what he meant. He explained. "The illusions leave afterimage hallucinations which interfere with visual perception."

Lucy said, "I'll make him recognize me."

She described several methods she would use. Hedrock considered them, then shook his head. "It's obvious," he said, "that you've never been in a House. These people are perpetually, endlessly, suspicious. Until you are actually in a state of illusion your chances of saying anything that is not overheard are dim. Once the automatic machines begin radiating stimuli they don't worry about you any more. Bear that in mind and adjust yourself to any situation that may come up."

Lucy was recovered from her shock. After the afternoon she and Cayle had spent together she had felt sure of him. "He'll recognize me," she said firmly.

Hedrock said nothing to that. He had merely wanted to point out the problem. Three days and nights of illusions was a long time. Even if there were no afterimages, the brain was dulled, the body's capacity for life temporarily at low ebb, no energy for memory.

Lucy was speaking again. "I'd better get ready. Goodbye, Mr. Hedrock."

"All the luck in the world, Lucy," said Hedrock. "But don't call for help unless it's absolutely necessary."

Hedrock did not leave the 'stat the moment the connection was broken. During this period of emergency he lived in an apartment adjoining the coordination office. His work was his life. Virtually all his waking hours were spent at his desk. Now he called the Weapon Shop naval headquarters and ordered them to dispatch a protective warship. And still he was not satisfied. Frowning, he considered the potentialities of Lucy's position and finally called for her secret file. In two minutes, by Weapon Shop interspatial transportation, the remote Information Center precipitated the plate onto the table in front of him. First, he checked the facts—comprehension 110, horizon 118, plethora 105, dominance 151, ego 120, emotional index 150—

Hedrock paused there. Compared to the norm of 100, not forgetting the average of 85, Lucy was a fine, intelligent girl with a somewhat high-category emotional capacity. It was that that had brought her into the affair. After Cayle Clark was identified (by a routine check-up on the crowds that gathered before a new Weapon Shop) as a callidetic giant it was decided to contact him through the medium of an unmarried woman with a high emotion index.

Deliberately, the Weapon Makers' Council anticipated that the callidetic would excite fixation in Lucy. There were other factors involved in her selection, mostly sanity safeguards for a young woman who was going to be subjected to unnatural stresses. For one thing it was desirable, from the point of view of the girl's happiness, that the attraction be mutual for the time being. Permanency, of course, could not be guaranteed in a changing world.

One by one Hedrock examined the factors applicable to the present situation. At last he sighed. He felt sorry for Lucy. The Weapon Shops did not normally interfere with the private lives of their members or of anyone. Only the unparalleled emergency justified using an individual; human being as a pawn.

Thought of the emergency drew his mind. He returned the file to Information Center, then switched on the 'stat again. He manipulated it intently, rejected several images that resulted from the "draw" of energy in the room he was aiming at and finally had what he wanted, the map of time. He had no difficulty locating the large shadow. It was lying six weeks and a day in the future. The tiny shadow was harder to find. He saw it then, a minute black point on the curving vastness of the map. It seemed to be approximately a million years in the past. Hedrock closed his eyes, and strove to visualize the span of time. He couldn't. The energy locked up in McAllister was too great now for planetary comparisons. The problem of exploding it was a logic nightmare.

When at last he shut off the 'stat, he experienced a great weariness, and an incredulous wonder that, after all this time he still didn't have even a tentative solution to the deadliest danger that had ever confronted the entire solar system.

He spent the next hour studying precis of reports that had been filed by other agents throughout the day. Lucy didn't know that she was among the few dozen agents who obtained immediate and direct access to him at any time of the day or night. Those not so favored talked to machines or to any one of a dozen executives who alternated on a three-shift basis.

Again and again the condensed accounts required more thorough investigation. Not once did he begrudge the time. Not once did he let himself feel rushed. Each report was examined in the detail that he considered necessary.

Ten-thirty came and, though he was aware that Lucy must now have arrived at the House, he paused only briefly and called the Weapon Shop warship, which was hovering high above the place. For a moment he examined the House itself as it showed through a telescope, a toylike structure in a suburban estate that seemed all garden. Then, the picture of it clear in his mind, he returned to his work.

FOURTEEN

As she pushed open the gate, Lucy felt a warm glow sweep through her. She stopped, almost in mid-stride.

The sensation of warmth, she knew, had been artificially induced. This was the first step of pleasure leading up to the strange heights of sensory joys offered by a House of Illusion. There would be scarcely a moment from now until she left the grounds that some new, perhaps insidious and unsuspected manipulation of her nervous system would not be occurring.

The brief indecisiveness yielded to her purpose. Slowly, she walked forward, studying the house as she did so. The House of Illusion was set well back from the street in grounds that were beautifully landscaped. Flowers and shrubs protruded cunningly from a score of breaks in the abundant stone that made up the larger part of the yard. A massive screen of gigantic green-fronded plants started about a hundred feet from the entrance of the building, and almost hid it from view.

She walked under them, and came presently to an entrance that built up gradually, beginning as a low fence that soon towered higher than her head, and finally curved up above her to form a gleaming roof. She could see the end of it nearly fifty yards ahead.

Twice, involuntarily, she slowed. The first time, something soft seemed to caress her face. It was almost as if a loving hand reached out and delicately touched her, with affectionate fingers. The second time, the result was more dramatic. She caught her breath suddenly. A flush burned her face and spread warmly down her body. She felt embarrassed yet happy, a little shy but excited. She couldn't help wondering if this could be how a young girl might feel on her wedding night.

It was in just such nuances that the Houses of Illusion excelled. Here, tired old roues—men and women both—could recapture for a price otherwise lost emotions of their abused bodies.

She reached the turning of the corridor, and found herself confronted by an alcove fitted with scores of mirrors. She moved toward them hesitantly, wondering if they could be doors, disturbed by the possibility that she might choose the wrong one. She paused finally, and waited for one of the doors to open. But after a minute or so, nothing had happened; so she began to push against the face of first one mirror, then another.

The first six were solid, as if there was an unmoveable wall behind them. The seventh opened easily, and proved to be a swinging door. She went through it into a corridor that was only a little wider than her body. Her shoulders kept brushing the walls, and she had an uneasy feeling of being closed in, a distinct sensation of the space being too narrow for comfort. It was more than a physical feeling. It was in her mind, associated with fears of confined places, somehow connected with all the unknown things that could happen to a person who, if anything went wrong, could only move forward or backward.

She wondered if the uneasiness might possibly derive from her own tension, the knowledge that she was here for a purpose that had nothing to do with the normal business of the establishment. She was against what went on in such a place. She intended to disrupt at least a part of their organization. Her anxiety might well derive from the possibility that her motives could be discovered before she could do what she wanted to do. It seemed reasonable that the regular customers of this abode would not be alarmed by a narrow passageway, knowing as they undoubtedly did where it ended.

Her fears faded as quickly as they had begun. She felt a sudden anticipation of immeasurable joy about to be experienced. Breathlessly, she came to the end of the corridor, and pushed at the narrow wall-end that was there. It opened easily, and this time, to her relief, she saw that she had come to a small though nicely furnished room. As she entered, she saw that a woman sat behind a desk just left of the door. Lucy stopped, and the woman said:

"Sit down, please. Naturally, there has to be an interview the first time someone visits our establishment."

She was a woman of forty or so, with a classically good looking face, except that her eyes were narrowed and her lips drawn into a thin line. Silently she indicated a chair, and Lucy sat down without a word. The woman began:

"You understand, my dear, that everything you tell me will be kept confidential. In fact—" Her lips made the motions of a smile, and she touched her forehead with a manicured finger—"it never gets beyond here. But I must tell you that I have a perfect memory. Once I hear somebody talk, or see someone, I never forget them."

Lucy said nothing. She had met a number of individuals with eidetic memories; and she accepted the woman's statement that she had such a memory. From all the accounts she herself had heard of the Houses of Illusion, no record had ever been found of the customers. Apparently, this House kept its records inside the mind of someone who could remember such things.

The woman went on, "This means, of course, that we operate on a strictly cash basis. What is your annual income?"

"Five thousand credits." Lucy did not hesitate.

"Where do you work?"

Lucy named a firm well-known in the city. All this was simple, and long prepared for by the Weapon Shops. Every Weapon Shop member was listed as a worker in an organization which was either secretly owned by the shops or else owned by a Weapon Shop supporter. Thus, if a member was questioned in the normal routine of Isher commercial life, legitimate and checkable answers could be given.

"How much rent do you pay?" asked the woman.

"One hundred credits a month."

"And your food bills come to what?"

"Oh, fifty, sixty—something like that."

The woman said thoughtfully, half to herself "Transportation, ten; clothes, twenty-five; miscellaneous, ten—that leaves you a good twenty-five hundred a year for extras. If you wanted to come here once a week, you could do it at fifty credits each. However, we'll make you a discount for emergencies. Thirty-five credits, please."

Lucy counted out the money, startled by the ruthlessness of

the calculations involved. Actually, her income had other charges on it—a thousand credits income tax, for instance. Her clothes bill was much higher than twenty-five credits. And yet—and yet, she could, if necessary, if her craving for pleasure overreached her caution, get by on even less than the woman had indicated. Inherent in the other's calculations was the obvious fact that a person on the downward path would want to come oftener than once a week. In such an event, she could move to cheaper quarters, buy less expensive clothes, eat less—there were many short cuts possible, and all of them as old as human corruption.

The woman placed the money in a drawer, and stood up. "Thank you, my dear. I hope we have a long and mutually satisfying association. Through this door, please."

It was another concealed door, and it led to a broad corridor with an open doorway at the end of it. As she approached it, Lucy saw that it was a large and luxurious bedroom. The size of it was apparent even before she reached it. Several things about it made her suspicious, and so she did not enter immediately, but paused instead on the threshold, and studied the interior. She must, she told herself, remember that this was a House of *Illusion*. Here, what would normally seem real, might be nothing but fantasy. She recalled the clues Hedrock had given her as to how to detect the mechanically-induced delusions. And presently she saw that if she let herself look at the room out of the corners of her eyes, the scene blurred curiously, particularly at the very edge of her vision. She seemed to see the figure of a woman, and there was a suggestion of the room being larger than it appeared now.

Lucy smiled, walked towards the far wall, straight through it—solid though it seemed—and found herself in an enormous room that glittered with mirrors along three of its walls. A woman attendant hurried towards her, and bowed apologetically. "You will please pardon us, Miss. But since this is your first visit to our establishment, it was necessary to assume that you kne / nothing of our little bag of tricks. Did you learn about this particular illusion from a friend, or have you been to other Houses?"

It was a pointed question; and Lucy knew better than to evade it. "I heard a friend describe it," she said truthfully.

The answer seemed satisfactory. The woman, a small, vivacious looking blonde, led the way to what turned out to be a mirror door.

"Please change your clothes," she said, "and then go through the door on the far side."

Lucy found herself in a small dressing room. An attractive white dress hung on a hanger against one wall. A pair of sandals were on the floor. Nothing else. She undressed slowly, beginning suddenly to feel committed. It was going to be difficult indeed to get out of this situation. If she failed to contact Cayle during the time that would be available, then she might find herself experiencing what this House had to offer whether she wanted to or not.

The white dress was wonderfully soft to her touch; and, as she slipped it over her head, the feel of it on her skin brought a gasp of delight from her lips. The creation was made of a special costly cloth that was designed to affect only the pleasure nerves of the body. Its cost was more than a hundred credits a yard.

She stood for a long moment, letting the sensation of pleasure creep over her. Abruptly, excitement swept her. She swayed dizzily, and thought: "It really doesn't matter. Whatever happens here tonight, I'm going to have some fun."

She slipped her feet cosily into the sandals, staggered a little as she fumbled for the catch of the door; and then, steady again, opened it, and stood blinking at a vistalike room where men sat at tables along one wall and women along the opposite wall. The walls glittered with colorful plastic designs. A great liquor bar spread all across the side of the room facing her. Lucy made a halfhearted attempt to test for illusion by looking at the scene out of the corners of her eyes. But she didn't worry about it. This was it. Here was the concourse room. In a few minutes she would have her chance to get Cayle. If she didn't make contact—well, it didn't matter. There were other nights. So she told herself hazily.

She walked out into the room, swaggering a little. Scornfully, she surveyed the other women, sitting at their little tables, drinking from tiny glasses. Most were older than she was, older by a great deal. Abruptly bored by her competition, she glanced towards the men on the far side of the room. She saw with momentary interest that what had seemed one room was in reality two. A transparent barrier ran the full length of the room from ceiling to floor, dividing the men from the women. It was possible, of course, that the barrier also was an illusion. And that it would disappear either for individuals or for the entire group at the right moment. Lucy, who knew something of the energies involved in the processes by which the Houses achieved their effects, guessed that such a joining of the two sections would eventually occur.

The thought faded from her mind, as she ran her gaze rapidly along the line of men. Without exception, they were relatively young people. Her eyes were past Cayle before she recognized him. She started to bring them back for a second look, but just in time a basic pattern of caution stopped her. Already beginning to sober up after her brief emotional intoxication, she turned toward one of the small tables, and walked to it carrying with her the mental image of him.

She sat down, the high exhilaration gone out of her. She felt miserable with a remembrance of the disaster she had seen on his face. Haggard, worn-out, unhappy Cayle Clark—that was the vision she had. She wondered doubtfully if by any chance his glazed eyes had seen her. She thought finally: "I'll look again in a minute. And this time, I'll try to attract his attention."

She looked steadily at her watch, determined not to be rushed. The hands showed five seconds of the end of the minute when a slim little man came out of the alcove, and raised his hand. Lucy glanced hastily toward Cayle, saw with a sudden lift that he was watching her, and then heard the little man say in a cheerful tone:

"Down goes the barrier, folks. Now's the time to get acquainted."

There were different reactions to the signal. Most of the women remained seated. Several, however, got up hastily and hurried across the room. Lucy, seeing that Cayle was coming toward her, stayed where she was. He sank down into the chair opposite her, and said steadily, "I think you're very attractive, Miss."

She nodded her acceptance of the compliment, not trusting herself to speak. An attendant bent down beside her. "Satisfactory, Miss?" The question was softly spoken.

Lucy inclined her head again. The attendant said, "This way."

She stood up, thinking: "As soon as we're alone, we can start to plan."

There was a sudden flurry of excitement at one of the doors. The woman who had originally interviewed Lucy rushed in, and spoke in a low tone to the little man. A moment later, a bell began to ring. Lucy half-turned; and, doing so, in some curious fashion lost her balance. She felt herself falling into darkness . . .

Hedrock was still in his office at five minutes after eleven when the 'stat buzzed, and Lucy's face came on the screen. She shook her head in bewilderment. "I don't know what happened. Things seemed to be going along all right. He recognized me without giving away that he knew me, and we were apparently about to be led to some private room, when everything went black. The next thing I knew I was here in my apartment."

"Just a moment," Hedrock said.

He broke the connection, and called the warship. The commander shook his head. "I was just about to call you. There was a police raid, and the warning must have been very short, because they loaded the women into carplanes—half a dozen to a machine—and carted them off to their homes."

"What about the men?" Hedrock was tense. In emergencies the House sometimes had nasty habits.

"That's why I didn't call you immediately. I saw them pile the men into a truckplane, and cart them off. I followed, but they used the usual method."

"I see," said Hedrock. He covered his eyes with one shielding hand, and groaned inwardly. The problem of Cayle Clark was becoming complex again, and there was nothing to do but to let him go. "Okay, Captain," he said gloomily. "Good work."

He clicked off, called Lucy again, and gave her the news. "I'm sorry," he said, "but that eliminates him from the picture. We don't dare interfere."

"What'll I do?" she asked.

"Just wait," he said. "Wait."

That was all there was to say.

FIFTEEN

Fara worked. He had nothing else to do, and the thought was often in his mind that now he would be doing it till the day he died. Fool that he was—he told himself a thousand times how big a fool—he kept hoping that Cayle would walk into the shop and say:

"Father, I've learned my lesson. If you can ever forgive me, teach me the business, and then you retire to a well-earned rest."

It was on August 26 that the telestat clicked on just after Fara had finished lunch. "Money call," it sighed. "Money call."

Fara and Creel looked at each other. "Eh," said Fara finally, "money call for us."

He could see from the gray look in Creel's face the thought that was in her mind. He said under his breath: "Damn that boy!"

But he felt relieved. Amazingly, relieved! Cayle was beginning to appreciate the value of parents. He switched on the viewer. "Come and collect," he said.

The face that came on the screen was heavy-jowled, beetle-browed and strange. The man said: "This is Clerk Pearton of the Fifth Bank of Ferd. We have received a sight draft on you for ten thousand credits. With carrying charges and government tax, the sum required will be twelve thousand one hundred credits. Will you pay it now or will you come in this afternoon and pay it?"

"B-but . . . b-but—" said Fara. "W-who—" He stopped, conscious of the heavy-faced man saying something about the money having been paid out to Cayle Clark, that morning, on emergency call. At last Fara found his voice:

"But the bank had no right," he expostulated, "to pay out the money without my authority."

The voice cut him off coldly. "Are we then to inform our central that the money was obtained under false pretenses? Naturally, an order will be issued immediately for the arrest of your son."

"Wait . . . wait—" Fara spoke blindly. He was aware of Creel beside him, shaking her head at him. She was white, and her voice was a sick, stricken thing, as she said:

"Fara, let him go. He's through with us. We must be as hard. Let him go."

The words rang senselessly in Fara's ears. They didn't seem to fit into any normal pattern. He was saying: "I . . . I haven't got— How about my paying . . . installments?"

"If you wish a loan," said Clerk Pearton, "naturally we will be happy to go into the matter. I might say that when the draft arrived, we checked up on your status, and we are prepared to loan you eleven thousand credits on indefinite call with your shop as security. I have the form here, and if you are agreeable, we will switch this call through the registered circuit, and you can sign at once."

"Fara, no!"

The clerk went on: "The other eleven hundred credits will have to be paid in cash. Is that agreeable?"

"Yes, yes, of course. I've got twenty-five hund—" He stopped his chattering tongue with a gulp; then: "Yes, that's satisfactory."

The deal completed, Fara whirled on his wife. Out of the depths of his hurt and bewilderment, he raged: "What do you mean, standing there and talking about not paying it? You said several times that I was responsible for him being what he is. Besides, we don't know why he needed the money. He said it was an emergency."

Creel said in a low, dead voice, "In one hour he's stripped us of our savings. He must have done it deliberately, thinking of us as two old fools who wouldn't know any better than to pay it."

"All I see," Fara interrupted, "is that I have saved our name from disgrace."

His high sense of duty rightly done lasted until mid-afternoon, when the bailiff from Ferd came to take over the shop.

"But what—" Fara began.

The bailiff said, "The Automatic Atomic Motor Repair Shops,

Inc., took over your loan from the bank and are foreclosing."

"It's unfair," said Fara. "I'll take it to court." He was thinking dazedly: If the empress ever learned of this, she'd . . . she'd—

The courthouse was a big, gray building; and Fara felt emptier and colder every second, as he walked along the gray corridors. In Glay, his decision not to give himself into the hands of a lawyer had seemed a wise act. Here, in these enormous halls and palatial rooms, it seemed the sheerest folly.

He managed, nevertheless, to give an account of the criminal act of the bank in first giving Cayle the money, then turning over the note to his chief competitor, apparently within minutes of his signing it. He finished with, "I'm sure, sir, the empress would not approve of such goings-on against honest citizens."

"How dare you," said the cold-voiced person on the bench, "use the name of Her Holy Majesty in support of your own gross self-interest?"

Fara shivered. The sense of being intimately a member of the empress's great human family yielded to a sudden chill and a vast mind-picture of the ten million icy courts like this, and the myriad malevolent and heartless men—like this—who stood between the empress and her loyal subject, Fara. He thought passionately: If the empress knew what was happening here, how unjustly he was being treated, she would—

Or would she?

He pushed the terrible doubt out of his mind—came out of his reverie with a start, to hear the Cadi saying: "Plaintiff's appeal dismissed, with costs assessed at seven hundred credits, to be divided between the court and the defense solicitor in the ratio of five to two. See to it that the appellant does not leave until the costs are paid. Next case."

Fara went alone the next day to see Creel's mother. He called first at "Farmer's Restaurant" on the outskirts of the village. The place was, he noted with satisfaction in the thought of the steady stream of money flowing in, half full, though it was only mid-morning. But madam wasn't there. Try the feed store.

He found her in the back of the feed store, overseeing the weighing out of grain into cloth measures. The hard-faced old woman heard his story without a word. She said finally, curtly:

"Nothing doing, Fara. I'm one who has to make loans often from the bank to swing deals. If I tried to set you up in business,

I'd find the Automatic Atomic Motor Repair people getting after me. Besides, I'd be a fool to turn money over to a man who lets a bad son squeeze a fortune out of him. Such a man has no sense about worldly things. And I won't give you a job because I don't hire relatives in my business." She finished, "Tell Creel to come and live at my house. I won't support a man, though. That's all."

He watched her disconsolately for a while, as she went on calmly superintending the clerks who were manipulating the old, no longer accurate measuring machines. Twice her voice echoed through the dust-filled interior, each time with a sharp: "That's overweight, a gram at least. Watch your machine."

Though her back was turned, Fara knew by her posture that she was still aware of his presence. She turned at last with an abrupt movement, and said, "Why don't you go to the Weapon Shop? You haven't anything to lose, and you can't go on like this."

Fara went out then, a little blindly. At first the suggestion that he buy a gun and commit suicide had no real personal application. But he felt immeasurably hurt that his mother-in-law should have made it. Kill himself? It was ridiculous. He was still a young man, just going on fifty. Given the proper chance, with his skilled hands, he would wrest a good living even in a world where automatic machines were encroaching everywhere. There was always room for a man who did a good job. His whole life had been based on that credo.

He went home to find Creel packing. "It's the common sense thing to do," she said. "We'll rent the house and move into rooms."

He told her about her mother's offer to take her in, watching her face as he spoke. Creel shrugged. "I told her 'No' yesterday," she said thoughtfully. "I wonder why she mentioned it to you."

Fara walked swiftly over to the great front window overlooking the garden with its flowers, its pool, its rockery. He tried to think of Creel away from this garden of hers, this home of two thirds a lifetime, Creel living in rooms. And knew what her mother had meant. There was one more hope. He waited until Creel went upstairs, then called Mel Dale on the telestat. The mayor's plump face took on an uneasy expression as he saw who it was. But he listened pontifically, said finally, "Sorry, the council does not loan money; and I might as well tell you, Fara—I have nothing to do with this, mind you—but you can't get a license for a shop any more."

"W-what?"

"I'm sorry!" The mayor lowered his voice. "Listen, Fara, take my advice and go to the Weapon Shop. These places have their uses."

There was a click, and Fara sat staring at the blank face of the viewing screen.

So it was to be death!

SIXTEEN

It took two months of living in one room to make up his mind. He waited until the street was deserted, then slipped across the boulevard, past a design of flower gardens, and so to the door of the Weapon Shop. The brief fear came that the door wouldn't open, but it did, effortlessly. As he emerged from the dimness of the alcove into the shop proper, he saw the silver-haired old man sitting in a corner chair, reading under a softly bright light. The old man looked up, put aside his book, then rose to his feet.

"It's Mr. Clark," he said quietly. "What can we do for you?"

A faint flush crept into Fara's cheeks. He had hoped that he would not suffer the humiliation of being recognized. But now that his fear was realized, he stood his ground stubbornly. The important thing about killing himself was that there be no body for Creel to bury at great expense. Neither knife nor poison would satisfy that basic requirement. "I want a gun," said Fara, "that can be adjusted to disintegrate a body six feet in diameter in a single shot. Have you that kind?"

The old man turned to a showcase and brought forth a sturdy revolver that glinted with all the soft colors of the inimitable Ordine plastic. The man said in a precise voice, "Notice the flanges on this barrel are little more than bulges. This makes the model ideal for carrying in a shoulder holster under the coat. It can be drawn very swiftly because, when properly attuned, it will leap toward the reaching hand of its owner. At the moment it is attuned to me. Watch while I replace it in its holster and—"

The speed of the draw was amazing. The old man's fingers moved; and the gun, four feet away, was in them. There was no blur of movement. It was like the door the night that it had slipped from Fara's grasp, and slammed noiselessly in Constable Jor's face. *Instantaneous!*

Fara, who had parted his lips, as the old man was explaining, to protest the needlessness of illustrating any quality of the weapon except what he had asked for, closed them again. He stared in fascination. And something of the wonder that was here held his mind and his body. He had seen and handled the guns of soldiers, and they were simply ordinary metal or plastic things that one used clumsily like any other material substance, not like this at all, not possessed of a dazzling life of their own, leaping with an intimate eagerness to assist with all their superb power the will of their master.

With a start, Fara remembered his purpose. He smiled wryly, and said, "All this is very interesting. But what about the beam that can fan out?"

The old man said calmly, "At pencil thickness, this beam will pierce any body except certain alloys of lead up to four hundred yards. With proper adjustment of the firing nozzle, you can disintegrate a six-foot object at fifty yards or less. This screw is the adjuster."

He indicated a tiny device in the muzzle itself. "Turn it to the left to spread the beam, to the right to close it."

Fara said, "I'll take the gun. How much is it?"

He saw that the old man was looking at him thoughtfully. The oldster said finally, slowly, "I have previously explained our regulations to you, Mr. Clark. You recall them, of course?"

"Eh!" said Fara, and stopped, wide-eyed. "You mean," he gasped, "those things actually apply. They're not—" Tense and cold, he finished, "All I want is a gun that will shoot in self-defense, but which I can turn on myself if I have to—or want to."

"Oh, suicide!" said the old man. He looked as if a great understanding had dawned on him. "My dear sir, we have no objection to you killing yourself at any time. That is your personal privilege in a world where privileges grow scanter every year. As for the price of this revolver, it's four credits."

"Four . . . only four credits!" said Fara.

He stood astounded, his mind snatched from its dark purpose. Why, the plastic alone was—and the whole gun with its fine, intricate workmanship—twenty-five credits would have been cheap. He felt a thrill of interest. The mystery of the Weapon Shops suddenly loomed as vast and important as his own black destiny. But the old man was speaking again:

"And now, if you will remove your coat, we can put on the holster."

Automatically, Fara complied. It was vaguely startling to realize that, in a few seconds, he would be walking out of here, equipped for self-murder, and that there was now not a single obstacle to his death. Curiously, he was disappointed. He couldn't explain it, but somehow there had been in the back of his mind a hope that these Shops might, just might—what?

What indeed? Fara sighed. And grew aware again of the old man's voice:

"Perhaps you would prefer to step out of our side door. It is less conspicuous than the front."

There was no resistance in Fara. He was conscious of the man's fingers on his arm, half guiding him; and then the old man pressed one of several buttons on the wall—so that's how it was done—and there was the door. He could see flowers beyond the opening. Without a word he walked toward them. He was outside almost before he realized it.

SEVENTEEN

Fara stood for a moment in the neat little pathway, striving to grasp the finality of his situation. But nothing would come except awareness of many men around him. His mind was like a log drifting along a stream at night. Through that darkness grew a consciousness of something wrong. The wrongness was there in the back of his mind as he turned leftward to go to the front of the Weapon Shop. Vagueness transformed to a startled sense of shock. For he was not in Glay, and the Weapon Shop was not where it had been.

A dozen men brushed past Fara to join a long line of men farther along. But Fara was immune to their presence, their strangeness. His mind, his vision, his very being was concentrating on the section of machine that stood where the Weapon Shop had been. His brain lifted up, up in his effort to grasp the tremendousness of the dull-metaled immensity of what was spread here under a summer sun beneath a sky as blue as a remote southern sea.

The machine towered into the heavens, five great tiers of metal, each a hundred feet high; and the superbly streamlined five hundred feet ended in a peak of light, a spire that tilted straight up a sheer two hundred feet farther, and matched the sun for brightness.

And it *was* a machine, not a building, because the whole lower tier was alive with shimmering lights, mostly green, but sprinkled colorfully with red and occasionally blue and yellow. Twice, as Fara watched, green lights directly in front of him flashed unscintillatingly into red.

The second tier glowed with white and red lights, although there were only a fraction as many lights as on the lowest tier. The third section had on its dull-metal surface lights of blue and yellow; they twinkled softly here and there over the vast area.

The fourth tier was a series of signs, that brought the beginning of comprehension. The whole sign was:

WHITE—BIRTHS
RED—DEATHS
GREEN—LIVING
BLUE—IMMIGRATION TO EARTH
YELLOW—EMIGRATION

The fifth tier was all sign, finally explaining:

POPULATIONS

SOLAR SYSTEM	11,474,463,747
EARTH	11,193,247,361
MARS	97,298,604
VENUS	141,053,811
MOONS	42,863,971

The numbers changed, even as he looked at them, leaping up and down, shifting below and above what they had first been. People were dying, being born, moving to Mars, to Venus, to the moons of Jupiter, to Earth's moon, and others coming back again, landing minute by minute in the scores of spaceports. Life went on in its gigantic fashion—and here was the record.

"Better get in line," said a friendly voice beside Fara. "It takes quite a while to put through an individual case, I understand."

Fara stared at the man. He had the impression of having had senseless words flung at him. "In line?" he started, then stopped himself with a jerk that hurt his throat.

He was moving forward, blindly, ahead of the younger man, thinking a jumble about this having been the way that Constable Jor was transported to Mars, when another of the man's words penetrated.

"Case?" said Fara violently. "Individual case!"

The man, a heavy-faced, blue-eyed young chap of around thirty-five, looked at him curiously: "You must know why you're here," he said. "Surely, you wouldn't have been sent through here unless you had a problem of some kind that the Weapon Shop courts will solve for you; there's no other reason for coming to Information Center."

Fara walked on because he was in the line now, a fast-moving line that curved him inexorably around the machine; and seemed to be heading him toward a door that led into the interior of the great metal structure.

So it was a building as well as a machine.

A problem, he was thinking, why of course, he had a problem. A hopeless, insoluble, completely tangled problem so deeply rooted in the basic structure of Imperial civilization that the whole world would have to be overturned to make it right.

With a start, he saw that he was at the entrance. He thought with awe: In seconds he would be committed irrevocably—to what?

EIGHTEEN

Inside the Weapon Shop Information Center, Fara moved along a wide, shining corridor. Behind him, the young man said:

"There's a side corridor, practically empty. Let's go."

Fara turned into it, trembling. He noticed that at the end of the hallway were a dozen young women sitting at desks interviewing men. He stopped in front of one of the girls. She was older than she had looked from a distance, over thirty, but good looking, alert. She smiled pleasantly but impersonally, and said:

"Your name, please?"

He gave it, and added a mumble about being from the village of Glay. The woman said:

"Thank you. It will take a few minutes to get your file. Won't you sit down?"

He hadn't noticed the chair. He sank into it, and his heart was beating so wildly that he felt choked. There was scarcely a thought in his head, nor a real hope; only an intense, almost mind-wrecking excitement. He realized, suddenly, that the girl was speaking to him, but only snatches of what she said came through that screen of tension in his mind:

"—Information Center is . . . in effect . . . a bureau of statistics. Every person born . . . registered here . . . their education, change of address . . . occupation . . . and the highlights of their life. The whole is maintained by . . . combination of . . . unauthorized and unsuspected liaison with . . . Imperial Chamber of Statistics and . . . through medium of agents . . . every community—"

It seemed to Fara that he was missing vital information, and that if he could only force his attention and hear more—He strained, but it was of no use. His nerves were jumping too madly for him to focus his mind on what she was saying. He tried to speak, but before he could force words out of his trembling lips, there was a click, and a thin, dark plate slid onto the woman's desk. She took it up and examined it. After a moment, she said something into a mouthpiece, and in a short time two more plates precipitated out of the empty air onto her desk. She studied them impassively, looked up finally.

"You will be interested to know," she said, "that your son, Cayle, is on Mars."

"Eh?" said Fara. He half rose from his chair, but before he could say anything the young woman was speaking again, firmly:

"I must inform you that the Weapon Shops take no action against individuals. We are not concerned with moral correction. That must come naturally from the individual, and from the people as a whole—and now if you will give me a brief account of your problem for the record and the court."

Sweating, Fara sank back into his seat; most desperately, he wanted more information about Cayle. He began: "But . . . but what . . . how—" He caught himself; and in a low voice described what had happened. When he finished, the girl said:

"You will proceed now to the Name Room; watch for your name, and when it appears go straight to Room 474. Remember, 474—and now, the line is waiting, if you please—"

She smiled politely, and Fara was moving off almost before he realized it. He half turned to ask another question, but an old man was sinking into his chair. Fara hurried on, along a great corridor, conscious of curious blasts of sound coming from ahead.

Eagerly, he opened the door; and the sound crashed at him with all the impact of a sledgehammer blow. It was such a colossal, incredible sound that he stopped just inside the door, shrinking back. He stood then, trying to blink sense into a visual confusion that rivaled in magnitude the tornado of noise.

Men, men, men everywhere; men by the thousands in a long, broad auditorium, packed into rows of seats, pacing with an abandon of restlessness up and down the aisles, and all of them staring with frantic interest at a long board marked off into squares, each square lettered from the alphabet. The tremendous board with its lists of names ran the full length of the immense room. The Name Room,

Fara thought shakily as he sank into a seat. And his name would come up in the C's.

It was like sitting in at a no-limit poker game, watching the jewel-precious cards turn up. It was like playing the exchange with all the world at stake during a stock crash. It was nerve-wracking, dazzling, exhausting, fascinating, terrible.

New names kept flashing on to the twenty-six squares; and men would shout like insane beings and some fainted, and the uproar was shattering; the pandemonium raged on, one continuous, unbelievable sound. And every few minutes a great sign would flash along the board, telling everyone:

WATCH YOUR OWN INITIALS

Fara watched. Each second it seemed to him that he couldn't stand it an instant longer. He wanted to scream at the roomful of men to be silent. He wanted to jump up to pace the floor, but others who did that were yelled at hysterically. Abruptly, the blind savagery of it scared Fara. He thought unsteadily: "I'm not going to make a fool of myself. I—"

"Clark, Fara—" winked the board. "Clark, Fara—"

With a shout, Fara leaped to his feet. "That's me!" he shrieked. "Me!"

No one turned. No one paid the slightest attention. Shamed, he slunk across the room where an endless line of men kept crowding into a corridor beyond. The silence in the long corridor was almost as shattering as the noise it replaced. It was hard to concentrate on the idea of a number, 474. It was completely impossible to imagine what could lie beyond—474.

The room was small. It was furnished with a small, business-type table and two chairs. On the table were seven neat piles of folders, each pile a different color. The piles were arranged in a row in front of a large, milky-white globe, that began to glow with a soft light. Out of its depths, a man's baritone voice said:

"Fara Clark?"

"Yes," said Fara.

"Before the verdict is rendered in your case," the voice went on quietly, "I want you to take a folder from the blue pile. The list will show the Fifth Interplanetary Bank in its proper relation to yourself and the world, and it will be explained to you in due course."

The list, Fara saw, was simply a list of the names of companies. The names ran from A to Z, and there were about five hundred of them. The folder carried no explanation; and Fara slipped it automatically into his side pocket, as the voice came again from the shining globe:

"It has been established," the words came precisely, "that the Fifth Interplanetary Bank perpetrated upon you a gross swindle, and that it is further guilty of practicing scavengery, deception, blackmail and was accessory in a criminal conspiracy. The bank made contact with your son, Cayle, through what is quite properly known as a scavenger, that is, an agent whose job it is to find young men and women who are in financial difficulties but who have parents with money. The scavenger obtains for this service a commission of eight percent, which is always paid by the borrower, in this case, your son. The bank practiced deception in that its authorized agents deceived you by claiming that it had already paid out ten thousand credits to your son, whereas only one thousand credits was paid over and that not until your signature had been obtained. The blackmail guilt arises out of the threat to have your son arrested for falsely obtaining a loan, a threat made at a time when no money had exchanged hands. The conspiracy consists of the action whereby your note was promptly turned over to your competitor. The bank is accordingly triple-fined thirty-six thousand three hundred credits. It is not in our interest, Fara Clark, for you to know how this money is obtained. Suffice to know that the bank pays it, and that of the fine the Weapon Shops allocate to their own treasury a total of one half. The other half—"

There was a *plop*; a neatly packaged pile of bills fell onto the table. "For you," said the voice. Fara, with trembling fingers, slipped the package into his coat pocket. It required the purest mental and physical effort for him to concentrate on the next words that came.

"You must not assume that your troubles are over. The reestablishment of your motor repair shop in Glay will require force and courage. Be discreet, brave and determined, and you cannot fail. Do not hesitate to use the gun you have purchased in defense of your rights. The plan will be explained to you. And now, proceed through the door facing you."

Fara braced himself with an effort, opened the door and walked through. It was a dim, familiar room that he stepped into, and there was a silver-haired, fine-faced man who rose from a reading chair, and came forward in the dimness, smiling gravely.

The stupendous, fantastic, exhilarating adventure was over. He was back in the Weapon Shop of Glay.

NINETEEN

He couldn't get over the wonder of it. This great and fascinating organization established here in the very heart of a ruthless civilization, a civilization that had in a few brief weeks stripped him of everything he possessed. With a deliberate will, he stopped that glowing flow of thought. A frown wrinkled his solidly built face; he said:

"The . . . judge—" Fara hesitated over the name, frowned again in annoyance with himself, then went on: "The judge said that to re-establish myself I would have to—"

"Before we go into that," said the old man, "I want you to examine the blue folder you brought with you."

"Folder?" Fara echoed blankly. It took him a long moment to remember that he had picked up a folder from the table in Room 474.

He studied the list of company names with a gathering puzzlement, noting that the name Automatic Atomic Motor Repair Shops was well down among the A's, and the Fifth Interplanetary Bank only one of several great banks included. Fara looked up finally:

"I don't understand," he said. "Are these the companies you have had to act against?"

The silver-haired man smiled grimly, shook his head. "That is not what I mean. These firms constitute only a fraction of the eight million companies that are constantly in our books." He smiled again, humorlessly: "These companies all know that, because of us, their profits on paper bear no relation to their assets. What they don't know is what the difference really is, and, as we want a general improvement in business morals, not merely more skillful scheming to outwit us, we prefer them to remain in ignorance."

He paused, and this time he gave Fara a searching look, said at last: "The unique feature of the companies on this particular list is that they are every one wholly owned by Empress Isher." He finished swiftly: "In view of your past opinions on that subject, I do not expect you to believe me."

Fara stood quite still. He did believe it, with unquestioning conviction, completely, finally. The amazing, the unforgivable thing was that all his life he had watched the march of ruined men into the oblivion of poverty and disgrace—and blamed *them*.

Fara groaned. "I've been like a madman," he said. "Everything the empress and her officials did was right. No friendship, no personal relationship could survive with me that did not include belief in things as they were. I suppose if I started to talk against the empress I would receive equally short shrift."

"Under no circumstances," said the old man, "must you say anything against Her Majesty. The Weapon Shops will not countenance any such words, and will give no further aid to anyone who is so indiscreet. The empress is personally not as responsible as might appear. Like you, she is, to some extent, adrift on the tide of our civilization. But I will not enlarge upon our policy. The worst period of our relations with the Imperial power was reached some forty years ago when every person who was discovered receiving aid from us was murdered in some fashion. You may be surprised to learn that your father-in-law was among those assassinated at that time."

"Creel's father!" gasped Fara. "But—" He stopped. There was such a rush of blood to his head that for a moment he could hardly see. "But," he managed at last, "it was reported that he ran away with another woman."

"They always spread a story of some kind," the old man said; and Fara was silent.

The other went on: "We finally put a stop to their murders by killing the three men from the top down, *excluding* the royal family, who gave the order for the particular execution involved. But we do not again want that kind of bloody murder. Nor are we interested in any criticism of our toleration of so much that is evil. It is important to understand that *we do not interfere in the main stream of human existence.* We right wrongs; we act as a barrier between the people and their more ruthless exploiters. Generally speaking, we help only honest men; that is not to say that we do not give assistance to the less scrupulous, but only to the extent of selling them guns—which is a very great aid indeed, and which is one of the reasons why the government is relying almost exclusively for its power on an economic chicanery.

"In the four thousand years since the brilliant genius, Walter S. de Lany, invented the vibration process that made the Weapon Shops possible, and laid down the first principles of Weapon Shop political philosophy, we have watched the tide of government swing backward and forward between democracy under a limited monarchy to complete tyranny. And we have discovered one thing: *People always have the kind of government they want.* When they want change, they must change it. As always we shall remain an incorruptible core—and I mean that literally; we have a psychological machine that never lies about a man's character—I repeat, an incorruptible core of human idealism, devoted to relieving the ills that arise inevitably under any form of government.

"But now—your problem. It is very simple, really. You must fight, as all men have fought since the beginning of time for what they valued, for their just rights. As you know, the Automatic Atomic Motor Repair people removed all your machinery and tools within an hour of foreclosing on your shop. This material was taken to Ferd, and then shipped to a great warehouse on the coast. We recovered it, and with our special means of transportation have now replaced the machines in your shop. You will accordingly go there and—"

Fara listened with a gathering grimness to the instructions, nodded finally, his jaw clamped tight.

"You can count on me," he said curtly. "I've been a stubborn man in my time; and though I've changed sides, I haven't changed that."

TWENTY

Most of the Houses were known to the police. But there was an unwritten law in connection with them. When a raid was due to take place the owner was warned. But the names of the men who had been imprisoned on the premises *must* be discoverable in some easily accessible desk drawer. During the next few days a check-up would be made of passenger lists recording the names of indigents and criminals being sent to Mars, Venus, and the various moons. Government contractors were insatiably in need of men for work on other planets. And the Houses, frequented as they were by wealthy women who could not afford scandals, supplied a constant trickle of labor with no questions asked.

In their dealings with the Houses the police objected only to the idea that dead men tell no tales. Proprietors found themselves mercilessly hauled into court when they broke that one unalterable rule. After thousands of years, it had proved an effective method of keeping vice operating within the important limit, that the victim survived his grim experience.

Cayle stepped off the gangplank onto the soil of Mars. And stopped. It was an involuntary reaction. The ground was as hard as rock. The chill of it penetrated the soles of his shoes and somehow pierced the marrow of his being. With ice-cold eyes he surveyed the bleak town of Shardl. And this time a thought came, a hatred so violent that he shuddered. A determination so strong that he could feel the ice within him turning to steel.

"Get a move on you—" A stick prodded his shoulders. One of

the soldiers directing the disembarkation of the long line of sullen men bawled the words, his voice sounding strangely hollow in that rarefied air.

Cayle did not even turn around. He moved—that was his reaction to the insult and indignity. He walked along, keeping his place in the line; and with every step he took the chill off the ground penetrated more deeply into his being. He could feel the coldness of the air now in his lungs. Ahead of him other men felt the constriction. They began to run. Still others broke past him, breathing hoarsely, the whites of their eyes showing, their bodies clumsily responding to the lesser gravity. The ground was rough and uneven and those who fell cried out as the jagged edges tore at them. Human blood stained the iron-hard soil of ever-frozen Mars.

Cayle walked on, unheeding, contemptuous of those who had lost their heads. They had been warned against the gravity. And the great enclosed plastic compound was only a quarter of a mile away, the intervening cold shocking but bearable. He reached the compound, his flesh tingling, his feet numbed. It was warm inside and he made his way slowly to the side of the building from which the main section of the town was visible.

Shardl was a mining town. It stood on a flat plain that was just beginning to blossom here and there with the green of warm atomic gardens. The shrubbery, spotty and incongruous, only emphasized the near desolation of every visible horizon.

He saw that men were studying bulletin boards over against one wall. He moved closer, and read what he could see of one sign. It read:

OPPORTUNITY

Cayle pressed up to it and read the rest of the words, then smiled and turned away. So they wanted people to sign up for Martian farms. Agree to remain fifteen years and *"Her Gracious Majesty, Innelda of Isher, will supply you with a completely equipped atomic-heated farm. No down payment, forty years to pay."*

The offer concluded insinuatingly, "Go immediately to the Lands office, sign your application—and you will not have to do one minute's work in the mines."

Cayle was immune to the appeal. He had heard of this system

of colonizing the cold planet of Mars and the hot planet of Venus. Eventually every acre of soil would be occupied, and the planet subjected to the beneficent influence of atomic power. And so, over the millennia, men would at last thaw all the icy habitable worlds of the solar system and chill the burning deserts of Venus and Mercury. Men working out their lives on the drabber spawnings of their sun would create reasonable facsimiles of the far green Earth from which they had come.

That was the theory. In all those lazy days at public school, when he had read and listened to the accounts of colonization, he had not dreamed that he would one day be standing here, looking out at the half-light world of Mars, *standing here*, caught by a process too ruthless for any man, raised as he had been raised, to resist. He had no hatred now of his father. That was gone out of him into the hazy mists of the past, into that world of nothingness where his illusions had gone. The poor dumb fool—that was his thought now. Perhaps it was just as well some people never did comprehend the realities of life in the empire of Isher.

His own personal problem was solved in a simple, effective manner. He had been afraid. Now he wasn't. He had, astonishingly enough, been honest. Now, he wasn't. Well, in a way, he wasn't. It all depended on an individual's outlook on life as to how far he'd accept the theory that a human being must be strong enough to face the necessities of his era. Cayle Clark intended to face them all the way. Not for long would such a man as he had become remain on Mars. Meanwhile, he must sign nothing that would restrict his movements. He must be cautious, but seize opportunities instantly on an all-out basis.

Behind him a voice said slyly, "Am I addressing Cayle Clark, formerly of the village of Glay?"

Cayle turned slowly. He hadn't expected opportunity to come so quickly. The man who stood before him was small. He wore an overcoat of expensive material and he was very obviously not a person who had come on the boat, in spite of his shriveled and insignificant appearance. He spoke again.

"I am the local—uh—representative of the Fifth Bank. It may be that we can help you out of this unusual situation."

He looked like a toad, his gaunt face enframed in a high collar. His eyes, like black seeds, peered forth with a dull but avaricious light.

Cayle shrank involuntarily, not from fear but from loathing. There had been a woman who came to the House, a woman bedecked with jewels and furs—with a face like that and eyes like that. And all the whips they had used on his bare back while she looked on with greedy eyes had not broken his will to have nothing to do with her. It cost Cayle an effort of mind to realize that he must not necessarily compare the two people or believe that they had anything in common.

"Interested?" asked the creature.

Cayle started to nod. And then a word that hadn't really penetrated before came through to his consciousness.

"What bank did you say?"

The human caricature smiled with the look of a man who realized he was bearing precious gifts. "The Fifth Bank," he said. "You made a deposit in our central at Imperial City about a month ago. In the course of a normal investigation of the background of any new depositor we discovered that you were on your way to Mars under unpleasant circumstances. We therefore wish to place our loan department at your service."

"I see," said Cayle carefully.

His eyes, sharp and alert, made another more detailed examination of this agent of the great bank. But there was nothing new, nothing to inspire confidence. And yet he did not think of ending the conversation. "Just what would the bank do for me?" he asked quietly.

The man cleared his throat. "You are the son of Fara and Creel Clark?" he asked pompously.

Cayle admitted the relationship after a moment's hesitation.

"You desire to return to Earth?"

There was no hesitation about his answer to that. "Yes," he said.

"The base fare," said the man, "is six hundred credits for the trip when the distance between Mars and Earth permits a twenty-four-day journey. When the distance is greater the cost is ten credits a day extra. You probably knew that."

Cayle hadn't known. But he had guessed that the mine head wage of twenty-five credits a week would not provide a quick means of returning to Earth. He felt tense, conscious of how completely a man without resources could be confined to a planet. He had an idea of what was coming.

"The Fifth Bank," said the man in a grand tone, "will loan you the sum of one thousand credits if your father will guarantee the debt and if you will sign a note agreeing to pay back ten thousand credits."

Cayle sat down heavily. The end of hope had come more swiftly than he had expected. "My father," he said wearily, "would never guarantee a note for ten thousand credits."

"Your father," said the agent, "will be asked to guarantee only the one thousand. You will be expected to pay ten thousand out of your future earnings."

Cayle studied him with narrowed eyes. "By what method will this money be paid over to me?"

The gaunt face smiled. "You sign, then we give it to you. And just leave your father to us. The bank has a psychology department for handling co-signers and signers of notes. On some we use the dominating technique, on others—"

Cayle interrupted. "So far as I am concerned the money has to be paid over to me before I sign."

The other shrugged and laughed. "As you will. I see you are a sharp dealer. Come over to the mine manager's office."

He walked off, Cayle following thoughtfully. It was too easy and he didn't like it. Everything was happening too swiftly, as if—well, as if this were part of the routine of the end of a voyage. He slowed and looked around alertly. There was a long line of offices, he saw, where other men were being taken by well-dressed individuals.

It seemed to him that he could visualize the picture then. The first offer on the bulletin board. Volunteer to go on a farm. If they didn't get you that way, then along came a smooth-tongued man to offer a loan on the basis of your family credit. The loan money would either not be advanced at all or it would be stolen from you almost immediately afterwards.

Thereupon, having exhausted all your available resources, present and future, you were on Mars to stay.

"There'll be a couple of witnesses," Clark thought. "Big fellows with guns on them to make sure that you don't get your money."

It was a good way to colonize an unfriendly planet, possibly the only way, considering that human beings were not too interested any more in pioneering.

He walked into the office. And there were the two men, well-dressed, smiling, friendly. They were introduced as, respectively, the mine manager and a clerk from the bank. Clark wondered cynically how many other persons, shanghaied as he had been, were being introduced at this moment to the "mine manager." It sounded very impressive and it must be thrilling to have a chance to talk in heart to heart fashion with so important a personage, to realize that he was human after all. Cayle shook hands with him and then turned to look the situation over. The important thing was to get the money legally. That meant actually signing the document and getting a copy. Even that might not mean anything but, after all, there was a certain amount of law on the planets. The dangerous thing was to be without money and to arrive in court where other men could blandly deny one's story.

The room was not large but it was luxuriously furnished. It *could* have been a mine manager's office. There were two doors, the one through which he had come, and one directly opposite, where, presumably, the robbed individual made his exit without getting any chance to talk to people in the big room from which he had come. Clark walked over to the second door, opened it and saw that it led outside. There were scores of huts within sight and, standing in groups all around, were soldiers. The sight of them gave him pause, for obviously they would make it impossible for him to make a run for it if he succeeded in obtaining the money.

He used his body to block off the mob. With swift fingers he tested it to see if it were locked from the outside. It was. Quietly, he closed the door and, with a smile, turned back into the room. He shivered convincingly. "Sure chilly out there. I'll be glad to get back to Earth."

The three men smiled sympathetically and the reptilian bank agent held out a document with ten one hundred credit notes clipped to it. Clark counted the money and put it in his pocket. Then he read the contract. It was quite simple, apparently designed to ease the minds of people who were suspicious of involved forms. There were three copies, one to be sent to Earth, one for the Martian branch and one for him. They were properly signed and sealed and awaited only his signature. Clark tore off the bottom one and put it into his pocket. The others were inserted into the registered circuit. He signed the first one with a flourish—and then he stepped back and threw the pen, point first, into the face of the "manager."

The man screamed and put his hand up to his torn cheek.

That was all Clark saw. With a jump he reached the side of the toadlike man, grabbed at his neck just above the heavy coat collar and squeezed with all his strength. The creature yelped and struggled weakly.

For a moment then, Clark had the sharp fear that his plan of attack had been falsely based. He had assumed that the other had a gun also and would reach for it in panic. Long skinny fingers were clawing inside the voluminous coat. They came out clutching a little glittering blaster that Clark snatched, hand and all, and crushed into his own palm. Simultaneously, he squeezed the weapon away from the other's grasp.

He saw that the big "clerk" had his gun out, and was edging around, trying to get a chance to use it without harming the reptile. Clark took a snap shot at the man's foot. The radiant flame made a thin, bright beam. There was an odor of burning leather and a streamer of blue smoke. With a cry, the fellow dropped his weapon and sat down heavily on the floor. He writhed there, clutching at his foot. At Clark's urging, the "manager" held up his hands reluctantly. Swiftly, Clarke relieved him of his blaster, picked up the one on the floor and backed toward the door.

He explained his plan briefly. The toad would accompany him as a hostage. They would go to the nearest airline base and fly to the city of Mare Cimmerium, at which point he would catch a regular liner for Earth. "And if anything should go wrong," Cayle Clark concluded, "at least one person will die before I do."

Nothing went wrong.

And that day was August 26, 4784 Isher, two months and twenty-three days after Imperial Innelda launched her attack on the Weapon Makers.

TWENTY-ONE

Cayle Clark planned and schemed. The days of the journey from Mars to Earth wound their clockwise course. The ship time switched gradually from Cimmerium Daylight Time to Imperial City Time. But the night outside, with its flashingly bright sun off to one side and everywhere else starry darkness, was an unchanging environment. Meals were eaten. Clark slept and dreamed and moved and had his being. His thoughts grew more direct, more determined. He had no doubts. A man who had put away fear of death could not fail.

The sun grew brighter. It splashed spiral-like across the darkness. Mars receded to a point of smallness, a reddish dot in a sea of night—hard to find among the starry brilliants of the jewel-case sky. Gradually Earth became a large, shining ball of light, then a monstrous, misty, unbelievable thing that filled half the sky. The continents showed through. And on Earth's nightside, partly visible as the ship swung past the moon, the cities shone with intermittent glitter that rivaled the heavens themselves.

Clark saw that vision of Earth in snatches only. Five days from destination he had discovered a stud poker game in one of the holds. From the beginning he lost. Not every game—an occasional win helped him recuperate a few credits. But by the third day of the endless game, the second last of the trip, the direction of his fortune was so marked that he took alarm and quit.

In his cabin he counted the money that remained to him—eighty-one credits. He had paid eight percent commission on the thousand credits to the representative of the bank. The rest had gone on fare, poker losses and one Imperial-style gun. "At least,"

Clark thought, "I'll soon be back in Imperial City. And with more money than when I arrived last time."

He lay back, amazingly at ease. The poker losses did not disturb him. He hadn't, when he came right down to it, planned to try gambling again. He had a different picture of his life. He would take risks, of course, but on a higher level. He had won five hundred thousand credits—at least—in the Penny Palace. It would be difficult to collect it but he would succeed. He felt himself patient and capable, ready for all eventualities.

As soon as he had the money he would secure a commission from Colonel Medlon. He might pay for it and he might not. It depended upon the moment. There was no vengefulness in his plan. He didn't care what happened to two venal creatures like Fatty and the colonel. They were stepping stones, it seemed to Clark, in the most ambitious scheme that had ever been planned in the Empire of Isher. A scheme rooted in a fact that seemed to have escaped all the creature-men who had risen to positions of rank in the Imperial Service.

Innelda of Isher meant well by the country. In his one contact with her he had sensed a personality frustrated by the corruption of others. In spite of the talk against her, the empress was honest—on a Machiavellian level, of course. Clark did not doubt that she could issue an order of execution. But that was part of her function as a ruler. Like himself, she must rise to the necessities of her situation.

The empress was honest. She would welcome a man who would use her limitless authority to clean house for her. For two and a half months now he had been thinking over what she had said that day in Medlon's office and he had some pretty shrewd answers. There was her reference to officer-prospects staying away in droves because they had heard something was up. And her accusation of a pro-Weapon Shop conspiracy tied in with the inexplicable closing of the Shops. Something *was* up and, for a man who had made a personal contact, it spelled massive opportunity.

To all his planned actions Clark made but one qualification. First, he must seek out Lucy Rall and ask her to marry him.

That hunger would not wait.

The ship came down into its cradle a few minutes before noon on a cloudless day. There were formalities and it was two o'clock before Clark's papers were stamped and he emerged into the open.

A breeze touched his cheeks and, from the peak of metal that was the landing field, he could see the dazzling city to the west.

It was a view to make a man catch his breath, but Clark did not waste any time. From a 'stat booth, he called Lucy's number. A pause, then a young man's face came onto the screen. "I'm Lucy's husband," he said. "She went out for a minute, but you don't want to talk to her." Persuasively. "Take a good look at me and you'll agree."

Clark stared blankly. But the familiarity of the other's face would not penetrate through the shock of the words he had spoken.

"Look hard," the image in the 'stat urged.

Clark began, "I don't think that—"

And then he got it. He drew back like a man whose face has been slapped. He put out his hand as if he would defend his eyes from a vision that was too bright for them. He could feel the blood draining from his cheeks, and he swayed. The now familiar voice drew him back to normalcy.

"Pull yourself together!" it said. "And listen. I want you to meet me tomorrow night on the beach of the Haberdashery Paradise. Take one more look at me, convince yourself, and be there."

Clark didn't need the look but his eyes sought the image face. And there was no question. The face that was staring at him from the 'stat was his own.

Cayle Clark was looking at Cayle Clark—at 2:10 P.M., October 4, 4784 Isher.

TWENTY-TWO

October 6—the empress stirred, and turned over in bed. She had a memory. The night before she had told herself that by morning her mind would be made up. As she came out of sleep she realized the uncertainty was still there. She opened her eyes, already embittered against the day.

She sat up, composing the tension in her face. And as she did so half a dozen maids, who had been hovering behind a soundproofed screen, dashed forward. An energy drink was tendered. Sunlight adjustments were made, the great bedroom brightened for another morning. Massage, shower, facial, hair—and, again and again, as the routine proceeded, she thought, "I have got to get action or the attack will end in a personal humiliation. Surely, after four months, they cannot keep on delaying."

As soon as she had her dress on she began to receive palace officials. First, Gerritt, the chief of Palace Administration. He had a problem, many of them, and as usual, annoying ones. That was partially her own fault. Long ago she had insisted that all punishment of the palace staff be referred to her. Today the predominant motif was insolence. Servants defying their superiors and shirking their work. The offense was becoming common.

"For heaven's sake," Innelda said irritably, "if they don't like the limitations of their position, why don't they quit? Palace-trained servants can always obtain positions, if only for what they are believed to know about my private life."

"Why doesn't Your Majesty let me handle these personal matters?" said Gerritt. It was his stock remark, stolidly made. She knew that eventually he would wear her down but not to his own benefit.

No stubborn old conservative was going to have full control of the huge staff of palace servitors. A heritage from the regency period, he and all his kind were going to be asked to vacate. She sighed, and dismissed him—and was back with her problem. What to do? Should she order attacks wherever possible? Or wait in the hope that new information would turn up? The trouble was that she had been waiting now for so many weeks.

General Doocar came in, a tall, thin man with slate gray eyes. He saluted with an angular motion and said, "Madam, the building reappeared for two hours and forty minutes last night, only one minute from the estimated time."

Innelda nodded. That was routine now. The pattern of reappearance had been established within a week of the first disappearance. She still insisted on being kept informed of the building's movements, just why, she couldn't decide.

"I'm like a child," she thought self-critically. "I can't let anything get out of my control." The analysis darkened her mood. She made a few sharp remarks about the efficiency of the military scientists under his command, then asked the question. The general shook his head.

"Madam," he said, "an attack is out of the question at the moment. We have a power machine dominating the Weapon Shops in every large city on this planet. But during the past two and a half months eleven thousand officers have deserted. The power machines are manned by guards who do not know how to operate them."

The woman flashed, "The hypnotic machine could teach them en masse in one hour."

"Yes." The hard voice did not change. The thin lips became a little thinner. That was all. "Your Majesty, if we are prepared to hand such information over to common soldiers, that is your privilege. You have but to command and I will obey."

Innelda bit her lip, vexed. This grim old man had her there. It was annoying to have come out at last with a thought that she had restrained so often in the past. She said defensively, "It seems that the so-called common soldiers are more loyal than my commissioned officers, and braver."

He shrugged. "You allow these tax creatures of yours the privilege of selling commissions," he said. "You do, generally, get educated people that way, but you surely don't expect a man who has paid ten thousand credits for a captaincy to take the chance of getting himself killed."

The argument began to weary her. She had heard it all before in different words. The same old meanings, reinforced by the same dramatizations, though it was some weeks now since the problem of commissions in the armed forces had been mentioned. The subject was not a pleasant one. It reminded her now of something she had almost forgotten. "The last time we talked of this," she said slowly, "I requested you to contact Colonel Medlon and ask him whatever became of that officer he was about to commission when I called him one day? It isn't often that I make personal contacts with lower ranks." Suddenly she became savage—"I'm hedged in here by a brigade of old men who don't know how to mobilize an army." She fought down her anger. "But never mind that. What about him?" General Doocar said stonily, "Colonel Medlon informs me that the young officer-prospect did not return at the appointed hour. The colonel assumes that he must have got wind of what was up and hastily changed his mind."

There was silence. She found herself thinking—that the explanation sounded wrong. He wasn't like that. And besides the empress personally had talked to him.

She did not underestimate the power of such personal contact. People who met the empress of Isher felt not only her personal charm but experienced the abnormal aura of her position. The combination was overpowering, not to be lightly dismissed on the word of a suspected "wino."

She spoke at last with a quiet determination. "General, inform the colonel *today* that he will either produce this young officer or face a Lambeth in the morning."

The gaunt man bowed but there was a cynical smile on his face. "Madam," he said, "if it gives you pleasure to destroy corruption, one individual at a time, you have a lifelong task ahead of you."

She didn't like that. There was a brutality in the remark that reached deep into her. She drew back. "I've got to start somewhere." She made a gesture, half threat, half frustration. She said querulously, "I don't understand you anymore, General. When I was younger you used to agree that something ought to be done."

"Not by you." He shook his head. "The Imperial family must sanction, not personally direct, a moral housecleaning." He shrugged. "As a matter of fact, I have more or less come around to the Weapon Shop idea that this is an age where people take to corruption whenever their adventurous instincts are denied normal expression."

The green, imperial eyes flashed. "I am not interested in Weapon Shop philosophy."

She was abruptly astounded that he should have mentioned the Weapon Shops in such a fashion. She flung the accusation at him. The grand old man was immune.

"Madam," he said, "when I stop examining the ideas and philosophies of a power that has now existed for three thousand seven hundred years you may have my resignation."

The woman rejected the argument. Everywhere she turned was this semi-worship of the Weapon Shops. More, it was an acceptance of the shops as a legitimate facet of Isher civilization. *I must get rid of these old men,* she thought, not for the first time. *They treat me as a child and will always treat me that way.* Aloud she said icily, "General, I am not interested in hearing the moral teachings of an organization that at base is responsible for all the immorality in the solar system. We live in an age where productive capacity is so great that no one need ever starve. Crime because of economic need does not exist. The problem of psychiatric crime can be solved whenever we get hold of the afflicted person. But what is the situation?" She was hot now with remembered rage. "We discover that our psychopath has been sold a Weapon Shop gun. The owner of a House of Illusion is similarly protected. True, in that case there is an understanding between the police and the Houses whereby raids are allowed. But if any individual owner should decide to resist, we would have to bring a thirty-thousand-cycle cannon to defeat him." She paused to survey the job done by her hairdresser, felt satisfied, waved the woman away.

"Ridiculous and criminal!" she continued. "On every side, we are frustrated in our desire to end this eternal wickedness of millions of individuals, who sneer at the law because they have Weapon Shop guns. It would be different, if these—gun makers—would limit the sale of their products to respectable people. But when any sort of scoundrel can buy one—"

"A defensive gun!" interjected the general softly. "Defensive only."

"Exactly," said Innelda. "A man can commit any crime, then

defend himself against justice. Oh—" furiously—"why do I even talk to you? General, I'm telling you. We have the weapon that can destroy these Weapon Shops once and for all. You don't have to kill the members, but get the army organized to destroy the Shops. Get it organized, I say, for an attack within three days? A week?" She looked at him. "How long, General?"

He pleaded, "Give me until the new year, madam. I swear that the confusion which was caused by the desertions has temporarily ruined us."

She had forgotten the deserters for the moment. "You have captured some of these officers?"

He hesitated. "Some, yes."

"I want one available for questioning this morning."

General Doocar bowed.

"As for the rest," said Innelda, "keep the military police after them. As soon as this mess is over, I'll set up special courts-martial and we'll teach these traitors the meaning of their oaths of allegiance."

"Suppose," said Doocar, and his voice was soft again, "they have Weapon Shop guns?"

Her reaction to that was so violent that she grew calm in her anger. "My friend," she said gravely, "when army discipline can be set at nought by an underground organization, then even the generals must realize it is time to destroy the subversion." She made a motion with her right arm. A gesture of decisiveness. "This afternoon, General, I shall visit the laboratories of Olympian Field. I want to see what progress has been made in finding out just what the Weapon Makers did to that building. Tomorrow morning, at least, Colonel Medlon must procure for me the young man he was supposed to have commissioned. If he cannot do it, one corrupt head will roll. You may think I'm being childish, concerning myself with one individual. But I must start somewhere. And that young man I know about. Him I can check on. But now," she said, "you Weapon Shop admirer, get out of here before I do something drastic."

"Madam," protested Doocar mildly. "I am loyal to the House of Isher."

"I am glad to hear it," said Innelda scathingly.

She brushed past him and went out into the hallway without looking back.

TWENTY-THREE

As she entered the salon, she heard the faint sighing of relief of those already there. She smiled darkly. People who wanted to eat in the Imperial salon had to wait till she broke bread or sent word she wasn't coming. No compulsion existed for anyone to be present. But usually those who had access did not deny themselves the privilege. Innelda said, "Good morning!" Then sat down at the head of her table. She sipped a glass of water, which was the signal for the waiters to come in. After she had given her order, she looked around the room. Everywhere were graying heads; men and women over fifty; relics of the regency.

A half dozen young men and two of her younger secretaries sat at her own table. But they were a remnant; the residue of the emigration of young people that had followed the departure of Prince del Curtin.

"Did everybody have a nice sleep last night?" Innelda broke the silence sweetly. They hastened to assure her that they had. "How nice," she murmured—and settled into a moody silence. She wasn't sure just what she wanted of her companions. Lightness, perhaps. But how much? A year before, a newly introduced young man had asked her if she were still a virgin. And since she was, the incident still annoyed her.

Crudeness was definitely out of order. She had an instinctive feeling that immorality on her part would reflect on the reputation of the Isher family. But then what? She pecked at a piece of toast. What did she want? A positive approach—a belief in principles, with an ability to see the humorous side of life. Her own upbringing, severe and simple, had stressed the positive mind trainings.

Very important, but seriousness could be overdone. She stiffened with an old determination. "I've got to get rid of these humorless, do-nothing, let's-be-careful-and-not-rock-the-boat, think-twice-and-stop—" She paused, self-pitingly, and prayed to her private gods, "Give me one good joke a day to make me laugh and one man who can handle affairs of state and, in addition, know how to amuse me. If only Del were here."

She scowled in annoyance at the direction her thoughts were taking. Her cousin, Prince del Curtin, disapproved of the attack on the Weapon Shops. What a shock, when she had first discovered that. And what mortification when all the young men of his clique left the palace with him, refusing to participate in the adventure. Having killed Banton Vickers for threatening to inform the Weapon Shops of her plans, a treasonous utterance that would have destroyed her prestige if she had let it pass, she could not overlook the opposition. Tight-lipped, she recalled their final conversation, the prince cold and formal, marvelously good looking in his anger, herself uncertain but determined, as he said, "When you get over this madness, Innelda, you may call me back." He must have known that it was an opportunity for her to say, "That will be never." But she hadn't dared to say it. She had been like a wife, she thought bitterly. Wronged but unwilling to say too much, for fear that her husband might take her at her word. Not that she could ever marry the prince after such an action on his part. Still it would be nice to have him back—later—after the Weapon Shops were destroyed. She finished breakfast and glanced at her watch. Nine-thirty. She cringed, involuntarily. The long day was barely begun.

At half past ten, free of urgent correspondence, she had the officer-deserter brought in. He was a man of thirty-three according to his file, country born and holding the rank of major. He came in; a faint cynical smile on his lips, but his eyes looked depressed. His name was Gile Sanders. Innelda studied him gloomily. According to his file he had three mistresses and had made a fortune out of a peculiar graft involving army purchases. It was a fairly typical case history. And the part that was difficult to understand was why he, who had so much, had given it all up. She asked the question earnestly. "And please," she said, "do not insult me by suggesting that you were concerned with the moral issue of the war. Tell me simply and plainly why you gave up all your possessions for dishonor and disgrace. In one act you disinherited yourself. The very least that can happen to you is that you'll be sent to Mars or Venus permanently. Were you a fool or a coward or both?"

He shrugged. "I suppose I was a fool." His feet fumbled nervously over the floor. His eyes did not evade her direct stare, but his answer left her dissatisfied. After ten minutes she had got no real explanation out of him. It was possible that the profit and loss motivation had not influenced his decision. She tried a new approach. "According to your file," she said, "you were notified to report to building Eight Hundred A and, because of your rank, it was explained to you that at last a method had been found to destroy the Weapon Shops. An hour later, after having burned your private papers, you left your office and took up residence in a seaside cottage which you had purchased secretly—you thought—five years ago. A week later, when it was clear that you did not intend to do your duty, you were arrested. You have been in close confinement ever since. Is that picture fairly correct?"

The man nodded but said nothing. The empress studied him, biting her lips. "My friend," she said softly at last, "I have it in my power to make your punishment anything I desire. Anything. Death, banishment, commutation—" she hesitated—"reinstatement."

Major Sanders sighed wearily. "I know," he said. "That was the picture I suddenly saw."

"I don't understand." She was puzzled. "If you realize the potentialities of your act, then you were very foolish."

"The picture," he said in a monotone, as if he had not heard her interruption, "of a time when someone, not necessarily yourself, would have that power without qualification, without there being anywhere to turn, without alleviation, without—hope."

She had her answer. "Well, of all the stupidity!" said Innelda explosively. She leaned back in her chair, momentarily overcome, drew a deep breath, then shook her head in irritation. "Major," she said gently, "I feel sorry for you. Surely your knowledge of the history of my family must have told you that the danger of misuse of power does not exist. The world is too big. As an individual I can interfere in the affairs of such a tiny proportion of the human race that it is ridiculous. Every decree that I issue vanishes into a positive blur of conflicting interpretations as it recedes from me. That decree could be ultimately mild—it would make no difference in the final administration of it. Anything, when applied to eleven billion people, takes on a meaningless quality that is impossible to imagine unless you have studied, as I have, actual results."

She saw with astonishment that her words had not touched him. She drew back, offended. It was all so crystal clear and here was one more obstinate fool. She restrained her anger with an effort. "Major," she said, "with the Weapon Shops out of the way we could introduce steadying laws that could not be flouted. There would be more uniform administration of justice because people would have to accept the judgment of the courts, their only recourse being appeals to the higher courts."

"Exactly," said Sanders. That was all. His tone rejected her logic. She studied him for a long moment, all the sympathy gone from her. Then she said bitterly, "If you're such a firm believer in the Weapon Shops, why didn't you protect yourself by going to them for a defensive gun?"

"I did."

She hesitated; then asked coldly, "What was the matter? Did your courage fail you when it came to the point of using it to defend yourself from arrest?"

Watching him, she knew she shouldn't have said that. It left her open to a retort which, she realized, might be devastating. Her fear was justified.

Sanders said, "No, Your Majesty. I did exactly what some of the other—uh—deserters did. I took off my uniform and went to a Weapon Shop, intending to buy a gun. But the door wouldn't open. It appears that I am one of the few officers who believe that the Isher family is the more important of the two facets of Isher civilization."

His eyes had been bright as he spoke. Now they grew depressed again. "I am," he said, "in exactly the position you want to put everybody into. I have no way to turn. I must accept your law; must accept secret declarations of war on an institution that is as much a part of Isher civilization as the House of Isher itself; must accept death if you decree it, without a chance to defend myself in open battle. Your Majesty," he finished quietly, "I respect and admire you. The officers who deserted are not scoundrels. They were merely confronted with a choice and they chose not to participate in an attack on things as they are. I doubt if I could put it more honestly than that."

She doubted it too. Here was a man who would never understand the realistic necessity of what she was doing.

After she dismissed him she noted his name in her check-file, commenting that she wanted to hear the verdict of his court-martial. The action of writing the words reminded her of her inability to remember the name of the man whom Colonel Medlon was to produce by morning. She leafed the pages, and found it immediately. "Cayle Clark," she said aloud. "That's he." She realized that it was now time to go to the Treasury Department and hear all the reasons why it was impossible to spend more money. With a tired smile, she went out of the study and took a private elevator up to the fiftieth floor.

TWENTY-FOUR

We were married (said Lucy in her disjointed report to the coordination department of the Weapon Shops) shortly before noon, Friday, the day he landed from Mars. I do not know how to account for the fact that a later checkup revealed he had not landed until two o'clock, nor have I confronted him with this information. I will ask him about it only if I am specifically requested to do so. I do not desire to guess how he was able to marry me before the hour of the ship's arrival. There is no question in my mind, however. The man I married is Cayle Clark. It is impossible that I have been fooled by somebody representing himself to be Cayle. He has just made his daily 'stat call to me but he doesn't know that I am making this report. I'm beginning to feel that it is wrong for me to make any reports whatever about him. However, the general circumstances being what they are, I am as requested, trying to recall every detail of what happened. I will begin with the moment that I received a 'stat call from him on the morning of his arrival from Mars.

The time as I remember it was about half past ten. That conversation was extremely brief. We exchanged greetings, and then he asked me to marry him. My feelings about Cayle Clark are well known to the head of the coordination department. And I am sure Mr. Hedrock will not be surprised that I agreed instantly to the proposal, and that we signed our marriage declarations on the registered circuit a few minutes before noon the same morning. We then went to my apartment, where, with one interruption, we remained the rest of that day and that night. The interruption came at a quarter to two when he asked me if I would take a walk around the block while he used my 'stat for a call. He didn't say whether the call would be incoming or out-going but, on returning, I noticed on the 'stat meter that it had been an incoming call.

I do not apologize for leaving the apartment at his request. My acquiescence seems to me normal. During the course of the day and evening, he made no further reference to the call but instead described to me everything that had happened to him since I last saw him in the House of Illusion. I do confess that his account at times was not so clear as it might have been and he more than once gave me the impression that he was relating events which had happened to him a considerable time ago.

The morning after our marriage he was up early, and said that he had many things to do. Since I was anxious to call up Mr. Hedrock, I let him go without objection. The subsequent report of another Weapon Shop agent that a very expensive private carplane picked him up a block from the apartment and took off before the agent could summon transportation, puzzles me. Frankly, I cannot understand it.

Since then, Cayle has not been to the apartment but he has called me up every morning and told me that he cannot give me details as yet about what he is doing, but that he loves me as much as ever. I shall accept that until he himself tells me otherwise. I have no knowledge at all of the report that he has been for more than a month a captain in Her Majesty's Army. I do not know how he managed to obtain a commission, nor by what means he is pushing his interests. If it is true, as reported, that he has already been attached to the personal staff of the empress, then I can only express amazement and speculate privately as to how he has managed it.

In conclusion, let me affirm my faith in Cayle. I cannot account for his actions, but I believe that the end-result will be honorable.

(Signed) *Lucy Rall Clark*
November 14, 4784 I

TWENTY-FIVE

This was it. For a month Hedrock had delayed his reaction, waiting for new evidence. But now, reading Lucy's document, the conviction came. The unexpected turn of events that he had been waiting for was happening. What it was he had no idea. He felt a tensed alarm, the fear that he was missing vital clues. But doubt he had none—this was it.

Frowning, he reread the girl's statement. And it seemed to him then that Lucy was developing a negative attitude toward the Weapon Shops. It was not in what she had done but that she felt her actions might be misinterpreted. That was defensive, and therefore bad. The hold of the Shops on its members was psychological. Usually, when anyone wanted to break away, he was divested of vital memories, given a bonus depending on length of service and shooed off with the blessings of the organization. But Lucy was a key contact during a great crisis. The conflict between her duty to the Shops and her personal situation must not be allowed to become too disturbing.

Hedrock frowned over the problem, then dialed the 'stat. Lucy's face came onto the screen and Hedrock said earnestly, "I have just read your statement, Lucy, and I want to thank you for your cooperation. We appreciate your position thoroughly and I have been asked—" he worded it deliberately as if an executive group were behind what he was saying—"I have been asked to request that you hold yourself ready for a call from us night and day until the critical period is over. In return, the Weapon Shops will do everything in their power to protect your husband from any dangerous reactions that may result from what he is doing."

It was no light promise. He had already handed the assignment over to the protective branch. Insofar as it was possible to protect a man in the Imperial sphere the job was being done. He watched Lucy's face casually but intently. Intelligent though she was, she would never fully comprehend the Weapon Shop–Isher war. It didn't show. No guns were firing. Nobody was being killed. And even if the Weapon Shops were destroyed Lucy would not immediately notice the difference. Her life might never be affected and not even the immortal man could say what the pattern of existence would be when one of the two power facets of the culture was eliminated. He saw that Lucy was not satisfied with what he had said. He hesitated, then, "Mrs. Clark, on the day you were married you took your husband's callidity measurements and gave them to us. We have never told you the integrated result because we did not want to alarm you. I think, however, that you will be interested rather than anxious."

"They're special?" Lucy asked.

"*Special!*" Hedrock searched for adjectives. "Your husband's callidity at the time you measured him was the highest that has ever been recorded in the history of the Information Center. The index has nothing to do with gambling and we cannot guess what form it will take but that it will affect the whole world of Isher we have no doubt."

With troubled eyes he gazed at her. The devastating aspect of the affair was that Cayle Clark was not doing anything. There he was, attached to the personal staff of the empress, his movements accounted for by a host of spies—well, almost all his movements. Several 'stat calls he had made from the palace had proved too private for interference. And twice he had slipped away from the palace, and eluded his shadows. Minor incidents—they could scarcely account for the fact that, according to his callidetic measurement, what was happening was happening *now*. The great event, whatever it was, was taking place. And not even the No-men of the Shops were able to guess what it was.

Hedrock explained the situation, then, "Lucy," he said, "are you sure you have held nothing back? I swear to you it is a matter of life and death, particularly his life."

The girl shook her head. And though he watched closely her eyes did not change, showed not a trace of myopia. They widened, but that was another phenomenon. Her mouth remained firm, which was a good sign. It was impossible to tell definitely, of course, just by looking at her physical reactions—except that Lucy Rall was not known ever to have taken evasive training. Where Robert Hedrock could lie without giving one of the known lie-reactions, Lucy simply didn't have the experience or nerve-control training to stifle the unconscious signals of her muscles.

"Mr. Hedrock," she said, "you know that you can count on me to the limit."

That was a victory for his immediate purpose. But he broke the connection, dissatisfied, not with Lucy or with the other agents, but with himself. He was missing something. His mind was not seeing deep enough into reality. Just as the solution to the seesaw problem was eluding him, so now he was baffled by what must in reality be very apparent. Sitting here in his office, mulling over facts and figures, he was too far from the scene.

It was clearly time for an on-the-spot investigation by Robert Hedrock in person.

TWENTY-SIX

Hedrock walked slowly along the Avenue of Luck savoring the difference in its appearance. He couldn't recall just when he had last been on the street, but it seemed a long, long time ago. There were more establishments than he remembered, but not many changes otherwise. A hundred years did not affect the structural metals and material of a building made under the rigid Isher regulations. The general architectural designs remained the same. The decoration was different. New lighting facades, planned to attract the eye, confronted him in every direction. The science of refurbishing had not been neglected.

He entered the Penny Palace, undecided as to what level of action he should pursue. He favored the irresistible approach—he thought—better leave the decision about that for the moment. As he walked into the "treasure room" a ring on his little finger tingled. A transparency was probing him from his right. He walked on, then turned casually to examine the two men from whose direction the impulse had come. Were they employees or independents? Since he always carried about fifty thousand credits on him, independent sharpers would be a nuisance. He smiled gently as he came up to them.

"I'm afraid not," he said. "Forget any plans you had, eh?"

The heavier of the two men reached into a coat pocket, then shrugged. "You're not carrying a Weapon Shop gun," he said pointedly. "You're not armed at all."

Hedrock said, "Would you like to test that?" And looked straight at the man's eyes.

The gambler was the first to glance away. "C'mon, Jay," he said. "This job isn't the way I figured it."

Hedrock stopped him as he turned away. "Work here?"

The man shook his head. "Not," he said frankly, "if you're against it."

Hedrock laughed. "I want to see the boss."

"That's what I thought," the man said. "Well, it was a good job while it lasted."

This time Hedrock let them go. He felt no surprise at their reaction. The secret of human power was confidence. And the confidence they had seen in his eyes was rooted in certainties of which most men had never heard. In all the world there had never been a man armed as he was with mental, physical, emotional, neural and molecular defenses.

Lucy's description of Martin's office made it unnecessary for him to explore. He entered the corridor at the back of the gambling section. As he closed the door behind him, a net fell over him, neatly enveloping him. It drew instantly tight and pulled him several feet above the floor. Hedrock made no effort to free himself. There was enough light for him to see the floor five feet below, and the indignity of his position did not disturb him. He had time for several thoughts. So Harj Martin had become wary of uninvited visitors. It proved something; just what, he would leave to the moment of meeting.

He had not long to wait. Footsteps sounded. The door opened, and the fat man came in. He turned on a bright light and stood with a jolly look on his face, staring up at his prisoner. "Well," he said at last, "what have we got here?" He stopped. His eye had caught Hedrock's. Some of the jolliness faded from his expression. "Who are you?" he snapped.

Hedrock said, "On or about the night of October fifth, you were visited here by a young man named Cayle Clark. What happened?"

"I'll do the questioning," said Martin. Once again his eyes met Hedrock's. "Say," he said querulously, "who *are* you?"

Hedrock made a gesture. It was very carefully timed and estimated. One of the rings on his fingers dissolved the hard material of the net. It parted beneath him like a door opening. He landed on his feet. He said, "Start talking, my friend. I'm in a hurry."

Ignoring the gun that Martin snatched, he brushed past him

into the large office. When he spoke again the confidence was in his voice. It required only a few moments after that for the resigned gambling palace operator to decide on cooperation. "If all you want is information, okay." He added, "Your date is right. It was October fifth, about midnight, when this guy Clark came in here. He had his twin brother with him."

Hedrock nodded, but said nothing. He was not here for discussion.

"Boy," said Martin, "they were about the most coldblooded twins I ever saw and they worked together like a team. One of them must have had some army experience because he stood—well, you know the hypnotic posture they get. He was the one who knew everything, and was he ever tough! I started to say something about not being a sucker and I got a blast across my legs. I made a bit too fast a move when I turned to pump the money out of the safe and another blast took off some of my hair."

He pointed at a bald spot on one side of his head. Hedrock examined it briefly. It had been close but obviously trained shooting. Weapon Shop or army. By elimination, army.

"You're all right," he commented.

Martin shuddered. "That guy wasn't worrying whether I was all right or not." He finished, complaining, "Life is getting too tough. I never knew the normal defense devices of Isher could be so easily nullified."

Outside Hedrock headed for a carplane stop in a meditative mood. The existence of the two Cayles was now established. And one of them had been in the army long enough to receive more than the preliminary officer training. He had had that training on October fifth, a mere one day after Cayle Clark's arrival from Mars. By the morning of the sixth, the day Clark joined the army, according to the record, he had five hundred thousand credits.

It was a nice stake for a young man trying to get ahead. But it scarcely accounted for certain things that were happening. And, large though it was, it was a tiny sum when considered in its relations to Cayle Clark's callidetic index—if the callidity were due to follow a money pattern. His carplane arrived and the thought ended. He had one more call to make this morning—Colonel Medlon.

TWENTY-SEVEN

Robert Hedrock returned to his office in the Hotel Royal Ganeel shortly after midday. He examined the reports that had come in during his absence, then spent two hours on a private telestat with an economic expert at the Weapon Shop Information Center. Then he called the members of the Weapon Makers' Council, and requested an immediate plenary session.

It required about ten minutes for the full council to assemble in the council chamber of the hotel. Dresley opened the meeting. "Looks to me, gentlemen," he said, "as if our coordinator has struck a warm trail. Right, Mr. Hedrock?"

Hedrock came forward smiling. Last time, in speaking to a delegation of this council, he had had the pressure of the time map *and* the empress on his spirit. The map was still in the building, its problem unsolved, becoming more urgent every hour. But now he had one solution. He began without preliminary. "Gentlemen, on the morning of November twenty-seventh, twelve days hence, we will send a message to the Isher Empress, and request her to end her war. We will accompany our request with facts and figures that will convince her she has no alternative."

He expected a sensation, and he got it. These men knew that, when it came to his job, he was not one to raise false hopes (they had yet to discover that his efficiency was equally great in other fields). Feet stirred, and there was excitement.

Peter Cadron said explosively, "*Man!* Don't keep us in suspense. What have you discovered?"

"Permit me," said Hedrock, "to recapitulate."

He went on. "As you are aware, on the morning of June third, four thousand seven hundred and eighty-four Isher, a man from the year nineteen hundred and fifty-one A.D. appeared in our Greenway Weapon Shop. The discovery was then made that the empress was directing a new energy weapon against all Imperial City Weapon Shops. This energy was a form of atomic power, old in nature but new to science. Its discovery heralds another step forward in our understanding of the complex structure of the space-time tensions that make for the existence of Matter. The source of the energy in Imperial City was a building completed about a year ago and located on Capital Avenue. Its effect on the Greenway Shop differed from its effect on Shops further away. Theoretically, it should have destroyed any material structure instantly but, though the Isher rulers have never known it, Weapon Shops are not made of matter in the accepted sense. And so there was an intricate interplay of gigantic forces that took place predominantly in time itself. And so a man came seven thousand years out of the past."

He described briefly, using pure mathematical terms, the see-saw action of the man and the building, once they were launched into the abyss of time. He went on, "There are still people who cannot understand how there can be a time swing, when it is a macrocosmic fact that the sun and its planets move steadily through space-time at twelve-plus miles a second, in addition to which the planets follow an orbital course around the sun at varying speeds. By this logic it should follow that, if you go into the past or future, you will find yourself at some remote point in space, far from Earth. It is hard for people who think this to realize that space is a fiction, a by-product of the basic time-energy, and that a matter tension like a planet does not influence phenomena in the time stream, but is itself subject to the time energy laws.

"The reason for the balancing for two hours and forty minutes after every swing is obscure, but it has been suggested that nature unrelentingly seeks stability. The building, when it swings into the past, occupies the same 'space' as it did in normal time but there are no repercussions—for the reason that similarity is a function of time itself, not of its tension-product. McAllister started at seven thousand years, the building at two seconds. That is approximate.

"Today the man is several quadrillions of years away and the building swings at a distance of somewhat less than three months. The fulcrum, of course, moves forward in our time, so that we have the following situation—the building no longer swings back in time as far as June third, where the seesaw originally started. Please bear these facts in mind while I turn briefly to another division of this seemingly complicated but basically simple business."

Hedrock paused. There were quick minds in this room. It interested him to see that every face was still expectant. Now that he himself knew the truth it seemed queer that they had not yet grasped the reality. He continued: "Gentlemen, the coordination department discovered some months ago that there existed in the village of Glay a callidetic giant. With so much internal pressure pushing him we had no difficulty maneuvering him into coming to Imperial City. At first, our belief that he would influence events markedly was nullified by his ignorance of Isher realities. I won't go into the details but he was shipped to Mars as a common laborer. He was able to return almost immediately."

He went on to explain how Lucy Rall had been married to one Cayle Clark a few hours before the arrival of the ship that brought Cayle Clark back to Earth, how the two Clarks secured five hundred thousand credits, then visited Colonel Medlon, one of them disguised. The visit was a fortunate one for Medlon. He had just been asked by the empress to produce Clark, or else. A captaincy was conferred on Clark, with the usual hypnotic machine training for officers. The following day he reported to the empress.

"For a reason which she considers to have been impulse, but which is traceable to his callidity, she attached him to her personal staff and he is there now. Wherever his influence extends, he has followed a very interesting pattern of ruthlessly eliminating the more obvious corruption, and this has roused the interest of the ambitious Innelda. Even if nothing else worked in his favor, he would appear to be a young man destined to go far in the Imperial service."

Then Hedrock smiled. "Actually, the Cayle Clark to watch is not the one in the open but the one who remained elusively in the city. It is that Clark who has been making history since last August seventh. In the time since then he has achieved the following successes—and gentlemen, I warn you, you've never heard anything like this before."

In a few sentences, he described what had happened. When he had finished, the table buzzed with excited discussion. At last a man said, "But why marry Lucy Rall?"

"Partly love, partly—" Hedrock hesitated. He had asked Lucy

a pointed question and her answer made his reply possible now. "I would say he grew immensely cautious, and began to think of the future. Basic urges came to the fore. Suppose something happened to a man who in a few weeks had accomplished the miracle that he had. Gentlemen, he wanted an heir and Lucy was the only honest girl he knew. It may be a permanent arrangement. I cannot say. Clark, in spite of his rebellion against his parents, is essentially a well brought up young man. In any event, Lucy will not suffer. She will have the interesting experience of having a child. And, as a wife, she has community property rights."

Peter Cadron climbed to his feet. "Gentlemen," he said, "I move a vote of thanks to Robert Hedrock for the service he has rendered the Weapon Shops."

The applause was prolonged.

"I move further," said Peter Cadron, "that he be given the rank of unrestricted member."

Once more there were no dissenters. Hedrock bowed his appreciation. The reward was more than an honor. As an unrestricted member he would be subject only to the *Pp* machine examinations. His movements and actions would never be scrutinized and he could use every facility of the Shops as if they were his own property. He had been doing that anyway but in future there would be no suspicion. It was a mighty gift.

"Thank you, gentlemen," he said, when the clapping ended.

"And now," said Peter Cadron, "I respectfully request Mr. Hedrock to leave the council room while we discuss our remaining problem, the seesaw."

Hedrock went out gloomily. He had momentarily forgotten that the greatest danger remained.

TWENTY-EIGHT

It was November twenty-sixth, one day before the Shops intended to inform the empress that her war was lost. She had no premonition. She had come down to the building to see and, perhaps—perhaps to do as Captain Clark had suggested. She still felt repelled, though without fear. The feeling that she had was that the empress of Isher must not involve her own person in harebrained adventures. Yet the thought had grown, and here she was. At the very least she would watch and wait while Captain Clark and the scientists made the trip. She climbed briskly out of her carplane and looked around her.

In the near distance a concealing haze rose up lazily into the sky, an artificial fog that, for months now, had cut off this city district from the view of the curious. She walked slowly forward, her distinctive Isher face turning this way and that as she examined the scene. She beckoned Captain Clark. "When is the building due?"

The smiling young man saluted briskly. "In seven minutes, Your Majesty."

"Have you all the necessary equipment?"

She listened carefully to his recapitulation. Seven groups of scientists would enter the building, each with his own instrument. It was a pleasure to realize that Captain Clark had personally checked over the lists of machines in each group. "Captain," she glowed, "you're a treasure."

Cayle did not reply. Her praise meant nothing. This girl, who almost literally owned the world, surely did not expect intelligent people to be absolutely faithful to her in exchange for a few compliments and army pay. He had no sense of anticipatory guilt and in fact did not regard what he intended to do as being in any way damaging to her. In Isher you did what was necessary and for him there was no turning back. The pattern of his action was already set.

The woman was looking over the scene again. The hole in the ground where the building had been was to her right. To her left was the Greenway Weapon Shop with its park. It was the first time she had seen one in which the glitter signs were not working. That made her feel better. The Shop seemed strangely isolated there in the shadows of its trees. She clenched her hands and thought: *If all the Weapon Shops in the solar system were suddenly eliminated the few thousand parklike lots where they had been could so easily be converted into almost anything that—in one generation*, she told herself with a dark certainty—*they'd be forgotten. The new children would grow up wondering what mythological nonsense their elders were talking.*

"By all the gods of space," she said aloud, passionately, "it's going to happen."

Her words were like a cue. The air shimmered strangely. And where there had been an enormous symmetrical hole abruptly towered a building.

"Right on the minute," said Captain Cayle Clark beside her, with satisfaction.

Innelda stared at the structure, chilled. She had watched this process once on a telestat screen. It was different, being on the scene. For one thing the size showed up better. For a quarter of a mile it reared up into the heavens, solid in its alloyed steel-and-plastic construction, as wide and long as it was high. It had to be large, of course. The engineers had stipulated oversized vacuums between the various energy rooms. The actual living space inside was tiny. It took about an hour to inspect all the levels.

"Well," said Innelda in a tone of relief, "the place doesn't seem to have been damaged in any way by its experiences. What about the rats?"

The rats had been placed in the building during an earlier appearance. So far, they had showed no sign of being affected. It was wise, though, to verify that they were still unharmed. She waited now in an upper room, glancing intermittently at her watch, as the minutes fled by.

It was annoying to realize that she was nervous. But, standing there in the virtual silence of an almost empty building she felt that she was being foolish in that she was even considering going along. She glanced at the men who had volunteered to accompany her if she went. Their silence was not normal and they did not look at her but stood moodily gazing through the transparent wall. There was a sound of footsteps. Captain Clark came striding into view. He was smiling and in his cupped hands he held a white rat. "Your Majesty," he said, "just look at him. Bright as a button."

He was so cheerful that when he held the little animal out to her she took it and stared down at it thoughtfully. On abrupt impulse, she drew it up and pressed its warm body against her cheek.

"What would we do," she murmured, "without lovely little rats like you?" She glanced at Captain Clark. "Well, sir," she said, "what is the scientific opinion?"

"Every rat," Clark said, "is organically, emotionally and psychologically sound. All the tests that show rats for what they are were favorable."

Innelda nodded. It fitted. At the beginning, on the day the first attack was launched, before the men inside the building knew what was happening, the structure had disappeared, causing an immense confusion inside, of which she had never received a coherent account. The moment, on that occasion, the building reappeared, all personnel was withdrawn and no one had been permitted to take the "trip" since then. But physical examinations of the men proved them unharmed.

Still Innelda hesitated. It would look bad now if she failed to go along, but there were so many factors to be considered. If anything happened to her the Isher government might fall. She had no direct heir. The succession would fall to Prince del Curtin, who was popular but known by many people to be out of her favor. The whole situation was ridiculous. She felt hedged in, but there was no use denying the reality.

"Captain," she said firmly, "you have volunteered to take this—journey—whether I go or not. I have definitely decided not to go. I wish you luck and wish, too, that I could go with you. But I'm afraid that I must not. As empress I do not feel free for light-hearted adventures." She held out her hand. "Go with my blessing."

Less than an hour later, she watched as the building flicked into nothingness. She waited. Food was brought. She ate it in her carplane, read several state papers she had brought along and then, as darkness fell over the capital city of her empire, saw by her watch that once more the building was due back.

It flashed into view and presently men began to troop out. One of the scientists came over. "Your Majesty," he said, "the journey was accomplished without incident except for one thing. Captain Clark, as you know, intended to leave the building for exploration purposes. He did leave it. We received one message from him, spoken into his wrist 'stat to the effect that the date was August seventh, four thousand seven hundred and eighty-four Isher. That was the last we heard. Something must have happened to him. He failed to come back in time to make the return journey with us."

"But—" said Innelda. She stopped blankly. Then, "But that means, from August seventh to November twenty-sixth there were two Cayle Clarks in existence, the normal and the one who went back in time."

She paused, uncertain. *The old time paradox,* she thought to herself. *Can man go back in time and shake hands with himself?* Aloud, she said wonderingly, "But whatever became of the second one?"

TWENTY-NINE

August 7—it was a bright day with a soft blue sky; and a faint breeze blew into Clark's face as he walked rapidly away from the building that had brought him to a period of his own past life. No one bothered him. He wore a captain's uniform with the special red insignia that indicated an Imperial staff member. Sentries posted on streets adjoining the building snapped to attention as he walked by.

In five minutes he was in a public carplane heading purposefully into the heart of the city. He had more than two and a half months to pass before he would be back where he had started, but for what he had in mind the time would be short indeed.

It was late afternoon, but he was able to rent a four-room office before the close of business that day. An employment agency promised to have several stenographers and bookkeepers report by 9 A.M. the following morning. And though the place was furnished as an office only, he was able to obtain a cot before dark from a twenty-four-hour rental service. That night, he planned into the early morning hours, and then slept restlessly on the cot. He rose shortly after dawn and, carrying with him the sheet of paper on which he had his calculations, took an elevator down to the exchange room of one of the largest stockbrokerage firms in the city. In his pockets were some five hundred thousand credits which had been given to him by the "second" Cayle Clark. The money was mostly in bills of large denomination, and there were as many of them as one man could burden himself with, and still be able to move.

Before that day had run its course, he had made thirty-seven hundred thousand credits. And the bookkeepers upstairs were busy making records of his stock transactions; the stenographers were beginning to write letters; and a chartered accountant, hastily hired as office manager, hired more help and took on more office space on adjoining floors.

Tired but jubilant, Cayle spent the evening preparing for the next day. He had had one experience of what a man could do who had brought with him from the future complete stock market reports for a period of two and a half months. He slept that night with a sense of exhilaration. He could scarcely wait for the next day. And the next. And the next and the next.

During that month of August, he won ninety billion credits. In that series of deals, he took over one of the chain banks, four billion-credit industrial establishments and obtained partial control of thirty-four other companies.

During the month of September he made three hundred and thirty billion credits, and absorbed the colossal First Imperial Bank, three interplanetary mining corporations and part ownership of two hundred and ninety companies. By the end of September, he was established in a hundred-story skyscraper in the heart of the financial district, and he gave Employment Incorporated the job of setting him up as a big business. On September thirtieth, over seven thousand employees were working in the building.

In October he diverted his cash resources to investment in available hotel and residential properties, a total of three and one-eighth trillion credits worth. In October also, he married Lucy Rall, answered the call from himself—just back from Mars—and made an appointment to meet the "other" Clark. The two young men, equally grim and determined, visited the Penny Palace, and secured from Harj Martin the money that had been stolen by the gambling house owner. Actually, the money mattered little at this stage, but there was an important principle involved. Cayle Clark was out to conquer the impersonal world of Isher. And no one who had ever put anything over on him was going to have that satisfaction for long. After Harj Martin, it was a natural step to seek out Colonel Medlon and so prepare the groundwork for the journey into the past.

Two Cayle Clarks—really only one, but from different times—and that was the story that Robert Hedrock gave to the Weapon Shop Council. That was the phenomenal incident that forced the empress to end her war lest other officers or men wreck the financial stability of the solar system by trying to repeat the success of Cayle Clark.

THIRTY

Outside, it was night. Fara walked along the quiet streets of Glay, and for the first time it struck him that the Weapon Shop Information Center must be halfway around the world, for there it had been day.

The picture vanished as if it had never existed as he grew aware again of the village of Glay asleep all around him. Silent, peaceful—yet ugly, he thought, ugly with the ugliness of evil enthroned. He thought: The right to buy weapons—and his heart swelled into his throat; the tears came into his eyes. He wiped his vision clear with the back of his hand, thought of Creel's long dead father, and strode on, without shame. Tears were good for an angry man.

The hard, metal padlock yielded before the tiny, blazing power of the revolver. One flick of fire, the metal dissolved, and he was inside. It was dark, too dark to see, but Fara did not turn on the lights immediately. He fumbled across to the window control, turned the windows to darkness vibration, and then clicked on the lights. He gulped with awful relief as he saw that the machines, his precious tools that he had watched the bailiff carry away, were here again, ready for use.

Shaky from the pressure of his emotion, Fara called Creel on the telestat. It took a little while for her to appear; and she was in her dressing gown. When she saw who it was she turned very pale.

"Fara, oh, Fara, I thought—"

He cut her off grimly: "Creel, I've been to the Weapon Shop. I want you to do this: go straight to your mother. I'm here at my shop. I'm going to stay here day and night until it's settled that I *stay* . . . I shall go home later for some food and clothing, but I want you to be gone by then. Is that clear?"

Color was coming back into her lean, handsome face. She said: "Don't you bother coming home, Fara. I'll do everything necessary. I'll pack all that's needed into the carplane, including a folding bed. We'll sleep in the back room at the shop."

Morning came palely but it was ten o'clock before a shadow darkened the open door; and Constable Jor came in. He looked shamefaced.

"I've got an order here for your arrest," he said.

"Tell those who sent you," Fara replied deliberately, "that I resisted arrest—with a gun." The deed followed the words with such rapidity that Jor blinked. He stood like that for a moment, a big, sleepy-looking man, staring at that gleaming, magical revolver; then:

"I have a summons here ordering you to appear at the great court of Ferd this afternoon. Will you accept it?"

"Certainly."

"Then you will be there?"

"I'll send my lawyer," said Fara. "Just drop the summons on the floor there. Tell them I took it."

The Weapon Shop man had said: "Do not ridicule by word any legal measure of the Imperial authorities. Simply disobey them."

Jor went out, seemingly relieved. It took an hour before Mayor Mel Dale came pompously through the door. "See here, Fara Clark," he bellowed. "You can't get away with this. This is defiance of the law."

Fara was silent as His Honor waddled farther into the building. It was puzzling, almost amazing that Mayor Dale would risk his plump, treasured body. Puzzlement ended as the mayor said in a low voice:

"Good work, Fara; I knew you had it in you. There's dozens of us in Glay behind you, so stick it out. I had to yell at you just now because there's a crowd outside. Yell back at me, will you? Let's have a real name calling. But first, a word of warning: the manager of the Automatic Atomic Motor Repair shop is on his way here with his bodyguards, two of them."

Shakily, Fara watched the mayor go out. The crisis was at hand. He braced himself, thought: Let them come, let them—

It was easier than he had expected, for the men who entered

the shop turned pale when they saw the holstered revolver. There was a violence of blustering nevertheless, that narrowed down finally to:

"Look here," the man said, "we've got your note for twelve thousand one hundred credits. You're not going to deny you owe that money."

"I'll buy it back," said Fara stonily, "for exactly one thousand credits, the amount actually paid to my son."

The strong-jawed young man looked at him for a long time. "We'll take it," he said finally, curtly.

Fara said: "I've got the agreement here."

His first customer was old man Miser Lan Harris. Fara stared at the long-faced oldster with a vast surmise, and his first, amazed comprehension came of how the Weapon Shop must have settled on Harris's lot by arrangement. It was an hour after Harris had gone that Creel's mother stamped into the shop. She closed the door.

"Well," she said. "You did it, eh? Good work. I'm sorry if I seemed rough with you when you came to my place, but we Weapon Shop supporters can't afford to take risks for those who are not on our side.

"But never mind that. I've come to take Creel home. The important thing is to return everything to normal as quickly as possible."

It was over. Incredibly, it was over. Twice, as he walked home that night, Fara stopped in midstride, and wondered if it had not all been a dream. The air was like wine. The little world of Glay spread before him, green and gracious, a peaceful paradise where time had stood still.

THIRTY-ONE

The empress said, "Mr. de Lany."

Hedrock bowed. He had disguised himself slightly, and taken one of his long discarded names so that she would not recognize him at some future date.

"You have sought an interview?" said the empress of Isher.

"As you see."

She toyed with his card. She had on a snow-white gown that accentuated the tan of her face and neck. The room in which she received him had been made up to resemble a small south sea island. Palms and green growth surrounded them. And on every side was water, lapping on a beach as real as nature. A cool wind blew from that restless sea onto Hedrock's back and into her face. The woman gazed bitterly at Hedrock. She saw a man of earnest mien and commanding appearance. But it was his eyes that startled her. They were strong and kind and infinitely brave. She hadn't expected such special qualities. The visitor took on sudden importance. She looked down at the card again.

"Walter de Lany," she said thoughtfully. She seemed to listen to the name as she spoke it, as if she expected it to acquire meaning. Finally she shook her head, wonderingly. "How did you get in here? I found this appointment on my list and took it for granted that the chamberlain must have arranged it because it involved necessary business."

Hedrock said nothing. Like so many Imperials, the chamberlain lacked the defensive mind trainings. And, though the empress herself had them, she did not know that the Weapon Shops had developed energy methods for forcing instantaneous favorable response from the unprotected. The woman spoke again.

"Very strange," she said.

Hedrock said, "Reassure yourself, Madam. I have come to solicit your mercy on behalf of an unfortunate, guiltless man."

That caught her. Once more her eyes met his, flinched from the strength that was there, then steadied.

Hedrock said quietly, "Your Majesty, you are in a position to do an act of unparalleled kindness to a man who is nearly five million million years from here, swinging from past to future as your building forces him ever further away."

The words had to be spoken. He expected her to realize instantly that only her intimates and her enemies would know certain details about the vanishing building. The way the color drained from her cheeks showed that she was realizing.

"You're a Weapon Shop man?" she whispered. She was on her feet. "Get out of here," she breathed. "Out!"

Hedrock stood up. "Your Majesty," he said, "control yourself. You are in no danger."

He intended his words to be like a dash of cold water. The suggestion that she was afraid brought splotches of color into her face. She stood like that for a moment and then, with a quick movement, reached into the bosom of her dress and drew out a gleaming white energy weapon. "If you do not leave instantly," she said, "I shall fire."

Hedrock held his arms away from his body like a man being searched. "An ordinary gun," he said in amazement, "against a man who carries a Weapon Shop defensive? Madam," he said, "if you will listen to me for a moment—"

"I do not," said the empress, "deal with Weapon Shop people."

That was merely irritating. "Your Majesty," said Hedrock in a level voice, "I am surprised that you make such immature statements. You have not only been dealing with the Shops the last few days, you have yielded to them. You have been compelled to end the war and to destroy your time-energy machines. You have agreed not to prosecute the officer-deserters but only to discharge them. And you have granted immunity to Cayle Clark."

He saw in her face that he had not touched her. She was staring at him, frowning. "There must be a reason," she said, "that you dare to talk to me like this."

Her own words seemed to galvanize her. She turned back to

her chair and stood with finger poised over the ornamented arm. "If I should press this alarm," she said, "it would bring guards."

Hedrock sighed. He had hoped she would not force him to reveal his power. "Why not, then," he suggested, "press it?" It was time, he thought, that she found out her true situation.

The woman said, "You think I won't?" Firmly, her extended finger pressed downward.

There was silence except for the lapping of the waves and the soft sound of the lifelike breeze. After at least two minutes, Innelda, ignoring Hedrock as if he did not exist, walked twenty feet to a tree, and touched one of the branches. It must have been another alarm, because she waited—not so long this time—and then walked hurriedly over to the thick brush that concealed the elevator shaft. She activated its mechanism and, when there was no response, came slowly back to where Hedrock waited, and sat down in her chair. She was pale but composed. Her eyes did not look at him but her voice was calm and without fear. "Do you intend to murder me?"

Hedrock shook his head, but said nothing. More strongly now, he regretted that he had had to reveal to her how helpless she could be, particularly regretted it because she would undoubtedly start modernizing the defenses of the palace in the mistaken belief that she was protecting herself against superior Weapon Shop science. He had come here this afternoon prepared for any emergency, physical or mental. He could not force her to do what he wanted but his fingers blazed with offensive and defensive rings. He had on his "business" suit and even Weapon Shop scientists would have been amazed at the variety of his armor. In his vicinity no alarm energies would come to life and no guns would operate. It was the day of the greatest decision in the history of the solar system, and he had come mightily girded.

The woman's eyes were staring at him with somber intensity. "What do you want?" she said. "What about this man you mentioned?"

Hedrock told her about McAllister.

"Are you mad?" she whispered when he had finished. "But why so far? The building is only—three months."

"The ruling factor seems to be mass."

"Oh!" Silence, then, "But what do you want me to do?"

Hedrock said, "Your Majesty, this man commands our pity and

our mercy. He is floating in a void whose like no human eyes will ever see again. He has looked upon our Earth and our sun in their infancy and in their old, old age. Nothing can help him now. We must give him the surcease of death."

In her mind Innelda saw the night he pictured. But she was more intent now, seeing this event in its larger environment. "What," she said, "about this machine you have?"

"It is a duplicate of the map machine of the Weapon Shops." He didn't explain that he had built it in one of his secret laboratories. "It lacks only the map itself, which was too intricate to fashion swiftly."

"I see." Her words were automatic, not a real response. She studied his face. She said slowly, "Where do you fit into all this?"

It was a question that Hedrock was not prepared to answer. He had come to the empress of Isher because she had suffered a defeat and, her position being what it was, it was important that she should not remain too resentful. An immortal man, who was once more interfering in the affairs of mortals, had to think of things like that. "Madam," he said, "there is no time to waste. The building is due here again in one hour."

The woman said, "But why cannot we leave this decision to the Weapon Shop Council?"

"Because they might make the wrong decision."

"What," persisted Innelda, "is the right decision?"

Sitting there, Hedrock told her.

Cayle Clark set the controls so that the carplane would make a wide circle around the house.

"Oh, my goodness!" said Lucy Rall Clark, "Why it's one of these up-in-the-air places—"

She stopped and stared with wide, wondering eyes at the grounds below, at the hanging gardens, at the house floating in the air. "Oh, Cayle," she said, "are you sure we can afford it?"

Cayle Clark smiled. "Darling, I've explained to you a dozen times. I'm not going to do it again."

She protested, "That isn't what I mean. Are you sure the empress will let you get away with it?"

Cayle Clark gazed at his wife with a faint, grim smile. "Mr. Hedrock," he said slowly, "gave me a Weapon Shop gun. And besides, I did a great deal for Her Majesty which—at least, so she told me on the telestat today—she appreciates. She doesn't dissemble very much, so I have agreed to continue to work for her in much the same way."

"Oh!" said Lucy.

"Now, don't get yourself upset," said Cayle. "Remember, you yourself told me that the Weapon Shops believed in one government. The more that government is purified the better off the world will be. And believe me—" his face hardened—"I've had just enough experience to make me want to purify it."

He landed the carplane on the roof of the five-story residence. He led Lucy into the interior, down into the world of bright, gracious rooms where she and he would live forever.

At least, at twenty-two or -three, it seemed as if it would be forever.

EPILOGUE

McAllister had forgotten about the personal decision he intended to make. It was so hard to think in this darkness. He opened his tired eyes, and saw that he was poised moveless in black space. There was no Earth under him. He was in a time where the planets did not yet exist. The darkness seemed to be waiting for some colossal event.

Waiting for him.

He had a sudden flash of understanding of what was going to happen. Wonder came then, and a realization of what his decision must be: resignation to death.

It was a strangely easy decision to make. He was so weary. Bitter-sweet remembrance came of the days in far-gone time and space, when he had lain half-dead on a battlefield of the middle twentieth century, resigned to personal oblivion. Then he had thought that he must die so that others might live. The feeling now was the same, but stronger and on a much higher level.

How it would be worked he had no idea. But the seesaw would end in the very remote past, with the release of the stupendous temporal energy he had been accumulating with each of those monstrous swings.

He would not witness but he would aid in the formation of the planets.

THE WEAPON MAKERS

ONE

Hedrock almost forgot the spy ray. It continued to glow, the picture on the screen showing the Imperial conference room as clearly as ever. There were still men bowing low over the hand of the cold-faced young woman who sat on the throne chair, and the sound of their voices came distinctly. Everything was as it should be.

For Hedrock, however, all interest in that palatial room, that courtly scene, had faded. The icy words of the young woman spun around and around in his mind, though minutes had now passed since she had spoken them.

"—Under the circumstances," she had said, "we cannot afford to take further risks with this Weapon Shop turncoat. What has happened is too important. Accordingly, General Grall, you will, as a purely precautionary measure, arrest Captain Hedrock an hour after lunch and hang him. The time sequence is important, as he will, as usual, sit at my table during lunch, and also because I wish to be present at the execution."

"Very well, Your Majesty—"

Hedrock paced back and forth in front of his viewing machine. Finally, he stared again at the screen, which, in its present materialized form, occupied an entire corner of the apartment. He saw, with a somber awareness, that the young woman was still in the conference room, alone now. She sat, a faint smile on her long face. The smile faded as she touched an instrument on her chair and began to dictate in a clear, bell-like voice.

For a moment, Hedrock allowed the meaning of the routine palace matters she was discussing to penetrate his mind; then he withdrew his attention. There was a purpose in his mind, a hardening determination not to accept the failure that was here. Very carefully, he began to adjust his machine. The scene showing the young empress faded. The viewing plate flickered with formless light, finally caught the face of a man, and steadied. Hedrock said, "Calling the High Council of the Weapon Makers."

"It will take a minute," said the man on the screen, gravely, "to bring the various councilors to their locals."

Hedrock nodded stiffly. He was suddenly nervous. His voice had been steady enough, but he had the feeling that it would deteriorate into a quaver. He stood very still, consciously relaxing the tension. When he looked again at the screen, a dozen faces had replaced the one; enough members for a quorum. He began at once an account of the sentence of death that had been pronounced on him. He finished, finally: "There is no doubt that something important is happening. Time and again during the last two weeks, when an Imperial conference has been called, I have found myself headed off into tedious conversations with superior officers, prevented from returning to my rooms. To my mind, however, the significant factor of the hanging order is the time element involved. Note that I am not to be arrested until an hour after lunch, that is, about three hours from now. And then, too, I was allowed to return to my apartment in time to hear the sentence pronounced. If they know the Weapon Shops, they must realize that, given three hours warning, I have ample time to escape."

"Are you suggesting," said Councilor Peter Cadron sharply, "that you are going to remain?"

The cold, stiff feeling came back to Hedrock. When he spoke again, his voice shook the faintest bit though the words themselves were precise and, in their essence, confident: "You will remember, Mr. Cadron, that we have analyzed the empress's character. The abnormal sociotechnical pressures of the age have made her as restless and as adventure-minded as are her nineteen billion subjects. She wants change, excitement, new experiences. But above everything else she is the Imperial power, representative of the conservative, antichange forces. The result is a constant tug of mind, a dangerous state of unbalance, which makes her the most difficult enemy the Weapon Shops have had in many centuries."

"The hanging, no doubt," said another man coldly, "will supply a fillip to her jaded nerves. For the few moments that you jerk and bounce in the noose, her life will seem less drab."

"What I had in mind," said Hedrock steadily, "was that one of our No-men might resolve the various factors and advise on the practicability of my remaining."

"We will consult Edward Gonish," said Peter Cadron. "Now please have patience while we discuss this matter privately."

They withdrew, but not visually, for their faces remained on the viewer, and though Hedrock could see their lips move, no voice came through. The conversation went on for a very long time, and there was a seemingly endless period when something was being explained to somebody not on the screen. The time grew so long that Hedrock stood finally with teeth clamped tight, and clenched hands. He sighed with relief as the silence ended, and Peter Cadron said:

"We must regretfully report that the No-man, Edward Gonish, considers that there are not sufficient known factors for him to offer an intuition. This leaves us with only logic, and so we wish to ask one question: At what time will your present chances of escaping from the palace begin to deteriorate sharply? Can you possibly stay for lunch?"

Hedrock held himself steady, letting the shock of the report of the No-man's verdict drain out of him. He hadn't realized how much he was depending on that superbly trained intuitive genius to decide on *his* life or death. In an instant, the situation had become uncertain and dangerous beyond his previous conception. He said at last, "No, if I stay to lunch I'm committed. The empress likes to play cat and mouse, and she will definitely inform me of the sentence during the meal. I have a plan, dependent on her emotional reactions and based on the fact that she will consider it necessary to justify herself."

He paused, frowning at the screen. "What were the conclusions of your discussion? I need every possible assistance."

It was Councilor Kendlon, a thick-faced man who had hitherto not spoken, who said, "As you know, Hedrock, you are in the palace for two purposes, one being to protect the Weapon Shops from a surprise attack during what we have all agreed is a dangerous time for our civilization. Your other purpose is, of course, your own pet scheme of establishing a liaison between the Weapon Shops and the Imperial government. You are a spy, therefore, only in a minor sense. Any lesser information you may gain is yours alone. We do not want it. But think back in your mind: Have you heard anything—*anything*—that might provide a foundation for your theory that something tremendous is being planned?"

Hedrock shook his head slowly. Quite suddenly, he felt no emotion. He had a sense of being physically detached. He spoke finally as out of a remote, cold region, precisely, evenly, conclusively, "I can see, sirs, that you have come to no decision, yet you cannot deny that you are reluctant to have my connection here broken. And there is no doubt of your anxiety to learn what the empress is concealing. Finally, there is, as you say, my pet scheme. Accordingly, I have decided to remain."

They were not so quick as that to agree. The strange, restless character of the empress made it possible that the slightest wrong word on his part would be fatal. Details—details—they discussed them with a painstaking thoroughness. There was the fact that he was the first apparent traitor to the Weapon Shops in history, one who nevertheless refused to give any information to the curious ruler. His striking appearance, mental brilliance and strong personality had already fascinated her, and should continue to do so. Therefore, except for the fact that she was engaged in something secret and important, the threat of hanging was a test, product of suspicion. But be careful. If necessary, give her secret Weapon Shop information of a general nature, to titillate her appetite for more and—

At that point the door buzzer broke off the conversation. With a start, Hedrock flicked off the controls, and shut off the power. Then, acutely conscious that he had allowed himself to become jumpy, he deliberately removed the plain gold pin from his tie, and bent down over the table. The ring lay there, a small, bright design, its ornamental head an exact duplicate of the spy ray machine, the image of which was built up into solid form by the atomic forces manufactured by the perfect power plant inside the ring. It would be quicker to release the tiny, automatic lever that was attached to the ring for that very purpose, but his own nervous condition was more important.

It was as delicate a task as threading a needle. Three times his hand trembled the slightest bit and missed the almost invisible depression that had to be contacted. The fourth time he got it. The spy ray machine winked out like a smashed light, except that there was no debris, nothing but empty air. Where it had stood on the corner table was only the blanket he had used to protect the table top from scratches. Hedrock whisked the blanket back to the bedroom, and then stood for a moment with the ring in his palm, undecided. He put it finally in a metal box with three other rings, and set the controls of the box to dissolve the rings if there were any tampering. Only the ring gun remained encircled on his finger when at last he walked coolly to answer the insistent buzzer.

Hedrock recognized the tall man who stood in the corridor as one of the empress's orderlies. The fellow nodded recognition, and said, "Captain, Her Majesty asks me to inform you that lunch is being served, and will you please come at once."

For a moment, Hedrock had the distinct impression that he was the object of a practical joke, and that Imperial Innelda was already playing her little thrill game. It couldn't be lunch time so soon. He glanced at his wrist watch. The little dial showed twelve thirty-five. An hour had passed since he had heard the sentence of death from the empress's firm, finely shaped mouth.

Actually, the question of whether or not he remained till lunch had not been his to decide. The event had rushed upon him even as he was telling the council that it was an hour away. The reality of his position became clear as he walked along past scores of soldiers who stood in every corridor on his way to the royal dining hall; and that reality was that he was staying. It was so final that Hedrock stopped on the threshold of the great room, stood for a moment, smiling sardonically, and was himself.

Quietly, still smiling faintly, he made his way among the tables of noisy courtiers, and sank into his place five chairs down from the empress at the head table.

TWO

The cocktail and soup courses were already past. Hedrock sat, more pensive now that he was not physically on the move, waiting for whatever was next. He studied the men around the table, the young, strong, arrogant, intelligent thirty-year-olds who made up the personal following of Her Imperial Majesty.

He felt a pang of regret at the thought that it must now end. He had enjoyed his six months among this brilliant gathering. It had been exciting again to watch young people tasting the fruits of stupendous power, an untamed enjoyment of joy that was reminiscent of his own distant past. Hedrock smiled wryly. There was a quality about his immortality that he had not allowed for, a developing disregard of risks until the crisis was upon him, a pre-danger casualness about the danger. He had known, of course, that he would sooner or later involve himself beyond even his secret powers. Now as in the past, only his overall purpose, as distinct from the purposes that people thought he had, was important.

The empress's voice rose for the first time above the clamor of conversation and cut off his reverie. "You seem very thoughtful, Captain Hedrock."

Hedrock turned his head slowly to face her. He had been wanting to give her more than the cursory glance he had allowed himself so far. But he had been aware of her green eyes watching him from the moment he had seated himself. Hers was a striking, almost a noble countenance. She had the high-cheeked, firm-chinned facial structure of the famous Isher family; and there was no doubt at all that here was only the latest, not the last member of a star human line. Willful passions and power unlimited had twisted her handsome face. But already it was apparent that the erratic, brilliant Innelda, like all the remarkable men and women who were her ancestors, would carry on through corruption and intrigue, in spite of character defects, and that the extraordinary Isher family would survive another generation.

The important thing now, Hedrock thought with a sharpening alertness, was to bring her out into the open under the most advantageous—for him—circumstances. He said, "I was thinking, Innelda, of your grandmother seven times removed, the lovely Ganeel, the golden-haired empress. Except for your brown hair, you're very like her as she was in her younger days."

The green eyes looked puzzled. The empress pursed her lips, and then parted them as if to say something. Before she could speak, Hedrock went on, "The Weapon Shops have an entire pictorial of her life. What I was thinking of was the rather sad idea that some day you, too, would be but a pictorial record in some dusty Information Center."

It struck deep. He had known that this young woman could not bear the thought of old age or death in connection with herself. Anger brought a gleam to her eyes, and produced as it always had in the past what she was really thinking.

"You at least," she snapped in a brittle, yet ringing voice, "will not live to see any pictorial of my life. You may be interested to know, my dear captain, that your spy work here has been found out, and you are to be hanged this afternoon."

The words shocked him. It was one thing to theorize in advance that here was nothing but a cunning, murderous test, a determined attempt to draw him out—and quite another to sit here beside this woman, who could be so cruel and merciless and yet whose every whim was law, and hear her pronounce his death sentence. Against such a flesh and blood tyrant, all logic was weak, all theory unreal and fantastic.

Abruptly, it was difficult to understand the reasoning that had made him place himself in such a predicament. He could so easily have waited another generation, or two, or more, for a woman to turn up again in the Isher line. It was true, of course, that this was the logical point, both biologically and historically. He ended the thought and fought off the black mood. He forced himself, then, to relax and to smile. After all, he had drawn that answer out of her, clearly before she really wanted to announce the sentence. In a grisly sort of way, it was a psychological victory. A few more victories like that, however, and he'd be all set for a nervous breakdown.

There was still conversation going on in the great dining room, but not at the royal table. That brought Hedrock back to full awareness of his environment. Some of the young men were sitting staring at the empress. Others looked at Hedrock, then at the empress, then at Hedrock again. All were transparently puzzled. They seemed uncertain as to whether it was a bad joke or one of the damnable real-life dramas that the empress precipitated from time to time, seemingly for the sole purpose of ruining everybody's digestion. The important thing, Hedrock thought tightly, was that the situation now had the full attention of the men whom he expected to save his life.

It was the empress who broke the silence. She said softly, tauntingly, "A penny for your *latest* thoughts, Captain."

She couldn't have put it better. Hedrock suppressed a savage smile, and said, "My earlier statement still holds. You're very like the lovely, temperamental, explosive Ganeel. The main difference is that she never slept with a live snake when she was sixteen."

"What's this?" said a courtier. "Innelda sleeping with snakes? Is this intended symbolically or literally? Why look, she's blushing."

It was so. Hedrock's cool gaze studied the empress's scarlet-cheeked confusion with amazed curiosity. He had not expected to obtain so violent a response. In a moment, of course, there would be a flood of bad temper. It wouldn't disturb most of the bold young men, who had, each in his own way, found that middle path between yes-man and individual that the young woman demanded of all her personal followers.

"Come, come, Hedrock," said the mustachioed Prince del Curtin, "you're not going to keep this splendid tidbit to yourself. I suppose this also is derived from the pictorial files of the Weapon Shops."

Hedrock was silent. His smile of acknowledgment seemed to be directed at the prince-cousin of the empress, but actually he scarcely saw the man. His gaze and attention were concentrated on the only person in the room who mattered. The Empress Isher sat, the flush on her face slowly yielding to anger. She climbed to her feet, a dangerous glint in her eyes, but her voice had in it only a fraction of the fury that he had hoped for. She said grimly: "It was very clever of you, Captain Hedrock, to twist the conversation the way you did. But I assure you it won't do you the slightest good. You're swift response merely confirms that you were aware in advance of my intention. You're a spy, and we're taking no more chances with you."

"Oh, come now, Innelda," said a man. "You're not going to pull a miserable stunt like that."

"You watch out, mister," the woman flared, "or you'll join him on the scaffold."

The men at the table exchanged significant glances. Some of them shook their heads disapprovingly, and then all of them fell to talking among themselves, ignoring the empress.

Hedrock waited. This was what he had been working for, but now that it was here, it seemed inadequate. In the past, ostracism by the men whose companionship she valued had had a great emotional effect on the ruler. Twice since his arrival he had seen it influence her decisively. But not this time. The realization penetrated to Hedrock with finality as he watched the woman sink back into her chair, and sit there, her long, handsome face twisted satirically. Her smile faded. She said gravely: "I'm sorry, gentlemen, that you feel as you do. I regret any outburst which would seem to indicate that my decision against Captain Hedrock was a personal one. But I have been greatly upset by my discovery that he is a spy."

It was impressive. It had a convincing ring to it, and the men's private conversations, which had died while she was speaking, did not resume. Hedrock leaned back in his chair, his sense of defeat stronger with each passing second. Quite clearly, whatever was behind the execution was too big, too important, for mere cleverness to over-balance.

Drastic, dangerous, deadly action was in order.

For a while, then, he was intent on his own thought. The long table with its satin-smooth white linen covering, its golden dishes, its two dozen fine-looking young men, yielded before that intensity, became a background to his ever grimmer purpose. He needed words that would change the whole design of the situation, plus action that would clinch it. He grew aware that Prince del Curtin had been speaking for some moments:

"—You can't just make a statement that a man is a spy, and expect us to believe it. We know you're the biggest and best liar this side of creation when it suits you. If I'd suspected this was coming up, I'd have attended the cabinet meeting this morning. How about a little fact?"

Hedrock felt impatient. The men had already accepted the sentence, though they didn't seem to realize it. The quicker they were cut out of the conversation the better. But careful now. Wait until the empress had committed herself, regardless of how well she did it. She was, he saw, sitting stiffly, her expression grave, unsmiling. She said quietly: "I'm afraid I shall have to ask you all to trust me. A very serious situation has arisen; it was the sole subject of our council meeting today, and I assure you the decision to execute Captain Hedrock was unanimous, and I am personally distressed by the necessity."

Hedrock said, "I really thought better of your intelligence than this, Innelda. Are you planning another of your futile forays against the Weapon Shops, and think that I might find out about it and report it to the Weapon Shop Council?"

Her green eyes blazed at him. Her voice was like chipped steel as she snapped, "I shall say nothing that might give you a clue. I don't know just what kind of a communications system you have with your superiors, but I know that one exists. My physicists have frequently registered on their instruments powerful wavelengths of extremely high range."

"Originating in my room?" asked Hedrock softly.

She stared at him, her lips drawn into an angry frown. She said reluctantly, "You would never have dared come here if you had to be as obvious as that. I will inform you, sir, that I am not interested in continuing this conversation."

"Though you do not realize it," said Hedrock in his steadiest tone, "I have said all that was necessary to prove my innocence when I disclosed to you that I knew that, at the age of sixteen, you slept one night with a live snake."

"Ah!" said the empress. Her body shook with triumph. "Now the confession begins. So you expected to have to put up a defense, and you prepared that little speech."

Hedrock shrugged. "I knew something was being planned for me. My apartment has been searched every day for a week. I've been subjected to the most boring sustained monologues by the prize dunderheads in the army office. Wouldn't I be a simpleton if I hadn't thought of every angle?"

"What I don't understand," chimed in a young man, "is the snake business. Why do you think your knowledge of that proves you not guilty? That's too deep for me."

"Don't be such an ass, Maddern," said Prince del Curtin. "It simply means that the Weapon Shops knew intimate details of Innelda's palace life long before Captain Hedrock ever came. It shows the existence of a spy system more dangerous than anything we ever suspected, and the real charge against Captain Hedrock is that he has been remiss in not telling us that such a system existed."

Hedrock was thinking: Not yet, not yet. Somewhere along here the crisis would come suddenly, and then his action must be swift, perfectly timed, decisive. Aloud, he said coolly, "Why should you worry? Three thousand years have proven that the Weapon Shops have no intention of overthrowing the Imperial government. I know for a fact that the spy ray is used with great discretion, and has never been employed at night except on the occasion that Her Majesty had the snake smuggled in from the palace zoo. Curiosity made the two women scientists in charge of the machine on that occasion continue their watch. The story was, of course, too good to keep in a file. And you may be interested, Your Majesty, to know that two psychological articles were written about it, one by our greatest living No-man, Edward Gonish."

From the corners of his eyes Hedrock saw that the slim, lithe body of the woman was leaning forward, her lips were slightly parted, her eyes wide with an intense interest. Her whole being seemed to move according to his words. "What," she half whispered, "did he say about me?"

With a shock, Hedrock recognized his moment. Now, he thought, *now!*

He was trembling. But he couldn't help his physical condition, nor did he care. A man threatened with death was expected to show agitation, or else he was considered unhuman, cold—and received no sympathy. His voice rose against the pattern of babble from distant tables, a little wildly and passionately. But that, too, was good, for a woman was staring at him with wide eyes, a woman who was half child, half genius, and who hungered with all her intense emotional nature for the strange and the exotic. She sat with shining eyes, as Hedrock said:

"You must be mad, all of you, or you would not constantly underestimate the Weapon Shops and their lineally-developed science. What a petty idea it is that I have come here as a spy, that I am curious about some simple little government secret. I am here for one purpose only, and Her Majesty is perfectly aware of what it is. If she kills me she is deliberately destroying her better, greater self; and if I know anything about the Isher line in the final issue they draw back from suicide."

The empress was straightening, frowning. "The presumption of your purpose," she snapped, "is only equalled by your cleverness."

Hedrock paid no attention to the interruption. He refused to give up the initiative. He rushed on, "It is apparent that you have all forgotten your history, or are blinding yourself to the reality. The Weapon Shops were founded several thousand years ago by a man who decided that the incessant struggle for power of different groups was insane, and that civil and other wars must stop forever. It was a time when the world had just emerged from a war in which more than a billion people had died, and he found thousands of individuals who agreed to follow him to the death. His idea was nothing less than that whatever government was in power should not be overthrown. But that an organization should be set up which would have one principle purpose: to ensure that no government ever again obtained complete power over its people.

"A man who felt himself wronged should be able to go somewhere to buy a defensive gun. What made this possible was the invention of an electronic and atomic system of control which made it possible to build indestructible Weapon Shops, and to manufacture weapons that could only be used for defense. That last ended all possibility of Weapon Shop guns being used by gangsters and criminals, and morally justified placing dangerous instruments in the hands of anyone who needed protection.

"At first people thought that the Shops were a sort of underground anti-government organization that would itself protect them from harm. But gradually they realized that the Shops did not interfere in Isher life. It was up to each individual or group of individuals to save their own lives. The idea was that the individual would learn to stand up for himself, and that in the long run the forces which would normally try to enslave him would be restrained by the knowledge that a man or a group could be pressed only so far. And so a great balance was struck between those who govern and those who are governed.

"It turned out that a further step was necessary, not as a protection against the government, but against rapacious private enterprise. Civilization became so intricate that the average person could not protect himself against the cunning devices of those who competed for his money. Accordingly, a system of Weapon Shop courts was set up, to which people could turn when they felt themselves aggrieved in this fashion."

Out of the corner of his eye, Hedrock saw that the empress was becoming restive. She was not a Weapon Shop admirer, and since his purpose was to impress with the absurdity of her suspicions, and not to change her basic attitude, he came to his point:

"What is not clearly realized by the government forces is that the Weapon Shops are, because of their scientific achievements, more powerful than the government itself. They understand of course that if they should be foolish enough to overthrow the empress they would not necessarily have the support of the population, and that in fact they would upset the stability which their presence has made possible. *Nevertheless, the superiority is a fact.* For that reason alone, the empress's accusation against me is meaningless, and must have some other motivation than the one she has stated."

Hedrock had too sharp a sense of dramatic values to pause there. His main point was made, but the reality was so harsh that he instantly needed a distraction, something on a different level entirely; and which, yet, would appear to be part of the whole. He rushed on: "To give you some idea of the great scientific attainments of the Weapon Shops, I can tell you that they have an instrument which can predict the moment of death of any person. Before I came to the palace six months ago, for my own amusement I secured readings as to the death moments of almost every person at this table and of the members of the Imperial Council."

He had them now. He could see it in the strained faces that looked at him with a feverish fascination. But still he could not afford to lose control of the conversation. With an effort, he forced himself to bow at the white-faced ruler. Then hastily he said. "I am happy to announce, Your Majesty, that you have a long and increasingly honorable life ahead of you. Unfortunately—" His voice took on a darker tone, as he raced on: "Unfortunately, there is a gentleman present who is destined to die—within minutes."

He did not wait to see the effect of that, but turned in his chair, a tigerishly swift movement. For there was no time to waste.

Any instant his bluff might be called; and his show end in a ludicrous failure. His voice bawled across the space that separated him from a table where sat a dozen men in uniform:

"General Grall!"

"Eh!" The officer who was to carry out the hanging order whipped around. He looked startled when he saw who it was.

It struck Hedrock that his bellow had brought complete silence to the room. People at every table had stopped eating, stopped their private conversations, and were watching the royal table, and him. Conscious of his greater audience, Hedrock pushed his voice forward in his mouth, tightened his diaphragm, and brought forth the ringing question, "General Grall, if you were to die this minute, what would be the cause?"

The heavy-faced man two tables away stood up slowly. "I'm in perfect health," he growled. "What the devil are you talking About?"

"Nothing wrong with your heart?" Hedrock urged.

"Not a thing."

Hedrock thrust his chair back and climbed to his feet. He couldn't afford errors due to awkward positions. With a jerk, he raised his arm and pointed at the general with his finger, rudely.

"You're General Lister Grall, are you not?"

"That's right. And now, Captain Hedrock, I resent most violently this—"

Hedrock cut him off, "General, I regret to announce that, according to the records of the Weapon Shops, you are due to die at exactly one fifteen o'clock *today* from heart failure. That's this minute, this—second."

There was no stopping now. With a single, synchronized motion, Hedrick bent his finger, shaped his hand to receive the gun materialized on an invisible plane by the gun ring on his finger.

It was no ordinary, retail-type gun, that unseen, wizard's product, but a special Unlimited never sold across counters, never displayed, never used except in extreme crises. It fired instantly on a vibration plane beyond human vision; and, as the general's heart muscles were caught by the paralyzing force, Hedrock unclenched his hand. The invisible gun dematerialized.

In the pandemonium that followed, Hedrock walked to the throne chair at the head of the royal table and bent over the empress. He could not suppress a tingle of admiration, for she was completely, abnormally calm. Emotional, erotic woman she might be, but in actual moments of excitement, during the hour of vital decision, all the great, basic stability that was her Isher inheritance came to the fore. It was that quality of utter sanity in her that he had appealed to; and here it was, like a precious jewel, shining at him from the quiet viridescence of her eyes. She said finally: "I suppose you realize you have, by implication, confessed everything by your killing of General Grall."

He knew better than to deny anything to the supernal being she had for that sustained moment become. He said, "I was advised of the sentence of death, and by whom it was to be carried out."

"Then you admit it?"

"I'll admit anything you wish so long as you understand that I have your best interests at heart."

She looked incredulous. "A Weapon Shop man, whose organization fights me at every turn, talking about my interests?"

"I am not, never have been, never will be, a Weapon Shop man." Hedrock spoke deliberately.

A startled look came into her face, then, "I almost believe that. There's something strange, and alien, about you, something I must discover—"

"Some day, I'll tell you. I promise."

"You seem very sure that I shall not have somebody else hang you."

"As I said before, the Ishers do not commit suicide."

"Now you're on your old theme, your impossible ambition. But never mind that. I'm going to let you live, but for the time being you must leave the palace. You can't convince me that an all-purpose spy ray exists."

"Can't I?"

"You may have had such a machine prying into the palace when I was sixteen, but since then the whole palace has been fitted with defense screens. Those can be pierced only by a two-way communication machine. In other words, there must be a machine inside as well as out."

"You're very clever."

"As for the pretense," the empress went on, "that the Weapon Shops can see into the future, let me inform you that we know as much about time travel, and its impossible limitations, as the Weapon Shops. The seesaw principle involved is only too clearly recognized, with all its ever-fatal end results. But again, never mind that. I want you to leave for two months. I may call you back before then, but it all depends. Meantime, you may transmit this message to the Weapon Shop Council: What I am doing is not in the faintest degree harmful to the Weapon Shops. I swear that on my honor."

For a long moment, Hedrock gazed at her steadily. He said at last, softly, "I am going to make a very profound statement. I haven't the faintest idea of what you are doing, or going to do, but in your adult life I have noticed one thing. In all your major political and economic moves, you are actuated by conservative impulses. Don't do it. Change is coming. Let it come. Don't fight it, but lead it, direct it. Add new laurels of prestige to the famous name of Isher."

"Thank you for your advice," she said coldly.

Hedrock bowed, and said, "I shall expect to hear from you in two months. Goodbye."

The hum of renewed conversation was mounting behind him as he reached the series of ornate doors on the far side of the room. He passed through, and then, out of sight, quickened his pace. He reached the elevators, stepped into one hurriedly, and pressed the express button for the roof. It was a long trip, and his nerves grew jumpy. Any minute, any *second*, that mood of the empress could wear off.

The elevator stopped, the door opened. He was stepping out before he noticed the body of men. They came forward at the double march and instantly hemmed him in. They were in plain clothes, but there was no mistaking that here were police.

The next instant one of the men said, "Captain Hedrock, you are under arrest."

THREE

As he stood there on the palace roof facing that score of men, his mind, adjusted to victory, could not accept the threatening defeat. Here were enough men to handle any resistance he might attempt. But that did not slow his purpose. The empress *must* have known when she gave the order to intercept him that he could only draw the worst conclusions, and fight with every power that he could muster. The time for subtlety, injured innocence and cleverness was past. His deep baritone clashed across the silence:

"What do you want?"

There were great moments in the history of the world when that bellow of his had produced a startled lull in the will to action of better men than any that stood here before him. It had no such effect now.

Hedrock felt astounded. His muscles, dynamically ready for the run that was to take him through the ranks of the men while they stood paralyzed, tensed. The large carplane which had seemed so near a moment before, only twenty-five feet, tantalized him now. His purpose, to reach it, collapsed into an awareness of his desperate situation. One man with one gun against twenty guns! True, his was an Unlimited, and like all Weapon Shop guns projected a defensive half circle around its owner, sufficient to counteract the fire of eight ordinary weapons, but he had never underestimated the capacity of a blaster.

His hard, mental assessment of his position ended as the huskily built young man who had pronounced him under arrest stepped forward from the group and said crisply, "Now, don't do anything rash, Mr. Weapon Shop Jones. You'd better come quietly."

"Jones!" said Hedrock. Shock made the word quiet, almost gentle. Shock and relief. For a moment, the gap between his first assumption and the reality seemed too great to bridge without some superhuman effort of will. The next second he had caught hold of himself and the tension was over. His gaze flashed with lightning appraisal toward the uniformed palace guards who were standing on the fringe of the group of plain-clothes men, interested spectators rather than participants. And he sighed under his breath as their faces remained blank of suspicion. He said, "I'll go quietly."

The plainclothesmen crowded around him, and herded him into the carplane. The machine took off with a lurch, so swiftly was it maneuvered into the air. Breathless, Hedrock sank into the seat beside the man who had given him the Weapon Shop password for that day. He found his voice after a minute.

"Very bravely done," he said warmly. "Very bold and efficient, I may say, though, you gave me a shock."

He laughed at the recollection, and was about to go on when the odd fact struck him that his hearer had not smiled in sympathetic response. His nerves, still keyed to unnatural sensitivity, examined that small, jarring fact. He said slowly, "You don't mind if I ask your name?"

"Peldy," the man said curtly.

"Who thought of the idea of sending you?"

"Councilor Peter Cadron."

Hedrock nodded. "I see. He thought if I had to fight my way to the roof, I'd be needing help by the time I got there."

"I have no doubt," said Peldy, "that that is part of the explanation."

He was cold, this young man. The chill of his personality startled Hedrock. He stared gloomily down through the transparent floor at the unreeling scene below. The plane, conforming to speed regulations, was slowly heading deeper into the city. Two-hundred-story skyscrapers seemed to gaze the bottom of the machine as Hedrock thought bleakly: Suppose they were suspicious of him. It was not impossible. In fact—Hedrock smiled with humorless certainty—all that had ever been needed was for some of the Weapon Shop mental wizards to turn their full attention to his case. Abruptly, that was depressing. For despite all his years of experience, these Weapon Shop supermen with their specialized training had inexorably forged ahead of him in a dozen fields. He could not even plan for his own protection because the techniques of education that had molded their brains from childhood were useless applied to his mind, which had been cluttered with confused, unplanned integrations ages before the techniques now so dangerous to him were invented. Some of the weariness of his long years sagged over his spirit. The strain of his transcendental purpose, which required that he keep from all men the knowledge that he was immortal, was briefly hard to bear. Hedrock roused himself finally and said, "Where are you taking me?"

"To the hotel."

Hedrock considered that. The Hotel Royal Ganeel was the city headquarters of the Weapon Makers. To be taken there indicated that something serious had happened. He watched the plane settle toward the broad garden roof of the hotel, his mind tense with the realization that the Weapon Shops took no chances. *They couldn't!* Their existence depended on their secrets remaining secrets. If they ever doubted anyone who knew certain basic things about their organization, as he did, the life of one man would be considered as nothing before the safety of all in an implacable world.

He must not, of course, forget the hotel itself. The Hotel Royal Ganeel was about two hundred years old. It had cost, if he remembered correctly, seven hundred and fifty billion credits. Its massive base spread over four city blocks. From this beginning, it went up in pyramidic tiers, streamlined according to the waterfall architecture of its age, leveling off at twelve hundred feet into a roof garden eight hundred feet long by eight hundred feet wide, the hard squareness of which was skillfully alleviated by illusion and design. He had built it in memory of a remarkable woman who was also an Isher empress, and in every room he had installed a device which, properly activated, provided a vibratory means of escape.

The activating instrument, unfortunately, was one of the three rings he had left behind him in the palace. Hedrock grimaced in vexation as he headed with the others from the plane to the nearest elevator. He had spent careful moments deciding not to wear more than the ring gun lest suspicion fall upon those remarkable secret machines of the Weapon Shops. There were other rings in secret panels scattered through the hotel, but it was doubtful if a man with twenty guards escorting him to the great section of the building occupied by the Imperial City headquarters of the Weapon Makers would have any time for side trips.

His reverie ended as the elevator stopped. The men crowded him out onto a broad corridor before a door on which glowing letters spelled out:

THE METEOR CORPORATION
HEAD OFFICES

The sign, Hedrock knew, was only half false. The gigantic mining trust was a genuine firm, doing a vast metal and manufacturing business. It was also an unsuspected subsidiary of the Weapon Shops, which was aside from the main point except, as in the present instance, where its various offices served as fronts behind which facets of the Weapon Shop world glittered in uninterrupted, unhindered activity.

As Hedrock walked into the great front offices, a tall, fine-looking, middle-aged man was emerging from an opaque door fifty feet away. Recognition was almost simultaneous. The man hesitated the faintest bit, then came forward with a friendly smile.

"Well, Mr. Hedrock," he said, "how's the empress?"

Hedrock's smile was stiff. The great No-man's hesitation had not been lost on him. He said, "I am happy to say that she is in good health, Mr. Gonish."

Edward Gonish laughed, a rich-toned laughter. "I'm afraid there are thousands of people who are always saddened when they hear that. At the moment, for instance, the council is trying to use my intuitive training to track down the secret of the empress. I'm studying *Pp* charts of known and potentially great men. It's miserable data to go on, far less than the ten percent I need. I've only reached the letter M as yet, and I have only come to tentative conclusions. If it's an invention, I would say interstellar travel. But that isn't a full intuitive."

Hedrock frowned. "Interstellar travel! She would be opposed to that—" He stopped; then, in an intense voice: "You've got it! Quick, who's the inventor?"

Gonish laughed again. "Not so fast. I have to go over all the data. I've got my attention on a scientist named Derd Kershaw, if you're interested."

His laughing eyes grew abruptly grave. The No-man stood frowning at Hedrock. He said finally, anxiously, "What the devil's up, Hedrock? What have you done?"

The secret police officer, Peldy, stepped forward quickly and said, "Really, Mr. Gonish, the prisoner can't—"

The proud face of the No-man turned coldly on the young man. "That will do," he said. "Step back out of hearing. I wish to talk to Mr. Hedrock alone."

Peldy bowed. "I beg your pardon, sir. I forgot myself."

He backed away, then began to wave his men off. There was a milling, and murmured questions. In less than a minute, however, Hedrock was alone with the No-man, the first shock fading in a series of little, mental pain waves. A prisoner! He had known it, of course, in a kind of a way, but he had tried to think of himself as being under suspicion only, and he had hoped that if he pretended not to recognize it, the Weapon Shop leaders might not force the issue into the open.

Actually, that stage was long past if indeed it had ever existed. The suspicion was already beyond the inner circle of the council. Definitely, the sands of his time were running out. But Gonish was speaking again, swiftly, "The worst part of it is, they refused to listen when I suggested that the whole business be left over for me to investigate in my capacity as No-man. That's bad. Could you give me some idea?"

Hedrock shook his head. "All I know is that two hours ago they were worried that I might be killed by the empress. They actually sent a rescue force, but it turned out I was, and am, under close arrest."

The tall Gonish stood thoughtful. "If you could only put them off some way," he said. "I don't know enough about the individual psychologies of the councilors or about the case to offer one of my intuitive opinions, but if you can possibly twist the affair into a trial of evidence and counterevidence, that would be a partial victory. They're a pretty highhanded outfit, so don't just knuckle under to their decision as if it were from God."

He walked off, frowning, toward a distant door, and Hedrock grew aware of Peldy striding forward. "This way, sir," the young man said. "The council will see you immediately."

"Eh?" said Hedrock. The sense of warmth produced by the No-man's friendly intent faded. "You mean, the council is in the local chamber?"

There was no answer, nor did he really expect one. The sharp question had been purely rhetorical. But put it off indeed! Stiffly erect, he followed the secret police officer to the door of the council chamber.

The men sitting at the V-shaped table lifted their eyes and started at him as he crossed the threshold into the room. The door closed behind him with a faint click as he walked forward toward the table. It seemed strange to be thinking that two years before he had refused to run for a seat on the council. The councilors were of every age, ranging from the brilliant thirty-year-old executive, Ancil Nare, to hoary-headed Bayd Roberts. Not all the faces were familiar to him. Hedrock counted noses, thinking about what the No-man had said: "Make it a trial!" That meant, force them out of their smug rut. He finished his counting, shocked. Thirty! The full Council of the Weapon Makers. What could they have found out about him, to bring all of them here? He pictured these leaders at their headquarters far and near, on Mars, Venus, on those moons that rated so exalted a representative—*everywhere* councilors stepping through their local vibratory transmitters, and instantly arriving here.

All for him. Abruptly, that was startling again. And steadying. With shoulders thrown back, fully conscious of his leonine head, and of his unmistakably notable appearance, aware, too, of the generations of men like this who had lived and died, and lived and died, and died, and died, since his own birth—Hedrock broke the silence. "What's the charge?" he asked resonantly. And into those words he put all the subtle, tremendous power of his trained voice, his vast experience in dealing with every conceivable type and group of human beings.

The three vibrantly spoken words were immeasurably more than just a question. They were an expression of will and determination, the essence of pride and superiority. And dangerous as death itself. They accepted in full the implication that his presence here meant execution. They were designed to take advantage of a great basic reality, the natural, time-proven reluctance of highly intelligent men to destroy a human being recognizably their peer. Here before him were the supremely intelligent men. And who else in all the universe could better act, feel and think superior than the one immortal man sprung from Earth's proud race?

There was a stirring along the gleaming V-table. Feet shuffled on the dimly glowing dais. Men turned to look at each other questioningly. It was Peter Cadron who finally climbed to his feet. "I have been asked," he said quietly, "to speak for the council. It was I who originated the charge against you." He did not wait for a reply, but turned slowly to face the men at the table. He said gravely, "I am sure that everyone present has suddenly become acutely aware of the personality of Mr. Hedrock. It is interesting to note how exactly this exhibition of hitherto concealed power verifies what we have discovered. I must confess by own amazement at the vivid force of it."

"That goes for me, too," interrupted the heavy-faced Deam Lealy. "Until this minute I thought of Hedrock as a soft-spoken, reserved sort of fellow. Now, suddenly, he's cornered and he flashes fire."

"There's no doubt," said the youthful Ancil Nare, "that we've uncovered something remarkable. We should strive for a thorough explanation."

It was disconcerting. His entire action was being enlarged upon beyond his intent, distorted by an expectation that he was not what he seemed. The truth was that he was no more superior to these men than they were to each other. The knowledge that he was immortal had always given a dynamic quality to his confidence. And there was, of course, that genuinely supernormal, over-the-ages development of his personality, an electrical, abnormal manifestation of aura that he could suppress, and nearly always had suppressed, by an unassuming mien. By revealing its full force, when they were looking for it, he had made them think him alien. Here was a dangerous backfire, requiring instant modification. He said: "This is ridiculous. An hour ago I was in the gravest danger of my years of service with this organization. The situation was so grave that I think I can truthfully say that no one else would have come out alive. Within minutes after undergoing that nerve-racking strain, I find myself arrested by my friends on an unnamed charge. Angry? Of course I'm angry. But what particularly startles me is this curious nonsense about my inhuman personality. Am I standing before the High Council of the Weapon Makers, or by some primeval fireside where the voodoo doctors are busily exorcising demons? I demand to be treated as a loyal Weapon Shop human being without a single black mark against his record; as a man, not a monster. But now I repeat: *What is the charge?*"

There was silence. Then Peter Cadron said, "You will learn that in due time. But first—Mr. Hedrock, where were you born?"

So they had got *that* far.

He felt no fear. He stood there, a little sad, conscious of amusement that his oldest bogey had at last come home to roost. For a long moment all the names he had ever had made a kaleidoscopic picture before his mind's eye. How carefully he had chosen them in the early days, with a meticulous attention to assonance, rhythmic quality, and how they looked in print. And then impatience with high-sounding nominals had produced a whole series of satiric reactions: Petrofft, Dubrinch, Glinzer. That phase, too, had passed until now, for ages, simple names unadorned by any really pleasing attributes had distinguished his unchanging form. There was, of course, the fact that every name had always required a birthplace and a host of relevant data, a wearing business. And it was possible also that he had grown careless.

He said, "You have my records. I was born in Centralia, Middle Lakeside States."

"You took a long time answering that question," snapped a councilor.

"I was," Hedrock said coolly, "trying to imagine what lay behind the question."

Cadron said, "What was your mother's name?"

Hedrock studied the man's even-featured countenance in the beginning of puzzlement. Surely they didn't expect to confuse him with anything so simple as that. He said, "Delmyra Marlter."

"She had three other children?"

Hedrock nodded. "My two brothers and sister all died before reaching their majority."

"And your father and mother died when?"

"My father eight years ago, my mother six."

Amazingly, that came hard. For a bare moment, it was difficult to employ those intimate terms for two pleasant middle-aged people whom he had never met, but about whom he had forced himself to learn so much. He saw that Cadron was smiling with dark satisfaction at the other councilors.

Cadron said, "You see, gentlemen, what we have here: A man whose people are deceased, who has no living relatives, and who less than ten years ago, after all his family was dead, entered the Weapon Shop organization in the usual manner—and by means of talents considered extraordinary even then, when we didn't know how much of himself he was holding back, quickly rose to a position of great trust. Subsequently he persuaded us to sponsor his present adventure. We agreed to do so because we had become alarmed that the empress might do us harm unless she was watched more carefully than previously. One of the important factors to consider now is that it is doubtful if, in all our vast organization, with its tens of thousands of able men, a single other person could have been found who was capable of sustaining the interest of the empress Innelda for six long months."

"And even now," Hedrock interrupted, "has only been temporarily banished from her circle." He finished sardonically, "You have not been interested, but *that* was the result of the turmoil in the palace today. The time involved, if I may add the information, is two months."

Peter Cadron bowed at him politely, then turned back to the silent men at the table. "Bear that in mind while I question Mr. Hedrock about his education." His gray gaze glowed at Hedrock. "Well?" he said.

"My mother," said Hedrock, "had been a university professor. She taught me privately. As you know, that has been common practice among the well-to-do for hundreds of years, the controlling factor being that periodic examinations must be passed. You will find that I handed in my examination certificates with my application."

The dark smile was back on Cadron's face. "A family on paper, an education—on paper; an entire life history verifiable only by documents."

It looked bad. Hedrock did not need to look at the faces of the councilors to realize how bad. Actually, of course, it was unavoidable. There never had been an alternative method. To have trusted to a living person to back up his identity in a crisis would have been suicidal. People, however friendly to you, however much they had been paid, could be made to tell the truth. But no one could ever more than cast suspicion on a properly executed certificate. He refused to believe that they had guessed even near the real truth.

"Look here!" he said. "What are you trying to prove? If I'm not Robert Hedrock, who am I?"

He gained a bleak content from the baffled expression that crept over Cadron's face. "That," the man rapped finally, "is what we are trying to find out. However, one more question. After your parents were married, your mother didn't keep in touch with her university friends, or any former colleagues?"

Hedrock hesitated, staring straight into the councilor's glinting eyes. "It fits in, doesn't it, Mr. Cadron?" he said at last in a tight, hard voice. "But you're right. We lived in apartments. My father's work kept us moving every few months. It is doubtful if you can find anyone who will remember having met them or me. We truly lived a shadow existence."

There was a subtle psychological victory in having spoken the indictment himself but—Hedrock smiled grayly—if ever he had heard a damning build-up of innuendo, here it was. He grew aware that Cadron was speaking.

"—We recognize, Mr. Hedrock, that this is not evidence, nor is that what we are after. The Weapon Shops do not hold trials in any real sense. They pass judgments. And the sole criterion always is, not proof of guilt, but doubt of innocence. If you had attained a less exalted position with the Shops, the punishment would be very simple. You would be given amnesia and released from service. As it is, you know too much about us, and accordingly the penalty must be very severe. You know that, in our position, we *cannot* do otherwise. Fortunately for our peace of mind, we have more than suspicion. Is it possible that you have anything to add to what has already gone?"

"Nothing," said Hedrock.

He stood very still, letting his mind settle around the situation. It was almost instinct, that attunement, but behind it was the synthesization of experience that recognized the possible importance of every phase of his immediate environment. Somehow, he had to seize the initiative. He saw the floor, the walls, the panel to his right—and there he paused in ironic bitterness. He had originally, by secret maneuvering, persuaded the Meteor Corporation to take offices near the roof of the Hotel Royal Ganeel because it had seemed to him that their unsuspected Imperial City headquarters would be safer in a building of his than anywhere else. For his own protection, however, he had had removed out of their part of the building all those ring activators and vibratory devices which now he needed so desperately. If he hadn't had that forethought, there would now be a ring behind *that* panel.

Peter Cadron was speaking, the charge at long last. It was hard at first for Hedrock to keep his mind on the man's words. They seemed to move about, eluding his hearing. Or else he was too jumpy, too conscious of his own necessities. There was something about dispatching the rescue force, and simultaneously setting psychologists the task of fixing the exact moment for the landing on the basis of Hedrock's statement that the issue would be forced out into the open by the empress during lunch. Naturally in arriving at their decision, the psychologists made a swift though careful examination of his psychology chart. It was this examination that brought out an extraordinary fact.

Peter Cadron paused. His gaze fixed on Hedrock's face, and for a moment he seemed to be probing in its lineaments for secret information. He finished weightily, "There was a variation between your courage in action and the *Pp* record of your potential courage. According to the *Pp* you would never even have considered staying for that dangerous luncheon at the palace."

Cadron stopped, and Hedrock waited for him to finish. The seconds passed, and suddenly he was startled to see that dozens of the men were leaning forward tensely, sharp eyes fixed on him. They were waiting for his reaction. It was all over. This was the charge. For a moment, then, he felt like a man delivered. Why, it was ridiculous. The dream yielded to the reality of the presence of the thirty. They wouldn't be here, sitting in full dress judgment, unless a great basic protective of the Weapon Shops was threatened.

The *Pp* record technique! Hedrock tried to concentrate his mind on remembering what he had heard about the machine. It was one of the original inventions, many thousands of years old. In the beginning it had been similar to the Imperial Lambeth Mind Control. There had been improvements from time to time, a widening of its scope, the power to assess intelligence, emotional stability, and other things. But it had never worried him, who had a partial ability to control his mind. At the time of the examination he had simply attempted to synchronize his intellectual attributes with the character he had decided would best suit his purpose among the Weapon Makers.

Hedrock shook himself like a stag at bay. Damned if he'd believe they had anything. "So," he said, and his voice sounded harsh in his own ears, "so I'm five percent braver than I ought to be. I don't believe it. Bravery is a matter of circumstances. A coward becomes a lion given the proper incentive."

In spite of himself, his voice was suddenly more forceful. Some of the fire of his convictions, his dark anxieties, thickened and deepened his tone. "You people," he snapped, "do not seem to be alive to what is going on. What is happening is no idle whim of a bored ruler. The empress is a mature personality in all except minor meanings of the terms, and it must never be forgotten that we are now entering into the fifth period of the House of Isher. At any hour mighty events could erupt from the undercurrents of human unrest. Twenty billion minds are active, uneasy, rebellious. New frontiers of science and relations among men are beyond the near horizon, and somewhere out of that chaotic mass will grow the fifth crisis of cosmic proportions in the history of the Isher civilization. Only a new development on a high level could bring the empress to such sustained, forceful action at this stage of her career. She said that in two months she would call me back, and suggested it might be less. It *will* be less. My impression, and I cannot emphasize it too strongly, is that we shall be lucky to have two days. Two weeks is the outside limit."

He was roused now. He saw that Cadron was trying to speak, but he plunged on, unheeding. His voice filled the room. "The entire available trained strength of the Weapon Shops should be concentrating in Imperial City. Every street should have its observer. The fleet should be mobilized within striking distance of the city. All this should be already in ceaseless operation. But what do I find instead?" He paused, then finished scathingly, "The mighty Weapon Shop Council is frittering its time away on some obscure discussion of whether or not a man should have been as brave as he was."

He ended, drably conscious that he had not influenced them. The men sat unsmiling, cold. Peter Cadron broke the silence quietly. "The difference," he said, "is seventy-five percent, not five. That's a lot of bravery, and we shall now discuss it briefly."

Hedrock sighed his recognition of defeat. And felt better. Wryly, he recognized why. Against all reason, there had been hope in him. Now there wasn't. Here was the crisis, product of a scientific force which he had thought under control. And it wasn't. It had become one more of a whole pattern of superbly accurate techniques that had created a steadily widening gap between their positive menace to his person and his capacity for counteraction. His attempts to persuade them were defeated. His life now depended on moment to moment developments. He listened intently as Cadron spoke again.

"I assure you, Mr. Hedrock," the man said with quiet sincerity, "we are all distressed by the duty that devolves upon us. But the evidence is relentless. Here is what happened: When the psychologists discovered the variation, two cerebro-geometric configurations were set up on the *Pp* machine. One used as a base the old record of your mind; the other took into account a *seventy-five percent increase in every function of your mind*, EVERY FUNCTION, I repeat, not only courage. Among other things, this brought your I.Q. to the astounding figure of two hundred seventy-eight."

Hedrock said, "You say, *every* function. Including idealism and altruism, I presume?"

He saw that the men were looking at him uneasily. Cadron said, "Mr. Hedrock, a man with that much altruism would regard the Weapon Shops as merely one factor in a greater game. The Weapon Shops cannot be so broad-minded. But let me go on. In both the cerebro-geometric configurations I have mentioned, the complicated configuration of the empress was mechanically woven into the matrix, and because speed was an essential, the possible influence on the situation of other minds was reduced to a high level Constant, modified by a simple, oscillating Variable—"

In spite of himself, Hedrock found himself becoming absorbed. His conviction that he ought to interrupt as often as was psychologically safe yielded before a gathering fascination in the details of a science that had so greatly outstripped his capacity even for learning about it. Graphs of brain and emotional integers, curious mathematical constructions whose roots delved deep into the obscure impulses of the human mind and body. He listened and watched, intently, as Cadron went on with his damning words:

"The problem, as I have said, was to insure that the rescue party did not arrive at the palace too soon, or too late. It was found that the graph based on your old *Pp* proved that you would never leave the place alive, unless an Unknown of the third order intervened in your favor. That configuration was instantly abandoned. Science cannot take account of possible miracles. The second projection centralized on the hour of 1:40 P.M., with a concentric error possibility of four minutes. The landing, therefore, was effected at

1:35, the false Imperial credentials were accepted within two minutes. At 1:39 you emerged from the elevator. You will agree, I think, that the evidence is conclusive."

It was a nightmare. All these years while he had been living and planning, carefully building up the structure of his hopes, he had actually already committed his fortunes to the *Pp* machine, possibly the greatest invention ever developed in the field of the human mind. Distractedly, Hedrock realized that one of the councilors, not Cadron, but a little gray-haired man, was saying:

"In view of the fact that this is not a criminal case in an ordinary sense of the term, and particularly because of Mr. Hedrock's past services, I think he is entitled to assurance that we are taking seriously what the empress is doing. For your information, young man, our staff here has been enlarged fivefold. Perhaps in your personal anxiety at the time, you did not notice that the elevator from the airport went down much farther than usual to reach here. We have taken over seven additional floors of the hotel and our organization *is* in ceaseless operation. Unfortunately, in spite of your stirring appeal, I must agree with Mr. Cadron. The Weapon Shops, being what they are, must handle cases like yours with cruel dispatch. I am compelled to agree that death is the only possible sentence."

There were nods along the table, voices murmuring: "Yes, death—death—immediate—"

"Just a minute!" Hedrock's voice made a strong pattern above the quiet medley. "Did you say that this council room is now in a part of the hotel not previously occupied by the Meteor Corporation?"

They stared at him blankly, as he ran, not waiting for a reply, straight at the ornamental panel on the darkly gleaming wall to his right. It was simpler than he had expected in his wildest imaginings. No one stopped him; no one even drew a gun. As he reached the panel, he adjusted his four fingers, accurately fitted them against the panel, twisted—and the ring slid out of its hidden groove onto his index finger. In one continuous, synchronized motion, he turned its pale-green fire on the vibratory device—and stepped through the transmitter.

Hedrock wasted no time examining the familiar room in which he found himself. It was located in underground vaults twenty-five hundred miles from Imperial City, filled with softly pulsing machines and glittering instruments. His hand closed on a wall switch.

There was a hiss of power as he plunged it home. He had a brief mind picture, then, of all the rings and devices in the Hotel Royal Ganeel dissolving out of existence. They had served their purpose. One surprise escape was all he could ever hope to make from the Weapon Shops. He turned, walked through a door; and then, at the last instant, saw his deadly danger and tried to leap back.

Too late. The twenty-foot monster pounced on him. Its sledge-hammer paws sent him spinning along one wall, dizzy, sick, half unconscious. He tried to move, to rise—and saw the gigantic white rat darting toward him, its great teeth bared for the kill.

FOUR

Grimly, Hedrock waited until the last possible moment. And then the roar of his voice filled the room with its threatening echoes. There was a massive squealing as the rat dodged aside into the far corner. It crouched there, and he could see that its violent movement had incremented its already speeded up life processes. Slowly, it began to keel over. Its glazed eyes peered at Hedrock as he staggered over to the rat inclosure, straight for the line of power switches. It made no effort to follow him; and, in a moment, he had pulled the lever that furnished the force for its size.

More slowly, he walked back into the large room. He had already noticed where the wall had been smashed but he did not pause to examine the break. It required half a minute to find the creature, now that it was no longer physically magnified. But he finally saw the six-inch glint of dirty white, where it had crawled under a broken chair. It was still alive, a very old-looking rat. It twisted weakly as he picked it up and carried it through the rat inclosure into the laboratory beyond. The feeling that came to him then had very little to do with the miserable creature he was placing in his data-gathering machine. It was pity, but on a vast scale, not for any individual. The compassion embraced all life. He felt, suddenly, alone in a world where people and things lived and died with heartbreaking rapidity, ephemeral shadows that blinked in the strong light from the sun, and then faded and were gone forevermore.

With an effort, he fought off that black mood and, turning away from the data machine, went to examine his rat inclosure. The four rat houses were doing well. Each had a new batch of young ones, and from the size of them he guessed that they had been born since the mechanical process had been interrupted by the rat that had broken out.

It would take too long to repair the break in the big metal pen, but the rest of the process resumed with automatic precision the moment he threw the switches back into position. The process was simplicity itself. He had begun it a thousand years before by introducing a dozen rats (six males and six females) into each of four specially constructed houses. Food was provided at intervals. The pens were kept clean by an ingenious pusher device that worked on a gear system. Nature had her own automatic methods, and every little while youngsters appeared and grew up, adding to the weight of the delicate balances that held up the floor. As soon as the weight of rats on the poised floor reached a set point, a little door would open, and sooner or later a rat would go into the narrow corridor beyond. The door would close behind it; and no other door in any of the four houses would open until it was disposed of. At the far end of the corridor was bait, inside which was a tiny Weapon Shop magnifier. When swallowed, the magnifier warmed from the rat's body heat and set off a relay which opened the door into an inclosure forty feet long, wide and high. It also set the little corridor floor moving. Like it or not, the rat was precipitated immediately into the open. That door shut too, blocking the way back.

More food in the center of the room activated the power that set off the magnifier. With a bang, the rat plummeted into size, becoming a twenty-foot monster, whose life functions speeded up in almost direct proportion to the difference in size. In that accelerated life-world, death came swiftly. And, as the corpse cooled below a certain temperature, the magnifying power was shut off, the floor tilted, and the small white body slid onto a conveyor belt which transported it to the data-gathering machine, from whence it was precipitated into a ray bath and disintegrated.

The process then repeated. And repeated and repeated and repeated. It had been going on for a millennium; and its purpose was tremendous. Somewhere along the line, the enlarging rays of the vibrator would do to a rat purposely what they had done accidentally to Hedrock fifty-five centuries previously. A rat would become immortal, and provide him with a priceless subject for experiment. Some day, if he succeeded in his search, all men would be immortal.

The data card of the rat that had so nearly killed him turned up in the "special" rack. There were three other cards with it, but the special quality about them was the continued functioning of some organ after death. Long ago, he had explored similar freak happenings to exhaustion. The fourth card excited Hedrock. The rat that had attacked him had lived the equivalent of ninety-five years. No wonder it had had time to break out. It must have lived several hours as a giant.

He calmed himself because—because he couldn't go into the matter now. The rat would have been precipitated, not into the dissolver, but into the preserver with the other specials, and would be waiting for his examination at some future date. Right now there were things to do, vitally important things affecting the existing human race; and he, who worked so hard for the future, had never yet let the might-be interfere at decisive moments with the *now*.

There were things to do, and they must be done before the Weapon Shop Council could completely nullify his position and his power in the Weapon Shop organization. Swiftly, Hedrock donned one of his "business" suits, and stepped through a transmitter.

He arrived in one of his secret apartments in Imperial City, and saw by his watch that ten minutes had passed since he had escaped from the Hotel Royal Ganeel. He'd be reasonably safe in assuming that the tens of thousands of Weapon Shop members would not yet have been notified that he was now regarded as a traitor. Hedrock seated himself at the apartment 'stat, and called the Weapon Shop Information Center.

"Hedrock speaking," he said when an operator answered. "Get me the address of Derd Kershaw."

"Yes, Mr. Hedrock." The response was quick and courteous, with no indication that his name was now anethema to the Shops. There was a pause, and then he heard the familiar click at the other end.

Another woman spoke, "I have Mr. Kershaw's file here, sir. Would you like it sent to you, or shall I read it to you?"

"Hold it up," said Hedrock, "I'll copy the information I want."

The image of a file sheet slid onto his 'stat plate. He noted down Kershaw's most recent address, "1874 Trellis Minor Building." The rest of "page" one was devoted to previous addresses of Kershaw, and to information about his birthplace, parentage, and the childhood trainings he had received.

There was a gold star stamped on the lower right corner of the "page." It was a Weapon Shop designation of merit, and indicated that Derd Kershaw was regarded by the shop scientists as one of the two or three greatest men in his field of physics.

"All right," said Hedrock, "next page, please."

The metal plate, many times thinner than an equal weight of paper, disappeared, and then reappeared again. "Page" two took up the story of Kershaw's life where the first page had left off. Teen-age training, college training, character and intelligence evaluations, early achievements, and finally lists of scientific discoveries and inventions.

Hedrock did not pause to read the list of Kershaw's discoveries. He could check on the details later. He had secured Kershaw's name from Edward Gonish, the No-man, and that was a stroke of luck that must not be lightly cancelled by any slow action now. Because of that accidental meeting he had information about which, he had reason to believe, no one else was as yet doing anything. It was true that Gonish did not regard his intuition about Kershaw and interstellar travel as complete. But his words provided a working basis. Accordingly for another hour, or even a day, Robert Hedrock could follow up the clue without interference from the Shops.

"Turn to the last page," he said quickly. The page came on. Hedrock's gaze flashed to the list of names at the right. They were the names of individuals who had most recently made use of the file. There were only two names, Edward Gonish, and below that, Dan Neelan. He stared at the second name with narrowed eyes and because he was alert and keyed up he noticed something that he might ordinarily have missed. Behind the name of Gonish there had been stamped a tiny symbol. It indicated that the Noman had made use of the file and that it had subsequently been returned to its cabinet. There was no such symbol after the name of Neelan. He asked swiftly, "When did Neelan make use of this file, and who is he?"

The girl was calm. "Mr. Neelan's call is not completed, sir. When you requested the file we withdrew it from that section and transferred it over here. One minute, please. I'll connect you with the operator involved."

She spoke to someone Hedrock couldn't see and he did not catch her words. There was a pause and then another girl's face came on the 'statplate. The new operator nodded when she understood what was wanted. "Mr. Neelan," she said, "is waiting at this moment in the Linwood Avenue Weapon Shop. His first inquiry was about his brother, Gil Neelan, who, it seems, disappeared about a year ago. When we told him that his brother's last known address was the same as that of Derd Kershaw, he asked for information about Kershaw. We were in process of searching for that information when your call with its higher priority came through."

Hedrock said, "Then Neelan is still waiting at the Linwood Shop?"

"Yes."

"Hold him there," said Hedrock, "until I can get to the Shop. I am not in a position to use a transmitter so it will take about fifteen minutes."

The girl said, "We'll take our time giving him his information."

"Thank you," said Hedrock. And broke the connection.

Regretfully but swiftly Hedrock removed his "business" suit. He stepped with it back through the transmitter into the laboratory and then returned to the apartment. He dressed in a normal cloth suit and headed for the roof of the apartment block to the hangar where he kept a private carplane.

It was a model he hadn't used for several years, so precious minutes slid by while he checked the motor and the controls. In the air he had time to consider what he had done. What disturbed him most was the change from the "business" suit. And yet, there had been no alternative. The suit, which operated on the same energy principles as the "material" of which a Weapon Shop was made, was large enough to set up an energy disturbance in any part of a Weapon Shop, and was in its turn easily affected by the Shop. Even that wouldn't matter particularly by itself. But the disturbance was dangerous when it occurred close to the skin. It was possible to carry Weapon Shop energy guns and ring devices into a Shop without ill effects, but a "business" suit was impractically large. There was another unfortunate aspect to his wearing such a suit into a Weapon Shop. He had incorporated into it features and inventions not known to the Weapon Makers. The possibility that some of those secrets might be analyzed by detector instruments was in itself sufficient reason for leaving the suit in a safe place.

There was no sign of anything unusual as he approached the Linwood Shop. His carplane was fitted with extremely sensitive detectors and if there had been a Weapon Shop warship hovering out of sight in the blue mists anywhere above the city they would have spotted it. That gave him, he estimated, a leeway of approximately five minutes, allowing for acceleration and deceleration of a spaceship in the atmosphere near the surface of the Earth.

Hedrock brought his machine down beside the Shop and glanced at his watch. Twenty-three minutes had passed since he had broken the 'stat connection with the Weapon Shop Information Center. And that meant it was now three quarters of an hour since his escape from the council room of the Weapon Makers. Warnings about him would be spreading farther through that vast organization. The time would come when the attendants of this Weapon Shop before him would also be advised. That put a pressure on him. And yet, despite the need for quick action, Hedrock stepped down from the carplane without haste and paused for another more searching examination of the Shop. The usual sign glowed above it:

FINE WEAPONS
THE RIGHT TO BUY WEAPONS
IS THE RIGHT TO BE FREE

Like all similar glitter signs, it seemed to turn to face him as he walked toward it. The illusion was one of the commoner aspects of a main thoroughfare, and yet a few hundred such signs could make so dazzling a spectacle that people had been known to become light-intoxicated. It was a pleasant experience, with colors and the sensation of floating on air, and no dangerous aftereffects. There was a pill you could take to normalize the vision centers quickly.

The shop stood in a glade of green and floral vegetation. It made a restful and idyllic picture in its gardenlike setting. It all seemed very normal and as of old. The window sign when he approached it was the same as it had always been. The letters were smaller than those on the outside sign, but the words were equally positive:

THE FINEST ENERGY WEAPONS
IN THE KNOWN UNIVERSE

Hedrock knew that that was true. He gazed at the gleaming display of revolvers and rifles and he was briefly shocked to realized that more than one hundred years had passed since he had last visited a Weapon Shop. It made the Shop itself more interesting than it might otherwise have been. He had a sudden awareness of what a wonderful organization the Weapon Makers were, with their Shops existing in tens of thousands of cities and towns in the far-flung Isher Empire, an independent, outlawed, indestructible, altruistic opposition to tyranny. It was sometimes hard to believe that every Weapon Shop was an impregnable fort and that bloodily earnest attempts had been made by the Isher governments in the past to smash the organization.

Hedrock walked quickly now toward the door. It wouldn't open when he pulled at it. He let go, and stared at it, startled. And then he realized what was the matter. The sensitive door was condemning him because there were so many thoughts near the surface of his mind of the action taken against him by the Weapon Shop Council. The door worked by thought and no enemy of the Shops, no servant of the empress, had ever been admitted.

He closed his eyes and let himself relax, let all the tense thoughts of the past hour drain from him. Presently, he tried the door again.

It opened gently, like a flower unfolding its petals, only faster. It was weightless in his fingers, like some supernally delicate and insubstantial structure, and when he stepped through the opening it crowded his heels without touching them and closed behind him silently as a night in space.

Hedrock stepped gingerly through a little alcove into a larger room.

FIVE

It was quiet inside. Not a sound penetrated from the busy daylight world from which he had come. His eyes swiftly accustomed themselves to the soft lighting, which came like a reflection from the walls and ceiling. He glanced around alertly, and at first he had the impression that there was no one in the outer room. That tensed him, for it seemed to indicate that they had been unable to hold Neelan.

It might even be that the expected warning had come through, and that this was a trap.

Hedrock sighed, and relaxed. Because if it was a trap then his chances of escape would depend on how many men they were prepared to sacrifice. They must know he would fight to avoid capture. On the other hand, if it was not a trap there was nothing to worry about.

He decided not to worry, for a time anyway.

He gazed curiously at the showcases which stood against the walls or were neatly arranged around the floor. They were shining structures, about a dozen of them altogether. Hedrock stepped up to the one nearest the door, and gazed at the four rifles that were mounted inside it. The sight of them thrilled him. He had had much to do with the development of these intricate energy weapons, but with him familiarity with machines had never bred contempt.

Many of these weapons still carried the old names. "Guns" they were called, or "revolvers," or "rifles," but there the resemblance ended. These "guns" did not shoot bullets, they discharged energy in many forms and quantities. Some of them could kill or destroy at a thousand miles if necessary, and yet they were controlled by the same sensitive elements as the Weapon Shop door. Just as the door refused to open for police officers, Imperial soldiers or people unfriendly to the Shops, so these guns had been set to fire only in self-defense, and against certain animals during open season.

They also had other special qualities, particularly as to defense and speed of operation.

Hedrock moved around the edge of the case, and saw that there was a tall man sitting in a chair almost out of sight behind another showcase. He presumed it was Neelan, but before he could go over and introduce himself, there was an interruption. The door to the rear of the Shop opened, and an older, heavily built man emerged. He came forward with an apologetic smile on his lips.

"I beg your pardon, Mr. Hedrock," he said. "I was aware of the outer door opening, and guessed it was you. But I had started a mechanical operation which I could not leave."

He was still being treated as if he was a major Weapon Shop personage. Hedrock gave the attendant one sharp glance, and decided that the man had not yet been advised that Robert Hedrock no longer had Weapon Shop privileges. The attendant raised his voice, "Oh, Mr. Neelan, this is the gentleman I mentioned to you."

The stranger climbed to his feet, as Hedrock and the clerk came over. The clerk said, "I took the liberty of informing Mr. Neelan a few minutes ago that you were coming." He broke off. "Mr. Neelan, I want you to meet Robert Hedrock, an executive officer of the Weapon Shops."

As they shook hands, Hedrock was aware of himself being examined by a pair of hard, black eyes. Neelan's face was heavily tanned, and Hedrock guessed that he had recently been to planets or on meteors that had little or no protection from the direct rays of the sun.

He began to regret that he had not taken the time to find out a little more about Dan Neelan and his missing brother. Having failed to do so, the important thing now was to take Neelan out of the shop to a place where they could talk in safety. Before he could speak, the attendant said: "For your information, Mr. Hedrock, we are securing Mr. Neelan's mail for him from his Martian postal address. You'll have plenty of time to talk to him."

Hedrock did not argue the matter. The words had a fateful clang. But what had happened was natural enough. The women at

Information Center had sought a simple solution to the problem of holding Neelan for him in this shop. So they had offered to secure his mail from Mars by way of a Weapon Shop transmitter.

They had set a limited objective, and they had achieved it. It was possible that Neelan could be lured out of the Shop for a short time. But there was a stubborn twist to the man's lips, and his eyes were ever so faintly narrowed, as if he had had to accustom himself to watch for trickery. Hedrock knew that breed of men, and it was unwise to try to put them under pressure. A suggestion to leave the shop would have to wait, but the need for speed could be indicated. He turned to the attendant.

"Great issues are at stake, so I hope you won't think me impolite if I start to talk immediately to Mr. Neelan."

The older man smiled. "I'll leave you two alone," he said, and went into the back room.

There was another chair in a nearby corner. Hedrock dragged it over, motioned Neelan back into his own chair, and settled down himself. He began immediately: "I'm going to be very frank with you, Mr. Neelan. The Weapon Shops have reason to believe that Derd Kershaw and your brother have invented an interstellar drive. There is evidence that the empress of Isher would be unalterably opposed to the release of such an invention. And, accordingly, Kershaw and your brother are in serious danger of being killed and imprisoned. It's vitally important to find out where they were building this drive and what has happened to them." He finished quietly, "I hope you will be able to tell me what you know of the affair."

Neelan was shaking his head. His smile was ironic, almost grim. "My brother is in no danger of being killed," he said.

"Then you know where he is?" Hedrock was relieved.

Neelan hesitated. When he finally spoke, Hedrock had the feeling that the words were not those that the man had first intended to utter. Neelan said, "What do you want of me?"

"Well, for one thing, who are you?"

The determined face relaxed the faintest bit. "My name is Daniel Neelan, I am the twin brother of Gilbert Neelan. We were born in Lakeside . . . Is that what you mean?"

Hedrock smiled his friendliest smile. "A development of that. There are lines in your face that indicate a lot has happened since then."

"Right now," said Neelan, "I could be classified as a meteor miner. For the past ten years I've been away from Earth. Most of that time I spent as a gambler on Mars, but two years ago I won a meteorite from a drunken fellow named Carew. I gave him back half of it out of pity, and we became partners. The meteor is three miles in diameter, and it's practically a solid chunk of 'heavy' beryllium. On paper we're worth billions of credits, but it needs another couple of years of development before we can start to cash in. About a year ago I had a very special reason for believing that something had happened to my brother."

He paused. There was an odd expression on his face. Finally, he said, "Have you ever heard of the experiments conducted by the Eugenics Institute?"

"Why, yes," said Hedrock, with the beginning of understanding. "Some remarkable work has been done, particularly with identical twins."

Neelan nodded. "That makes it easier to tell you what happened."

He stopped again, and then slowly began his account. The scientists had taken them at the age of five, Daniel and Gilbert Neelan, identical twins already sensitive to each other, and magnified the sensitivity until it was a warm interflow of life force, a world of dual sensation. The interrelation grew so sharp that at short distances, thought passed between them with all the clarity of the electronic flux in a local telestat.

Those early years had been pure joy of intimate relation. And then at the age of twelve began the attempt to make them different without breaking the nervous connection. Like a kid tossed into a deep pool to sink or swim, he was subjected to the full impact of Isher civilization, while Gil was secluded and confined to studious ways. Over those years, their intellectual association declined. Thoughts, though still transmittable, could be concealed. Neelan developed a curiously strong, big-brother attitude toward Gil, while Gil—

The grim man paused in his account, glanced at Hedrock, and then continued, "I guess I noticed the diffident way in which Gil tackled adulthood by the way he reacted to my experiences with taking out women. It shocked him and so I began to realize that we had a problem." He shrugged. "There never was any question as to which of us would leave Earth. On the day that the contract with the Eugenics Institute terminated, I bought a ticket for Mars.

I went there in the belief that Gil would have his chance at life. Only—" he finished in a drab voice "—it turned out to be death."

"Death?" said Hedrock.

"Death."

"When?"

"A year ago. That's what brought me to Earth. I was on the meteor when I *felt* him die."

Hedrock said, "It's taken you a long time to get here." The remark sounded too sharp, so he added quickly, "Please understand, I'm only trying to obtain a clear picture."

Neelan said wearily, "We were caught on the far side of the sun, because the meteor's velocity almost matched that of Earth. It only recently came into a position where we could figure out an acceptable orbit for our simple type freighter. A week ago Carew set me down at one of the cheap northern spaceports. He departed at once, but he's due to pick me up in about six months."

Hedrock nodded. The account was satisfactory. "Just what did you feel when your brother died?" he asked.

Neelan shifted in his chair. There had been pain, he explained uneasily. Gil had died in agony, suddenly, without expecting it. The anguish had bridged the multimiles between Earth and the meteor, and twisted his own nerves in dreadful sympathy. Instantly, there had been an end to that neural pressure which had constituted, even at that distance, the bond between his brother and himself.

He finished, "I haven't felt so much as a tingle since then."

In the silence that followed, Hedrock realized that his time must be running short.

For minutes the necessity for concentrating on Neelan's words had kept the pressure of urgency away from his mind. Now that barrier was no more, and the pressure was on. Time to leave! Leave now! The purpose was steady and intense; and because of his sharp awareness of things Weapon Shop he knew that he dared not ignore the warning impulse. And yet—he leaned back in his chair, and stared at the other man soberly. When he departed he wanted to take Neelan with him, and that meant the process must be orderly. He made a mental calculation, and slowly shook his head.

"I can't quite see this affair as having gone through a major crisis as far back as a year ago."

Neelan's black eyes were suddenly dull as tarnished metal.

"I've noticed that the death of one man seldom produces a crisis," he said in a drab voice. "I hate to say that in connection with my own brother, but it's the truth."

"And yet," said Hedrock, "something happened. For Kershaw is also missing."

He did not wait for a reply, but climbed to his feet and walked to the control board, which was located on the wall to his left. All these minutes he had been acutely conscious that Weapon Shop soldiers might swarm through the transmitter that was there. He couldn't take the chance of that happening while he was organizing his retreat.

He stepped close to the board, with its winking lights. He intended to make sure Neelan couldn't see what he was doing. Quickly, he activated one of his rings, and burned a needle-small hole in the delicate transmitter circuit. Instantly, a tiny light behind the paneling went dead.

Hedrock turned away from the board, relieved but as intent on his purpose as ever. He had protected his flank, nothing more. There was another transmitter in the rear of the Shop, and for all he knew men were coming through it at this very moment. And other men in armored warships could be swinging in to cut him off from his carplane.

The risks he was taking were measured in just such desperate terms. He walked back to Neelan, and said, "I have an address of your brother's that I'd like to check right away. And I want you to come with me." He spoke earnestly. "I assure you speed is important. You can tell me the rest of your story on the way, and I can drop you back here afterwards to pick up your mail."

Neelan stood up. "Actually, there's not very much more to tell," he said. "When I arrived in Imperial City, I located my brother's old address, and learned something that—"

"Just a moment," said Hedrock. He walked to the door that led to the rear, knocked on it, and called, "I'm taking Mr. Neelan with me, but he'll be back for his mail. Thank you for your cooperation."

He didn't wait for a reply, but returned to Neelan. "Let's go," he said briskly.

Neelan headed for the front entrance, talking as he went. "I discovered that my brother had maintained a false residence for registration purposes."

As they were going out of the door, Hedrock said, "You mean he didn't live at his registered address?"

"His landlady told me," said Neelan, "that he not only didn't live there, but gave her permission to rent the room. He turned up one evening a month, as required by law, and so her conscience was clear."

Out of the Shop and along the walk that led toward the carplane. . . . Hedrock knew that Neelan was talking, and presently the meaning would penetrate. But his attention now was on the heavens. Planes flitted across them, but no long dark shape; no torpedo-like structure darting in on wings of atomic energy. . . . He held the door of his small machine open for Neelan, and stepped in after him. A moment later, he sank into the control chair; and from its vantage point saw that there was no movement around the Shop. It stood there, and its magic sign flamed in the sun, symbol of a freedom that had now endured for thousands of years, a strange and curious freedom that had withstood that most dangerous of all the assaults that could be directed against it: the unlimited ambition of those who wielded the scepters of power.

As the carplane climbed into the air, under his guidance, the Weapon Shop seemed small and unimportant in its garden setting. It was quickly lost to view in a veritable wilderness of commercial structures that mushroomed on every side. Hedrock saw that Neelan was examining the controls. There was a confidence about his exploration that spoke "expert" louder than words. The man caught his gaze, and said, "There're a couple of new things here. What's this gadget?" He indicated the detector system.

That particular device was a Weapon Shop secret. It was not a very important one, however, so Hedrock had risked putting it in a plane that could conceivably fall into the hands of people hostile to the Shops. The Imperial government had similar devices but of slightly different construction.

Hedrock countered Neelan's question. "I see you're familiar with machinery?"

"I majored in atomic engineering," said Neelan. He added with a faint smile, "The Eugenics Institute does well by its protégés."

In this case, they had indeed. Until this instant Hedrock had considered Neelan important because of the information he might have. He was impressed by the obviously tough fiber of the other's character, but he had met so many hard and capable men in his long career that that quality of itself had not seemed of outstanding interest. The degree was. It changed his attitude. A man who knew atomic energy in the all-embracing way it was taught at the great universities could practically name his own price if he went into industry. And if they ever found the interstellar drive he'd be of inestimable value. Accordingly, Neelan was a man to be cultivated. Hedrock began at once. He drew out of his pocket the slip of paper that had Kershaw's last known address written on it. He handed it to Neelan with the remark, "That's where we're heading."

Neelan took the paper, and read it aloud, "Room 1874, Trellis Minor Building—Good God!"

"What's the matter?"

"I've been there three times," said Neelan. "I found the address in a suitcase my brother kept at the boarding house."

Hedrock could almost feel his search coming to a dead stop. Nevertheless, his comment went unerringly to the root of the other's words, "*Three* times?" he said.

"It's a room," Neelan said. "Every time I went there the door was locked. The building manager told me the rent had been paid ten years in advance, but that he hadn't seen anyone there since the contract was signed. That was three years ago."

"But you didn't go in?"

"No, he wouldn't let me, and I had no desire to get put in jail. And, besides, I don't think I could have gotten in. The lock was a protected one."

Hedrock nodded thoughtfully. He had no intention of letting any lock stop him. But he could appreciate the obstacle that such devices presented to even the most determined men who lacked his facilities. There was another thought in his mind. Somewhere along here he would have to drop in at one of his apartments and don his "business" suit. It was desperately important that he protect himself, and yet so long as the Weapon Shops could trace his movements he dared not slow his pace. In the final issue the half hour it would take to secure his own safety might make all the difference. Even a ten-minute advantage in time could be decisive.

The risks involved had to be taken.

They came to where a hundred-story building flashed up at them the sign: TRELLIS MAJOR BUILDING. The wrongness of the name did not immediately strike Hedrock. He was only a few hundred yards above the stupendous structure when he saw the smaller, fifty-story, spired monster that was the Trellis Minor Building. The sight jarred his memory. He recalled for the first time that Trellis Major and Minor were two meteors revolving around each other somewhere beyond Mars. The larger was contraterrene matter, the smaller terrene. They were being mined assiduously by a single company; and these massive buildings were but two by-products of the still unended treasure that flowed in a steady stream from that remote region of solar space.

Hedrock guided the carplane to a roof landing on the smaller building, and the two of them took an elevator down to the eighteenth floor. Hedrock needed only one glance at the outside of room 1874 to realize that it was indeed well protected. The door and its frame were of a steel-strong aluminum alloy. The lock was an electronic tube, and there was printing on it which read, "When tampered with, this lock mechanism flashes warnings in the office of the building manager, the local police station, and on all passing patrol planes."

The Weapon Shops had developed a dozen devices to circumvent such electronic circuits. The best one was the least complicated. It involved absolute faith in a curious characteristic of matter and energy. If a circuit was broken—or established—swiftly enough (the speeds involved were faster than light) the current would, in the former instance, continue to flow just as if there had been no break, and in the latter would establish a flow between two distant points in space just as if there was no distance. The phenomenon was no minor incident of science. The intricate matter transmitter that had made the Weapon Shops possible was based on it.

Hedrock motioned Neelan back, and stepped close to the door. He used a different ring this time, and a glow of orange flame reflected for several feet from the point of contact. The light died into nothingness, and he shoved at the door. It opened with a faint squeal of its long unused hinges. Hedrock stepped across the threshold into an office twenty feet long by ten wide. There was a desk at one end, and several chairs as well as a small filing cabinet. In the corner beside the desk was a telestat, its plate blank and lifeless.

The room was so bare, so obviously unlived in and unused that Hedrock walked forward a short distance and then stopped. Involuntarily, he turned to glance back at Neelan. The gambler was bending down beside the lock, studying it thoughtfully. He looked up at Hedrock, and shook his head wonderingly. "How did you do that?"

It cost Hedrock a mental effort to realize that the other was referring to the way he had opened the door. He smiled, then said gravely, "I'm sorry, that's a secret." He added quickly, "Better come inside. We don't want to rouse anyone's suspicions."

Neelan straightened with alacrity, stepped into the room and closed the door. Hedrock said, "You take the desk, and I'll examine the file cabinets. The faster we do this the better I'll like it."

His own job was over in less than a minute. The file drawers were empty. He pushed the last one shut, and walked over to the desk. Neelan was peering into a bottom drawer, and Hedrock saw instantly that it was empty also. Neelan closed the drawer, and stood up.

"That's it," he said. "What now?"

Hedrock did not reply immediately. There were things that could still be done. There were probably new leads to be found in the terms of the lease under which the room had been rented. A checkup could be made with the telestat company. What calls had been made from and to this office? Given time, he could probably re-establish a very solid trail.

That was the trouble. Time was the one thing he didn't have. Once more, standing there, he was amazed that the Weapon Shops had not caught up to him long before this. In the days when he had been head of the coordination department, he'd have had his facts about Kershaw within minutes of the first notification from the council. It seemed incredible that his successor, the able and brilliant No-man trainee, John Hale, was not equally successful. Whatever the meaning of the delay, it couldn't possibly last much longer. The sooner he departed the better.

He turned and started for the door. And stopped. Because if he left now where else would he go? Slowly, then, he straightened and faced the room again. Perhaps his search hadn't been quite thorough enough. Perhaps in his anxiety he had overlooked the obvious.

He would remain and find out.

At first there was nothing. As his gaze moved from the window behind the desk, he rejected each object in turn: the desk with its empty drawers; the filing cabinet, also empty; the chairs, the room itself, barren except for a minimum of furniture and no mechanisms except a telestat. He paused there. "Telestat," he said out loud. "Why, of course."

He started towards it, and then stopped as he grew aware of Neelan's eyes following him questioningly. "Quick," he said, "against that wall." He motioned to the area behind the 'stat. "I don't think he should see you."

"Who?" said Neelan. But he must have been convinced, for he walked to the indicated position.

Hedrock switched on the 'stat. He was furious at himself for not having made the test on entering the room. For years he had lived in the Weapon Shop world of channeled 'stats, 'stats that were connected only in series, 'stat that did not have dial systems, and he had lived in his own secret world of private, building-to-building 'stat. And therefore his slow understanding of the possibilities of *this* 'stat was almost a form of suicide.

A minute passed, and the plate remained blank. Two minutes—was that a sound? He couldn't be sure, but it seemed to be coming from the speaker, a padded movement as of—that was it—footsteps. They stopped abruptly, and there was silence. Hedrock tried to visualize a man staring uncertainly down at it undecided about answering it. The third minute went by. The sense of defeat began to weigh on him, for these were priceless minutes that were passing.

At the end of five minutes, a man's harsh voice said, "Yes, what is it?"

The thrill of that reached clear down to Hedrock's toes. He had his story prepared, but before he could reply the voice spoke again, more sharply, "Are you answering the ad? They told me it couldn't go in till tomorrow. Why didn't they ring me up and tell me they'd been able to get it in today?"

He sounded furious, and once more he failed to wait for a reply. "Are you an atomic engineer?" he asked.

"Yes," said Hedrock.

It was easy to say. The swift way the other had jumped to a false conclusion made it as simple as that to change the story he had organized. His intention had been to pass himself off as Dan Neelan and explain that he had found the address of this office in his brother's personal effects. He had in mind to be callous about his brother's death, and take the attitude that his interest was in the estate. It had seemed reasonable to him, and still seemed so, that the reaction to such a frank account would be highly significant. It would either show friendly awareness of Gil Neelan's brother—in which case he'd tone down the callousness—or unfriendly awareness. And if there was no recognition at all, that also would have a meaning.

He waited, but not for long this time. "You must," said the voice from the telestat, "be wondering the why of this queer method of employment."

Hedrock felt vaguely sorry for the man. The other was so sharply conscious of the queerness of his own actions that he took it for granted that everyone else was conscious of them also. The best method of dealing with such a projection was to play along with it. "I did wonder," he said, "but I don't really give a damn."

The man laughed, not too pleasantly. "Glad to hear that. I've got a job here that'll take just about two months; and I'll pay you eight hundred credits a week, and no question asked. How's that?"

More and more curious, Hedrock thought. It was a moment when caution would seem reasonable. He said slowly, "What is it you want me to do?"

"Just what the ad said. Repair atomic motors. Well—" Peremptorily "—what do you say?"

Hedrock asked *the* question, "Where do I report?"

There was silence. "Not so fast," the answer came at last. "I'm not going to hand out a lot of information, and then you not take the job. You realize that I'm paying you twice the going rate? Are you interested?"

"It's just the kind of job I'm looking for," said Hedrock.

He felt remote from the illegality that seemed to lie behind the other's carefulness. Even Neelan's problem was only incidental. There would be details of murder to investigate, but he who had watched generations of human beings die could never be too concerned with a few more dead men. His purpose were on a different level.

The voice was saying, "Five blocks north along One Hundred Thirty-first Street. Then about nine blocks east to 1997 Two Hundred Thirty-second Avenue, Center. It's a tall, narrow, grayish building. You can't miss it. Ring the bell, and wait for an answer. Get that?"

Hedrock wrote the precious address down swiftly. "Got it," he said finally. "When shall I report?"

"Right away." The voice was threatening. "Understand me, I don't want you rushing off somewhere else. If you want this job you'll come over by public carplane, and I know just how long it will take, so don't try to fool me. I expect you over here in about ten minutes."

Hedrock thought, *My God. Am I never going to get back to my apartment?*

Aloud he said, "I'll be there."

He waited. The 'stat plate remained blank. Evidently, the other man was not interested in seeing what the applicant looked like. Abruptly, there was a click, and he knew that the connection had been broken.

The interview was over.

Quickly, he used one of his rings to insure that the telestat would not be used by anyone else—and turned as Neelan came forward. He was smiling, a lithely built man, almost as tall, almost as big as Hedrock himself. "Good work," he said. "That was a smooth job. What was that address again? Ninety-seven what street?"

Hedrock said, "Let's get out of here."

His mind worked swiftly as they walked rapidly to the elevator. He had been wondering what he was going to do with Neelan. The man was valuable and might prove to be a wonderful ally for a normally lone operator like himself. But it was too soon to take him into confidence. Besides, there wasn't time to make the detailed story out of it that would be necessary to gain Neelan's support.

As their elevator raced towards the roof, Hedrock said, "My idea is that you go back to the Linwood Shop and pick up your mail, while I go and see the unpleasant individual I talked to. Afterwards rent a room at the Hotel Isher—I'll call you there. That way we'll do both jobs in half the time."

There was more to it than that. The sooner Neelan returned to the Weapon Shop the greater the likelihood that he would get there before a Weapon Shop search team. And if he waited in a hotel instead of his room, it would take just so much longer for any searchers to locate him. His failure to remember the address the voice had given made sending him considerably less dangerous.

Neelan was speaking. "You can drop me off at the first public carplane platform. But what about that address?"

"I'll write it for you as soon as we get on my ship," said Hedrock.

They were on the roof now, and he had a moment of terrible tension as several carplanes swooped down and landed with a rush. But the men and women who climbed out of them paid no attention to the two men heading for the carplane on the north runway.

As soon as they were up the air, Hedrock saw the flashing sign of a carplane platform. He dived towards it, and simultaneously pulled a slip of paper towards him, and wrote, "97 131st Street." A moment later they were on the pavement. He folded the paper, and gave it to Neelan as the latter climbed out of the carplane. They shook hands.

"Good luck," said Neelan.

"Don't go back to your brother's room," said Hedrock.

He hurried back to the control chair, closed the door, and instants later manipulated his machine above the traffic. Through the rear view plate of the control board, he watched Neelan climb aboard a public carplane. It was impossible to tell whether he was aware that he had been given the wrong address.

The Weapon Shop experts could use associative techniques to get the real one out of him, of course. He undoubtedly remembered it on some level of awareness. But it would take time to persuade him to cooperate, and time to induce the necessary associations. Hedrock actually had no objection to the Shops having the information. As he guided his machine slowly towards the address given him by the voice, he wrote another, longer note, with the real address on it. This one he placed in an envelope. On the envelope he wrote: *Peter Cadron, The Meteor Corporation, Hotel Ganeel, Imperial City—Deliver noon mail, the 6th.* That was tomorrow.

Under normal circumstances he would have been working with the Shops. Their purposes were basically his also, and it was unfortunate that an entire council had allowed itself to be frightened by one man, himself. But they had, and the emotion might conceivably interfere with their efficiency. Their very slowness in following up the Kershaw lead seemed to prove that their action had already endangered their cause. Hedrock had no doubts about what he was doing. In a crisis he trusted himself. Other people were skillful and brave, but they lacked his vast experience, and his willingness to take prolonged risks.

It was possible that he was the only one as yet who really believed that this was one of the great crises of the critical reign of Innelda Isher. In the final issue a few minutes might make all the difference between success or failure. No one was better equipped than he to make those minutes count.

His plane crossed Two Hundred Thirty-second Avenue, Center, and he brought it down in a carplane parking area on Two Hundred Thirty-third. He walked swiftly to the nearest corner, and mailed his letter, and then, satisfied, proceeded on to his destination. It was, he saw by his watch, exactly eleven minutes since he had talked to his prospective employer. Not too long.

So that was the building! Hedrock continued walking, but he studied it with a frown. It was an ungainly structure in that it was out of proportion, much too long for its width. Like a great, gray dull needle it poked into the lowering sky three, four hundred feet, a curiously sinister construction. There was no sign outside it to indicate what went on inside, simply a narrow walk leading from the sidewalk to a single, unimposing door that was level with the street. As he rang the doorbell, he tried to visualize Gilbert Neelan walking along this street on the day of his death, striding forward up to the door and disappearing forever. The mental picture did not seem complete, and he was still considering it when the now familiar harsh voice said from a hidden speaker above the door:

"You took your time about arriving."

Hedrock said steadily, "I came straight here."

There was a brief silence. Hedrock imagined the man measuring in his mind the distance from the Trellis Minor Building. The result seemed to be satisfactory, for he spoke again:

"Just a minute."

The door began to open. Hedrock saw a wide, high alcove, just how high he couldn't make out from where he was standing. He forgot the alcove as he found himself staring at a thick, partly open door made of dark, mottled metal. The entire inner wall, in which the big door was set, was smoothly wrought in the same metal. Hedrock stepped through the outer door, and paused as he realized what the overall unnatural effect was. The inner wall was Fursching steel, the structural alloy that was used exclusively for the superhard shells of spaceships.

The strange building was a hangar for a spaceship. And the ship was *in*.

Kershaw's ship! It was a guess, but the speed with which he was moving required that he act as if all his guesses and assumptions were realities. Subsidiary thoughts raced through his mind.

Gil Neelan, the brother of Dan, had not died on Earth but in a flight through space. Which would seem to mean that the interstellar drive had been tested a whole year before. But, then, why were the people aboard acting as they did? Surely, Kershaw, the inventor, would not be cowering nervously inside because somebody had been killed in an experiment, or because he was afraid of the empress? He must know that he could obtain the assistance of the Weapon Shops. All starred scientists were secretly advised that the "open" facilities of the Shops were secretly available to them. On rare occasions even "confidential" information had been given certain trusted men.

Poised there, Hedrock guessed grimly that Kershaw also was dead. His thoughts grew even swifter, and turned now toward decisive action. Should he try to get inside while he had the opportunity? Or retreat to go after the precious "business" suit?

The questions almost answered themselves. If he left now, he would arouse the suspicions of the man to whom he had talked. If he remained and seized the ship, the entire problem of the drive would be solved.

"What's the matter?" The harsh voice came as he reached that point in his thoughts. "What are you waiting for? The door's open."

So he was already suspicious. But there was anxiety in his tone, also. This man, whoever he was, was definitely eager to have an atomic engineer come aboard. It placed him subtly in Hedrock's control. It made it possible for Hedrock to say truthfully: "I've just discovered that this is a spaceship. I don't want to leave Earth."

"Oh!" There was silence. Then the voice said urgently, "Just a minute. I'll be right out. I'll prove to you that everything is as it should be. The ship can't fly till the motors have been gone over."

Hedrock waited. He had an idea that the proof was going to involve a gun. The question was, how big would it be? Not that it made any difference. He was going in, even if at the beginning he was at a disadvantage. Sooner or later his ring weapons would give him the opportunity he needed. As he watched, the inner door that had been fractionally open swung wide. It revealed a third door, which was also open, and beyond that, floating in the air, was a mobile energy gun, mounted and riding easily on antigravity plates. The three-noded muzzle of the gun pointed with a mechanical steadiness at Hedrock. From an inner speaker, the man said in a tight, hard voice:

"You probably carry a Weapon Shop gun. I hope you realize the futility of such a weapon against a ninety-thousand-cycle unit. Just toss your revolver through the door."

Hedrock, who did not carry ordinary guns, said, "I'm unarmed."

"Open your coat." Suspiciously.

Hedrock did so. There was silence, then, "All right, come on in."

Without a word, Hedrock stepped through the two inner doors, each of which, in turn, clanged behind him with heavy finality.

SIX

As Hedrock advanced, the gun withdrew sideways, and he had a kaleidoscope of swift impressions. He saw that he was in the control room of the spaceship, and that was startling. A control room was, by law, located in the center of a ship. That meant this hangar extended about four hundred feet underground, as well as above. This was an eight-hundred-foot spaceship, a veritable monster.

"Well," the stranger's voice cut raspingly across his thought, "what do you think of it?"

Slowly, Hedrock turned toward his captor. He saw a long, pale-faced individual, about thirty-five years old. The man had maneuvered the mobile unit toward the ceiling, and he was standing behind a transparent energy insulator. He regarded Hedrock with large, brown, suspicious eyes. Hedrock said, "I can see there's something damn funny going on here. But I happen to need money quick, so I'll take the job. Does that make sense?"

He had struck, he realized, the right note. The man relaxed visibly. He smiled wanly. He spoke finally with an attempt at heartiness that didn't quite come off. "Now you're talking. You can see how it was. I thought you weren't going to come in."

Hedrock said, "The spaceship startled me, located here in the heart of the city." It was a point, it seemed to him, that he should press hard. The fact that all this was new and strange to him would emphasize that he had no advance knowledge of the existence of a spaceship. He went on, "So long as we understand each other, I guess we'll get along. The eight hundred credits a week still goes, does it?"

The man nodded. "And it'll be clear, too," he said, "because

I'm taking no chances on you not coming back here."

Hedrock said, "What do you mean?"

The man smiled sardonically. He seemed to be more pleased with the situation. His voice sounded cool and confident as he said, "You're going to live aboard till the job is done."

Hedrock was not surprised. But he made a protest as a matter of principle. He said, "Now, look here, I don't really mind staying aboard, but you're taking a pretty high-handed manner. What's up? It's all very well for me to keep saying it's none of my business. But every few seconds you keep pushing something new at me until—well, I think I have a right to a few general facts."

"Like hell you have." the man snapped.

Hedrock persisted, "What's your name? I don't think it will hurt you if I know who you are."

There was a pause. The other's long face twisted into a frown. He shrugged finally. "I guess I can tell you my name." He smiled with a sudden savage exultation. "After all, *she* knows it. My name is Rel Greer."

It meant nothing, except that it wasn't Kershaw. Hedrock didn't have to be told who *she* might be. Before he could speak, Greer said curtly: "Come along! I want you to change your clothes. Over there." He must have noticed Hedrock's almost imperceptible hesitation. "Or maybe," he sneered, "you're too modest to undress out in the open."

"I'm not modest," said Hedrock.

He walked over and picked up the work clothes he was supposed to change into, and he was thinking, *Shall I take a chance and keep my rings on? Or take them off?*

He looked up, and said aloud, "I'd like to examine this insulated suit before I put it on."

"Go ahead. It's your funeral if there's anything wrong with it."

"Exactly," said Hedrock.

The interchange, brief though it was, had already brought him a vital piece of information. He had taken one glance at the suit, and recognized that it was in good repair. These insulated suits for atomic workers had a long history; if anything went wrong they lost their gloss. This one positively shone; and Greer's casual acceptance of his suggestion that he examine it seemed to signify that the man didn't know anything about such things. The implications were tremendous. As he went over the material, Hedrock's mind was busy.

Greer had indicated that the ship was not capable of flight. If that were true it could only mean that the motors had been taken apart. And that there was an uncomfortably large amount of radiation flooding the engine room. Because of the decision he had to make, it was a point that needed checking. He looked up, and asked the question.

Greer nodded, but there was a wary expression in his eyes. He said, "Yes, I took them apart, and then I realized the job was more than I cared to undertake."

That sounded reasonable enough, but Hedrock chose to misunderstand. "I don't get that. The work is simple enough."

Greer shrugged. "I just didn't want to be bothered."

Hedrock said, "I never heard of an authorized trade school—let alone a college—graduating an atomic motor repairman who couldn't put an engine together again. Where did you get your training?"

Greer was impatient. "Look," he said flatly, "get into that suit."

Hedrock undressed quickly. He was not satisfied with the results of his attempt to find out how good a mechanic Greer was. But the brief conversation gave direction to the decision he had to make. If there was free radiation in the engine room, then he couldn't take his rings with him. An insulation suit was efficient only if there was no metal inside it; and, while it was possible that he might be able to use his rings against Greer before there was any danger, the risk was too great. It was much safer to slip the tiny weapons into a pocket of his suit just as if they were simple ornaments. There would be other opportunities to use them.

It required only a few moments to change his clothes. It was he who led the way down into the bowels of the ship.

They came to a world of engines. Titanic drivers of the approved point-expand-point design, glistening, oval-shaped monsters that filled all of one great room, clustering almost belly to sleek belly over the floor. Hedrock counted them from the bottom of the stairs. There were seventeen of them; and he knew that he would be expected to show surprise. "But these are thirty-million-cycle engines," he said, and his amazement was not altogether put on. "Since when has a ship under a thousand feet long needed more than two such supers, and one of those for emergency only—let alone seventeen?"

He saw that Greer was enjoying his astonishment. "The ship

is a new invention," he said smugly. "I'm selling it. I'm negotiating, and have been for some weeks, with the empress herself." His lips tightened, then he went on, "I decided to tell you that on the way down. It isn't any of your business, but I don't want you worrying your head about it, and maybe prowling around. Now you know where you stand. It's *her* idea that the whole thing be kept quiet. And I pity any interloper who goes counter to her wishes in anything. The Earth wouldn't be big enough to hold such a fool unless he were a Weapon Shop man. There, is everything clear?"

It was much clearer than Greer realized. The great scientist, Kershaw, had hired Gil Neelan and Greer and others whose names had not yet been mentioned to assist him in perfecting his invention. Somewhere along the line Greer had murdered everyone else aboard, and taken control of the ship.

Hedrock climbed out of the engine room and up to the repair shop on the level above. He began to examine the tools, aware of Greer watching him. In turn, but much more casually, he watched Greer. Once more he was testing to discover just how much the man knew. There were mobile cranes and clamping machines, and welders and de-welders, and serrated polishers, all on the necessary gigantic scale, and all—one glance at meters plus a surge of power through them sufficed to verify the fact—ready for action. The question was, did Greer know?

He showed no sign of it. He stood by while Hedrock deliberately, and amateurishly, took one of the tools apart; and he made no comment. It took half an hour to put it together again. Greer spoke again at last:

"I've fixed a place for myself in the empty room above this repair shop. I'll spend most of my time there during the next two months. It isn't that I don't trust you, or that there is very much you can do. But while I'm up there I'll *know* that you're not wandering around the ship, prying into secrets."

Hedrock said nothing. He did not quite trust himself to speak, for fear that he would say too much to a man who had now irrevocably revealed himself. No further tests were necessary. Greer was not a scientist. And in a few minutes, as soon as he climbed up to the chamber above, the problem of seizing the ship would be solved.

The irritating thing, then, was that Greer didn't go up to the next level right away. He stayed around like a man starved for company, but at the same time afraid of it. At any other time, with anyone else, Hedrock would have felt at least a bleak sympathy. Of all the emotions he could appreciate, it was loneliness.

He had another reason for wanting the man to depart. One of the amazing aspects of his various interchanges with Greer was that the other had not yet asked him for his name. Hedrock had no intention of saying that he was Daniel Neelan; he intended to claim that the whole situation was too unnormal for him to reveal his identity. But still that might make for unpleasantness and delay.

Greer broke the silence. "How come a man of your training is out of a job?"

It sounded like the beginning of an inquiry. Since his name was not involved, Hedrock replied quickly, "I've been wasting my time out on the planets. Damn fool!"

Greer seemed to consider that, for several minutes went by. At last he said, "What brought you back?"

There could be no hesitating over that. If Greer went "upstairs," and examined his clothes, he'd find the name of Daniel Neelan written in a notebook. It was a possibility that had to be taken into account. "My brother's death," Hedrock said.

"Oh, your brother died?"

"Yes." It was the story he had originally intended to tell. Now, he could tell it without naming names. "Yes, he used to send me an allowance. When that stopped, I made inquiries, and it seems he's been missing for a year, unregistered. It'll take about six months more to close the estate, but, as you probably know, the courts recognize non-registration as proof of death in these days of multiple assassinations."

"I know," was all Greer said.

In the silence that followed, Hedrock thought, Let him mull that over. It wouldn't do any harm, in the event he did find the notation about Neelan, for Greer to believe that Gil and Dan Neelan had no strong feelings for each other. "It's more than ten years," Hedrock said aloud, "since I saw him. I found I didn't have the faintest sense of kinship. I didn't give a damn whether he was dead or alive. Funny."

Greer said, "You're going back into space?"

Hedrock shook his head. "Nope. Earth for me from now on. There's more excitement, fun, pleasure."

"I wouldn't," said Greer, after a silence, "exchange my last year in space for all the pleasure in Imperial City."

"Each to his own taste—" Hedrock began.

And stopped. His will—to get the man up to the insulation room—collapsed to secondary importance. For here was information. The astonishing thing was that he hadn't guessed it before. It had been implicit in every facet of this affair. "My last year in space—" Why, of course. Kershaw, Gil Neelan, Greer and other men had taken this ship on a trial interstellar cruise. They had been to one of the near stars, possibly Alpha Centauri, or Sirius or Procyon—in spite of all his years of life, Hedrock trembled with excitement as he ran over the names of the famous nearby star systems.

Slowly, the emotional repercussions of Greer's words died out of him. The picture of what had happened was far from clear, except for one thing. Greer had volunteered the new fact. He wanted to talk. He could be led into saying more. Hedrock said, "My idea of life isn't cruising around space looking for meteors. I've done it, and I know."

"Meteors!" Greer exploded. "Are you crazy? Do you think the empress of Isher would be interested in meteors? This is a hundred billion credit deal. Do you hear that? And she's going to pay it, too."

He began to pace the floor, obviously stimulated. He whirled suddenly on Hedrock, "Do you know where I've been?" he demanded. "I—"

He stopped. The muscles of his face worked convulsively. Finally, he managed a grim smile. "Oh, no, you don't," he said. "You're not pulling anything out of me. Not that it really matters, but—" He stood there and stared at Hedrock. Abruptly, he twisted on his heel, climbed the stairway, and disappeared from view.

Hedrock gazed at the stairway, conscious that the time had come for action. He examined the ceiling metal with a modified transparency, and nodded finally in satisfaction. Four inches thick, the usual alloy of lead and "heavy" beryllium, atomically processed. The transparency also showed the exact spot where Greer was sitting, a blurred figure, reading a book. Or rather, holding a book. It was impossible to see whether he was reading.

Hedrock felt himself cold, grim. His only emotion was a remote, deadly pleasure that Greer was sitting up there, smugly imagining himself in control of the situation. To think that the man had brought an easy chair into an empty room without even considering why the room was empty. The insulation "gap," confining areas where power was developed or used in large amounts, was old both in law and of necessity. The legal restrictions had been so effective that most people were probably not even aware that the danger or the protection existed. And yet at the same time scientists like Gil Neelan or Kershaw would be so familiar with the idea of the restrictions that it probably never occurred to them that others might not know.

Which, Hedrock thought, was ideal.

He maneuvered the heavy polisher directly under the spot where Greer was sitting, and turned its finely toothed surface to point upward. Then he began his estimation. Greer had looked about one hundred and seventy pounds. Two thirds of that, roughly, was one hundred and fourteen. To be on the safe side, allow for a blow that would kill a man of a hundred pounds. Greer didn't look too physically fit. He'd need the handicap.

There was, of course, the four-inch floor to figure in. Fortunately, its resistance was a formula based on tension. He made the necessary adjustments, and then pressed the button control.

Greer crumpled. Hedrock went upstairs to where the man lay sprawled on a leg-rest chair. He examined the unconscious body with a color transparency, for detail. No bones broken. And the heart still beat. Good. A dead man wouldn't be able to answer questions. There were a lot of questions.

It required considerable mathematical work to plot a system of force lines that would bind Greer into a reasonably comfortable position, allowing his arms and legs to move, and his body to turn, and yet be capable of holding him forever if necessary.

SEVEN

Hedrock spent the next half hour going over the ship. There were many locked doors and packed storerooms which he temporarily bypassed. He wanted a general idea of what the inside looked like, and he wanted it quickly.

What he found in that cursory search did not satisfy him. He had a spaceship that couldn't leave its hangar; a ship, moreover, which it would be dangerous for him to leave now that he had control of it.

It might be guarded. The fact that he had not seen any of Innelda's soldiers proved nothing. They could be wearing invisibility suits. The empress would be desperately anxious not to draw the attention of Weapon Shop observers to concentrations of government forces. And so, Robert Hedrock had come along an apparently deserted street, and entered the ship of ships before the commander of the protecting forces could make up his mind to stop him.

If that picture was even close to the reality, then it would be virtually impossible for him to get away from the machine without being picked up for questioning. It was a risk he dared not take. Which left him where? He went thoughtfully down to the insulation room, and found Greer conscious. The man glared at him with mingled hate and fear.

"You don't think you're going to get away with this," he said in a voice that trembled. "When the empress finds out about this, she'll—"

Hedrock cut him off. "Where are the others?" he asked. "Where are Kershaw and—" He hesitated—"my brother, Gil?"

The brown eyes that had been glaring at him widened. Greer shuddered visibly, then he said, "Go to hell!" But he sounded frightened.

Hedrock went on in a steady voice, "If I were you I'd start worrying about what would happen to you if I should decide to turn you over to the empress."

Greer's face acquired a bleached look. He swallowed hard, and then said huskily, "Don't be a fool! There's enough here for both of us. We can both cash in—but we've got to be careful—she's got the ship surrounded. I figured they'd let somebody through, but that's why I greeted you with that ninety-thousand-cycle cannon—just in case they tried to come in, too."

Hedrock said, "What about the telestat? Is it possible to make calls outside?"

"Just through the 'stat in the Trellis Minor Building."

"Oh!" said Hedrock, and bit his lip in vexation. For once he had overreached himself. It had seemed logical to render that particular 'stat useless, and so head off all other candidates for the job that was being offered. Then he hadn't expected that the trail would lead directly to the interstellar ship itself.

"What do you get on any other 'stat?"

"A fellow named Zeydel," said Greer in a grim tone.

It required several seconds for Hedrock to recall where he had heard that name before. At the empress's table, some months earlier. One of the men had expressed abhorrence at the idea that Innelda would employ such a creature. Hedrock remembered her answer. "God made rats," she had said, "and God made Zeydel. My scientists have found a use for rats in their laboratories, and I have found a use for Zeydel. Does that answer your question, sir?" She had finished haughtily.

The man who had brought up the subject was known for his sharp tongue. He had flashed back at her, "I see. You have human beings in your laboratories who experiment on rats, and now you have found a rat to experiment on human beings."

The remark had brought a flush to Innelda's cheeks, and for the man two weeks' banishment from her table. But it was apparent that she still had a use for Zeydel. Which was unfortunate, because it seemed to preclude bribery, that important adjunct of recent Isher civilization. Hedrock did not accept the defeat as final. He loaded Greer, force lines and all, onto an antigravity plate, and carted him upstairs to one of the bedrooms in the upper half of the ship. And then he started on his second exploration of the ship. This time, though every minute now seemed valuable—and a crisis imminent—it was no cursory search.

He went through every room, using a power drill to break recalcitrant locks. The personal quarters above the control room held him longest. But Greer had been there before him. Nothing remained that gave any clue to the real owner's whereabouts. Greer must have had plenty of time to destroy the evidence, and he had used it well. There were no letters, no personal property, nothing that would ever cause embarrassment to a murderer. It was in the nose of the ship, in an airlock, that Hedrock made his prize find. A fully equipped lifeboat, powered by two replicas of the giant engines in the main machine, was snugly fitted there into a formfitting cradle. The little boat—little only by comparison; it was nearly a hundred feet long—seemed to be in perfect condition and ready to fly.

Hedrock examined the controls carefully, and noticed with excitement that, beside the normal accelerator, was a gleaming white lever, with the letters INFINITY DRIVE printed on it. Its presence seemed to indicate that even the lifeboat had the interstellar drive mechanism built into it. Theoretically, he could sit down at the controls, launch the lifeboat into the air, and escape into space at a speed which pursuing ships would not be able to match. He examined the launching devices. They were automatic, he discovered. The spaceboat need merely glide forward from its cradle under normal drive, and its movement would activate the electrically operated lock. At tremendous speed, the lock-door would slide open; the boat would race through it. And the airlock would close the moment it was clear.

No doubt about it. He could now make his escape. Hedrock climbed out of the lifeboat, and went down to the main control room at the ground level. He felt undecided. Within a few hours of escaping from the Imperial palace, he had captured the interstellar ship. He had succeeded, accordingly, where the forces of the empress and of the Weapon Makers had failed. He did not underestimate the accomplishment. Success had come as the result of his old policy of heading toward a goal during a crisis without regard for personal risks. It was time now to be more careful, and that brought up a number of problems, all interrelated. How could he turn the big ship over to the Weapon Makers without endangering himself, and without starting a battle between the navies of the government and of the Weapon Makers? The decisive factor was that the latter wouldn't receive his note, giving this address, until noon the following day.

Under normal circumstances, the interval would probably pass without incident. But unfortunately a stranger had been observed going aboard. When Zeydel reported that to Innelda, she'd become suspicious. She might give Greer a little while to get in touch with her agents, and explain the event. But she wouldn't wait very long. Perhaps already she had made several attempts to contact Greer. Hedrock seated himself in the control chair, watched the main 'stat for activity. And considered his situation.

After five and three quarters minutes there was a click, a call light began to blink, and a siren gave off a low musical hum. The activity continued for two minutes, and then ceased. Hedrock waited. At the end of thirteen minutes, there was the click again, and the process repeated. So that was the pattern. Zeydel must have been instructed to "call Greer every fifteen minutes." Presumably, if he failed to answer, further action would be taken.

Hedrock went down to the engine room and set to work refitting a motor. It seemed unlikely that he would have time to put together the two engines that would be needed to enable the big ship to fly, but it was worth making the attempt. At first he went up to the control room every hour to see if the call was still coming through. But finally he rigged up a 'stat in the engine room, and connected it to the one in the control room. From then on, he could follow the calls without ceasing work.

What Innelda would do when she ran out of patience was a matter of conjecture. But Hedrock could imagine her having already mobilized the fleet, with the hope that, if the interstellar ship tried to get away, the mighty guns of the battleships would knock it out of the sky before it could gather speed.

It was that possibility that made it dangerous for him to risk an escape in the lifeboat. If it were brought down, that would end man's hope of reaching the stars. His plan must be to hold off the empress's forces until a *number* of possibilities existed for success. And then, and not till then, make an all out effort to gain an unqualified victory for himself and the Shops. He couldn't expect to do anything until twelve noon tomorrow.

At six o'clock, eighteen hours before the deadline, the 'stat failed to call out. Fifteen minutes later, it was again silent. Hedrock hurried to the galley, had a bite to eat, and carried sandwiches and coffee to Greer. He removed one of the force lines, so that Greer could move one arm freely enough to feed himself. At six-twenty-nine Hedrock settled himself at the control board. Once more, that 'stat failed to show any activity. Either a further step would now be taken, or else Innelda was giving up for the night. It was a choice Hedrock dared not leave to chance. He switched on his end of the telestat, the voice connection only—the vision plate remained dark—and dialed the nearest police station. He intended to pretend that he knew nothing about what was going on, and it was interesting therefore that they let him dial the whole number. It was particularly interesting because he wanted them to believe that he was making an unsuspecting call to the police.

The familiar click was his first knowledge that he had made a connection. Before the person at the other end could say anything, Hedrock whispered loudly, "Is that the police department? I'm a prisoner aboard what seems to be a spaceship, and I want to be rescued."

There was a long pause, and then a man said in a low voice, "What address are you at?"

Hedrock gave it, and went on succinctly to explain that he had been hired to repair some atomic motors, but was now forcibly being detained by a man named Rel Greer. His account was interrupted, "Where's Greer now?"

"He's lying down in his cabin upstairs."

"Just a moment," said the man.

There was a pause, and then the unmistakable voice of the empress Innelda said, "What is your name?"

"Daniel Neelan," said Hedrock. He added urgently, "But please hurry. Greer may come down at any minute. I don't want to be caught here."

"Why don't you just open the doors and walk out?"

Hedrock had his answer for that, also. He explained that Greer had removed from the control board the devices for opening and shutting the doors. "He has them up in his room," he finished.

"I see." There was a momentary silence. He could imagine her swift mind visualizing the situation and its possibilities. She must have been in the process of making up her mind, for she said almost immediately, "Mr. Neelan, your call to the police station has been switched to the offices of the government secret service. The reason is that quite unwittingly you have walked in upon a situation in which the government is interested." She added quickly, "Do not be alarmed."

Hedrock decided to say nothing.

Innelda continued swiftly, "Mr. Neelan, can you turn on the vision plate? It is important that you see the person to whom you are talking."

"I can turn it on, so that I could see you, but the section of the 'stat which would enable you to see me has been removed."

Her reply was acid toned. "We are familiar with Greer's secretiveness about his personal appearance." She broke off. "But quick now, I want you to have a look at me."

Hedrock switched on the plate, and watched while the image of the empress of Isher grew onto it. He hesitated for a few moments, and then whispered, "Your Majesty!"

"You recognize me?"

"Yes, yes, but—"

She cut him off. "Mr. Neelan, you occupy a unique position in the world of great affairs. Your government, your—empress—require your loyal and faithful services."

Hedrock said, "Your Majesty, forgive me, but please hurry."

"I must make myself clear; you must understand. This afternoon, Dan Neelan, when I was informed that a strange young man—that is, yourself—had entered the Greer spaceship, I immediately ordered the execution of a Captain Hedrock, a Weapon Shop spy, whom I had previously tolerated in the palace."

She was mixing her times a little, it seemed to Hedrock, and also mixing truth with falsehood. But it was not up to him to correct her. What did interest him was her refusal to be hurried. He had an idea that she regarded this as an unexpected opportunity, but that she would not worry too much about what happened to Daniel Neelan. She must take it for granted that she could always go back to bargaining with Greer, and she was probably right. She went on, her face intent, her voice low but firm: "I tell you this to illustrate graphically the completeness and extent of the precautions I am prepared to take to insure that my will shall prevail. Consider Captain Hedrock's fate as symbolical of what will befall anyone who dares to oppose me in this matter, or who bungles his part of the job. Here is what you must and will do. As of this moment you are a soldier in the government service. You will continue to pretend to repair the drive motors of the ship, and actually you will do enough work to convince Greer that you are fulfilling your obligations to him. But every spare moment that you have will spend in taking apart those motors which can still operate. I am assured that it is possible to do this so skillfully that only an expert would notice that anything was wrong.

"Now, please listen carefully. As soon as you have paralyzed the motive power of the ship, you must take the first opportunity to advise us. A single word will do. You can switch on your 'stat, and say, 'Now,' 'Ready' or anything like that, and we will break in. We have eight one-hundred-million-cycle guns in position. These weapons are so powerful that each unit will fire only one shot, dissolving as it does so. But eight units smashing at one narrow portion of the wall will cause a breakthrough within three minutes. That is the plan. So it shall be. Within twenty-four hours of its successful conclusion, you will receive a tremendous reward for your assistance."

Her intense voice died away. Her tensed body relaxed. The flame died from her gaze. There was suddenly a warm and generous smile around her eyes and lips. She said in a quiet voice, "I hope, Dan Neelan, I have made myself clear."

There was no doubt of that. In spite of himself, in spite of his previous association with her, Hedrock was fascinated. He had made no mistake in believing that Imperial Innelda would play a foremost role in every crisis of this unsettled age. The tigress had shown her claws, and they were made of steel and quiescent violence. The soul of this woman must be pure fire.

His mind began to consider the implications of what she had said; and he was shocked. She had indicated that these mighty cannon she had mentioned were in place, ready to blast. It was possible that, by dialing the 'stat when he did, he had barely headed off an attack. And the worst of it was, if they should become suspicious, they were in a position to break through *at any time*. Actually, they had nothing to fear. The ship's motive power was already paralyzed and only their false beliefs would enable him to hold them off until the critical hour of noon tomorrow. The empress's voice interrupted his thoughts:

"—Zeydel, take over!"

The face, head and shoulders of a man of about forty-five replaced her image on the plate. Zeydel had slate-colored eyes, a thin beak of a nose, and lips that formed a long slit across his face. There was a faint, grim smile on his raffish countenance, but his voice had a flat quality as he said:

"You have heard our glorious ruler's commands. You must consider yourself a soldier who has been called to duty against a man for whom there can be no sympathy. This scoundrel Greer has deliberately set himself against the Crown. He has an invention which endangers the State, and which must be completely withheld from the knowledge of the public. Greer presumes to regard himself as a negotiator of equal rank with the government, and, from a position of temporary immunity, he argues arrogantly, demands impossible terms and otherwise conducts himself in a treasonous manner. It further appears that he has hired you to repair the ship which he is offering for sale, apparently for the purpose of getting it into a condition where he can fly off with it after he has secured the money he demands. The very type of long lasting repair he requires shows the careful nature of the betrayal he is planning.

"Accordingly—and listen well—if it should prove necessary, or if the opportunity occurs, you are herewith given permission to kill Greer as an enemy of the State, in the name of her Imperial Majesty, Innelda, Empress of the Solar System, Grand Descendant of the House of Isher. The full power of government authority is behind any act which you may take in support of the instructions you have received. And now, before I break off, are there any questions?"

They were taking his cooperation for granted. And, if it had been a chance motor repairman who had come into this situation, Hedrock could well believe that such a man would be awed and virtually overwhelmed by the rank and position of the people who had spoken to him. But unfortunately for Innelda it was she who was cooperating with his purpose, not he with hers.

He realized that he was expected to make an answer. "No questions," he whispered. "I am a loyal subject of Her Majesty. I understand everything."

"Good. If we don't hear from you by eleven tomorrow, we will attack anyway. May you prove worthy of the empress's trust."

There was a click. Hedrock broke the connection at his own end, and went down to the engine room again. He was disturbed at the time limitation that had been set. But it seemed to him that he ought to be able to delay the assault for an hour or even more.

He took an anti-sleep pill, and set to work on the motors. Shortly after midnight he completed the balancing adjustments on one of the drives, and so had half the power that was necessary to lift a ship as large as this one into the air. He went upstairs, cooked himself a steak; and then, having eaten, returned to the engine room.

As he labored on the second motor, he realized that he was working on the basis of assumptions that were not proven. He was assuming that these drives *could* operate. In a way it was a reasonable conclusion, because after all, the ship had made a return voyage from a nearby star, and had successfully lowered itself into this sheathlike hangar. But there was no question that he was depending on machinery which he could not hope to test until the moment of crisis.

All too swiftly the hours went by. At ten after nine, Hedrock realized suddenly how much time had passed. He estimated, then, that he was a good two hours away from readying the second motor, and that, for that reason alone, some kind of delay was in order. He fed Greer, ate a hurried breakfast, and then worked on the motor until twenty minutes to eleven.

At that time, perspiring from his efforts, his job still not completed, he switched on the 'stat connection and called Zeydel. The man's face image appeared on the plate almost instantly; he was like a fox in his eagerness. His eyes flashed, his mouth trembled. "Yes?" he breathed.

"No," said Hedrock. He spoke swiftly, "Greer has just now gone up to the control room. He's been with me all morning, so I'm only now in a position to start putting the motors out of commission. It'll take till twelve-thirty, or one. Make it one to be absolutely sure. I—"

Zeydel's image faded from the screen, and that of the empress Innelda replaced it. Her green eyes were narrowed the faintest bit, but her voice was calm as she said, "We accept the delay, but only till twelve. Get busy—and leave the 'stat on; not the vision plate, of course, just the voice—*and have those drives paralyzed in time!*"

"I'll try, Your Majesty," Hedrock whispered.

He had gained another hour.

He went back to his delicate task of adjusting an atomic motor back into working condition. He caught glimpses of his perspiring face in the gleaming metal of the tools he used. He felt himself tense, and no longer sure that the work he was doing would serve any useful purpose. In the sky above the great city, the government fleet would be out in force. And the chances of a last minute action by the Weapon Makers seemed more remote every passing instant. He pictured the noon delivery at the Meteor Corporation. His letter to Peter Cadron, giving this address would be passed on swiftly—but Cadron might be in conference; he might have stepped through a transmitter to the other side of the Earth; he might be at lunch. Besides, people didn't open their mail as if their lives depended on it. Accordingly, the possibility was strong that it would be one, or even two o'clock before the Weapon Shop councilor read the letter from Robert Hedrock.

It was eleven-thirty when the straining Hedrock realized that the second motor would not be ready in time. He continued working, because the sounds would convince the empress that he was obeying instructions. But he realized it was time to make decisions. He'd have to get up to the lifeboat, of course. Whatever else went wrong or right, it represented his personal hope of escape. And since it also included the interstellar drive it was by itself as valuable as the larger ship. If it got away, then man would reach the stars. If it didn't, if it was brought down, then—but there was no point in considering failure. Either he would be killed instantly, or he would be captured.

But how could he get up to the lifeboat while the 'stat was on? By fixing up a 'stat connection in the engine room, he had been able in a plausible fashion to carry on the illusion that he could only communicate with the outside when Greer was not around. And so he had delayed the attack an hour. Unfortunately, Innelda's insistence that contact be maintained was now an obstacle. If he should cease his noisy activity, she and Zeydel would immediately become suspicious. It would take him, he estimated, five minutes to climb to the lifeboat. Considering everything, that was a long time. So long, in fact, that a further effort to confuse Innelda was justified. Hedrock hesitated, and then approached the 'stat.

"Your Majesty," he said in a loud whisper.

"Yes?"

The reply was so prompt that he had a sudden vision of her sitting before a bank of telestats, keeping in touch with all the facets of this enterprise. With the men on the battleships, with the soldiers waiting beside the invisible cannon, with Zeydel, and with himself. He said quickly: "Your Majesty, it will be impossible for me to put all the motors out of commission by the time you have set me. There are seventeen drive engines down here, and I have only had time to work on nine of them. Do you mind if I make a suggestion?"

"Go ahead." Her tone was noncommittal.

"My idea is that I go upstairs and try to overpower Greer. I might possibly catch him by surprise."

"Yes." There was an odd note in her voice. "Yes, you might." She hesitated, then she continued firmly, "I may as well tell you, Neelan, that we are becoming suspicious of you."

"I don't understand, Your Majesty."

She seemed not to hear. "We have been trying since early yesterday afternoon to contact Greer. In the past he has always responded within an hour or so, and it is unusual, to say the least, that he has not even deigned to answer our attempts at communication. For all he knows we are prepared to meet his exorbitant terms and every one of his absurd conditions."

"I still don't see—"

"Let me put it like this," she said coolly. "At this final hour we do not take chances. You have permission to go upstairs and overpower Greer. In fact, I order you to take the risks of a soldier and prevent him from successfully launching this ship out of its hangar. However, just in case our vague suspicions of you have any basis, I am now, *this instant*, ordering the attack. If you have any private plans of your own, abandon them now, and cooperate with us. Climb up, while the attack is in progress, and do anything that is necessary against Greer. But you'll have to hurry."

Her voice grew stronger, and it was clear that she was giving orders into other 'stats, as she cried in a tone that was like a deep violin note, "All forces act. Break in!"

Hedrock heard that command as he started for the stairway. He had to pause to open the radiation door, and then he was racing up the steps, still hopeful, still convinced that in spite of what had happened he could climb up above the ground level before anybody could stop him.

The first shot struck then. It shook the ship. It was violent beyond his wildest preconception. It brought a moment of horrible daze, and the mind-racking thought that he had forgotten concussion. He raced on up, up, the fear of defeat already in his heart. The second titanic shot sent him reeling back. But he recovered and climbed on, conscious of lassitude. He was vaguely aware of what Innelda was risking, using such mighty weapons. A cycle of chain reactions of a million units' duration was dangerously close to an uncontrolled atomic explosion.

The third shot raged then. And blood spurted from his nose; a warm stream trickled out of his ears. The fourth shot—he was dimly aware that he was halfway to the control room—crumpled him in a heap. He half-rolled down an entire section of stairway. And the fifth shot caught him as he was staggering erect.

He knew his defeat now, a sick and deadly knowledge, but he kept moving his legs, and felt amazed when he reached the next level. The sixth intolerable explosion caught him there at the head of that long stairway, and sent him spinning down like a leaf engulfed in a storm. There was a door at the bottom; and he closed it with automatic intention. He stared dully as the great door lifted from its hinges, grazed him as it fell, and clanged to the floor. That was the seventh shot.

Like an animal now, he retreated from pain, down the next line of steps, instinctively locking the lower door. He was standing there, infinitely weary, half leaning against the wall when the shouts of men roused his stunned mind. Voices, he thought then, inside the ship. He shook his head, unbelievingly. The voices came nearer; and then abruptly, the truth penetrated.

They were in. It had only taken seven shots.

A man shouted arrogantly from the other side of the door beside which he was standing, "Quick, break it down! Capture everybody aboard. That's orders!"

EIGHT

Hedrock began to retreat. It was a slow business, because his mind wouldn't gather around any one thought, and his reflexes were disorganized. And that, he thought incoherently, was almost literally true. He had been reduced to an inchoate nervous organism by the greatest concentration of energy fire ever leveled at a machine containing a man.

His knees trembled as he kept going down the stairs. Down, down—the feeling came that he was climbing down into his grave. Not, he thought, that there was much farther to go now. The storerooms were past. Next would be the insulation room, then the repair room, then the engine room, then the drive chamber; and then—

And then—

Hope came. Because there was a way. The ship was lost, of course. And with it the chance of all the billions of human beings who might have carried the torch of civilization to the farthest stars of the universe—their chance, their destiny, their hope of greater happiness was gone. But once more there was hope for him. He reached the engine room, and forgot all else but the work that had to be done. It took a precious minute to discover which of the electric switches controlled the ship's lighting system and other power functions. During that minute the floors shuddered as another of the doors he had locked went down with a distant clang before the hissing roar of a mobile unit. Instantly, the shouting of men came nearer.

Hedrock began to pull switches. He wanted all the upper lights off. It should take them several minutes to get more. He had already visually located the six-foot drill he wanted. He floated it out on its antigravity base, pushing it urgently down the two flights of stairs from the repair room, where it had been, down past the engine room, into the great drive chamber that was the final room of the big spaceship. And there, in spite of himself, in spite of urgency, Hedrock paused and stared at what must be the stellar drive itself.

Here was the treasure that all the fighting was about. Yesterday—how long ago that seemed—he hadn't had time to come down to this room. Now, he had to make the time. He snatched the transparency bar of the giant drill and focused its penetrating light at that thirty-foot-thick drive shaft. He saw dark mist—and realized his failure. The metal was too hard, too thick. There were too many interlayers and reflectors. No known transparency would ever approach the core of that drive.

Defeated, he whirled and began to run, pushing the drill which, weightless though it was, nevertheless offered a "mass" resistance to his straining muscles. He got through the first door of the bottom lock, then the second, then the third, and then he stood there in a wild surmise. He had been gathering his reserves of strength and will for the job of drilling a six-foot hole through the Earth on a steep slanting thrust for the surface. He didn't have to. The hole, the passageway, was there. A line of dim ceiling lights made a straight but upward slanting path into the distance.

It was not the moment to think of why it was there. Hedrock grabbed the transparency bar, squeezed past the now unnecessary drill, and raced along the tunnel. It was much longer than he would have had time to drill. The angle of ascent was only about twenty degrees. But actually the greater distance was all to the good. The farther he got away from the ship before emerging into the open, the better.

He reached the end suddenly. It was a metal door; and, using the transparency, he could see that beyond it was an empty cellar. The door had a simple latch that opened at his touch and closed behind him like amorphous metal sinking tracelessly into a solid wall. It was the perfection of workmanship that brought understanding. Hedrock paused inside the cellar and studied the door. He had taken it for granted that Greer had been back from Centaurus for a long time. But there was another explanation. Not Greer, but Kershaw and the others, had built this. They, too, had been cautious about their contacts with the outside world. It was possible that Greer had not even known of this passageway. In fact—Hedrock felt suddenly positive—the man would never have left him alone in the engine room yesterday morning, so near an exit, if he had known. The other, the telestat contacts with the outside world had probably been handed into Greer's control as general handyman by those brilliant nitwits, Kershaw and Gil Neelan, who thought of every precaution against outside interference but had failed to protect themselves against their own employee.

It was an interesting but academic point in view of what had happened. Depressed, Hedrock headed for a set of stairs to his left. Halfway up, the stairs branched. The left way led up to a rather ornate door beyond which his transparency showed a vacant kitchen. The right way proved to be the one he wanted.

Hedrock laid the transparency down on the steps. He wouldn't be needing it any more. He straightened, opened the second door, and stepped into bright sunlight. He found himself in the backyard of a large, vacant house. There was the usual green wonder of lawn, the perpetually flowering garden, the carplane garage, and a high fence with a gate. The gate opened easily from inside onto a back-alley boulevard, the kind where the sidewalks hug the sides of the street. Farther along. Hedrock could see a broad thoroughfare.

He hurried toward it, anxious to identify it so that he could judge how far he was from the spaceship. Knowing where he was would give him a better idea of what he must do, *could* do, next. There would be a cordon of guards. But just how far they extended from the center of operations, and what degree of watchfulness they were exercising, was another matter. Suppose they had the entire area surrounded.

They did. There was a uniformed guard at the corner, and he wore the glittering viewer headpiece. He waved at Hedrock from a distance.

"How're things going?"

"We're in!" Hedrock called. "Keep your eyes peeled."

"Don't worry. There's a solid line of us out here."

Hedrock turned away, thoughtfully, and walked hastily back the way he had come. Trapped. The streets would be covered for blocks; and, in minutes, a yelling crew would smash the last of the hard doors that barred their way in the spaceship, realize what had happened and the search with its certainty of capture would be on. Or, worse still, perhaps they were already by the final barrier, and in minutes would break from the house, where the tunnel ended, and seeing him, swoop for the kill.

He vaulted a high fence into another backyard. There was a line of viewer-helmeted men along the front of the house. But now that he was heading for the ship, with the hope it suddenly offered, the spirit of retreat faded. Nobody tried to stop him. And, after a tense minute, he had to smile at the psychology that permitted a man to head toward a center of infection, but not away from it. He crossed boldly to the corner of the street, from where he could see the needle-shaped hangar just down the block. A few seconds later he reached the ship. No one tried to stop him as he climbed gingerly through the jagged gap the cannon had made, and so into the control room.

The lights he had turned off were on. That was the first thing Hedrock noticed. The searchers had reached the engine room. Presently, they would come surging up to explore the rest of the ship. Meanwhile, he had the opportunity he needed. Hedrock glanced around the control room. There were several dozen men standing around, and every one of them was dressed in the regulation insulation suit. There was no suspicion in their eyes.

To them he was just one more member of the secret police, wearing protective clothing in a radioactive area. They were too long away from battle, these men. The existence of the Weapon Shops had kept the army alive, but being an officer or a soldier had for ages been one of the sinecures sought after by all the ne'er-do-wells who had the influence or the bribe money. Here they stood and here they sat, idle-brained, waiting for the silly business to get over with, so they could go back to their mistresses and their games and the easy routine of their existence. It was an unfortunate by-product of his plan for ending war, but it was better than having men by the million die in battle.

Crash! The sound coming from deep in the ship galvanized Hedrock. *That must be the door to the drive chamber.* His freedom was just now being discovered. In seconds, the alarm would clamor forth. Hedrock walked without haste toward the stairway, jostled past several men waiting there, and began to climb up. It was as simple as that. There were men on each level, but they didn't seem to be guarding anything. Hedrock could not escape the impression that they had come up here to avoid any possible fighting. He forgot them as he came to the lifeboat. He searched it quickly. It was untenanted. With a sigh, he sank into the multipurpose chair before the control board, drew a shaky breath, and pressed the launching lever.

Like a ball rolling down a glass incline, the little ship slid up into the air.

The old and wonderful city, seen from the height of half a mile, sparkled in the sun. It semed very close, some of the spearheads of buildings almost scraping the bottom of his ship as he flew. Hedrock sat almost without thought. His first wonder that the warships had not attacked him had already yielded to the belief that they were on the lookout for an eight-hundred-foot spaceship; this tiny craft resembled at a distance a public carplane, or a dozen types of pleasure craft. He had two purposes. The first one was to escape, if he could, to one of his hiding places. Failing that he intended to use the special drive of the lifeboat to help him get away.

It was a dark spot on the upper rim of the rear-view 'stat that brought him out of his hopeful mood. The spot hurtled down out of the blue, became a ship, became a thousand-foot cruiser. Simultaneously, his general call 'stat (usable now that he was out in the open) broke into life. A stern voice said:

"Didn't you hear the universal order to ground? Carry on straight ahead, stay on your present level till you come to the military airport beacon due east. Land there, or be blown to bits."

Hedrock's fingers, reaching for the white accelerator, paused in midair. The command showed no suspicion of his identity. His gaze flashed to the telestat plates again and saw that, except for the cruiser, he was alone in the air. All traffic *had* been forced down. Was it possible that no one had yet glanced into the lifeboat cradle and noticed its absence? Hedrock held his ship steady, and sat there toying with the idea of actually landing at the military field. There must be a swarm of planes down there and he might conceivably lose himself among them. A grim smile touched his lips as he recognized the plan for the heady madness it was. They wouldn't be as foolish as that. The moment the news about the missing lifeboat was received, somebody in the cruiser would remember the lone ship that had been herded toward the field.

Hedrock flashed a frowning glance at the cruiser on the 'stat plate. It showed directly above him and startlingly close. Too close. His eyes narrowed. It blocked an entire section of the upper sky from him. He realized the truth as a second cruiser slipped down to his right, and a third cruiser slid to his left, and a small swarm of destroyers rocketed into view behind and in front of him. The first ship, in almost hugging him, had screened the approach of the others. And there was no doubt that, whatever the army might be, the fleet was efficient. A second time his hand reached toward the white accelerator. He clenched it, and then paused as the long, patrician face of the empress appeared on the general call plate.

"Neelan," she said, "I don't understand. Surely, you're not going to be foolish enough to oppose your government."

Hedrock made no reply. He was tilting his ship ever so slightly. He had his eye on an open space above and between the destroyers ahead. And, besides, his end of these conversations could no longer be carried on in whispers. Which meant that he would have to disguise his voice, something which he hadn't done for years. It was not the moment to risk his future relationship with her by an unskillful performance.

"Dan Neelan—" The empress's voice was low and intense—"think before you commit yourself irrevocably to ruin. My offer is still open. Simply land that lifeboat as directed and—"

Her voice went on, but Hedrock was intent on escape. Her interruption had given him time to make a further adjustment on his course, and his little ship was tilted now toward the southern hemisphere in the general direction of Centaurus. It was a rough aim, but he had a suspicion that the acceleration he'd need to escape the warships would black him out for a while; and he might as well be going somewhere that he knew about.

"—I offer you one billion credits—"

His fingers were clenched around the white lever on which were engraved the words INFINITY DRIVE, and now that the time had come he did not hesitate. With a flick of his arm, he pulled the lever all the way over.

There was a blow as from a sledgehammer.

NINE

The morning dragged. The empress paced the floor of her office in front of the mirrors that lined the walls, a tall, handsome young woman.

She thought once, "How strained I look, like an overworked kitchen maid. I'm beginning to feel sorry for myself and all the hard things I have to do. I'm getting old."

She felt older. For the dozenth time, she turned on one of the bank of telestats and stared at the men working in the drive chamber of the Greer spaceship. She had a frantic sense of wanting to shout at them, to urge them to hurry, *hurry.* Didn't they realize that any hour, any minute, the Weapon Shops might discover where the ship was hidden, and attack with all their power?

A score of times during that long morning, she thought, "Destroy the ship now, before it's too late."

But each time she caught the desperate defeatism with a tight-lipped resistance. The House of Isher could not afford to destroy such a secret. Some day, it might play a vital part in preserving the Imperial House from resurgent enemies. She smiled at the intensity of her indecision. And there was no doubt in her mind that so long as the ship remained in existence the hours would seem long, and the Crown would be in mortal danger.

With a nervous flick of her finger, she turned on her news 'stat and listened to the clamor that roared at her: *Weapon Shops charge that the empress has secret of interstellar travel. . . . Weapon Shops demand that the empress release to the people the secret of—*

She clicked it off, and stood briefly startled by the sharp silence. After a moment she felt better. They *didn't* know. That was the essence of the reports. The Weapon Shops didn't know the secret. It was true that they had somehow divined what she had. But too late. Minutes and minutes too late. That was the reality behind the barrage of demands they were making, behind the fury of their verbal attacks. As soon as the ship was destroyed—she felt another flare of anxiety—there would remain the one doubtful point, one man, the incomprehensible Dan Neelan. The thought was like a signal. Her buzzer sounded. A woman's voice said:

"Chan Boller, the physicist, to see you, Your Majesty. You said—"

"Yes, yes, send him in." She wondered if she sounded too eager.

Boller was an intense young man with dark eyes and a crisp manner. "I have, Your Majesty, completed the report on interstellar travel for which you asked." He stopped and stared at her sharply; and she realized that he knew all about the news flashes—who didn't?—and that he was wondering how much truth was in them. Her green eyes measured him coolly.

"Go on," she said.

She listened intently, as he began, pushing the sound of his voice away from her thought, ignoring even the exact words, letting only the meaning come through.

Alpha Centauri, the physicist explained, was about four and a third light-years from Earth. It was a four-star system, and it was known to have planets. The fastest ship built to date could cover the distance in about a hundred and thirty years, at an average of five hundred miles a second. Such a flight had never been attempted. To accomplish the journey in eleven days, "the figure Your Most Gracious Majesty mentioned," would mean an average speed of twenty-eight million miles a second. The effect on the human system of the full acceleration involved, given the present imperfect anti-acceleration efficiency of ninety-nine point nine percent plus, was impossible to evaluate.

"Impossible!" the woman ejaculated with a sharp dismay.

Boller explained: "The difference between one hundred percent and ninety-nine point nine percent is .0000000 plus, with the one swimming somewhere short of infinity, but just where, it is arithmetically impossible to state." But it would be a factor under really high accelerations, particularly as even the strongest men died from the shock of less than fifteen gravities. As for interstellar navigation, that required a known fixed point as a base. Once that contact was lost, so was the ship.

When the physicist had gone, she sat with her eyes half closed. Neelan was dead, or lost. During the two seconds that his little ship had been within range of the warship radar beams, technical officers had estimated its acceleration at well beyond that which a human being could endure and remain conscious. The pressure that had produced the unconscious state would continue for an indefinite period. Let the Weapon Shops rave and rant. The House of Isher had survived greater storms than this. She turned on the telestat connecting her with the Greer spaceship. But the men were still working in their laborious fashion. The greater danger remained.

It began to work on her mind again. The mental picture of the ship, and the disaster that would follow its seizure by the Weapon Shops, stayed with her as she went to the eleven o'clock cabinet meeting. It was that fear in the back of her thought that made her mood chilling as she listened to the latest reports of the effect of the propaganda.

She saw that the councilors were wary and soft-spoken. They acted as if she were about to explode. It had never struck her before what a barrier of fear existed between herself and even these high officers. Abruptly, that was startling. She pictured herself alone in the world, served by fools and cowards, who would turn against her if ever that intangible force which created an hierarchy was subjected to strong enough blows. Rats, she thought in a flame of anger, damned scurrying rats! She flared finally, "But what's being done? All I hear when I turn on the 'stat is a babble of commentators vying with each other to spread Weapon Shop propaganda. Stop it. Take control of all public communications. Organize a campaign of denial of the Weapon Shop charge that I am withholding the secret of interstellar travel, and launch counterpropaganda accusing them of revolutionary intent. And keep asking them what they really do want. That should start people wondering."

She stalked out of the meeting. When she reached her office, the telestat was barking that mobs were surging through the streets, yelling for the secret of interstellar travel. Her lip curled. The silly fools! Next thing, they'd be hanging her in effigy.

After a moment, that hurt. She bit her lip, and sat fighting to regain her self-assurance. Finally, she called up Prince del Curtin's apartment. He spoke first. "I'm on my way to lunch, Innelda. Are you coming?"

She was surprised. "Is it so late? But no, I'm having lunch brought here. I'm waiting for word about—about something."

He looked at her intently. "See here, Innelda, there are lines in your face. You're not letting this get you down."

"I've never," she replied, "played a more careful game."

After she had broken the connection, she sat back and thought tensely: Why not he? Nothing would have a greater effect on the present crisis than a swift but imposing marriage. She paused there, frowning with the memory of Dr. Snow's blunt words about just that subject. The old fool! Her lips came together defiantly. After a moment, she sighed her rejection of del Curtin. Captain Hedrock had been right when he'd said that the Imperial family did not commit racial suicide even by degrees, not knowingly anyway. Long ago she had decided that the prince was too closely related to be eligible. She mustn't allow herself to be stampeded by events into marrying even her likable cousin. Actually, there was no one yet unless—she frowned. Ridiculous. The man was simply a clever, presumptuous interloper. Even now it was difficult to grasp why she had permitted him to state his objective.

An involuntary glance at the 'stat, which was attuned to the Greer spaceship, jarred her mind back to her basic danger. For a long minute she stared at the uncompleted work. Then, trembling, she broke the connection. It was a nightmare, she thought, this waiting.

She ate a sandwich, and drank a glass of something that seemed tasteless; that was all she remembered of her lunch. It was heartening to listen to the early-afternoon news. It was more reassuring. Everything about the Weapon Shops was against them. She mustered a wry smile. How low she had sunk when her own propaganda could cheer her up.

But it did. So much so that her nerves quieted sufficiently for her to feel up to an interview she had been putting off all morning. The interview with Greer. She sat cold as rock while the frightened wretch poured out his story. The man was almost beside himself with terror, and his tongue kept running off into pleas for mercy. For a time that didn't bother her. There was only the thread of his tale about Kershaw and Neelan and—

And Neelan!

She sighed her understanding. What an impregnable wall of purpose she had smashed up against. The relationship, it seemed to her, explained the unexpected resistance he had offered her, though there was still no explanation of how he had located the ship. Whatever the details, within a few hours of boarding the machine he had had control of it. His efforts to get the drives working again had been herculean, but the odds against his success had been out of proportion to the enormousness of the task. That was particularly true, and even unfair, because in the final issue she herself had ordered the attack on the basis of her terrible anxiety. Logically, she should have accepted his reasons for delaying the assault. There was no question but that she had run up against a remarkable man.

She came out of her reverie, and said softly to Greer, "And where did you leave Kershaw and the others?"

The man broke into a frenzy of babbling, something about there being seven habitable planets altogether in the Alpha Centauri system, three of them lovelier than Earth—"And I swear I left them on one of those. They'll be all right. The first ship will pick them up. All I wanted was to get back here and sell the invention. It's a crime, of course. But these days everybody's out for himself."

She knew he was lying about where he had left the men. She felt cold and merciless. People who were afraid always did that to her. She had a sense of loathing, as if something unclean was near her. It didn't really matter whether such people lived or died. She hesitated in spite of the simple logic, and the simpler impulse involved. It took a long second to realize why. It was because, fantastically, she was afraid, too. Not in the way he was. Not for herself. But for the House of Isher. It was strange to sit here and admit that fear to herself. She felt repelled at the notion that she had a kinship with this creature who had been blatant and threatening when he was safe behind a fortress of steel, but who now shivered for the rag that was his life.

She stiffened. "Take him back to his cell," she said. "I shall decide later what to do with him."

But she knew that she was going to let him live. Contempt burned in her at the weakness. She was become one with the mobs that raged through the streets shouting for the secrets of the interstellar drive.

Her personal 'stat buzzed. She clicked it on; and her eyes widened as she saw that it was Admiral Dirn.

"Yes," she managed to say finally, "yes, I'll be right over."

She climbed to her feet with an unnatural sense of urgency. The spaceship was ready, waiting now for her to drain its secret. But in an affair like this, with the mighty Weapon Makers opposing her, one minute could be too late. She ran for the door.

The Greer spaceship—she continued to call it that irritably for want of a better name—seemed a tiny thing in that vast military hangar. But as her carplane with its attendant patrol vessels flew nearer, it began to take on size. It towered above her finally, a long, mottled-metal, cigar-shaped structure lying horizontally on the cradle in which it was berthed. She could see the gaping holes where the big energy guns had smashed through to conquer for her. She forgot that as she climbed into the control room. Now that the ship was horizontal, the stairways had automatically drawn back against the wall; and it didn't take long to walk the four hundred feet through door after shattered door. Her eyes studied the gigantic drive shaft. She saw that the plates had been loosened but not removed. And after a moment she looked questioningly at the uniformed officer who stood a respectful distance behind her. The man bowed.

"As you see, Your Majesty, your orders have been carried out to the letter. Nothing inside the drive has been touched or seen, and the workmen who disconnected the plates are the ones who were chosen by you personally from case histories submitted this morning. Not one has sufficient knowledge of science to analyze even an ordinary drive let alone a special type."

She nodded, then allowed herself a smile, which she tried to make warm. "You have done well, Admiral. You will receive a bonus of one million credits."

His evident pleasure gave her a brief fillip. Then he was speaking again, "Not one of these men has been allowed near a telestat all day. They are unaware of the turmoil outside."

"Good. Send them in as you go out."

For a minute she was alone. She stood, a faint smile on her long Isher face, content growing into her tired body. It shouldn't take too long. The men who, millennia ago, had planned the education of the members of the Imperial family had rightly judged that no ruler could survive in the age of science without some course of training that would synthesize all knowledge and discovery into one brain. The training had evolved slowly. It was far from perfect. Captain Hedrock had told her that it was similar to that of a Weapon Shop No-man, resembling the latter much as a caricature resembled a photograph. It was a bitter comparison, but she still felt pleased with it.

Hedrock had—once more she frowned. There she was again, thinking of that curious man. A sound interrupted her. She turned and saw that a troop of men was coming in. They all saluted. She nodded, flashing her public smile.

The men, she saw, had their orders. They began to remove the loosened plates with a quiet efficiency. In two hours, the job was done. The secret of the drive was carefully integrated into her brain. She stood finally behind a ray shield watching an energy gun dissolve the drive core into a mass of sagging, then molten metal. Her patience had no end. She waited until there was a splotchy mound of white-hot metal on the floor; and then, satisfied at last, climbed into her carplane.

Dark clouds rode the late afternoon sky as she returned to the palace.

TEN

It wasn't that the darkness lightened. Hedrock sagged for a long time with his eyes open. And the night was abysmal. But there was a difference. Why, of course, he thought finally, he was conscious. It was hard, for a moment, to grasp the idea of the two kinds of night involved. His brain seemed far away, his thoughts a dead-slow panorama. He had memories, but there was a remote quality to them, as if not he but some other facet of himself had experienced the physical sensations.

Slowly, Hedrock grew aware of a quietness around him, a lack of pressure, of movement. The elements of his mind gathered a little closer together. He straightened in the control chair, and glanced at the 'stat plates. He was staring into space. In every direction were stars. No sun, nothing but needle-sharp points of light varying in brilliance. And no pressure of acceleration, no gravity. It wasn't an unusual experience; but this time it was different. He glanced at the Infinity Drive, and it was still in gear. That was the trouble. It was in gear. The speedometer showed impossible figures; the automatic calendar said that the time was 7 P.M., August 28, 4791 Isher. Hedrock nodded to himself. So he had been unconscious for twenty-two days; and during that time the ship had gone—he glanced at the speedometer again—and turned away swiftly without hazarding even the beginning of an estimate.

The movement brought a whirling in his brain, and a blur of nausea. He sat for a while, being quietly but violently sick. Slowly, however, his body that had withstood so many strains, struck a metabolistic balance. And he realized that hunger had brought that painful dizziness. He made two attempts to get to his feet, and each time fell back ill and dizzy. The third time he lowered himself to the floor, and crawled toward the galley.

Eating required a full hour because, after the first few sips of a reviving dextrose liquid, he forced himself to a careful diet. Afterward, it struck him that he ought to sleep. He hesitated. There was the problem of his distance away from Earth, and the curious lack of acceleration pressure. Somewhere in the course of his flight, the stellar drive had attained a supernatural oneness with some great basic force. And the Point ooooo . . . 1 of inertia had vanished. He went back to the control board, switched off the lights again, and sat for minutes manipulating the telescopic adjustors on the 'stats. A few stars waxed brighter, but none grew in size. None showed any evidence of being really nearer. The speedometer still registered something over four hundred million miles a second. At that rate, he was covering the distance between Earth and Centaurus every eighteen hours. The problem was to retrace his course.

Thoughtfully, he eased the clutch of the automatic half-circle into the steering shaft. It whirred and then went *ticaticatic* a hundred and eighty times, very fast. The stars reeled, but settled into steadiness as the stop watch showed three seconds. A perfect hairpin turn in twelve hundred million miles. At that rate he would be within sight of Earth's sun in another twenty-two days. No, wait! It wasn't as simple as that. He couldn't subject himself again to the kind of pressure that had held him unconscious so long. After some estimations, he set the drive lever at three quarters reverse. And waited. The question was, how soon had he recovered consciousness after the pressure stopped? Two hours passed, and still nothing had happened. His head kept drooping, his eyes closing. But the blow of deceleration didn't come.

He went back to look at the engines. But the meters showed a seventy-five percent drain of power. The outer plate of the drive shaft felt normally warm and tense. It was disturbingly obvious that he had been a long time in the supernormal force field that had nullified the remnants of his inertia, much longer than seemed reasonable or safe. Uneasily expectant, Hedrock finally went to sleep on one of the couches.

There was a jar that shook his bones. Hedrock awakened with a start, but he calmed swiftly as he felt the steady pressure on his body. It was strong, like the current of a very heavy wind. But now that he had taken the first shock, it was bearable. What interested him was, at what point of speed had he emerged from the mysterious inertialess field back into the world of deceleration pressures? He ached to leap up and examine the speedometer. But he held himself where he was. He was acutely conscious of the tingling readjustments going on in his body, the electronic, atomic, molecular, neural, muscular readjustments. He gave himself thirty minutes before moving. Then he headed for the control boards and peered into the 'stats. But there was nothing to see. The calendar said August 29, 11:03 P.M., and the speedometer was down to three hundred and fifty million miles. He'd do the calculating on that later.

Things were at last on the way to being done. He'd have to be careful, of course, lie down again, and eat, and so gradually build up his strength. It was hard to stay in bed, but finally he slept. He woke up feeling strangely melancholy. His gloom deepened as he sat, a few minutes later, staring into the 'stats. Everything seemed very far away, very far. Against this background of immensity, how futile seemed the blind, mothlike fluttering of men toward the light of ultimate truth. The very violence of the struggle to suppress, and, conversely, to force into the open, the secret of the stellar drive, seemed to take on meaningless qualities. In the face of the terrific night of the universe, it didn't matter. Suddenly, it seemed incredible that such a woman existed as the Imperial Innelda Isher, with her almost mindless will to safeguard the power of her clan.

Hedrock shook off his unhappy mood, and stared out at the fixed stars, conscious that the days and the hours of flight were going to be long for one man alone in vastness. His velocity declined something less than twelve million miles a second during the next twenty-four hours. Hedrock frowned over that. A faint fear came that the time the ship had been in the inertialess space had introduced an element of dangerous uncertainty. At his present deceleration, the lifeboat should come to a full stop in about thirty-two days, at most.

The third day also showed a reduction of more than eleven million miles a second. The hollow feeling went slowly out of him, as he watched the average of deceleration develop steadily hour by dragging hour. It grew increasingly clear that, above three hundred and fifty million miles a second, increases and decreases in speed must be governed by far more potent laws than they were here.

Four times as much at least, though there seemed to be an upper limit.

As the days dragged by, he brought his calculations down to a fine point of accuracy. With satisfaction, Hedrock watched the light on the speedometer grow darker, darker, until the beam of force quivered gently, and stopped. A glowing sign flashed on the instrument board: DRIVE OFF. SHIP AT REST.

His estimates were an hour and nineteen minutes askew, a bull's-eye for the distance he had flown. His satisfaction dimmed somewhat as he peered into the 'stat plates. He manipulated the telescope adjustors and the automatic estimators. The nearest sun showed approximately two light years to his left, and its prismatic register showed little relation to Earth's Sol.

It was too yellow. It was the color of a deep-toned egg. And the effect grew as his machine plunged toward it. At nine hundred million miles, it was a jaundiced ball of fire whose ochroid no earthly eye had ever gazed on before him. That wouldn't have mattered so much except that the star seemed to have no recognizable distance connection with any of the nearer stars. It was seven light years from a faint red sun almost straight beyond it. There was a blue star seventeen light years to the right. The third nearest star in any direction that he could discover was more than forty light years beyond the blue sun.

He decided to check thoroughly. Space was ablaze, and it would be easy to miss Sol or Centaurus looking at the heavens from his present strange position. Three planets swam into his ken but, as with the stars, Hedrock knew there could be others. The telescope adjustors on so small a ship had not the capacity for first-class magnification. After critical examination, he selected a planet about eighty million miles from the sun. It was seven thousand miles in diameter, and it seemed to have an atmosphere.

It did. The lifeboat settled through a thick cushion of air, out over a sea, and then circled slowly back under his guiding fingers toward a continent. Hedrock came down within sight of the sea beside a virgin forest. Air pressure was seventeen pounds, oxygen content thirty percent, and nothing poisonous in deadly quantities. He ventured forth gingerly and stood on a carpet of thick, gray grass. A faint wind was blowing, but there was silence around him, broken only by the lapping of water on the nearby sandy beach.

He took a swim, and then watched the yellow sun sink toward the horizon of heaving waters. Night came suddenly, and brought with it a loneliness more intense than any he had known in space. All night long, the sea mourned on the lifeless beach, the eternal dirge of water meeting land. And, in the morning, as he soared up to continue his journey, the planet spun behind him emptily through the dark waste around its sun, one more uninhabited hostage to the fortune of worlds that Nature had spawned in her attempt to create intelligence. He had known, of course. Yellower was that planet's sun than old Sol would ever be. Yellow and strange and alien.

The blue sun hurtled nearer; and the hope that it would be Sirius died only when the 'stats confirmed definitely that there was no companion star. There *were* planets. A dozen pale orbs stood out in the first telescopic sweep, but they only emphasized the reality. He was lost. Lost in a night that grew more meaningless every hour. He slept restlessly, then returned to the control chair.

He had barely settled into it when there was a jar that shook every plate in the lifeboat. The little craft spun like driftwood in a whirlpool. It was the chair that saved Hedrock, the all-purpose chair. Light as thistledown, it twisted as fast as the ship, holding him always downward and steady; and with him the entire control board.

The surrounding space was aswarm with monstrously large torpedo-shaped ships. Every 'stat showed dozens of the mile-long things; and each stupendous machine was drawn up as part of a long line that completely enveloped his small craft. Out of that mass of machines came a thought. It boiled into the control room like an atomic gas bubble. It was so strong that, for an instant, it had no coherency. And even when it did, it was a long moment before Hedrock's staggered mind grasped that the titanic thought was not for him, but *about* him.

"—an inhabitant of . . . !!!—meaningless . . . Intelligence type nine hundred minus. . . . Study value Tension 1. . . . Shall it be destroyed?"

The mad, private thought that came to Hedrock, as he sat there with tottering reason, expecting death, was that this was the relation-value of all that desperate fighting on Earth to suppress the interstellar drive. It didn't matter. It was too late. Man was too slow by a measureless time. Greater beings had long since grasped all of the universe that they desired, and the rest would be doled out according to their savage will. . . . Too late, too late—

ELEVEN

It could have been one minute or many that passed as Hedrock sat there. When he finally began to observe again, he had the sensation of emerging from darkness. It was startling to realize that he wasn't dead. His will to live surged up into a bright pattern of purpose. His gaze narrowed on the 'stat plates. They were like windows through, which he peered out at the mass of spaceships that surrounded him. The fear that came was not for himself, but for man. There were so many, too many. The implication of their presence was deadly.

But he was alive. The conscious, second thought of life galvanized him. His fingers flashed toward the controls. He glanced along the sighting guides, aimed at an opening between two of the massive vessels, plunged home the adjustor, waited an instant for the lifeboat to swing into line—and deliberately snapped the white accelerator far over. Their control of him, he was thinking, would be a balance of forces based upon his partial acceleration, which would be overcome by putting on full speed.

His mind made a pause, for there was darkness, a gulf of physical, not mental darkness. Hedrock tore the drive out of gear. He recalled after a blank moment that there had been the faintest tug of movement. Now, there was nothing—no ships, no stars, not a sign of the fiery ball that had been the blue sun. Nothing at all. It wasn't that the 'stats were blank. They were on. But they registered blackness unqualified by light. After a moment, he touched a button on the instrument board. Almost immediately a word glowed up at him. It said simply: Metal.

Metal! Surrounded by metal. That meant he was inside one of

the mile-long alien ships. Just how it had been done was a mystery, but if the Weapon Makers on Earth had a vibratory transmission system, whereby material objects could be sent through walls and over distances, then the absorption of his lifeboat into the hold of a bigger machine was well within the realm of possibility.

He felt torn by a soaring comprehension of his situation. He sank back against the chair, weakened and exhausted by the intensity of his emotional conflict. After a while his mind steadied. He was obviously a prisoner, and in due course would learn his fate. He settled back and waited. But the minutes ticked away with no sign of his captors. He became hungry. He turned on the cooking tubes and prepared a meal. It was while he was waiting that he began to question his instinctive policy of sitting tight and awaiting developments. After all, these were intelligent beings. They were letting him live—which must mean that he had been found of some value. Hedrock finished eating, and then climbed into a spacesuit. He felt tense but very determined.

Ready finally, he opened the air lock, and stood for a moment thinking bleakly of how far he was from the Earth. And then he stepped down and out. There was no gravity, and so he floated down under the impetus of a push on the lock. His flashlight blazed an intense path downward, revealing a flat plain of metal, with walls sharply delineated in the near distance, walls with doors in them.

The picture was normal, even ordinary. He need only try all the doors, and if one opened, follow through. The first door opened effortlessly. After a moment, his nervous reflexes caught up with his staggered mind, and he felt an intense wonder. He was staring down at a city from a height of about two miles. The city glittered and shone from a blaze of hidden light, and it was set in a garden of trees and shrubs in bloom. Beyond was green countryside, bright with a profusion of brush and meadows and sparkling streams. The whole curved gently upward into a haze of distance on the three sides that he could see. Except for the limited horizon, it could have been Earth.

The second tremendous shock struck Hedrock at that point. A city, he thought, an Earthlike city in a ship so big that—his mind couldn't grasp it. The spaceship, which had seemed a mile long, was actually at least fifty, and it was cruising through space with several hundred of its kind, each machine the size of a planetoid, and manned by superbeings.

Hedrock remembered his purpose. He held his thought on a cold, practical level as he estimated the size of the largest door. It seemed to him that it was large enough. He went back to the lifeboat. He had a moment of doubt as to whether the mysterious beings would permit it to move. It all depended on what they wanted him to do. His doubt ended as the little machine slipped gently forward, cleared the door by several feet, and landed a few minutes later on the outskirts of the city.

Safely landed, he sat there, letting the unpleasant thrill tingle along his nerves, the realization that this was what they wanted. There was no doubt that some overall purpose was being worked on him; and while precautions seemed ridiculous, nevertheless they must be taken. He tested the atmosphere. Air pressure was slightly over fourteen pounds, oxygen content was nineteen percent, nitrogen seventy-nine percent, temperature seventy-four, and gravitational pressure one G. He stopped there, because the figures were the same as for Earth.

Hedrock divested himself of his spacesuit. The possibility of resistance did not exist. Creatures who could casually, in minutes, re-create an Earth setting for him had him, *had* him. He stepped out of the lifeboat into silence. Ahead were empty streets that stretched on every side, a deserted city. There was not a breeze, not a movement. The nearby trees stood in the deathly quiet, their leaves curled stiffly, their branches steady. It was like a scene under glass, a garden in a bottle, and he the tiny figure standing rigidly. Only he wasn't going to stand there.

He came to a white, glistening building, wide and long but not very high. His knock made a hollow sound, and after a moment he tried the latch. The door opened and revealed, without any preliminary of vestibule or hallway, a small metal room. There was a control board, and a multipurpose chair, and a man sitting in the chair. Hedrock stopped as he saw that it was he, himself, sitting there, and that this was a replica of his spaceboat. Hedrock walked forward stiffly, half expecting the body to vanish as he approached. But it didn't. He expected his hand to pass through that false version of his own body. *But it didn't.* The feel of the clothes was unmistakable, and the flesh of the face was warm with life as he touched it with his fingers. The Hedrock who was in the chair paid no attention but continued to stare fixedly at the general 'stat plate.

Hedrock followed that intent gaze, and sighed when he saw

the empress's passionately earnest face image on it. So they were re-enacting Innelda's final order to him, without sound effects, without her vibrant voice urging him to land the spaceboat. He waited, wondering what was next on the program, but though several minutes went by the scene did not change.

His patience was considerable, but finally he backed away toward the door. Outside, he paused to realize how rigid his muscles had become. It was a figment that he had seen, he told himself tautly, a scene out of his memory re-created in some fashion. But why that scene? Why any?

On impulse he opened the door again, and peered inside. The room was empty. He closed the door, walked swiftly into the city, and felt the silence again like a pall around him. Slowly, he relaxed. Because he must face every facet of strangeness that his unseen captors had in store for him. Something about him had roused their interest, and it was up to him to force issues and so hold their attention until he had discovered the secret of their control over him.

Hedrock turned abruptly into the imposing entrance of a thirty-story marble skyscraper. The ornate door opened like the one in the first building he had entered, not into an anteroom, but directly into a room. It was a larger chamber than the first. There were guns in floor and wall showcases, and in the corner sat a man opening a letter. The first shock had already come to Hedrock. This was the Linwood Weapon Shop, and the man in the corner was Daniel Neelan. The interview scene between Neelan and himself was about to be re-enacted.

He walked forward, conscious that something was wrong with the picture. It was not quite as he remembered it. He realized abruptly what was wrong. Neelan had not been reading a letter when they first met.

Was it possible that this was something that had happened afterwards?

As he paused directly behind the seated Neelan, and glanced at the letter the other was holding, Hedrock realized that it was very possible indeed. The envelope had a Martian post-office mark on it. This was the mail that the Weapon Shops had offered to obtain for Neelan, and this was Neelan *after* the two of them had been to 1874 Trellis Minor Building.

But how was it being done? It was one thing to build up a scene which they had obtained from his memory, quite another to enact something in which he had not participated, and which had taken place countless light years away, and nearly two months ago. Yet there must be a reason why they were performing so difficult a feat for his benefit. He decided that his captors wanted him to read the letter that Neelan had received.

He was bending forward to read it when there was a momentary blur before his eyes. It ended, and he realized he was sitting down instead of standing, and that he himself was now holding the letter. The changeover was so startling that Hedrock involuntarily turned in the chair, and looked behind him.

For long moments he stared at the body of himself that stood there, rigid, leaning slightly forward, eyes fixed and unwinking; and then, slowly, he faced about again, and stared down—at Neelan's clothes, Neelan's hands and Neelan's body. He began to feel the difference, to become aware of Neelan's thoughts and intense emotional interest in the letter.

Before Hedrock could more than realize that somehow—somehow—*his* "mind" had been put into Neelan's body, Neelan was concentrating on the letter. It was from his brother Gil, and it read:

Dear Dan:

Now I can tell you about the greatest invention in the history of the human race.

I had to wait till now, a few hours before we leave, because we could not take the risk of the letter being intercepted. We want to present the world with a *fait accompli*. When we come back, we intend to shout our news from the housetops, and have endless film and other records to support our story. But to get down to facts.

There are seven of us, headed by the famous scientist, Derd Kershaw. Six of us are science specialists. The seventh is a fellow called Greer, a sort of general handyman who keeps the books and the records, who turns on the automatic cookers, and so on. Kershaw is teaching him how to operate the controls, so that the rest of us can be relieved of that chore—

Hedrock-Neelan paused there, sick to his soul. "The children!" he muttered huskily. "Those damned grown-up children." After a moment he thought: *So Greer was a handyman. No wonder the man had known nothing about science.*

He was about to read on, when Hedrock momentarily disentangled his ego from that compound awareness. He thought, almost blankly, *But Neelan didn't know about Greer. How could he have a feeling about him?* That was as far as he got. Neelan's compulsion to continue reading the letter overwhelmed his will to separate thought. *They* read on:

> I got into the affair as a result of Kershaw noticing an article of mine in the *Atomic Journal*, in which I described that I had been doing some contraterrene research exactly along the lines of an idea that he had for the development of his invention.
>
> Right here I might as well say that the chance of this discovery being duplicated by other researchers is practically nil. It embraces, in its conception, too many specialized fields. You know what we were taught during our training period, that there are nearly five hundred thousand special science fields, and that undoubtedly by skillful coordination of knowledges countless new inventions would be forthcoming, but that no known mind training could ever coordinate a fraction of these sciences, let alone all of them.
>
> I mention this to emphasize once again the importance of secrecy. Kershaw and I had a midnight conference, and I was hired under the most confidential terms.
>
> Dan, listen—the news is absolutely stupendous. We've got a drive that's so fast it's like a dream. The stars are conquered. Almost as soon as I finish this letter, we leave for Centaurus.
>
> I feel sick and shaky and cold and hot at the mere idea of it. It means everything. It's going to blow the world wide open. Just think of all those people who were forcibly dumped on Mars and Venus and the various moons—it had to be done, of course; somebody had to live there and exploit their wealth—but now there's hope, a new chance on greener, finer worlds.

From this point onward, man will expand without limit, and put an end forever to all those petty murderous squabbles over ownership of property. Henceforth, there will always be more than enough.

The reason we have to be so careful is that the Isher Empire will be shaken to its foundations by the unprecedented emigration that would begin immediately, and the empress Innelda will be the first to realize, the first to attempt our destruction. We're not even sure that the Weapon Shops will support such a change. After all, they are an integral part of the Isher setup; they have provided the checks and balances, and so have helped to create the most stable government system ever devised for unstable man. For the time being we prefer that they also do not find out what we have.

One more thing: Kershaw and I have discussed the possible effect of light years of distance on your and my sensory relation. He thinks that our speed of withdrawal from the solar system will give the effect of an abrupt break, and of course there will be the agony of acceleration. We—

Neelan stopped there. Because that was what he had felt, the agony, then the break! *Gil wasn't dead.* Or rather—his mind rushed on—Gil hadn't died that day a year ago. Somewhere during the journey Greer had—

At that point, Hedrock once more tore his own consciousness clear of that integrated reaction. "My God," he thought shakily, "we're a part of each other. He's having emotions based on my knowledge, and I'm experiencing the emotions as if they're my own. It would be understandable if I was his brother, with whom he had long had an established sensory relationship. But I'm not. I'm a stranger, and we've only met once."

His thought paused there. Because it was possible that to the alien scientists who were manipulating their two minds and bodies, there was no more difference between Neelan and himself than there had been between the Neelan twins. After all, most human nervous systems were structurally similar. If the two Neelans could be "attuned" to each other, then apparently so could any two human beings.

This time, having rationalized it, Hedrock offered no resistance to the re-merging of their separate identities. He expected to finish reading Gil's letter. But instead the letter blurred. Hedrock-Neelan blinked, and then he started violently as fine, hot sand laced against his face.

He saw that he was no longer in the Weapon Shop, and there was no sign of the phantom city. He twisted in a spasm of muscular reaction and realized that he was lying on a flat red desert under an enormous bulging sun. Far to his left, through a thick haze of dust, was another sun. It seemed to be farther away and was smaller, but it looked almost the color of blood in that world of powdered sand. Men lay nearby on the sand. One of them turned weakly; he was a big, fine looking fellow, and his lips moved. There was no sound, but in a curious fashion his turning the way he did brought into Neelan-Hedrock's line of vision boxes, crates and metal structures. Hedrock recognized a water making machine, a food case and a telestat. His observation was interrupted.

"Gil!" he shrieked. Or rather, it was Neelan's reaction. "Gil, *Gil*, GIL!"

"Dan!" It seemed to come from far away. It was more a wisp of thought in his mind than a sound. It was a tired sigh that bridged the great night. It began again, faint, faraway but clear, and directed at Neelan, "Dan, you poor mug, where are you? Dan, how are you doing this? I don't feel that you're close. . . . Dan, I'm a sick man, dying. We're on a freak planet that's going to pass close to one of the Centauri suns. The storms will grow worse, the air hotter. We—oh, God!"

The break was so sharp, it hurt like fire. It was like an overstretched elastic—giving. Countless light years rushed in to fill the gap. Hedrock realized that "they" had not actually been at the scene. It had been a sensory connection between the two brothers, and the picture of that nightmarish world had come through the eyes of Gil Neelan.

Whoever was doing this had achieved a fantastic control and understanding of human beings. It took a long moment to realize that Neelan was still in the Weapon Shop, and still clutching the letter. There were tears in his eyes, but presently it was possible to see the letter again, and to finish reading it:

. . . We will probably be completely separated for the first time since we were born. It's going to feel very empty and lonely.

I know you're envying me, Dan, as you read this. When I think how long man has dreamed of going to the stars, and of how it has been proved time and again that it can't be done, I know exactly how you feel. Particularly you who were the adventurer of our family.

Wish me luck, Dan, and watch your tongue.

Your other half,
Gil.

Just when the transformation occurred, or by what stages, Hedrock wasn't sure. His first awareness of change was that he was no longer in the Weapon Shop. That was not immediately important to him. His mind was caught up in thought of Gil Neelan and of the miracle that had been wrought. Somehow, these mighty captors of his had intensified the flimsy bonds between the two brothers, and made a thought connection across light centuries, an incredible, instantaneous connection.

And, casually, *he* had been taken along on that fantastic journey.

Odd, how dark it was. Since he was not in the Weapon Shop, he should logically be back in the "city," or somewhere on the ship of the beings who had captured him. Hedrock lifted himself, and by that action realized that he had been lying face downward. As he moved, his hands and feet tangled in a network of intertwined ropes. He had to grab at the individual strands of rope to balance himself. He swayed there in pitch darkness.

He had been holding himself calm, fighting with all his strength to comprehend each separate experience. But this one was too much. Panic struck him like a physical blow. Instead of a floor there was a mesh of ropes like the rigging in the ships that sailed the seas of Earth in olden days, or like the web of some nightmare-sized spider. His thought paused, and a chill spread down his spine. *Like a spider's web.*

A vague bluish light began to grow around him, and he saw that the city was indeed gone. In its place was an unearthly dark-blue world, and webs, miles and miles of webs. They reared up toward the remote ceiling and vanished into the distance of the dimness. They spread out in all directions, fading into the seminight like things of some nether world. And, mercifully, they did not appear to be inhabited at first.

Hedrock had time to brace his brain for the most terrible shock its highly trained structure would ever have to face. He had time to grasp that this was the interior of the ship, and that there *must* be inhabitants. Far above him, there was suddenly a flicker of movement. Spiders. He saw them plainly, huge things with many legs, and grew tense with the bitterness of his realization. So a tribe of spiderlike beings were Nature's prize package, the supreme intelligence of the ages, rulers of the universe. The thought seemed to be in his mind a very long time, before a faint light focused on him from a hidden source. Abruptly, a very thunderbolt of mind vibrations rocked his brain:

"—examination negative. . . . There is no physical connection between these beings . . . energy only—"

"But the tensions were augmentable by energy. The connection was contrived across—xxx?!! distance."

"—my finding is that there is no physical connection—" Coldly.

"I was merely expressing amazement, mighty xx—!! (meaningless name). Here is undoubtedly a phenomenon closely related to the behavior of this race. Let us ask him—"

"MAN!"

Hedrock's brain, already strained under the weight of those enormous thoughts, cringed before that direct wave. "Yes?" he managed finally. He spoke aloud. His voice made a feeble sound against the blue-dark vastness, and was swallowed instantly by the silence.

"MAN, WHY DID ONE BROTHER MAKE A LONG JOURNEY TO FIND OUT WHAT HAD HAPPENED TO THE OTHER BROTHER?"

For a moment the question puzzled Hedrock. It seemed to refer to the fact that Dan Neelan had come from a remote meteor to the Earth to find out why the sensory connection with his brother Gil had been broken. It seemed a fairly meaningless question, because the answer was so obvious. They were brothers, they had been brought up together, they had a very special intimate relationship. Before Hedrock could explain the simple elements of human nature involved, the titanic thunder raged down again at his mind:

"MAN, WHY DID YOU RISK YOUR LIFE SO THAT OTHER HUMAN BEINGS CAN GO TO THE STARS? AND WHY DO YOU WANT TO GIVE THE SECRET OF IMMORTALITY TO OTHERS?"

In spite of the tattered state of Hedrock's thoughts understanding began to streak through. These spider beings were trying to comprehend man's emotional nature *without having themselves a capacity for emotion.* Here were blind things asking to have color explained to them, stone-deaf creatures being given a definition of sound. The principle was the same.

What they had done was explained now. The apparently meaningless re-enactment of the scene between himself and the empress had been designed so that his emotions could be observed while he was risking his life for an altruistic purpose. In the same way and for a similar reason, the sensory connection had been established between the Neelans and himself. They wanted to measure and assess emotions in action.

Once more a clamor of outside thought interrupted him: "IT IS REGRETTABLE THAT ONE OF THE BROTHERS DIED, BREAKING THE CONNECTION—"

"THAT NEED BE NO DETERRENT. NOR IS THE BROTHER ON EARTH NEEDED, NOW THAT WE HAVE ESTABLISHED A DIRECT CONNECTION BETWEEN OUR PRISONER AND THE DEAD ONE. A MAJOR EXPERIMENT IS IN ORDER—"

"X-XX?!X PROCEED AT ONCE."

"WHAT IS TO BE DONE FIRST?"

"GIVE HIM FREEDOM, OF COURSE."

There was a prolonged pause, then a blur. Hedrock grew taut, and involuntarily closed his eyes. When he opened them again, he saw that he was in one of his secret laboratories on Earth, the one in which the giant rat had nearly killed him.

TWELVE

He *seemed* to be back on the Earth. Hedrock climbed gingerly to his feet, and examined himself. He was still wearing the insulation suit, which Greer had given him, and in which he had dressed himself before leaving the lifeboat to wander around in the Earth-like "city" the spider beings had created for him. He looked around the room slowly, searching for tiny discrepancies that would indicate that this was another illusion.

He couldn't be sure. And yet he felt different than when they had been manipulating him. Then there had been an overall atmosphere of unreality. He had been like a man in a dream. He no longer felt that way.

He stood frowning, remembering the last thoughts he had received from them. One of the beings had definitely indicated that he was to be given his freedom for the next phase of their experiment. Hedrock was not sure what they meant by freedom, because it was clear that they were still studying human emotional behavior. But he had been in danger so often in his life that, in the final issue, he did not allow personal fear to alter his purposes. He did however want to test the reality of his surroundings.

He walked to the general 'stat in one of the study rooms, and tuned into a news channel. It was a drab account to which he listened then. The commentator was concerned with some new laws which were under discussion by the Imperial Parliament. There was no mention of the interstellar drive. If there had been any excitement at the time of his escape from Kershaw's ship it had apparently died down. Whatever effort had been made to force the empress to give up the secret seemed to have been abandoned.

He shut off the 'stat, and changed into a "business" suit. Carefully, he selected four more ring weapons, and then, arrayed for battle, he stepped through a transmitter into one of his apartments in Imperial City. He began to feel a lot better. In the back of his mind he had plans for experiments *he* was going to conduct if the spider beings tried to take control of him again, but he was still anxious about the exact nature of the "freedom" he had been given. He hurried to the great window that overlooked the city looking south. For more than a minute Hedrock gazed at the familiar scene of the tremendous metropolis; and then, turning slowly, he walked over to the apartment 'stat, and called Public News Service.

The news organization was associated with the Weapon Shops, and provided free information and news. The girl who talked to Hedrock answered all his questions without asking his identity. From her he learned definitely that the empress had publicly and repeatedly denied all knowledge of an interstellar drive, and that the Weapon Shops after two weeks of intense propaganda against her had dropped their campaign abruptly.

Hedrock broke the connection grimly. So Innelda had gotten away with it. He could understand why the Weapon Shops had ceased putting presure on her. Theirs would be an increasingly unpopular cause, for they had no evidence to offer; and they were too logical to pursue openly a matter which might turn people against them. It could be taken for granted that ninety percent of the population would long ago have lost interest in the affair. Of those who remained, the majority wouldn't know what to do, even if they believed that the drive existed. How did one force the hereditary ruler of the solar system to give up a secret?

Hedrock, who had his own ideas of how it would have to be done, became grimmer. He moved across to the library, and studied the century clock. He had several problems. It would take a little while to organize his campaign, and his time of action must be postponed until a Rest Day.

As for the spider beings, they were an unknown factor, whose movements he could not control. He'd have to act as if they did not exist.

"Let's see now," he muttered half to himself, "today is October first, and tomorrow is—*Rest Day!*"

That shocked him. It meant that he had one afternoon to prepare for the most sustained physical effort in his career. What disturbed him was that the preliminary would not be at all simple. Imagine facing men like Nensen, Deely and Triner when he was in a hurry. But there was no time to waste in regret that the situation wasn't different.

He returned to his underground laboratory, and began a detailed study of a very large 'stat which occupied one corner of his transport room. The 'stat was lined with row on row of glow points, slightly more than fifteen hundred. It took a while to punch out the score of individual numbers that he wanted. Seventeen of them turned a rich green. The other three flashed red, which meant that the three men at the other end were not in their offices. Seventeen out of twenty was better than he had expected. Hedrock straightened from his job of selection, and faced the 'stat as it started to glow.

"Take a good look at me," he said. "You will probably be seeing me today."

He paused, considering his next words. It would be foolish to indicate that he was talking to more than one individual. Undoubtedly, some of the shrewd men listening in probably knew that other firms were in the same position as their own, but it would be gratuitous folly to confirm their suspicion.

Satisfied, Hedrock went on, "Your firm will remain open until tomorrow morning. Provide sleeping quarters, entertainment and food for the staffs. Continue with normal business until the usual hour, or until further notice. Employees must be paid a twenty percent bonus for this week. For your private information, a great emergency has arisen, but if you do not hear further by 7 A.M. tomorrow, consider the matter closed. Meanwhile, read Article Seven of your incorporation papers. That is all."

He clicked off the 'stat and grimaced at the lateness of the hour. At least thirty minutes must lapse between his verbal and his first physical call. There was no other way. It was impossible that he appear in person a minute after his 'stat message. The message would have caused a big enough sensation as it was, without the added complication of his immediate arrival.

Besides, he still had to rig up a magnifier control, and swallow the magnifier. He stood finally with narrowed eyes, considering the potentialities of the interviews that he had to make. Some of the executives out there would be extremely hard to dominate quickly. He had been intending to take action against several of them for a long time. They'd been big bosses too long. His policy of letting a family operate for generations, merely paying into a central fund, but otherwise without control, had progressively weakened his authority. It couldn't be helped. Control of so many was a practical impossibility.

The half hour up, Hedrock plugged in a transmitter, examined the gleaming corridor that showed beyond. He stepped through. The door he finally came to had a sign on it:

STAR REALITY CO.
TRILLION CREDITS IN PROPERTIES
Office of the President
J. T. TRINER
Trespassers Forbidden

With his ring, Hedrock actuated the secret mechanism of the door. He walked in, straight past the pretty girl at the great reception desk, who tried to stop him. The rays of his ring automatically unlocked the second door. He stepped inside to find himself in a large and imposing office. A big, pale-faced, pale-eyed man rose from behind a curving monster of a desk, and stared at him.

Hedrock paid no attention. One of the other rings that he had put on his finger was tingling violently. He turned his hand slowly. When the tingling stopped, the ring stone was pointing directly at the wall behind the desk. It was a good job of camouflage, Hedrock decided admiringly. The wall design was unbroken, the enormous blaster behind it perfectly hidden. Without his finder ring, he would never have spotted it.

Abruptly, he felt grimmer. He allowed himself the icy and swift thought that his discovery only confirmed his opinion of the man. A veritable cannon hidden in his office—what damnable stuff! His private case history of Triner showed that he wasn't merely self-centered and ruthless, common traits in an age of gigantic administration trusts. Nor was he simply amoral; hundreds of thousands of Isher citizens had committed as many murders as Triner, but the difference in motive was like the difference between right and wrong. Triner was a prurient wretch, a lecherous skunk, a very hound of evil.

The man was coming forward, holding out his hand, a hearty smile on his pale face, a hearty tone to his voice, as he said, "I don't know whether to believe in you or not, but at least I'm willing to listen."

Hedrock strode toward the outstretched hand as if to shake it. At the last instant, he stepped past the man and in a moment had seated himself in the big chair behind the curving desk. He faced the startled executive, thinking savagely: So Triner was willing to talk, was he? That was nice. But first he'd get some psychological bludgeoning and a lesson in straightforward ruthlessness with emphatic punctuation of the fact that there were tougher men in the world than J. T. Triner. Keep pushing him; keep him off balance. Hedrock said curtly:

"Before you sit down *in that chair*, Mr. Triner, before we talk, I want you to start your staff on the job you're going to do for me—are you listening?"

There was no doubt about it. Triner was not only listening, he was shocked and angry and bewildered. Like so many strong men subjected for the first time to the full force of a personality aura that was almost an energy in itself, he seemed unable to adjust his mental and physical functions to the reality. Not that he looked cowed. Hedrock knew better than to expect fear. Triner's expression simply grew cautious, with a mixture of curiosity thrown in. He said, "What is it you want done?"

That was too important for ruthlessness of manner. Hedrock drew a folded paper from his pocket. "There," he said earnestly, "are the names of fifty cities. I want all my business properties in those cities listed according to avenues and streets. Never mind who's in them. Just get the street numbers, two, four, six, eight and so on. And only in cases where there are many in a row, such as a whole block, at least a dozen altogether. Do you follow that?"

"Yes, but—" Triner looked dazed. Hedrock cut him off:

"Give the order." He studied the man from narrowed eyes, then he leaned forward. "I—hope—Triner—that you have been living up to Article Seven of your constitution."

"But, man, that article was promulgated nearly a thousand years ago. You can't mean—"

"Can you provide that list, or can't you?"

Triner was sweating visibly. "I guess so," he said finally. "I really don't know. I'll see." He stiffened abruptly, added through clenched teeth, "Damn you, you can't come in here and—"

Hedrock realized when he had pushed a man far enough. "Give the order," he said mildly, "then we'll talk."

Triner hesitated. He was a badly shaken man, and, after a moment, he must have realized that he could always countermand any instructions. He said, "I'll have to use the desk 'stat."

Hedrock nodded and watched and listened while the order was transmitted to an underling chief. The man at the other end of the 'stat protested, but giving orders was more in Triner's line than receiving them. He barked like a sea lion, and seemed to recover more of his aplomb with every word. He drew up his chair alongside the desk. He smirked at Hedrock.

"What's the dope?" he asked in a confidential tone. "What's it all about?"

The man's seeming acquiescence gave him away. Hedrock sat icily thoughtful. So the controls of the gun were *in* the desk, somewhere beside where Triner had drawn his chair. Hedrock studied the physical situation thoughtfully. He was sitting at the desk, his back to the cannon, and with Triner to his left. The door leading to the outer office was about fifty feet away, and beyond it was the reception girl. The wall and door would protect her. Anybody else who came in would have to be kept well to the left, preferably behind and beside Triner. Hedrock nodded with satisfaction. His gaze had never left Triner; and now he said:

"I'm going to tell you everything, Triner—" that was an appetizer for the man's undoubted curiosity, and should restrain his impatience. Hedrock went on—"but first I want you to do one more thing. You have an executive accountant in the head office here, named Royan. Ask him to come up. After I've spoken to him, you'll have a better idea as to whether he'll be in the firm after today."

Triner looked puzzled, hesitated, and then spoke briefly into the 'stat. A very clear, resonant voice promised to come up immediately. Triner clicked off, and leaned back in his chair. "So you're the man behind that mysterious wall 'stat," he temporized finally.

He waved his hand at the design on the wall beside him, then said suddenly, his voice intense, "Is the empress behind us? Is it the House of Isher that owns this business?"

"No!" said Hedrock.

Triner looked disappointed, but said, "I'm going to believe that, and do you know why? The House of Isher needs money too badly and too continuously to let a treasure like this company vegetate the way it's been doing. All that stuff about dividing the profits with the tenants periodically, whatever else it is, it isn't Isher."

"No, it isn't Isher," said Hedrock. And watched the baffled look that came into Triner's face. Like so many men before him, Triner didn't quite dare defy the secret owner so long as there was a possibility that the owner was the Imperial family. And Hedrock had found that denial only increased the doubts of the ambitious.

There was a knock at the door, and a young man of about thirty-five came in. He was a big chap with a brisk manner. His eyes widened a little as he took in the seating arrangement of the men in the private office. Hedrock said:

"You're Royan?"

"Yes." The young man glanced at Triner questioningly, but Triner did not look up.

Hedrock motioned to the decoration that was the wall telestat. "You have been previously informed as to the meaning behind this 'stat?"

"I've read the incorporation articles," Royan began; and then he stopped. Understanding poured into his eyes. "You're not that—"

"Let us," said Hedrock, "have no histrionics. I want to ask you a question, Royan?"

"Yes?"

"How much money—" Hedrock articulated his words—"did Triner take out of the firm last year?"

There was a little hiss of indrawn breath from Triner, then silence. The two men, Royan and Triner, looked at each other steadily for a long moment, an unmistakable and violent clash of minds. Finally, Royan laughed softly, an almost boyish laugh, and said, "Five billion credits, sir."

"That's a little high, isn't it," Hedrock asked steadily, "for a salary?"

Royan nodded. "I don't think Mr. Triner regarded himself as being on salary, but rather as an owner."

Hedrock saw that Triner was staring fixedly down at the desk, and his right hand was moving casually toward a tiny ornamental statue.

Hedrock said, "Come over here, Royan." He motioned with his left hand, waited until the young man had taken up a position to the left of Triner, and then manipulated the ring control of his own magnifier. The magnification involved was small, not more than an inch all around. He could have gained the same physical effect by sitting up and swelling out his chest. What was important about it was that it changed the basic structure of his "business" suit and of his own body. Both became virtually as impregnable as a Weapon Shop itself. Six months before, on entering the palace, he had racked his brain for a method whereby he might safely take the suit in with him, but the danger of having it stolen by alert palace spies while he was not wearing it had made that impossible. From its structure, any competent physicist could have analyzed at a glance the basic vibrational secret of the Weapon Shops. The suit not only carried the considerable power plant necessary to such an intensive form of magnification, but its innate construction served to confine the entire process to itself and to what it inclosed, a very necessary precaution.

Almost everything that had happened to him after his escape from the Weapon Makers was the result of his not being able to wear the suit into a Weapon Shop.

Hedrock felt the greater rigidity of his body; and his throat was stiffer, his voice slower, as he said, "I would say the salary was much too high. See that it is cut down to five million."

There was a wordless sound from Triner, but Hedrock went on speaking to Royan in that slow, steely voice, "Furthermore, in spite of its cooperative structure, this firm has acquired an unenviable reputation for remorselessness, and the policy of its president of having pretty women picked up in the street and taken to his various secret apartments is—"

He saw the final movement as Triner convulsively grasped the statuette. Hedrock stood up, as Royan yelled a warning.

The fire from the cannon disintegrated the chair on which Hedrock had sat, spumed off the metal desk, drenched the ceiling with flame. It was immensely violent, at least ninety thousand cycles of energy, but it was not so strong that Hedrock did not notice the flash of Royan's gun. After a moment, the sequence of events was clear. Triner had manipulated and fired the cannon at Hedrock, then whirled, drawing his imperial gun with the intention of killing Royan. But Royan, using a Weapon Shop defensive model, had fired first.

Where Triner had been was a shiningness that twinkled and faded instantly as the powerful suction pumps (automatically set off by the cannon) drew great gulps of fresh air through the room. It was a standard process, so swift that the total volume of air in the room was actually changed five times a second.

In the office, between Hedrock and Royan, silence settled. "I don't see," said Royan finally, "how you escaped."

The man looked excited. His voice trembled. He was white and he obviously needed patient handling for a few minutes. Only, there wasn't time. No time at all. Already, it seemed to Hedrock, he had spent far too many precious minutes in one office. Hedrock switched off his magnification, said hurriedly:

"You're the new president of the company, Royan. Your salary is five million a year. What kind of mind-training course are you giving your son?"

Royan was recovering more rapidly than Hedrock had expected. "The usual," he said.

"Change it. The Weapon Shops have recently published the details of a new course, which is not very popular as yet. It includes the strengthening of moral functions. But now . . . when will the lists be ready that Triner ordered for me? Or don't you know about them?"

The speed of the conversation seemed to be dazing Royan again, but he carried the load. "Not before six. I—"

Hedrock cut him off. "You are going to get some awful shocks tomorrow, Royan, but bear up. Don't lose your head. We have incurred the wrath of a powerful secret organization. We are to be given a lesson. There will be great destruction of our property, but do not under any circumstances let on to anyone that it *is* our property, nor begin reconstruction for a month, or until further notice."

He finished grimly, "We must take our losses without outcry. Fortunately, tomorrow is Rest Day. The people will be away from their shops. But remember, have—those—lists—ready—at—six!"

He left the man abruptly. The reference to a secret organization was as good a story as any, and when the giant started moving, all its weaknesses would be dwarfed by the horrendous reality. But first, now, some other calls, a few of the easier ones, then eat, then the arrogant Nensen, and then take action on the vastest scale.

He killed Nensen an hour later by the simple method of reflecting the energy of the man's own gun back at him. The once indomitable Deely turned out harmless, a reformed monster of an old man who resigned swiftly when he saw that Hedrock was not interested in so delayed a conversation. The other men were obstacles whose curiosity and mental inertia had to be overcome. It was a quarter to seven the next morning when Hedrock took an energy drug, several vitamin shots and lay down for half an hour to let them work on his weary body.

He ate an enormous breakfast, and a few minutes before eight o'clock adjusted the magnifier of his "business" suit to full power. The day of the giant had come.

THIRTEEN

A few minutes before the first news came through, Innelda was saying coldly, "Why do we always need money? Where does it go? Our annual budget is astronomical, and yet all I ever see are statements showing that so much of it goes for one general department and so much of it for another, and so on *ad nauseum*. The solar system is wealthy beyond estimate; the daily turnover at the Exchange runs into hundreds of billions of credits; and yet the government has no money. What's the matter? Are tax receipts in arrears?"

There was silence. The lord of finance glanced helplessly around the long cabinet table. His gaze came to rest finally on the face of Prince del Curtin. His eyes lighted up with silent appeal. The Prince hesitated, and then said:

"These cabinet meetings are beginning to follow a pattern, Your Majesty. The rest of us are silent while you nag us. These days you have the perpetual complaining tone of a wife who, having spent all her husband's money, berates him for not having more."

She was slow in realizing the implications of that. She was so accustomed to plain speaking in private from her cousin that it did not strike her immediately that this comment was being made during an official meeting of the cabinet. She noted absently that the other men seemed relieved, but she was concentrating too hard on her own words for the full meaning to penetrate. She went on angrily:

"I am tired of being told that we haven't the money to carry on the normal expenses of government. The Imperial household expenses have been the same for generations. Any private property I have is maintained out of its earnings, and not by the State. I have been told many times that we have been taxing business and individuals to the limit, and that in fact business complains bitterly of the burden. If these astute businessmen would examine their books they would discover that there is another less obvious drain upon their resources. I refer to the levies of that outrageous, illegal organization, the Weapon Shops, which taxes the resources of this country fully as heavily as the legitimate government. Their pretense that they sell only guns is one of the greatest frauds ever perpetrated on a people. Their method is cunningly designed to enlist the support of grasping individuals among the unthinking masses. It is common knowledge that you need merely make an accusation that a business firm has swindled you, and the secret Weapon Shop courts will adjudicate for you. The question is, when does legitimate profit become a swindle? It is a purely philosophical problem, and could be argued endlessly. But these Shop courts all too easily assess triple damages, give half the money to the accuser, and keep the other half themselves. I tell you gentlemen, we must start a campaign. We must convince businessmen that the Weapon Shops are a greater drain on them than is the government. Actually, of course, if businessmen were honest, it would make no difference. In such an event, the sanctimonious Weapon Makers would be exposed for the thieves they really are. Because, of course, they would still have to have money to maintain their organizations."

She paused, momentarily breathless, and remembered what Prince del Curtin had said earlier. She frowned at him. "So I sound like a nagging wife, do I, cousin? Having spent all my loving husband's money, I—"

She stopped short. She had a sudden, startled remembrance of the expression of relief that had come to the faces of the cabinet members after the Prince's comment. In a flash she realized what had not struck her before, that she had been personally accused in front of her whole cabinet.

"Well, I'll be damned!" she said explosively. "So I'm responsible. So I've been spending government money like an irresponsible woman—"

Once more she paused for breath. She was about to speak again when the 'stat beside her chair came to life. "Your Majesty, an urgent news message has just come through from the Middle West. A giant human being, one hundred and fifty feet tall, is destroying the business section of the city of Denar."

"*What?*"

"If you wish, I will show you the scene. The giant is retreating slowly before the attacks of mobile units."

"Never mind—" Her voice was cool and incisive. She finished her curt dismissal, "It must be some robotic machine built by a madman, and the navy can handle it. I cannot give the matter my attention at the moment. Report later."

"Very well."

During the silence that followed, she sat like a statue, her face whitely immobile, her eyes feeling hot in their sockets. She whispered finally, "Can it be some new action of the Weapon Shops?"

She hesitated, and then broke the thrall of what had happened. With a rush her mind came back to what she had been saying before the interruption. Her first words struck at the heart of the implied accusation.

"Prince, am I to understand that you hold me responsible in this public fashion for the financial predicament in which the government finds itself?"

The Prince was cool. "Your Majesty is misreading my words. My point was that these cabinet meetings have become nothing but scolding parties. The various departmental lords have a responsibility to parliament, and no useful purpose is served by destructive criticism."

She stared at him, and realized angrily that he had no intention of elaborating on his original statement. She said quickly, "Then you do not regard my suggestion that we inform businessmen of Weapon Shop thieving tactics—you do not regard that as constructive?"

The Prince was silent so long that she snapped, "Well, do you, or don't you?"

He stroked his jaw, and then looked directly at her. "No!" he said.

She stared at him wide-eyed, and breathless again. For this was being said in front of the entire cabinet. "Why not?" she said finally, in her most reasonable voice. "It would at least ease the pressure of criticism against us because taxes are so high."

"If it will make you happy," said Prince del Curtin, "it would probably do no harm to launch such a propaganda campaign. It shouldn't put us very much further in the red."

Innelda was cold again. "It has nothing to do with my happiness," she snapped. "I am thinking only of the State."

Prince del Curtin held his silence; and she gazed at him with a gathering determination. "Prince," she said earnestly, "you and I are related by blood. We are good friends in private, and we have had violent disagreements on many matters. However, now you have implied that I allow my private interests to intrude upon my responsibility to the State. Of course, I have always taken for granted that one cannot have two personalities, and that an individual's every act reflects to some extent his or her private prejudice. But there is a difference between unconscious assumptions which influence the individual's opinions—between that and a policy calculated to further the person's private ends. In what way have I become calculating? What made you suddenly utter a statement with so many implications? Well, I'm waiting."

"Suddenly is hardly the correct description," the Prince said drily. "For more than a month I have sat here listening with a gathering amazement to your impatient tirades. And I have asked myself one question. Would you like to know what that question is?"

The woman hesitated. The answer had already taken a turn that made her uneasy. She took the plunge. "Tell me."

"The question I asked myself," said Prince del Curtin, "was, 'What is bothering her? What decision is she trying to come to?' Now, the answer to that was not immediately obvious. We are all aware of your obsession with the Weapon Shops. On two different occasions you have been prepared to spend enormous sums of government money to further some action against the Weapon Shops. The first such incident occurred some years ago, and cost so much money that only last year was it paid off. And then a few months ago you began to make mysterious remarks to me, and you finally asked the cabinet to vote a large sum of money for a purpose which you did not then state, nor have you stated it since. Abruptly the fleet was called out, there was a charge made by the Weapon Makers that you had secured and were suppressing an interstellar drive. We financed a counter-propaganda, and eventually the affair fizzled out, although the cost as our budget figures show was colossal. I'd still like to know why you felt it necessary to have eight one-hundred-million-cycle energy guns constructed at a cost of one billion eight hundred million credits each. Please don't misunderstand me. I am not asking you to explain that. I assume from certain remarks of yours that the incident was successfully concluded. The questions then remained: Why were you not satisfied? What was wrong? I decided that the problem was internal not external, personal not political."

The empty feeling was expanding inside her. But still she didn't know where he was heading. She hesitated, and was lost. The prince continued:

"Innelda, you are thirty-two years old, and unmarried. There are rumors—forgive me for mentioning them—that you have lovers by the hundred, but I know for a fact that those rumors are false. Accordingly, to put it bluntly, it is damn well time you got married."

"Would you suggest," she asked in a voice that was just a little off key, "that I call forth all the young men of the land to perform deeds of derring-do, and that I marry the one who makes the best plum puddings?"

"That is quite unnecessary," said the Prince calmly. "You are already in love."

There was a stirring around the table. Smiles. Friendly faces. "Your Majesty," one man began, "this is the best news I've heard in—" He must have seen the expression on her face, because he faltered into silence.

She said, as if she had not heard the interruptions, "Prince, I am amazed. And who is the lucky young man?"

"Possibly one of the most formidable men whom I have ever met, but charming for all of his vitality and well worthy of your hand. He came to the palace about eight months ago, and you were immediately impressed with him, but unfortunately because of his antecedents, politically speaking, there was a conflict in your mind between your natural desires and your obsession."

She was aware now of whom he was talking, and she tried to head him off, "Surely, you are not referring to that young man whom I ordered hanged two months ago, but to whom I subsequently granted mercy."

Prince del Curtin smiled. "I admit your violent judgment against him puzzled me for a while, but actually it was merely another facet of the equally violent conflict going on in your mind."

Innelda was cool as she answered. "I seem to remember that

you offered no great objections to the execution order."

"I was bowled over. I have an innate loyalty to your person, and your positive statements against him confused me. It was only afterwards that I realized it all fitted."

"You don't think I was sincere in giving the order?"

The Prince said, "In this world, people continually destroy those they love. They even commit suicide, thus destroying the one they love most of all."

"And what has all this to do with the conflict that is going on in my mind, and which—ironically—is making a shrew out of me?"

"Two months ago you told me that you had informed Captain Hedrock—" She tensed slightly as the name was mentioned for the first time—"that you would invite him back to the palace in two months. The time is up, and you cannot make your mind to do so."

"You mean, my love has dimmed?"

"No." He was patient. "You have suddenly realized that calling him back would be an act far more significant than anything you imagined when you first named the time limit. In your mind it will be tantamount to an admission that the situation is exactly as I have stated."

Innelda stood up. "Gentlemen," she said with a faint, tolerant smile, "all this has been a revelation to me. I am sure that my cousin means well, and in a way it might be an excellent thing for me to get married. But I confess that I had never thought of Captain Hedrock as the individual who would have to hear my nagging all the rest of his life. Unfortunately, there is another reason why I have hesitated to marry, and so a third conflict should be added to the two mentioned by the prince. I—"

Beside her chair the telestat clicked on. "Your Majesty, the Weapon Makers' Council has just issued a statement in connection with the giant."

Innelda sat down. She felt a vague shock at the realization that she had forgotten about the meaningless titan with his seemingly senseless program of destruction. Now she gripped the edge of the long table. "I'll obtain a copy of it later," she said. "What is the gist?"

There was a pause, and then another, deeper voice took over: "A special statement has just been issued by the Weapon Makers' Council denouncing the hundred-and-fifty-foot giant, who has now devastated the business districts of the cities of Denar and Lenton.

The Weapon Makers state that the rumor that the giant is a Weapon Shop machine is absolutely false, and they emphasize that they will do all in their power to help capture the giant. As was reported earlier, the giant ran—"

She shut it off with a flick of her fingers. "Gentlemen," she said, "I think you had all better go back to your headquarters and stand by. The State is in danger, and this time—" She stared at her cousin—"this time it does not seem to be a product of any calculation on my part."

She broke off. "Good day to you, gentlemen."

As was customary, the cabinet lords remained at their places until she had left the room.

When she got back to her apartment, she waited a few minutes, and then put a call through to Prince del Curtin's office. His face came onto the plate almost immediately. His eyes grew questioning.

"Mad?" he asked.

"Of course not. You know better than that." She broke off. "Del, is there any information yet as to what the giant wants?"

"He wants release of the interstellar drive."

"Oh! Then it is the Shops."

The Prince shook his head. "I don't think so, Innelda," he said seriously. "They've issued a second statement within the past few minutes, apparently realizing that their propaganda of six weeks ago would be connected with the giant. They reiterate their demand that you release the drive, but deny any connection with the giant, and once more offer to help catch him."

"Their denial is ridiculous on the face of it."

Prince del Curtin said earnestly, "Innelda, if this giant continues his destruction, you'll have to do something besides make accusations against the Shops."

"Are you coming down to breakfast?" she asked.

"No, I'm going to Denar."

She stared at him anxiously. "Be careful, Del."

"Oh, I have no intention of getting killed."

She laughed abruptly. "I'm sure of it. You can tell me later what your reason is for going."

"It's no secret. I've been invited by the navy. I think they want a responsible witness to the efforts they are making, so that no charges can later be made that they aren't doing everything in their power." He broke off. "So long."

"Goodbye," said Innelda. And clicked off her 'stat.

She spent the morning dictating letters. At lunch in the main salon, so many anxious glances were turned her way that, when she went back to her apartment, she immediately turned on the 'stat and had a look at the giant. Her first sight of him showed him ravaging a city street. He was like a gigantic madman, a veritable destroying demon. She stared at him in a gathering fascination of horror, almost of disbelief. Buildings crashed before his incredible advance. He shone in the sun like a monstrous knight in dazzling armor.

As she watched, a destroyer flashed near him, firing with all of its forty guns; and the flames splashed off the giant in an incandescent chromatic fury, as if he were a solid energy screen in himself. But she noticed with narrowed eyes that, after the attack, he stepped behind a tall building and partially crouched there as the destroyer came back. Baffled, the ship refrained from firing. It returned a minute later with two others, but the giant was farther away, leaving behind him a trail of destruction, a devastation of shattered buildings. He held up a small shop between himself and the ships' fire, and seemed immune and even unaware of the spumes of energy that bounced on him.

The woman thought, "He doesn't like direct fire, but he can stand it. Indirect energy doesn't bother him at all." With a shudder she snapped off the 'stat. The scene faded instantly from the plate.

She felt tired, and so she lay down for an hour. And she must have slept, because she work up to the sound of her private bedside 'stat. It was Prince del Curtin, looking and sounding very worried. "Innelda, have you been keeping track of the giant?"

She felt a sudden emptiness. It was still hard for her to grasp that such a menace had come out of nothingness only that morning, and was now threatening the nature of things Isher. She managed finally, "Is there anything special? I've been busy."

"Thirty-four cities, Innelda. Only one person killed yet, and that an accident. But think of it. It's real; it's no joke. The continent's beginning to boil like a toppled ant hill. He destroyed small establishments only, leaving the big companies untouched. A regular tidal wave of rumors have started about that, and I don't think any amount of propaganda is of value so long as the damned thing is at large." He broke off, "What is this about you hiding an interstellar drive? Is there any truth in it?"

She hesitated; then, "Why do you ask?"

"Because," he said grimly, "if it's true, and if that's what's behind the giant, then you'd better start thinking seriously of handing the secret over with the best possible grace. You can't stand another day of the giant."

"My dear—" she was cold, determined, "we'll stand a hundred days, if necessary. If an interstellar drive should be developed, the House of Isher would under present circumstances be opposed to it!"

"Why?"

"Because—" her voice was a resonant force, "our population would shoot off in all directions. In two hundred years, there'd be thousands of upstart royal families and sovereign governments ruling hundreds of planets, declaring wars like kings and dictators of old. And of all the people they would hate most would be the ancient House of Isher, whose living presence would make their loud pretensions ridiculous. Life on Earth would become one long series of wars against other star systems." She went on tautly, "It may seem silly to think of a situation as it would be two hundred years hence, but a family like ours, that has ruled in unbroken line for more than forty-seven hundred years, has learned to think in terms of centuries." She finished, "On the day that an administration method is developed whereby controlled stellar emigration is possible, on that day we could regard with approval such an invention. Until then—"

She stopped, because he was nodding, his lean, strong face thoughtful. "You're right, of course. That angle didn't occur to me. No chaos like that can be permitted. But our situation is becoming more serious every hour. Innelda, let me make a suggestion."

"Yes."

"You're going to be shocked."

A tiny frowned ceased her forehead. "Go ahead."

"All right. Listen: The Weapon Shops' propaganda is benefiting from the giant's handiwork, and at the same time they keep denouncing the giant. Let's take them up on that."

"What do you mean?"

"Let me get in touch with them. We've got to identify the people behind that giant."

"You mean, work with *them?*" She found her voice in an explosive outburst, "After three thousand years an empress of Isher begs the aid of the Weapon Markers? Never!"

"Innelda, the giant is at the present moment destroying the city of Lakeside."

"Oh!"

She was silent. For the first time, she felt dismayed. Glorious Lakeside, second only to Imperial City in splendor and wealth. She tried to picture the shining giant crashing through the wonder city of lakes. And, slowly, she nodded agreement. There was no longer any doubt. After one short day, the giant, with a single exception, had become the most important factor in a shattering world.

She hesitated; then, "Prince!"

"Yes."

"Captain Hedrock left me an address. Will you try to get in touch with him, and ask him to come to the palace, tonight if possible?"

Her cousin looked at her thoughtfully, said finally, simply, "What's the address?"

She gave it, and then sat back, forcing herself to relax. It was relieving after a minute to realize that she had made two great decisions.

It was a few minutes before five o'clock when the automatically relayed and recorded message from the empress reached Hedrock. The request that he come to the palace startled him. It was hard to believe that Innelda had become so panicky about the future of the House of Isher.

He ended his destructive campaign, and returned to his secret laboratory. Arrived there, he tuned in to the secret wavelength of the Weapon Makers' Council, or rather the wavelength they thought secret; and, disguising his voice, said, "Members of the Weapon Makers' Council, I am sure that you have already realized the great advantage to your own cause of what the giants are doing."

It seemed to Hedrock that he must keep stressing that there were more than one involved. The Weapon Shops knew only too well that a normal human being was aged five years every thirty minutes when enlarged. He went on urgently, "The giants need immediate assistance. The Weapon Makers must now take over, must send out volunteers to play the role of giant for fifteen minutes, or half an hour per person. They do not have to destroy, but their appearance will give an effect of continuity. It is also important that the Shops now resume in full force their propaganda to compel the empress to surrender the secret of the interstellar drive. It is essential that the first giant appear sometime early this evening. For the sake of the progressive forces of man, do not fail."

He was still in his hideout fifteen minutes later when the first of the giants appeared, so quick was the response. It was too quick. It showed private plans. It showed that the greatest power in the solar system was reacting like a finely poised steel spring; and he had no doubt that the plans included a determination to penetrate the identity of the person who knew their secrets. He was even prepared to believe that they knew who he was.

Accordingly, the time had come to bring into use one of his secret inventions. To begin with, he must make a trip through the one he had here in his hideout. Later, when the crisis came, he could make an attempt to utilize a replica that, long ago, he had secreted in the tombs of the palace. The next twelve hours would be decisive; and the great question was, would the spider beings let him carry through?

They showed no sign.

FOURTEEN

The warm, cloudy night was ablaze. The Long Street, the notorious Avenue of Luck, scintillated like a jewel as Gonish walked along it. Mile on mile of jewels, fusing in the remote distance in either direction to a shimmer of a mingled white and color. Signs glowed at the No-man, a glory of light-engraved messages:

WIN A FORTUNE
WALK IN WITH TEN CREDITS
WALK OUT WITH A MILLION

THE DIAMOND PALACE
10,000,000 DIAMONDS BLAZON INTERIOR

TRY YOUR LUCK IN A
SETTING OF DIAMONDS

There were more of that type as Gonish walked on: The RUBY PALACE—GOLD PALACE—EMERALD PALACE—intermingled with hundreds of no less gaudy structures. He came finally to his destination.

LUCK EMPORIUM
BETS AS LOW AS FIVE PENNIES
NO LIMIT

The No-man paused, smiling gravely. It was fitting that the empress had selected as their rendezvous one of her properties that catered to the masses. He must find out if she knew where Hedrock was, draw the information out of her, and escape with his life.

Gonish studied the crowds of predominantly young people who were streaming in and out of the garish building. Their laughter, the rich young voices of them, quickened the splendor of the blazing night. It all seemed normal, but he stood with practiced patience measuring the faces that moved by, assessing the characters of the loungers from their expressions; and it didn't take long to grasp the reality. The sidewalks swarmed with Imperial Government agents.

Gonish stood grim. The Weapon Makers' Council had insisted that the place of meeting be public. It was understandable that great precautions should be taken by the government secret police, and also that Her Majesty would not be anxious to have it known that she was dealing with the Weapon Shops so soon after the appearance of the giants. The conference was scheduled for the small hour of 2:30 A.M. It was now—Gonish glanced at his watch—exactly 1:55.

He remained where he was, conscious of a gathering sadness that it was his duty to attempt to ensnare Hedrock. But the identification of Hedrock from his message, as the man behind the giants had been shockingly convincing and, it seemed to Gonish, fully justifying the fears of the council. Hedrock had shown by his actions that he was dangerous, and since he had made no attempt to explain his purposes when given the opportunity to do so, he must be considered guilty as charged.

It was unthinkable that a man who possessed the basic secrets of the Weapon Shops could be permitted at large. And if, as the council believed, the empress knew his whereabouts, the information would have to be cleverly extracted from her at the meeting which she herself had suggested. His friend Hedrock must die. And meanwhile he had better go inside and look around.

The interior sparkled with gardens and fountains and mechanical games. It was bigger than it had seemed from outside, both longer and wider. It was crowded with about equal numbers of men and women. Many of the women wore masks. Gonish nodded with comprehension. The Empress Isher would be simply one more masked woman. He paused before a game that was all flashing fire, a spray of violently glittering numbers twisting over the velvet blackness of a great board. Thoughtfully, the No-man watched several games run their course, trying each time to impress the overall structure of the game into the ultra-trained region that was his brain. Finally, he placed ten credits on each of three numbers.

The fire slowed its gyrations in its coruscating fashion, and became a dazzling pillar of numbers piled one on top of another. The croupier intoned: "seventy-four, twenty-nine, eighty-six, paying odds this time of seventeen to one."

As Gonish collected his five hundred ten credits, the croupier stared at him. "Say," he said in an astonished voice, "that's only the second time since I've been at this table that anybody's ever won on all three numbers."

The No-man smiled. "Mind over matter," he said gently; and, disinterested, wandered off. He could almost feel the croupier's astounded gaze boring into his back. What he wanted was a game he couldn't solve with his special abilities. And there was still nearly twenty-five minutes in which to find it. He came to an enormous machine with balls and an involved series of wheels under wheels. The balls, sixty of them, all numbered, started at the top, and, as the wheels spun, the balls rolled gradually downward, progressing from wheel to wheel. The farther down they went, the more they paid; but the first half of that complicated though swift journey didn't count, and few ever got lower.

The great attraction, so far as Gonish could make out, was the sensation of watching one's ball go down, down, with hope not fading until the last second. It turned out to be too simple. His ball went farthest four times in a row. Gonish pocketed his winnings, and came finally to a game that was a sphere of black and white light. The two lights merged into a single, spinning beam, and came out all white or all black. The bet was, which would it be?

Not once was he sure. He finally laid his first wager on the gambler's basis that white was the symbol of purity. White lost. He watched his money whisked off, and decided to forget the purity. Black lost. Beside him, a woman's rich laughter tinkled; and then, "I hope, Mr. Gonish, that you can do better than that with the giant. But please follow us to the private rooms."

Gonish turned. Three men and a woman stood there. One of the men was Prince del Curtin. The woman's face under its mask seemed long and the mouth itself was unmistakably Isher. Her eyes through the mask slits glinted green and her familiar, golden voice completed the recognition picture.

The No-man bowed low and said, "I'm sure I shall."

They went in silence to a luxuriously furnished drawing room, and sat down. Gonish took his time. There were questions he wanted to ask. The strange thing was, his casual references to Hedrock produced only silence. After a while, that was astounding. Gonish leaned back, studying the faces of the three men and the woman, genuinely disturbed. He said at last, very carefully, "My feeling is that you are withholding information."

It wasn't, he thought after he had spoken, that they could be doing it consciously. Their earnestness was unmistakable. And they couldn't possibly suspect that it was Hedrock he was after. Yet there seemed to exist among them a tacit understanding that nothing be said about Hedrock.

It was Prince del Curtin who made the denial. "I assure you, Mr. Gonish, you are quite mistaken. Among us four is every scrap of information that has come in about the giant. And, of course, any clue that may have turned up in the past as to his identity will probably be somewhere in our minds, too. You have only to ask the proper questions and we will answer."

It was convincing. This was going to be harder than he had thought, and it was just possible that, dangerous though it was, he might have to come out into the open. Gonish said slowly, "You are mistaken in assuming that you are the only reliable sources of information. There is a man, probably the greatest man now living, whose extraordinary abilities we of the Weapon Shops are just beginning to appreciate. I am referring to Robert Hedrock, who holds the rank of captain in Your Majesty's army."

To Gonish's amazement, the empress leaned toward him. Her gaze was intense, her lips parted breathlessly, her eyes shining.

"You mean," she whispered, "the Weapon Shops consider Robert—Captain Hedrock—as one of the world's great men?" She did not wait for a reply, but turned to Prince del Curtin. "You see," she said. *"You see!"*

The prince smiled. "Your Majesty," he said quietly, "my opinion of Captain Hedrock has always been high."

The woman faced Gonish across the table, said in a strangely formal tone, "I will see to it that Captain Hedrock is advised of your urgent desire to interview him."

She knew! He had that much. As for the rest—Gonish leaned back in his chair ruefully. She would advise Hedrock, would she? He could just imagine Hedrock's sardonic reception of the information. Gonish straightened slowly. His situation was becoming desperate. The entire Weapon Shop world was geared to act on the results of this meeting. And still he had nothing.

There was no doubt that these people were as anxious to get rid of the giant as the Weapon Makers were to get hold of Hedrock; and the irony was that the death of Hedrock would simultaneously solve both problems. With an effort, Gonish mustered his best smile, and said, "You seem to have a little mystery among yourselves about Captain Hedrock. May I ask what it is?"

Surprisingly, the question brought a puzzled stare from Prince del Curtin. "I should have thought," the man said finally, politely, "that in your fashion you would long ago have put two and two together. Or is it possible that, of all the people of the solar system, you are not aware of what happened tonight. Where have you been since 7:45?"

Gonish was startled. In his desire to keep his mind clear for this meeting, he had come early to Imperial City. At 7:30 he had gone into a quiet little restaurant. Emerging an hour and a half later, he had attended a play. That ended at 11:53. Since then, he had wandered along sightseeing. He had ignored the news. He knew nothing. Incredibly, half the world could have been destroyed and he wouldn't know. Prince del Curtin was speaking again:

"It is true that the identity of the man in such a case is traditionally withheld, but—"

"Prince!"

It was the empress, her voice low and tense. The men looked at her, startled, as she went on, more grimly, "Say no more. There is something wrong. All this questioning about Captain Hedrock has an ulterior motive. They're only partly interested in the giant."

She herself must have realized that her warning was too late. She stopped and looked at Gonish, and the look in her eyes brought pity welling up in him. Until this moment, he had never regarded the Empress Isher as quite human. But there could be no pity. With a jerk, Gonish brought his hand up near his mouth, tore back the sleeve, and said ringingly into the tiny radio that was strapped there:

"Captain Hedrock is in the empress's personal apartment—"

They were quick, those three men. They bowled him over in one concerted rush; and then they were on top of him. Gonish offered no resistance, but submitted quietly to arrest. After a moment, he felt relief that he, who had been compelled by inexorable duty to betray his friend, would now die too.

FIFTEEN

The ruins consisted of a breakthrough into a main corridor of the palace, and of gaping energy holes along the corridor itself where the fighting had taken place.

Beside the empress, Prince del Curtin said anxiously, "Hadn't you better get some sleep, Your Majesty? It's after four. And, as the Weapon Makers have not answered our repeated calls, there is nothing more that can be done tonight about your husband... about Captain Hedrock."

She waved him away, vaguely. There was a thought in her mind, a thought so sharp that it seemed to have physical qualities; so painful that every moment it existed it was a bit of hell. She must get him back; no matter what the sacrifice, she must have Hedrock back. Strange, she thought finally, how she who had been so cold and steely and calculating, so almost inhumanly imperial—strange how in the ultimate issue she should prove to be like all the women who had ever become emotional over a man. As if the first shock of committing herself to one man had literally changed the chemistry of her body. When Hedrock had been announced at six o'clock the night before, her mind was already made up. She thought of her decision as intellectual, product of the need for an Isher heir. Actually, of course, she had never thought of anyone but Hedrock as the father. In the first audience she had granted him eight months earlier, he had coolly announced that he had come to the palace for the sole purpose of marrying her. That amused, then angered, then enraged her, but it had put him in the special category as the only man who had ever asked for her hand. The psychology involved had always been plain; and she sometimes felt acutely the unfairness of the situation for other men who might have the ambition or desire. Court etiquette forbade that they mention the subject. The tradition was that she must ask. She never had.

In the final issue she had thought only of the man who had actually proposed; and, at six o'clock he had come in response to her urgent call and agreed instantly to an immediate marriage. The ceremony had been simple but public. Public in that she took her vows before the telestat, so that all the world might see her and hear her words. Hedrock had not appeared in the telestat. His name was not mentioned. He was referred to as "the distinguished officer who has won Her Majesty's esteem." He was a consort only, and as such must remain in the background.

Only the Ishers mattered. The men and women they married remained private persons. That was the law; and she had never thought there was anything wrong with it. She didn't now, but for nearly ten hours she had been a wife, and during those hours her mind and metabolism adjusted. The thoughts that came had no relation to any she had ever had before. Curious thoughts about how she must now bear the chosen man's children, and mother them, and of how the palace must be transformed spiritually so that children could live there. After six hours she had told him of her appointment to meet Edward Gonish. And went off with the memory of the odd expression in his eyes—and now this ruin, and the gathering realization that Hedrock was gone, snatched irresistibly from the heart of her empire by her old enemies. She grew aware that someone, the court chancellor, was recounting a list of precautions that had been taken to prevent leakage of the news that the palace had been attacked.

No reports had been permitted to be broadcast. Every witness was being sworn to silence under strict penalties. By dawn, the repair work would be completed without trace, and thereafter any story that did come out would seem a barefaced rumor, to be laughed at, and ridiculed. It had been, she realized, fast, effective suppression. Very important, that. The prestige of the House of Isher might have been dealt a damaging blow. But the success of the censorship made it all remote, secondary. There would be rewards and honors to dole out, but what mattered now was, she must get him back.

Slowly, she emerged from her dark mood. Her party, she saw,

was clear now of the muttering repair machines, and was moving along the wrecked corridor. Her mind withdrew further from itself, grew more intent on her surroundings. She thought: the important thing was to find out what had happened, then act. Frowning from her new purpose, she examined the mutilated walls of the hallway. Her green eyes flashed. She said with a semblance of her old sardonicism, "From the slant of the ray burns, our side seems to have done all the damage, except for the initial breach in the main wall."

One of the officers nodded grimly. "They were after Captain Hedrock only. They used a peculiar paralyzing ray that toppled our soldiers over like ninepins. The men are still recovering with no harmful effects visible, much as General Grall did after Captain Hedrock seemed to cause him to die from heart failure at lunch two months ago."

"But what happened?" she demanded sharply. "Bring me someone who saw everything. Was Captain Hedrock asleep when the attack came?"

"No—" The officer spoke cautiously. "No, Your Majesty, he was down in the tombs."

"Where?"

The soldier looked unhappy. "Your Majesty, as soon as you and your party left the palace, Captain Hed . . . your consor—"

She said impatiently, "Call him Prince Hedrock, please."

"Thank you, Majesty. Prince Hedrock went down in the tombs to one of the old storerooms, removed part of one wall—"

"He what? But go on!"

"Yes, Your Majesty. Naturally, in view of his new position, our guards gave him every assistance in removing the section of metal wall and transporting it to the elevators, and up to this corridor."

"Naturally."

"The soldiers who reported to me said the wall section was weightless but it offered some quality of innate resistance to movement. It was about two feet wide and six and a half feet long; and when Cap . . . Prince Hedrock stepped through it and vanished, and then came back, it—"

"When he what? Colonel, what are you talking about?"

The officer bowed. "I regret my confusion, Madam. I did not see all of this, but I have pieced together varied accounts. My mind of course persists in regarding as more important what I myself saw.

I actually saw him enter the detached wall shield, disappear, and return a minute later."

The empress stood there, her mind almost a blank. She knew she would get the story eventually, but right now it seemed beyond her reach, buried deep in a muddle of phrases that had no meaning in themselves. Captain Hedrock had gone to the tombs deep below the palace, removed a section of wall, and then what?

She put the question incisively; and the colonel said, "And then, Your Majesty, he brought it up to the palace proper and stood waiting."

"This was before the attack?"

The officer shook his head. "During it. He was still in the tombs when the wall was breached by the concentrated fire of the Weapon Shop warships. I warned him personally in my capacity as chief of the palace guards of what was happening. The warning only made him speed his return to the surface, where he was captured."

Briefly again she felt helpless. The description seemed clear enough now. But it made no sense. Hedrock must have known something was going to happen, because he had gone purposely down into the tombs immediately after her own departure to meet Edward Gonish. That part was all right. It seemed to indicate a plan. The strange thing was that he had come up and, right before the eyes of the Weapon Shop forces and the palace guards, had apparently used the wall section to transmit himself somewhere, as the Weapon Makers were reputed to be able to do. But, instead of staying away, he had come back. Insanely, he had come back, and permitted the Weapon Makers to take him prisoner.

She said finally, hopelessly, "What happened to the section of wall?"

"It burned up right after Prince Hedrock warned the Weapon Shop councilor, Peter Cadron, who led the attackers."

"Warned—" She turned to del Curtin. "Prince, perhaps you can obtain a coherent story. I'm lost."

The prince said quietly, "We're all tired, Your Majesty. Colonel Nison has been up all night." He turned to the flushing officer. "Colonel, as I understand it, guns from Weapon Shop warships breached the gap in the outer wall at the end of the corridor. Then one of the ships drew alongside, and sent men into the corridor, men who were immune to the fire of our troops—is that right?"

"Absolutely, sir."

"They were led by Peter Cadron of the Weapon Makers' Council, and when they reached a certain point in the corridor, there was Prince Hedrock standing waiting. He had brought some kind of electronic plate or shield, six feet by two feet, from a hiding place in the tombs. He stood beside it, waited until everybody could see his action, then stepped *into* the plate, vanishing as he did so.

"The plate continued to stand there, apparently held in place from the other side; this would account for the resistance it offered when the soldiers carried it up from the tombs for Prince Hedrock. A minute after his disappearance, Prince Hedrock stepped back out of the shield and, facing the Weapon Shop men, warned Peter Cadron."

"That is correct, sir."

"What was the warning?"

The officer said steadily, "He asked Councilor Cadron if he recalled the Weapon Shop laws forbidding any interference, for any reason, with the seat of Imperial Government, and warned him that the entire Weapon Shop Council would regret its high-handed action, and that it would be taught to remember that it is but one of two facets of Isher civilization."

"He said *that!*" Her voice was eager, her eyes ablaze. She whirled on del Curtin. "Prince, did you hear that?"

The prince bowed, then turned back to Colonel Nison. "My last question is this: In your opinion did Prince Hedrock give any evidence of being able to fulfill his threat against the Weapon Makers?"

"None, sir. I could have shot him myself from where I stood. Physically he was, and I presume is, completely in their power."

"Thank you," said the prince. "That is all."

There remained the fact that she must rescue Captain Hedrock. She paced up and down, up and down. Dawn came, a gray muggy light that peered through the huge windows of her office apartment shedding vague pools of light in its shadowy corners, and making no impression at all where there were artificial lights. She saw that Prince del Curtin was watching her anxiously. She slowed her rapid pacing, and said, "I can't believe it. I can't believe that Captain Hedrock would say things out of bravado. It is possible that there exists some organization of which we know nothing. In fact—" She faced him wildly. "Prince," she said in an intense voice, "he *told* me that he was not, never had been, never would be a Weapon Shop man."

Del Curtin was frowning. "Innelda," he said pityingly, "you are exciting yourself uselessly. There can't be anything. Human beings, being what they are, sooner or later manifest any power they may have. That is a law as fixed as Einsteinian gravitation. If such an organization existed, we would have known of it."

"We have missed the clues. Don't you see?" Her voice trembled with the desperation of her thought. "He came to marry me. And he won there. That shows the caliber of the organization. And what about the section of wall that he removed from the storeroom in the tombs—how did that get there? Explain that."

"Surely," said the prince in a stately voice, "the Ishers cannot but be mortal enemies of any secret organization that may exist!"

"The Ishers," said the woman icily, "are learning that they are human beings as well as rulers, and that the world is a big place, too big for one mind or group of minds to comprehend in its entirety."

They stared at each other, two people whose nerves were frayed to the utmost. It was the empress who recovered first. She said wearily, "It seems incredible, Prince, that you and I who have been almost truly brother and sister, should be on the verge of a quarrel. I'm sorry."

She came forward and placed her hand on his. He took it and kissed it. There were tears in his eyes as he straightened. "Your Majesty," he said huskily, "I beg your forgiveness. I should have remembered the strain you are undergoing. You have but to command me. We have power. A billion men will spring to arms at your command. We can threaten the Weapon Makers with a generation of war. We can destroy any man who has dealings with them. We can—"

She shook her head hopelessly. "My dear, you do not realize what you are saying. This is an age that would normally be revolutionary. The necessary disorganized mental outlook exists. The evils are there: selfish administration, corrupt courts, and rapacious industry. Every class contributes its own brand of amoral and immoral attributes, which are beyond the control of any individual. Life itself is in the driver's seat; we are only passengers. So far our marvelous science, the immensity of machine production, the intricate and superb organization of law, and—" she hesitated, then went on reluctantly—"the existence of the Weapon Makers as a stabilizing influence, have prevented an open explosion. But for a generation at least, we mustn't rock the boat. I am counting particularly upon a new method of mind training recently released by the Weapon Shops, which strengthens moral function as well as performing everything that other methods are noted for. As soon as we get rid of the menace of the giant organization we—"

She stopped because of the startled expression that flashed into the prince's lean face. Her eyes widened. She whispered, "It's impossible. He . . . can't be . . . the giant. Wait . . . wait, don't do anything. We can prove it all in a minute—"

She crossed swiftly to her personal 'stat, said in a tired, flat voice, "Bring the prisoner, Edward Gonish, to my office."

For five minutes she stood almost unmoving until the door opened and Gonish was ushered in. The guards departed on her command. She relaxed sufficiently then to ask the questions.

The No-man answered her steadily. "I do not understand the electronic shield through which you say he disappeared, but yes, Your Majesty, Captain Hedrock is one of the giants, or—" he hesitated, then added slowly, "or, and this thought has just come, *the* giant."

The significance of the hesitation was not lost on her. She swayed wearily. "But why should he want to marry the woman whose empire he is trying to ruin?"

"Madam—" Gonish spoke quietly—"it was only two months ago that we discovered Captain Hedrock was deceiving the Weapon Shops. It was the accidental disclosure of his remarkably superior intelligence that proved him to be a man to whom the Isher line and the Weapon Makers are but a means to an end. What that end is, I am only beginning to suspect. If you will answer a few questions, I shall be able to tell you in a few minutes who Captain Hedrock is, or rather, was! I say 'was' of necessity. I regret to say that the intention of the Weapon Makers was to question him in a specially constructed chamber; then immediately execute him."

Silence settled over the room. Actually, the capacity of her body for shock was gone. She stood, cold and numb, without thought, waiting. She noticed finally, absently, that the No-man was an extremely distinguished looking individual. She studied him, and then forgot his personal appearance as he began to speak:

"I have, of course, all the information about Captain Hedrock that is known to the Weapon Makers. My search led into very unusual byways. But if similar curious paths exist in the Isher annals, as I believe they do, then the section of wall Hedrock removed from the tombs is only the final clue. But let me ask: Is there any picture, or film, *any* physical record available of the husband of the empress Ganeel?"

"Why—no!" The breathlessness was accompanied by a dizziness, almost a spinning of her brain; for her mind had made an improbable leap. She spoke blurrily, "Mr. Gonish, he said that, except for my dark hair, I reminded him of Ganeel."

The No-man bowed gravely. "Your Majesty, I see you have already plunged into these strange waters. I want you to run your mind back and *back* through the history of your line, and remember—whose pictorial record is missing, husband or emperor?"

"They're mostly husbands of empresses," she said slowly, steadily. "That is how the tradition began, that consorts should remain in the background." She frowned. "So far as I know there is only one emperor, of whom picture, portrait or film record is not available. That one is understandable. As the first of the line, he—"

She stopped. She stared at Gonish. "Are you crazy?" she said. "Are you *crazy?*"

The No-man shook his head. "You may now regard it as a full intuition. You know what my training is. I take a fact here and a fact there, and as soon as I have approximately ten percent, the answer comes automatically. They call it intuition, but actually it is simply the ability of the brain to co-ordinate tens of thousands of facts in a flash, and to logicalize any gaps that may exist.

"One of the facts in this case is that there are no less than twenty-seven important pictorial records missing in the history of the Weapon Shops. I concentrated my attention on the writings of the men in question, and the similarity of mental outlook, the breadth of intellect, was unmistakable." He finished, "You may or may not know it, but just as the first and greatest of the Ishers is only a name, so our founder, Walter S. de Lany, is a name without a face."

"But who is he?" said Prince del Curtin, blankly. "Apparently, somewhere along the line the race of man bred an immortal."

"Not bred. It must have been artificial. Had it been natural, it would have been repeated many times in these centuries. And it must have been accidental, and unrepeatable, because everything the man has ever said or done shows an immense and passionate interest in the welfare of the race."

"But," said the prince, "what is he trying to do? Why did he marry Innelda?"

For a moment, Gonish was silent. He stared at the woman, and she returned his gaze, the color in her cheeks high and brilliant. Finally she nodded, and Gonish said:

"For one thing, he has tried to keep the Isher strain *Isher*. He believes in his own blood, and rightly so, as history has proven. For instance, you two are only remotely Isher. Your blood is so diluted that your kinship to Captain Hedrock can hardly be called a relation. Hedrock remarked to me once that the Isher emperors tended to marry brilliant and somewhat unstable women, and that this periodically endangered the family. It was the empresses, he said, who always saved the line by marrying steady, sober, able men."

"Suppose—" The woman did not think of her words as an interruption; the thought came; she spoke it. "Suppose we offered to trade you for him?"

Gonish shrugged. "You can probably obtain his corpse for me."

That burned and chilled by turns, but the brief fever left her colder, more remote from emotion. Death was something that she had seen with icy eyes, and she could face it for *him* as well as for herself.

"Suppose I were to offer the interstellar drive?"

Her intensity seemed to astound the man. He drew back and stared at her. "Madam," he said finally, "I can offer you no intuition one way or the other, nor any logical hope. I must admit that I am puzzled by the electronic shield, but I get nothing, no sense of what it could be, or why it should help him. Whatever he did when he was *within* it could not to my knowledge assist him to escape through the impregnable walls of a Weapon Shop battle cruiser, or out of the metal room where he was taken. All the science of the Weapon Makers and the Isher Empire is arrayed against him. Science moves in spurts, and we are in the dynamic middle of the latest one. A hundred years from now, when the lull has set in, an immortal man may begin to get his bearings, not before."

"Suppose he tells them the truth?" It was Prince del Curtin who spoke.

"Never!" the woman flashed. "Why, that would be begging. No Isher would think of such a thing."

Gonish said, "Her Majesty is right, but that is not the only reason. I will not explain. The possibility of a confession does not exist."

She was only vaguely aware of his words. She whirled on her cousin. She held herself straight, her head high. She said in a thrillingly clear voice, "Keep trying to contact the Weapon Makers. Offer them Gonish, the interstellar drive and legal recognition, including an arrangement whereby their courts and ours establish a liaison, all in exchange for Captain Hedrock. They would be mad to refuse."

The passion sagged. She saw that the No-man was gazing at her gloomily. "Madam," he said sadly, "you have obviously paid no attention to my earlier statement. The intention was to kill him within a maximum of one hour. In view of his previous escape from the Weapon Makers, that intention will not be deviated from. The greatest human story in history is over. And, Madam—"

The No-man stared at her steadily. "For your sake, it is just as well. You know as well as I do that you cannot have children."

"What's this?" Said Prince del Curtin in a vast amazement. "Innelda—"

"Silence!" Her voice was harsh with mortified fury. "Prince, have this man returned to his cell. He has really become intolerable. And I forbid you to discuss your sovereign with him."

The prince bowed. "Your Majesty commands," he said coldly. He turned. "This way, Mr. Gonish."

She had wondered if she could be hurt further; and here it was. She stood, after a moment, alone in her shattered world. Long minutes dragged before she realized that sleep at least would be kind.

SIXTEEN

It was not so much a room in which Hedrock found himself as a metal cavern. He stopped short in the doorway, beside Peter Cadron, a sardonic smile on his face. He saw that the councilor was watching him from narrowed eyes, and his lips curled.

Let them wonder and doubt. They had surprised him once by an unexpected arrest. This time it was different. This time he was ready for them. His gaze played boldly over the twenty-nine men who sat around the V-table which the Weapon Makers' Council used in their public hearings. He waited until Peter Cadron, the thirtieth of that high council, had walked over and seated himself; waited while the commander of the guards reported that the prisoner was stripped of all rings, that his clothes had been changed and his body subjected to a transparency and found to be normal, with nowhere a hidden weapon. Having spoken, the commander and his guards withdrew, but still Hedrock waited. He smiled as Peter Cadron explained the reason for the precautions; and then, slowly, coolly, he walked forward and faced the open end of the V-table. He saw that the men's eyes were on him. Some looked curious, some expectant, some merely hostile. All seemed willing for him to speak.

"Gentlemen," Hedrock said in his ringing voice, "I'm going to ask one question: Does anyone present know where I was when I stepped through that shield? If not, I would suggest that I be released at once because the mighty Weapon Makers' Council is in for a devil of a shock."

There was silence. The men looked at each other. "I would say," said young Ancil Nare, "that the sooner the execution is carried out the better. At the present moment, his throat can be cut; he can be strangled; a bullet can smash his head; an energy gun disintegrate him. His body is without protection—if necessary we could even club him to death. We know that all this can be done *this instant.* We do not know, in view of his strange statements, that it can be done ten minutes from now." In his earnestness, the youthful executive stood up as he finished, "Gentlemen, let us act now!"

Hedrock's loud clapping broke the silence that followed. "Bravo," he said, "bravo. Such well-spoken advice merits being acted upon. Go ahead and try to kill me in any fashion you please. Draw your guns and fire; pick up your chairs and bludgeon me; order knives and pin me against the wall. No matter what you do, gentlemen, you're in for a shock." His eyes were chilling. "And deservedly so.

"Wait!" His thunderous voice drowned the attempt of the solid-faced Deam Lealy to break into speech. "*I'll* do the talking. It is the council that is on trial, not I. It can still win leniency for its criminal action in attacking the Imperial Palace by recognizing now, without further offense, that it has broken its own laws."

"Really," a councilor wedged in the words, "this is beyond toleration."

"Let him talk," Peter Cadron said. "We shall learn a great deal about his motives."

Hedrock bowed gravely. "Indeed you shall, Mr. Cadron. My motives are concerned entirely with the action of this council in ordering the attack on the palace."

"I can understand," said Cadron ironically, "your vexation that this council did not respect a regulation more than three thousand years old when apparently you had counted upon it and upon our natural reluctance to make such an attack, and accordingly felt yourself safe to pursue your own ends, whatever they are."

Hedrock said steadily, "I did *not* count upon the regulation or the reluctance. My colleagues and I—" it was just as well to suggest once more that he was not alone—"have noted with regret the developing arrogance of this council, its growing belief that it was not accountable for its actions, and that therefore it could safely flout its own constitution."

"Our constitution," said Bayd Roberts, the senior councilor, with dignity, "demands that we take any action necessary to maintain our position. The proviso that this be done without an attack on the person or residence of the reigning Isher, her heirs or successors, has no meaning in an extreme emergency such as this. You will notice that we did secure the absence of Her Majesty during the attack."

"I must interrupt." It was the chairman of the council. "Incredibly, the prisoner has succeeded in concentrating the conversation according to his own desires. I can understand that we all have a guilty feeling about the attack on the palace, but we are not required to defend our actions to the prisoner." He spoke curtly into his chair-arm 'stat, "Commander, come in here and put a sack over the prisoner's head."

Hedrock was smiling gently as the guard of ten came in. He said, "We will now have the shock."

He stood perfectly still as the men grabbed him. The sack came up and—

It happened.

When Hedrock, in the palace half an hour before, had stepped through the section of wall which he had brought up from the tombs, he found himself in a dim world. He stood for a long time letting his body adjust, hoping that no one would attempt to follow him through that electronic-force field. It was not a personal worry. The vibratory shield was tuned to his body and his alone; and during all the years that it had been part of the wall in the underground palace storeroom, the only danger had been that someone might unknowingly wander into it, and suffer damage. Hedrock had often wondered what would happen to such an unlucky innocent. Several animals that he had tagged and put through an experimental model had been sent back from points as far away as ten thousand miles. Some had never been returned despite the high reward offer printed on the tag.

Now that he himself was in, there was no hurry. Normal time and space laws had no meaning in this realm of half-light. It was nowhere and it was everywhere. It was the quickest place in which to go mad, because the body that intruded on it experienced time; *it* didn't. He had found that a six-hour session made serious inroads on his sanity. His incursion earlier in the evening, through the shield in his hideout, had been for what would have been two hours normal time, and the trip had revealed to him that the empress wanted to marry him. Temporarily, that had guaranteed his safety; what was more important, it also guaranteed he would have access to the shield in the palace tombs. Accordingly, he had withdrawn swiftly, conserving the remaining four hours of the six that was the human limit.

His present incursion mustn't occupy more than four hours, preferably three, more preferably two. After which, he'd have to stay away from the mind destroying thing for months. The idea for the invention had been broached to him during one of his terms as chairman of the Weapon Makers' Council, an enormously autocratic position that had enabled him to assign an entire laboratory of physicists to assist the brilliant young man whose brain child it was. Simply, the problem had been: The Weapon Shop vibratory transmitter bridged the spatial gap between two points in interplanetary space by mechanically accepting that space had no material existence. Why not then, the inventor had expounded, why not reverse the process and create an illusion of space where there had been nothing?

The research was a success. The inventor reported the details to Hedrock, who thought it over and informed the man and his colleagues that the council had decided on secrecy. To the council itself, he made a negative report on the invention. And had it. The subject, once explored, was considered one more closed door, was entered as such in the files of Information Center for the future reference of men who might have a repetition of the idea. Accordingly, it would never again be the subject of Weapon Shop research. Some day, he would release the knowledge.

It was, Hedrock reflected, as he stood there patiently letting his body adjust, not the first time that an invention had come into his possession and been withheld from the public. His own discovery, vibratory magnification, he had kept as a personal secret for twenty centuries before finally using it to establish the Weapon Shops as a counterbalance to the Isher emperors. He still had several others. And his main rule for withholding or not had always been: Would release for general use be of benefit to the progressive spirit of man? Or would the power that it represented merely assist some temporal group in tightening a tyranny already too rigid? Quite enough dangerous inventions were carelessly produced during the inventive spurts that came every few centuries by scientists who never thought in a practical fashion of what the effect of their discoveries might be.

Damn it, why should a billion people die because some inventor had a brain that couldn't see an inch into human nature?

Then, of course, there were the people who saw an invention in terms of their own private or group welfare. If they were withholding, as the empress was withholding the interstellar drive, they must be forced by all means to yield their secret. Sometimes, the decision had been a hard one, but who else had the power, the experience to decide? For better or for worse, he was the arbiter.

He let the thought drain slowly out of him. His body was ready. The time had come for action. Hedrock began to walk forward in the mist. He could see the people in the palace, standing rigidly like carved figures seen at late dusk. His time relation to them had not changed a single instant. He paid them no attention, even when they were in his way, but stepped through their bodies as if they were clouds of gas. Walls yielded before his mass, but that had to be carefully done. It would have been just as easy, too easy, to sink through the floor, and so on into the Earth. The laboratory experiments of the inventor and his assistants had produced one such casualty; and repetition was not desired. To avoid the calamity, the research staff finally designed that the initial creation of new space should be on a partial scale only. A ring was provided which, when activated, would increase or decrease the original apportionment at will, for use when heavy materials had to be penetrated.

The ring, one of two—the other had a different purpose—was what Hedrock used when he came to walls. First, an easy jump, followed as his feet left the floor by a touch on the activator of the ring, then swift release of the activator, and then a gentle landing on a floor that gave like thick mud under his feet. It was simple for muscles so perfectly coordinated as his own. He reached the cache of machines which he had long ago tuned to this space, and secreted in the palace. There was a small spaceship, with lifting devices, magnetizers large and small, particularly there were dozens of machines that could snatch and hold things. There were various weapons and, of course, every tool, every instrument from spaceship to mechanical fingers had its own equivalent of the two adjustors necessary to their complete operation. Every instrument in the ship, the ship itself, and the two adjustor rings on Hedrock's finger, were attuned to a master control on the switchboard of the spaceship.

The second ring and the matching adjustors on the machine comprised the second valuable function of the invention. By controlling the second ring, it was possible to go backward and forward in time for a short distance. Theoretically, years could be covered; actually, the shattering effect of the entire experience to the human brain limited a trip to a few hours backward or forward.

Hedrock had discovered that, in nine hours forward in time, and nine backward, eighteen altogether, the body lived the six normal hours that it could endure without going too insane. Three for one. The method of time travel had no relation to the seesaw system of time travel unwittingly devised by the empress's physicists seven years before, wherein the body collected time-energy which could never again quite be balanced off, with the result that the time traveler was always destroyed. There was no time in *this* space; there was only a method of adjusting the space to a given time in the normal world.

Hedrock eased the little spaceship and everything in it around to where the Weapon Shop cruiser lay-to beside the break in the palace wall. Through the hard shell of the cruiser, he nosed his machine; then switched off the engines, and turned on the master time adjustor to full power, thrice the rate of normal time. He waited tensely, watching the Sensitives, which were nothing but automatic relays converted to use in this space. It shouldn't take long. The Sensitive lights flashed; the master switch clicked instantly down to one third its full power, adjusting the whole ship to normal-time rate. Simultaneously, Hedrock felt movement. The great Weapon Shop cruiser was rising; and he and his small machine were with it, perfectly matched as to time rate, and just far enough out of the special space to keep from falling through the walls of the cruiser.

If he was right, there were now two Hedrocks in the cruiser, himself here in the gray-dark realm, and himself returned to the palace *from* this very spy trip, made prisoner by the Weapon Makers and brought aboard the cruiser. It was unwise to take that for granted. One of the difficulties of moving around in time was that of locating people, and keeping track of them in crowds, or just keeping track. He had once wasted an entire six-hour period searching for a person who had gone to a theater. Accordingly, even now, it was best to make sure. He peered into the 'stats; and, yes, there he was, surrounded by guards. The Hedrock out there was already back from this time trip, and knew what had happened. Which was more than *he* did. It shouldn't take long, though.

The cruiser flashed to the fortress that was its destination. Prisoner and guards emerged and went down into the building, where the thick metal room had been constructed. Hedrock forced his ship through the heavy walls and got busy. First, he put out a sound collector; and while listening to the argument in the room, unloaded some of his machines. When the guards rushed in with the "sack," which was simply a gagging device, he waited till it was about to be fastened, then lowered a mechanical hand and snatched it into his own space. He sat then, with his fingers on the time control, waiting for developments.

In the room itself, the silence was a thing of tensed nerves and startled looks. Hedrock, the prisoner, stood still, a faint, sardonic smile on his lips, making no effort to break the grip of the guards who held him. He felt remorseless. There was a job to be done, and he intended to do it thoroughly. He said icily, "I won't waste any time on verbal argument. The determination of this organization to kill me, despite the fact that the *Pp* machine proved my altruism and good will shows a defensive conservatism that always tries to destroy when confronted by something it does not completely understand. That conservatism shall be taught by overwhelming force that there exists an organization capable of overthrowing even the mighty Weapon Makers."

Peter Cadron said coldly, "The Weapon Shops recognize no secret organization. Guards, destroy him!"

"You fool," Hedrock cried. "I thought better of you, Cadron, than that you would give such a command after what I have said."

He went on talking, paying no attention to what was happening. Without looking around at the guards, he *knew*.

In that other space, his earlier self simply cut the time-adjustor switch, whereupon everything in the room stabilized. Without haste, his earlier self relieved the guards of their weapons, and then proceeded to disarm every member of the Council including the removal of the rings from their fingers and the 'stat radios from their wrists and chairs. Next, he slipped handcuffs onto their wrists, chaining them all together in a long row around the table. The guards he handcuffed arms to legs, and set outside in the hallway. Then he closed and locked the door. The whole job took no time. Literally.

He returned to the control board, adjusted his time rate from zero to normal and listened to the uproar of the men discovering their situation.

The dismay was vast. Chains clanked. Men cried out in wonder and alarm, and then sank back looking pale and terrified. Hedrock knew there was very little personal fear involved. It was all too plain that every man present had suddenly had a terrible vision of the end of the Weapon Shops. He waited for their startled attention to jerk back to him, then spoke swiftly, "Gentlemen, calm your fears. Your great organization is not in danger. This situation would never have arisen if you had not pursued me with such singleness of purpose. For your information, it was your own founder, Walter S. de Lany, who recognized the danger to the State of an invincible body such as the Weapon Makers. It was he who set a group of friendly watchers over the Shops. That is all I will say, except to emphasize our friendliness, our good will, our resolve not to interfere so long as the Weapon Makers live according to their constitution. It is that constitution which has now been violated in its one inflexible article."

He paused there, his gaze sweeping the faces before him, but mentally he was coolly appraising his words. It was a good story withal, the lack of detail being its safest feature. All he desired from it was that it conceal the fact that an immortal man was the only watcher. He saw that several of the men had recovered sufficiently to attempt speech, but he cut them off.

"Here is what must be done. First, keep silent about what you have learned today. The Watchers do not wish it known that they exist. Secondly, resign *in toto*. You can all stand for re-election, not for the next term, but thereafter. The mass resignation will serve as a reminder to the rank and file of the Shops that there is a constitution and that it is one to respect. Finally, no further attempt to molest me must be made. About noon tomorrow, inform the empress that you have released me, and ask her to give up the interstellar drive. I think myself that the drive will be forthcoming before that hour without any urging, but give her the chance to be generous."

His voice must have been holding them in thrall. As he finished, there was an angry clamor, then silence, and then a lesser clamor, and silence again. Hedrock did not fail to notice that three or four men, among them Peter Cadron, did not join in either manifestation of that confusion. It was to Cadron that Hedrock addressed himself, "I am sure that Mr. Cadron can act as spokesman. I have long regarded him as one of the most able members on the council."

Cadron climbed to his feet, a strongly built man in his middle forties. "Yes," he said, "I believe I can be spokesman. I think I speak for the majority when I say that we accept your terms."

No one dissented. Hedrock bowed and said loudly, "All right, Number One, pull me out!"

He must have vanished instantly.

They attempted no experiments, the two Hedrocks who were briefly together in that misty partial space. The human brain suffered too greatly from the slightest interference with time. Numerous tests had proved that fact long before. The "earlier" Hedrock sat at the controls of the little ship, driving it hard back in time and toward the palace. The other stood beside him, looking down gloomily.

He had done what he could. As a result the psychological direction events were taking was so marked that the issue was no longer in doubt. It was possible that Innelda would hold the interstellar drive back for bargaining purposes. But that didn't matter. Victory was sure.

The trouble was that greater beings had "freed" him to see what he would do. Somewhere out in space a vast fleet manned by a spider race had paused to study man and his actions. Having captured him they had instantly traced him back to his planet of origin, and manipulated him as if distance did not exist. Having watched him carry out his original purpose, and realizing that there would be little point in further observation of a person who had completed an action, they would undoubtedly re-assert control of him.

Theoretically they might now be bored with human beings, and destroy the solar system and all its intensely emotional inhabitants. Such destruction would be a mere incident in their coldly intellectual existence.

With a grimace, as he reached that point in his thought, Hedrock saw that they were at their destination. The shield loomed up in the dim reaches of the shadowy palace, a rectangular shape of soft brilliance. The two Hedrocks tried no trickery, attempted no paradox. It was his "earlier" self who stepped through the shield and became one more misty form in the palace room. Hedrock sprayed the combustible shield with a sticky explosive powder, and set it afire. He waited till it had burned, and then he sent the little ship hurtling across the dark city toward one of his dozen secret apartments. Swiftly, he set the Sensitives to hold the ship at normal time rate for possible future use, then he focused the power of the lifter on himself, and felt it lower him into the apartment.

The moment he was on his feet, he headed for a comfortable armchair. When he had settled himself, he called in a savage tone, "All right, my spider friends, if you have any further plans, better try to carry them out now."

The greater struggle had still to be made.

SEVENTEEN

His first awareness of the presence of the aliens was a thought, not directed at him, but which was intended for him to understand. The thought was on the old titanic level, so violent that his brain was shocked by the impact:

"—AN INTERESTING EXAMPLE OF AN ENERGY IMPULSE CONTINUING AS IF NO OUTSIDE FORCE HAD BEEN APPLIED—"

"NO!" The answer was cold. "THE MAN WAS AWARE OF US. THE PURPOSE DRIVING HIM WAS CARRIED THROUGH IN SPITE OF HIS KNOWLEDGE OF OUR EXISTENCE."

"CLEARLY, THEN, HE ACTED ILLOGICALLY."

"POSSIBLY. BUT LET US BRING HIM BACK.... HERE..."

Hedrock recognized that the critical moment had come. For many hours he had been thinking of what he would do when it arrived, and for more than a minute, ever since he had sat down, he had been doing it.

His eyes were closed, his body calm, his mind slow and blank. It was not a perfect state of what the ancient Hindu fakirs had called Nirvana but it was a condition of profound relaxation; and millennia before, the great institutes for mind and sensory study had used it as the basis for all mind training. Sitting there, Hedrock grew conscious of a steady and enormous pulsing that shook his brain with its thunder. But that physical phase, that pounding of his heart with its attendant murmurs of blood flow, and all the tens of thousands of muscular tensions each with its own tiny sounds—that phase, also, passed. He was alone with utter calm and utter peace.

His first impression, then, was that he was sitting in a chair—but not the chair of his apartment. The picture grew so clear that he knew after a few seconds that the chair was in the control room of the lifeboat which in turn was inside one of the huge alien-controlled spaceships.

Hedrock sighed, and opened his eyes. He sat there letting the familiarity of the surroundings figuratively suffuse his being. So his resistance had failed. It was too bad, but of course he had not positively counted on success. He continued to sit in the multi-purposed control chair, because relaxation was his only method of resistance; and he intended to resist from now on.

While he waited, he glanced lazily into the glowing 'stats. Three of the view plates showed starry space, but there was an image of a ship in the rear view plate. Odd, he thought. His lifeboat must no longer be inside the alien machine. He considered that with a faint frown, and then he noticed something else. There was only one ship. But, then, where were the hundreds of others?

He fought down a rising excitement, as he realized what was happening. The relaxation process was working. *Had* worked to some extent. The spider beings had succeeded in bringing him back to his lifeboat, but their domination of his mind was partially broken; and so several of their illusions had faded from his mind.

The first illusion had been that there was more than one ship. Now, free of their control, he could see that there was only one. The second illusion had been that his lifeboat had been inside their machine. Now, free of their control, he could see that it wasn't. He was about to go on in that orderly fashion when his mind leaped to the possibility that their control of him was probably very tenuous at this moment. He closed his eyes, and he was about to think himself back in his apartment when there was an interruption.

"Man, do not compel us to destroy you."

He had been expecting a mental interference, instinctively cringing in anticipation of the titanic impact of it. The shock was different from his expectation. The alien thought lacked force. It seemed far away, weak. Hedrock was conscious of astonishment, and unsteady, wide-eyed comprehension: *This* was the reality. Earlier, they must have established over him an instantaneous and complete rapport. Now, they had to reach at him from the outside. His situation was showing continuous improvement. The spider creatures that had seemed so supreme were being deflated every instant. Four hundred ships had become one. A seemingly superhuman mind control was now reduced to reachable size. He had no doubt that their threat to destroy him was on a physical level. What they meant was that they would use energy beams against him.

It was a far cry from their irresistible domination of his entire nervous system, but it was as dangerous as ever. He must play his game cautiously, and await an opportunity. He waited, and presently a thought was directed at him:

"It is true that you have successfully released yourself from our mental thrall, and have discovered that there is but one ship. However, we have further use of you, and therefore we must ask you to cooperate under the threat of immediate extermination if you refuse."

"Naturally," said Hedrock, an old and successful cooperator, "I'll do what is required unless it involves a near equivalent of extermination such as dismemberment."

"We have in mind," came the precise answer, *"a further sensory study of the Neelan twins. Since you were connected with the relationship when you were under our control, we can dispense with the twin on Earth, and work directly through you. There will be no pain, but you must yield yourself to the investigation."*

Hedrock protested, "I heard one of you say that Gil Neelan was dead. That was before I was put back on Earth. How can you work with a dead man?"

The reply was icy. *"Please allow us to handle the cell growth problems involved. Do you submit yourself?"*

Hedrock hesitated. "Are you going to let me live—afterwards?"

"Naturally not."

He had expected that answer, but it was a shock nonetheless. Hedrock countered, "I don't see how you can expect me to cooperate on such a basis."

"We will advise you of the moment of death. That will give you the emotional excitement you crave, and will thus conform to your requirements."

Hedrock said nothing for a moment. He was fascinated. These monsters thought they would be catering to human nervous requirements by telling him when he was due to die. That was as far as they had gotten in their investigation of man's emotional nature. It seemed incredible that anyone could miss the mark so completely. The intellectual approach of these creatures to life and death must be stoical in the extreme. Instead of trying to bite the hand that was reaching forth to destroy it, each individual spider probably examined all methods of escape and, finding none, accepted death without a struggle.

Hedrock said finally with a crisp ferocity, "You seem to have done pretty well, you and your kind. Here you are in a ship the size of a small moon. You obviously come from a mentally superior civilization; I'd like to see the planet that spawned you, its industries, its ordinary way of life. It should be interesting. Beyond doubt, your brand of logic has done well by you. Nature can pat herself on the back for a successful experiment in producing intelligence, but you've missed the point about man if you think that all I'm interested in is when I can expect to be killed."

"*What more would you like to know?*" There was interest in the questioning thought.

Hedrock said wearily, "All right, you win. I'd like to know when I can get something to eat."

"*Food!*" His questioner was excited. "*Did you hear that,—Xx-Y—* (meaningless)?"

"*Most interesting,*" came another thought. "*At a critical moment the need for food is uppermost. It seems significant. Reassure him, and proceed with the experiment.*"

Hedrock said, "You don't have to reassure me. What do you want me to do?"

"*Yield.*"

"How?"

"*Submit. Think of the dead body.*"

It was a relief to do that, and the picture grew remarkably sharp. He thought suddenly: Poor Gil, lying lifeless on a limitless sea of sand, his cells already collapsed from the ever rising pall of heat as the speedy planet drew ever nearer to one of its two parent suns. It was a strangely agonizing visualization for him, and yet, at the same time, thank God he was dead. The suffering was over. The mortal remains were beyond the pain of heat, beyond the ceaseless worry of the stinging sand, beyond thirst and hunger, beyond fear and unreasonable hope. Death had come to Gilbert Neelan as it must to all men. God bless him and keep him.

Hedrock deliberately stopped that intense emotional reaction. "Just a minute," he said, amazed. "I'm beginning to feel as if I *am* his brother."

"That," came a thought, *"is one of the astonishing characteristics of human beings. The easy way that one nervous system responds to the impulses from another. The sensory equipment involved has no parallel in the world of intelligence. But now, sit up and look around you."*

Hedrock studied his 'stat plates. He saw that there had been a change in the scene. The big ship, whose captive he was, had rolled upward; its immense bulk filled the forward and rear plates, and was visible also on the upper right and left panels. Where it had been before was a gulf of space, and deep in that gulf swam two white, yellow-tinged suns. They were tiny at first, little more than bright stars. But they grew. They grew. And far to the left another, tinier sun appeared. The two larger stars showed after a while six inches in diameter. They had seemed a foot apart; they separated farther. One remained small while the other drew nearer and took on more size. The second sun swung farther and farther to the left; his estimators showed it finally as about three billion miles away.

Further tests showed the angular diameter of both the nearer suns of the system to be larger than that of Sol, though only one was brighter. The third sun was a mere blur of light in the distance. It would have taken a long time for his inadequate instruments to compute its character. But the fact that it was there made Hedrock frown. He searched for, and presently found a red point in the distance, the fourth sun of that system. He was beginning to feel excited, when the alien mind directed its cold vibrations at him again.

"Yes, man, you are correct. These are the suns of the system you call Alpha Centauri. The two nearest are Alpha A and Alpha B. The third white sun is Alpha C, and the red point is, of course, the insignificant Proxima Centauri, known for centuries to be the nearest star to the solar system. These latter two do not concern us. What matters is that the dead twin is on a freak planet of this system. There is only one freak. It is a planet which, by describing a figure eight, revolves in turn around the Centauri suns Alpha A and Alpha B. It does this by traveling at the unusual speed of three thousand miles a second. In its eccentric orbit, it passes very close to each star, much as a comet might. But unlike a comet it is forever unable to break away. The gravitational fields of Alpha A and Alpha B alternately whip it on its way. It is now approaching ever nearer

to Alpha A, the star almost directly ahead, and we must work swiftly if we are to revive the dead body—"

"If we are to *what?*" said Hedrock.

There was no answer, nor did he need one. He leaned weakly back in his chair, and he thought, *Why, of course, it's been obvious from the beginning. I took it for granted they were going to try to rig up some sensory connection between a living and a dead body, but that was an assumption based upon my conviction that a man who has been dead two days is not only dead but decomposing.*

He felt genuinely awed. For thousands of years he had been striving to prolong the lives of living men to some approximation of the immortality that he had accidentally achieved. Now, here were beings who could undoubtedly not only solve that problem but could also resurrect the dead.

Curiously, the discovery dimmed his hope that he would be able to survive in spite of their determination to kill him. He had been trying to imagine some method of defeating them based on their extremely logical approach to existence. But, while that still seemed the only possible way out, it had become a remote chance, an opportunity to be planned for because the alternative was so final. Their scientific achievements made the result extremely doubtful.

"*You will now,*" said a thought impulse, "*submit to the next phase.*"

He lay under a light. Just where he was, or even where they wanted him to think he was, he had no idea. His body rested comfortably in what could have been a form-fitting coffin. The comparison made a gruesome titillation along his nerves, but he quieted that jumpiness. He lay steady, determined, cold with his own intentions, and watched the light. It hung in blackness above him or—the thought made a curious pattern—was he staring *down* at it? It didn't matter. There was only the light, shining out of the darkness, shining, shining. It was not, he noticed after a long while, a white light; and yet, conversely, it seemed to have no definite color. Nor was it bright, nor was it warm. His thought paused; he flinched. It was the notion of heat that did it, that brought consciousness of how cold it was. The light was icy.

The discovery was like a signal, like a cue. "*Emotion,*" said a spider's mind vibrations from afar, "*is a manifestation of energy. It acts instantaneously over any distance. The reason why the connection between the twins diminished in intensity, so far as their reception of it was con-*

cerned, was their mutual expectation that it would so diminish. This expectation was almost entirely unconscious. Their respective nervous systems naturally recognized the widening distance when one set out for Centaurus. Instinctively, they yielded their connection, though the emotional rapport between them remained as strong as ever. And now, since you have become a part of the relationship . . . accept the connection."

It seemed instantaneous. He was lying, Hedrock saw, on a grassy bank beside a stream. The water gurgled and babbled over rocks. A gentle breeze blew into his face, and through the trees to his left a glorious sun was rearing above the horizon. All around him on the ground were boxes and packing cases, several machines, and four men lying quietly asleep. The nearest man was Gil Neelan. Hedrock controlled his mind again, thinking desperately, *Steady, you fool, it's only an image, a* thing *they've put into your brain. Gil is on sand, on a freak planet, headed into hell. This is a dream world, an Eden, Earth in its sweetest summertime.*

Several seconds passed, and the body of Gil Neelan slept on with flushed face, breathing stentoriously, as if it couldn't get enough air into it, as if life was returning the hard way, and clinging with effort. A faint thought came into Hedrock's mind. "Water," it said. "Oh, God, water!"

He hadn't thought that. Literally Hedrock threw himself at the stream. Twice, his cupped hands trembled so violently that the precious water spilled onto the green grass. At last a measure of sanity came, and he searched one of the boxes and found a container. He kept letting the water trickle in and around Gil Neelan's mouth. Several times, the emaciated body contorted in dreadful coughing. But that too, was good—dead muscles jarring back to life. Hedrock, eyes glinting, persisted. He could feel Gil's slow heartbeat, could see all the mind pictures that pushed hesitantly into the brain that had scattered far. It was the sensory relation that, until now, had belonged exclusively to the brothers. Gil stirred in awareness.

"Why, Dan—" there was a vast amaze in Gil's thought—"you old devil! Where did you come from?"

"From Earth." Hedrock spoke aloud into the breeze that blew in his face. Later he would explain that he was not Dan.

The answer seemed all that Gil needed. He sighed, smiled, and turning over, withdrew mentally into a deep sleep. Hedrock began to prowl around the boxes, looking for dextrose tablets. He found a bottle of the quick-acting food, and slipped a tablet into Gil's mouth. It should, he thought, dissolve gradually. Satisfied that he had done all he could for the moment, he turned to the other men. He doled out water to each of the three in turn, and then dextrose tablets. He was straightening from the work when a spider-thought touched him, matter-of-fact in its steely overtones.

"You see," it said, *"he did attend the others, too. The emotion involved is more than just an artificial extension of paired spermatozoa reacting sympathetically."*

That was all there was, just that comment. But it stopped Hedrock in his tracks. It wasn't that he had forgotten the spiders. But the memory of them had been pressed into the background of his mind by the urgency of events. And now here was the reality again. He stared up into the blue sky, up at that glorious, yellow-white sun, up into the spider folk. But that, he realized, was like savages of old shaking their fists and mouthing their maledictions at the evil demons who lurked in the heavens.

He grew calmer, and again fed his sick charges, this time a liquid made of highly digestible fruit juice concentrates dissolved in water. One of the men, a lean, handsome fellow, revived sufficiently to smile up at him in a puzzled fashion, but he asked no questions and Hedrock volunteered no information. When the patients were sleeping again, Hedrock climbed the tallest tree he could find, and studied his surroundings. But there were only trees and rolling hills and far, far away, almost lost in the midst of distance, a wider glint of water. What interested him more were patches of yellow color on a tree a quarter of a mile along the creek. He shinnied to the ground and walked with some excitement, following the stream bed. It must have been farther than he had estimated, for when he came back with a container full of fruit, the sun was past the zenith.

But the trek had done him good; he felt better, more alive; and he was thinking shrewdly: Gil and Kershaw—if one of these chaps was Kershaw—must have visited this planet. They must have tested the fruits they found, and as soon as they recovered sufficiently, they'd be able to tell him whether this yellow stuff was edible. There might even be a pocket analyzer in one of the packing cases.

If there was, he couldn't find it. But he did uncover a number of instruments, including a recorder for communication disks, used in surveying and marking land sites. They probably had left a lot of those on their various points of landing. The sun lowered itself toward, well, the west. He'd call it that, Hedrock decided wryly. Late in the afternoon, the second sun came up in the east, tinier, a pale orb. For a while, then, it grew warmer, but cooled off when the larger sun sank behind the horizon, and "night" set in. It was like a dull day on Earth, with a ghost of a sun peering through heavy clouds, only the sky wasn't cloudy and there was none of the humidity and closeness of a dull day. Soft winds blew. The third sun came up, but its dim light seemed to add nothing. A few faint stars showed. The bright gloom began to get on Hedrock's nerves. He paced along the creek bank, and he thought finally: How long would this . . . this sensory investigation continue? And why did they want to kill him?

He had not intended it as a direct question to his captors, but, surprisingly, he received an answer at once. It seemed to float at him out of the dim, cloudless sky, precise and supernally dispassionate:

"*We are not quite what we seem,*" the spider-thought said. "*Our race is not, as you suggested, one of Nature's successes. In this ship is actually the remnant of our people. All of us here present are immortal, the winners in the struggle for supremacy and existence on our planet. Each and every one of us is supreme in some one field by virtue of having destroyed all competition. We intend to remain alive, our existence unsuspected by the several other races in the universe. Because of an accident that precipitated you into our midst, you must die. Is that clear?*"

Hedrock had no answer, for here at long last was a completely understandable logic. He was to be killed because he knew too much.

"*It is our intention,*" said the cold mind at him, "*to make a final investigation of man's sensory equipment on the basis of what we have discovered through you, and then leave this portion of space forever. The investigation will take some time. You will please have patience until then. There will be no answers meanwhile to your petty appeals. Conduct yourself accordingly.*"

That, too, was clear. Hedrock went back slowly to the camp. The lean, tired-looking man who had smiled at him earlier was sitting up.

"Hello," he said cheerfully. "My name is Kershaw. Derd Kershaw. Thanks for saving our lives."

"You're thanking me too soon," said Hedrock gruffly.

But the sound of the human voice brought a gathering excitement and, just like that, an idea. He worked, now that the hope had come, with an intense anxiety. He expected to be destroyed momentarily.

The job itself was simple enough. With Gil's energy gun, he cut trees into little round disks about an inch thick. The disks he kept feeding into the survey recording machine, which imprinted on the elements of each a message stating the position of himself and his companions, describing the spider folk and the threat they had made. For some of the disks, he set the recorder to various antigravity pressures, ten feet, twenty feet, fifty—up to five hundred—and watched them float up into the sky to the level their atoms had been adjusted for. They drifted in the vagrant currents of the air. Some just hung around and made him sweat with anger at the slowness with which they scattered. Others whisked out of sight with a satisfying rapidity. Some of them, Hedrock knew, would lodge on hillsides, some in trees, some would float for years, perhaps centuries, prey to every breeze that blew, and every hour that passed they would be more difficult to find, would take longer to search out. The spider folk were going to have a hell of a time preventing the knowledge of their presence from being spread abroad.

The precious days dragged by, and soon there was no doubt that enough time had gone by for the disks to scatter widely.

His patients were slow in recuperating. It was apparent that their bodies were not capable of absorbing properly the food he gave them, and that they needed medical care which was not available. Kershaw was the first to reach the convalescent stage where he wanted to know what had happened. Hedrock showed him the message on one of the disks, which, after three weeks, he was still sending out spasmodically. Kershaw read it and then lay back thoughtfully.

"So that's what we're up against," he said slowly. "What makes you think the disks will do any good?"

Hedrock said, "The spiders are logic hounds. They'll accept an accomplished fact. The problem is when will the process of distribution of the disks have reached a point where they'll instantly realize that they can't possibly ever find all of them? Every little while I think that surely I've done enough, and then I begin to wonder just how intricate will distribution have to be before they'll accept it as decisive. The reason they haven't bothered us so far is that they're near Earth studying man's emotional structure. At least that was their intention, and I was told they wouldn't talk to me for a while. My guess is they're too far away for their brand of telepathy."

"But what are they after?" Kershaw asked.

It was hard to explain what his own experiences with the spiders had taught him, but Hedrock made the attempt. He was careful to give no inkling of his activities on Earth. He finished, "I can break their mental control at any time, so that their only threat against me is physical force."

Kershaw said, "How do you explain their ability to draw you back to the lifeboat in spite of your resistance?"

"I can only suggest that the nervous system is slow in setting patterns. I was back in the lifeboat before my method of opposition actually went into operation. When it did they recognized what was happening and threatened to destroy me unless I cooperated."

"Do you think they'll get anywhere in their attempt to understand human emotional nature?"

Hedrock shook his head. "For thousands of years men have been trying to gain ascendancy over their emotional impulses. The secret, of course, is not to eliminate emotion from life but to channel it where it is healthy and sane: sex, love, good will, enthusiasm, alertness, personality, and so on. These are apparently aspects of existence which are not within the possible experience of the spider beings. I don't see how they can ever understand, particularly because they have no method of distinguishing between a man who is willing to risk his life for a cause, and a man who takes risk, for example, for gain. This inability to understand variations of human nature is a basic flaw, and forever bars them from real comprehension."

Kershaw was thoughtful. At last he said, "What are our chances of rescue?"

Hedrock said grimly, "Very good. I know it looks bad for us, but the spiders said they were definitely leaving this part of space. Why would they leave unless they have some reason to believe that soon great ships from Earth will be plying the Centauri traffic lanes? In my opinion the empress will release the interstellar drive, and in these days of speedy manufacture they'll have hundreds of drives installed into spaceships within a few weeks. And the trip itself could be completed in little more than two days, if necessary."

"I think," said Kershaw quietly, "we'd better get busy. You've put a lot of those disks out, but a few thousand more can't hurt. You cut the trees and pile the disks. I'll feed them into the machine."

He stopped, and swayed in a curious fashion. His gaze flashed wildly up beyond Hedrock's head. Hedrock whirled and stared into the sky. He saw a ship. For a moment he thought it was the spider ship as seen from far away. And then the mottled hue of it in the sun, and the great letters on its bottom snatched his attention. The letters said:

WS—CENTARUS—719

The ship was not far away, but low down. It skimmed over them less than half a mile up; and turned slowly back toward them in response to their urgent telestat calls. It made the return run to the Earth in just over forty-one hours of flight. Hedrock had taken the precaution of having Kershaw and Neelan identify him as Gil's brother, and so he landed without incident at Imperial City, and proceeded to one of his apartments.

A few minutes later he was connecting the apartment 'stat to one of his relay systems. By that roundabout fashion he called the Weapon Makers.

EIGHTEEN

It was Peter Cardron's image that appeared on the plate. He was not looking at the screen at the moment of contact, but was talking with animation to someone who was out of Hedrock's line of vision. There was no sound, and Hedrock made no attempt to guess at what the former councilor was saying. He had time to wonder again how Cadron would receive him.

Nearly a month had passed since that night when he had been compelled to act against the Weapon Makers in self-defense. In spite of his personal admiration for the majority of the councilors, he had no regrets. Earth's immortal man must assume his life was worth saving. For better or for worse he was what he was, and all the world must put up with him so long as he could protect himself.

Cadron was turning toward the 'stat plate. He froze as he saw who it was, and then hurriedly he clicked on the sound control. "Hedrock," he said, "it's you!"

A smile of pleasure came into his face. His eyes lighted up. "Hedrock, where have you been? We've been trying to contact you by every means."

Hedrock said, "What is my status with the Weapon Makers?"

Cadron straightened a little. "I have been authorized," he said, "by the *retiring* council to apologize to you for our hysterical actions against you. We can only assume that we were all caught up in a kind of mob attitude based on tension. I am personally sorry for what happened."

"Thank you. That means definitely no plotting?"

"Our word of honor." He broke off. "Hedrock, listen, we've been sitting on tenterhooks waiting for you to call. The empress, as you know, released the drive unconditionally on the morning following the attack."

Hedrock had learned that on the ship coming back to Earth, but all he said was, "Proceed."

Cadron was excited. "We have received from her a most remarkable offer. Recognition for the Shops and a share in the government. It's a surrender of the first order."

Hedrock said, "You're refusing, of course."

"Eh?" Cadron's image stared.

Hedrock went on firmly, "You don't really mean that the Council considered accepting. You must realize there can never be a meeting ground between two such diametrically opposed forces."

"But," protested Cadron, "that's one of the things you suggested yourself as a reason for your going to the palace."

Hedrock said steadily, "That was a blind. During this crisis of civilization we *had* to have somebody in both the Shops and the palace. Wait!"

He went on in a ringing voice before the other could interrupt, "Cadron, the Weapon Shops constitute a permanent opposition. The trouble with the opposition of the old days was that they were always scheming for power; all too frequently their criticism was dishonest, their intentions evil; they *lusted* for control. The Weapon Shops never must allow such emotions to be aroused in their followers. Let the empress rebuild her own chaos. I do not say she is responsible for the corrupt state of the empire, but the time has come for her to attempt a vigorous housecleaning. Throughout, the Weapon Makers will remain aloof, interested, but maintaining their great standards for the relief *throughout the galaxy* of those who must defend themselves from oppression. The gunmakers will continue to sell their guns and stay out of politics."

Cadron said slowly, "You want us then to—"

"Go about the routine of your normal business; nothing more nor less. And now, Cadron—" Hedrock smiled. "Cadron, I have enjoyed knowing you personally. Pass on my felicitations to the retiring council. I intend to present myself at the palace one hour from now; and none of you will hear from me again. Goodbye to all of you, and good luck."

He shut off the 'stat with a jerky movement and sat there conscious of that old, old pain of his. Once more he was withdrawing himself. He forced the great loneliness out of his soul at last and put his carplane down on the palace exactly on the hour. He had already called Innelda, and he was admitted at once to her apartment.

He watched her from half-closed eyes, as they talked. She sat stiffly beside him, a tall, graceful, long-faced woman whose green eyes hid her thoughts. They sat under a palm tree in the garden that was the reception room of the thirty-fourth floor. Soft breezes blew against them; the shaded lights shed a gentle glow over the quiet scene. Twice, he kissed her, conscious that her diffidence had an inner meaning that he must bring into the open. She took the kisses with all the passivity of a slave woman.

Hedrock drew back. "Innelda, what's the matter?" She was silent; and he pressed on, "The first thing I find, when I come back, is that Prince del Curtin, who has been almost literally your right hand, has been banished from the palace. Why?"

The words seemed to rouse her out of some depth. She said with a shadow of fire in her tone, "My cousin has had the temerity to criticize and oppose a project of mine. I will not be badgered even by those I love."

Hedrock said, "Badgered you, did he? That doesn't sound like the prince."

Silence. Hedrock stared at her slantwise, then said in a persistent tone, "You practically gave up the interstellar drive for me, and yet now that you have me, I can't feel that it means anything."

During the long silence that followed, he had his first thought of what all this rigidity might be. Was it possible that she knew the truth about him? Before he could speak, her low voice came, "Perhaps all I really need to say, Robert, is that there will be an Isher heir, an *Isher* heir."

The child part of the revelation hardly touched him. She knew. That was what counted. Hedrock sighed finally. "I forgot. You caught Gonish, didn't you?"

"Yes, I caught him; and he didn't need very much more information than he had. A few words; and the intuition was complete."

He said at last, "What are you going to do?"

Her answer came, remote-toned, "A woman cannot love an immortal man. The relation would destroy her soul and her mind." She went on, almost as if speaking to herself, "I realize now I never did love you. You fascinated me, and perhaps repelled me a little, too. I'm proud, though, that I selected you without knowing. It shows the enormous instinctive vitality of our line. Robert!"

"Yes?"

"Those other empresses—what was your life like with them?"

Hedrock shook his head. "I won't tell you. I want you to make up your mind without even thinking of them."

She laughed in a brittle tone. "You think I'm jealous. It's not . . . not that at all." She added in a disjointed manner, "Henceforth, I'm a family woman who intends to have the respect as well as the affection of her child. An Isher Empress can do no other. But I won't press you." Her eyes darkened. She said with sudden heaviness, "I'll have to think it over. Leave me now, will you?"

She held out her hand. It felt limp under the pressure of his lips, and Hedrock went frowning to his apartment. Sitting there alone, he remembered Gonish. He put a call through the Weapon Makers exchange, and asked the No-man to come to the palace. An hour later, the two men sat facing each other. "I realize," Gonish said, "that I am going to receive no explanations."

"Later," said Hedrock; then, "What are *you* going to do? Or rather, what have you done?"

"Nothing."

"You mean—"

"Nothing. You see, I understand just what the knowledge would do to the average and even the higher-type human being. I shall never say a word, not to the council, not to anyone."

Hedrock was relieved. He knew this man, his enormous integrity. No fear was behind that promise, simply a stark honesty of outlook that would never be more than equalled. He saw that Gonish's eyes were studying him. The No-man said, "With my training, I would have quite naturally known better than to make a test of the effect of immorality on others. But you made it, didn't you? Where was it? When?"

Hedrock swallowed hard. The memory was like fire. "It was on Venus," he said in a flat voice, "during the early days of interplanetary travel. I set up an isolated colony of scientists, told them the truth, and set them to work to help me discover the secret of my immortality. It was horrible, oh—" His voice thickened in distress. "They couldn't stand watching my perpetual youth as they grew old. Never again."

He shuddered; and the No-man said quickly, "What about your wife?"

Hedrock was silent for a long minute. He said then, slowly, "The Isher empresses in the past have always been proud of their relation to the immortal man. For the sake of the children, they put up with me. I can say no more."

His frown deepened. "I've sometimes thought I should marry oftener. The immortal strain might, just might, repeat that way. This is only my thirteenth marriage. Somehow, I didn't have the heart even though—" he looked up—"I've developed a perfect method of aging my appearance, enough to have a psychological effect on those who actually know the truth."

There was a look on Gonish's face that narrowed Hedrock's eyes. He said quickly, "What's the matter?"

The No-man said, "She loves you, I think; and that makes it very bad. You see, she can't have any children."

Hedrock rose up out of his chair, took a step forward as if he intended the No-man bodily harm. "Are you in earnest? Why she told me—"

Gonish was bleak. "We of the Weapon Shops have studied the empress from childhood. Her file, of course, is accessible only to the three No-men and to the members of the council. There is no doubt of it."

The No-man's gaze fixed Hedrock sharply. "I know this wrecks your plans, but don't take it so hard. Prince del Curtin is next in line and will carry on, rather strongly, I think. There'll be another empress along in a few generations, and you can marry her."

Hedrock ceased his pacing. "Don't be so damned callous," he said. "I'm not thinking of myself. It's these Isher women. The trait hasn't shown clearly in Innelda, but it's there. She won't give up that child; and that's what I'm worrying about." He swung directly toward the No-man again. "Are you absolutely sure? Don't play with me, Gonish."

The No-man said steadily, "Hedrock, I'm not playing. The Empress Isher is going to die in childbirth and—" He stopped; his eyes fixed on a point beyond Hedrock.

Hedrock turned slowly, and faced the woman who stood there. The woman said in a cold voice, "Captain Hedrock, you will take your friend, Mr. Gonish, and depart from the palace within the hour, not to return until—"

She stopped and stood for a moment like a figure of stone. She finished with a rush, "Never," she said thickly. "Never come back. I couldn't stand it. Goodbye."

"Wait!" Hedrock cried piercingly. "Innelda, you mustn't have that child."

He was talking to a closed door.

NINETEEN

It was del Curtin who got Hedrock into the palace on the final day. "We've got to," the prince had whispered, "get somebody near her. She must listen to reason. My friends are going to advise that new doctor of hers, Telinger, that you're in. Just stick to your rooms until you're called."

Waiting was dreary. Hedrock paced the thickly carpeted floor, thinking of the months since he had been banished from the palace. Actually, it was the last few days that had been worst. The whisper had spread abroad. Hedrock heard it far and wide. It didn't come over the telestats. No official word was given out; just how it became known definitely was impossible to say. He had heard it sitting in the restaurants he sometimes frequented. He heard it walking along quiet streets. It drifted on thin breezes, and rose in briefly heard voices above the clamor of conversations on carplanes. It had not been evil in intent or in actuality. It was simply, there was going to be an Isher heir *any day*, and the excited world of Isher was waiting for the announcement. They didn't know it, but the day was now. The crisis came at ten o'clock at night. A message from Dr. Telinger brought Hedrock out of the study and up into the Imperial apartments.

Telinger, Hedrock found, was a middle-aged man with a thin face, which was wrinkled in dismay as he greeted his visitor. Dr. Telinger, Hedrock knew, was guilty of nothing but weakness. He had been dragooned into the Imperial service as a replacement for Dr. Snow, who had been summarily dismissed after being court physician for thirty years. Hedrock could still remember one day at the dinner table when Innelda had inveighed against Dr. Snow, calling him "an outdated practitioner who's still palming himself off as a doctor on the strength of having delivered me into the world."

There was no doubt that old Dr. Snow had told her the exact situation; and Innelda hadn't liked it. And there was also no doubt, Hedrock realized as he listened to Dr. Telinger, that the new doctor had never been granted the privilege of a too thorough examination. She had picked well. He looked the kind of man who would be too awed to override the resistance of his Imperial patient.

"I've just discovered the truth," he almost babbled at Hedrock. "She's under antipain, but I've left a communication gap. Prince Hedrock, you must persuade her. It's the baby or she, and her conviction that she will live is utterly unfounded. She has threatened me," he finished whitely, "with death if the baby does not survive."

Hedrock said, "Let me talk to her."

She lay in the bed, calm and still. There was no color in her cheeks, and the rise and fall of her chest was so infinitesimal that she seemed already dead. Hedrock was conscious of relief when the doctor placed the communicator mask gently over that quiet yet intense face. Poor tyrant, he thought, poor, wretched, unhappy tyrant, caught up by inner forces too great for her to command or think through.

He picked up his end of the communicator. "Innelda," he said tenderly.

"It's—you—Robert." The answer was slow in coming and yet fierce. "I told—them—not—to—let—you—come."

"Your friends love you. They want to keep you."

"They—hate—me. They think—I'm—a fool. But I shall show them. I *will* myself to live, but the child must live."

"Prince del Curtin has married a lovely and wonderful woman. They will have beautiful children, worthy of the succession."

"No child but mine—and yours—will rule in Isher's name. Don't you see, it is the direct line that matters. There has never been a break. There will not be now. Don't you see?"

Hedrock stood sad. He saw even more clearly than she did. In the old days when, under various aliases, he had persuaded Isher emperors to marry women to whom family was vitally important, it had not seemed possible that the trait could ever become too strong. Here was proof that it could be tragic. And what this unhappy woman did not realize was that the reference to her "line" was only a rationalization. She wanted a child of her own. That was the simple reality.

"Robert—will you stay—and hold my hand?"

He stayed, and watched the life force ebb away. Waited till death lay heavily on the chilling body, and the baby was a thing whose raucous yowling made him angry.

Half a light year distant, a hundred-mile-long ship got under way. Inside it, thoughts vibrated from mind to mind:

"*. . . The second general examination is almost as futile as the first in its basic results. We know some of the laws—but why did this ruler who possessed a world give her life for her child when in actuality she shrank from personal death? Her reasons that she personally must carry on her line are logically inadequate. It is only a matter of slight atomic rearrangement. Many men and women are alive who could carry forward her tribal progression.*

"*It remains but to bring her back to life, and make a record of the emotional reactions of those around her to her resuscitation.*

"*. . . X-x??—has investigated the appearance of our former prisoner Hedrock at the palace, and it appears that he nullified by an ingenious method the logic that required his destruction. Accordingly, we can leave the galaxy within one . . . period.*

"*This much we have learned. Here is the race that shall rule the sevagram.*"